Pardee Butler, Rosetta Butler Hastings

Personal Recollections of Pardee Butler

With reminiscences

Pardee Butler, Rosetta Butler Hastings

Personal Recollections of Pardee Butler
With reminiscences

ISBN/EAN: 9783337219161

Printed in Europe, USA, Canada, Australia, Japan

Cover: Foto ©Raphael Reischuk / pixelio.de

More available books at **www.hansebooks.com**

Pardee Butler

PERSONAL RECOLLECTIONS

OF

PARDEE BUTLER

WITH REMINISCENCES, BY
HIS DAUGHTER,

MRS. ROSETTA B. HASTINGS

AND ADDITIONAL CHAPTERS

BY

ELD. JOHN BOGGS AND ELD. J. B. McCLEERY.

CINCINNATI

STANDARD PUBLISHING COMPANY

1889

Copyright, 1889, by
STANDARD PUBLISHING CO.

PREFACE.

I have not attempted to write a complete biography of my father, but merely to supplement his "Recollections" with a few of my own reminiscences. He was a man who said little in his family about his early years, or about any of the occurrences of his eventful life. Nor did he ever keep any journal, or any account of his meetings, or of the number that he baptized. He seldom reported his meetings to the newspapers. I think it was only during the few years that he was employed by missionary societies, that he ever made reports of what he accomplished. He had even destroyed the most of his old letters. And so, for nearly all information outside of my own recollections, I have been indebted to the kindness of relatives and friends.

The later chapters have been written by men who knew my father intimately, and men whose reputations are such as to give weight to their testimony.

To all of these friends I now offer my thanks for their kind assistance.

And to the public I offer this book, not for its literary merit, but as the tribute of a daughter to a loved father, whose earnest devotion to duty was worthy of imitation.

MRS. ROSETTA B. HASTINGS.

Farmington, Kansas, April 23, 1889.

INTRODUCTION.

In this country inherited fortunes, or ancestral honors, have little effect on a man's reputation; but inherited disposition and early sourroundings have much effect on his character.

My father's ancestors were from New England. His father, Phineas Butler, came from Saybrook, Connecticut, where the Congregational Churches framed the Saybrook platform. His mother's people, the Pardees, came from Norfork, Connecticut. The Pardees were said to have been descendants of the French Huguenots. Ebenezer Pardee emigrated to Marcellus, now known as Skaneateles, Onondaga Co., New York. There he died in 1811, leaving his wife Ann Pardee, (known for many years as grandmother Pardee) a widow, with nine sons and two daughters. The eldest daughter, Sarah Pardee, was there married in 1813, to Phineas Butler; and there my father, who was the second of seven children, was born, March 9, 1816.

In the autumn of 1818, Phineas Butler, of whom I shall hereafter speak as grandfather Butler, went to Wadsworth, Medina Co., Ohio. There a settlement had been begun three years before in the heavy timber, and there were only a few small clearings here and there in the woods.

My grandmother came on with her brother the following spring. She had three small children, but they made the journey in a sled, in bad weather, cutting their own roads, and camping in the woods at night. Grandmother Pardee came on later. She was a woman of great energy, and brought up her sons so well that they all became leading men in the communities in which they lived. Grandmother Butler was also a capable, fearless woman, and so calm and firm that it was said no vexation was ever known to ruffle her temper.

Their cabins were built of logs, with hewed puncheon floors and doors; and on the roof, in the place of nailed shingles, were split shakes, fastened on with poles and wooden pins. But grandfather had brought a few nails (made by a blacksmith) from New York, and used them in his house. When a neighbor died they hewed out puncheons to make a coffin, and finding only eighteen nails in the neighborhood, grandfather, by torchlight, pulled fourteen more out of his house to finish the coffin.

Their lives were full of hardship and ·privation. Grandfather was a famous hunter, and his well aimed rifle sometimes furnished game that kept the neighborhood from starvation. He was dependent on bartering furs at some distant trading post, for his supplies of salt, needles, ammunition and other necessary articles that could not be made at home.

Often, after a hard day's work, he hunted half of the night to obtain coonskins and other furs. Father said that one night grandfather and Orin Loomis were out hunting coons with the dogs, having taken their axes to chop down coon trees, but no guns, when they found a bear, on a small island, in the middle of a swamp. But I find his bear story so well told in the "*Wadsworth Memorial*" that I will quote from that:

"In the fall of 1823, as Butler and Loomis were returning after midnight from one of their hunts, and had arrived within a mile or two of home it was noticed that the dogs were missing. Presently a noise was heard, far back in the rear.

"'Hark! What was that?' said Loomis. They listened awhile, and agreed it was dogs, sure.

"'Orr, let's go back,' said Butler.

"'No, it is too late,' answered Loomis.

"'But,' said Butler, 'I'll warrant the dogs are after a bear; don't you hear old Beaver? It sounds to me like the bark of old Beaver when he is after a bear.'

"Butler was bound to go back, and so they started. The scene of the disturbance was finally reached, after traveling two or three miles. The dogs had found a bear; but it was in the middle of Long Swamp, and the alders were so thick that there was scarcely room for man, dog or bear to get through. This did not deter Phin. Butler, however. They got near enough to find that the bear was stationed on a spot a little drier than the main swamp, surrounded by alder bushes, and that she was determined not to leave it. The dogs would bay up close, when the old bear would run out after them. They would retreat, and then she would run back to her nest again.

"We can't kill her to-night," said Loomis, 'we will have to go home and come down again in the morning.'

"No,' replied Butler, 'I am afraid she will get away. We can kill her to-night, I guess. You can go and hiss on the dogs on one side, and I will come up on the other; and when she runs out after them, I'll cut her back-bone off with the ax.'

"They concluded to try this plan, and came very near succeeding. As the old bear rushed past, Butler put the whole bit of the ax into her back, but failed to cut the back-bone by an inch or two. Enraged and desperate, she sprang upon the dogs, who, emboldened by the presence of their masters, came too close. With one of her enormous paws she came down on old Beaver, making a large wound in his side, which nearly killed him. He was hardly able to crawl out of the swamp.

"The fight was then abandoned until morning, as without Beaver to lead the dogs it was useless to proceed. It was difficult to get the old dog home, but he finally got well. Early in the morning the hunters were on the ground.   This time they had their guns with them, but found the old bear was gone.   On examining her nest of the night before, her unusual ferocity was explained.   She had a litter of cubs, which, however, she had succeeded in removing, and must have carried them off in her mouth.   In a short time the dogs had tracked her out.   She was found a half mile lower down the swamp, where she had a new nest.   Butler's rifle soon dispatched her ; but her cubs, four in number, and not more than three or four weeks old, were taken alive, and kept for pets."

Father said that he could remember when they brought the bears home, growling, snarling—the crossest little things he ever saw.

Strange as it may seem, my father did not inherit grandfather's love for hunting.   I never saw him shoot a gun, and he has never owned one within my recollection.

Orin Loomis was often heard to say that Phin. Butler was the most courageous man he ever knew. He was quick-tempered, but warm-hearted, and full of fun, and as honest and sincere as he was bold and fearless.   One time he was traveling, and stopped at a tavern.   The strangers present were discussing the statement that every man has his price, and each man was telling what was the least price for which he would tell a lie.   Finally one man said that he would tell a lie for five dollars.   Grandfather's impetuous nature could stand it no longer, and he burst out scornfully: "Tell a lie! Tell a lie for five dollars! Sell your manhood! Sell your soul for five dollars! You must rate yourself very cheap!" And then, they said, he fairly preached them a sermon on the nobility of perfect truthfulness, and the littleness and meanness of lying and deceitfulness.

My grandmother was also very conscientious, which was illustrated by the fact that on her death-bed, after giving some good advice to her daughters, she charged them to carry home a cup of coffee that she had borrowed.

An old Wadsworth friend, writing to us since father's death, says of him: "From a boy Pardee was remarkable for his uprightness, and bold and strict honesty, and it was a maxim among the boys to say, 'As honest as Pard Butler.' He and his father before him were specimens of puritanical honesty and courage, and had they lived in the days of Cromwell and in England, would doubtless have been in Cromwell's army."

Scarcely was the settlement begun when a school was taught in one room of a log dwelling-house. When but three years old, father was a pupil in the first school that was taught in the new school-house, by Miss Lodema Sackett, and continued to attend school a part of every year. Books were scarce, but he was fond of reading, and read, over and over, all that he could obtain.

The Western Reserve was settled mainly by New Englanders, who were intelligent and God-fearing men; and religious meetings were held from the first; printed sermons being read aloud when there was no preacher. A Sunday-school was organized in Wadsworth in 1820.

The most influential man in the neighborhood was Judge Brown, an uncle of " John Brown of Ossawatomie." He was noted for the purity of his life, the dignity of his demeanor, and the firmness with which he defended his views. He was a bitter opponent of slavery, and, what was strange in those days, a strong temperance man. Before leaving Connecticut he had heard Lyman Beecher deliver his famous temperance sermons, and he came to Wadsworth with his soul ablaze with temperance zeal. The community was strongly influenced by him, and father said that he was much indebted to Judge Brown for his temperance and anti-slavery principles.

Even in those early days Wadsworth contained a public library, a lyceum where the young men discussed the questions of the day, and an academy. Father took part in the lyceum debates, though he was said to be slow of speech; and attended the Wadsworth Academy from its beginning, in 1830. One of its most successful teachers was a shrewd Scotchman named John McGregor. Father and several young men from a distance, who boarded at grandfather's and attended this school, spent their evenings studying their lessons, or reading and discussing some good book. Dick's scientific works were among the books thus read.

There were many Lutherans, Dutch Reformers, and Mennonites near Wadsworth, and there was a perfect ferment of religious discussion.

During father's boyhood, Alexander Campbell and Walter Scott had been preaching the union of Christians on the Bible alone, and there was great enthusiasm.

Eld. Newcomb, an honored Baptist preacher, together with my grandfather, and Samuel Green—the father of Almon B. Green and Philander Green—had been reading the writings of A. Campbell for several years. Almon B. Green had been made skeptical by the unintelligible orthodox preaching. But one day, after reading the first four books of the New Testament, he exclaimed, ''No uninspired man ever wrote that book.'' He read on until he came to Acts ii. 38, which he took to Eld. Newcomb, asking him its meaning. '' It means what it says,'' was his reply. In a few days Almon was baptized by Eld. Newcomb, simply on his confession of faith in Christ, without telling any experience, as usually required by the Baptists. Soon afterwards four families, the Newcombs, Greens, Butlers and Bonnels, all Baptists, united to form a church on the apostolic pattern. Then William Hayden came with his fiery eloquence and wondrous songs ; the people were stirred up, opposition aroused, the various creeds were discussed with re-newed energy, and the church grew and multiplied.

But father and his uncle Aaron, who was eight years older than himself, had been made skeptical by orthodox mysticism and the disputes of so many wrang-ling churches.

In September, 1833, A. Campbell came to Wads-worth to attend a great yearly meeting held in William Eyle's barn. The following account of an incident that occurred at that time, I quote from "History of the Disciples on the Western Reserve."

"An incident occurred at this time which displays Mr Campbell's character for discernment and candor. Aaron Pardee, a gentleman residing in the vicinity, an unbeliever in the gospel, attracted by Campbell's abili-ties as a reasoner, and won by his fairness in argument, resolved to obtain an interview and propose freely his difficulties. Mr. Campbell received him with such frankness that he opened his case at once, saying, 'I discover, Mr. Campbell, you are well prepared in the argument and defenses of the Christian religion. I confess to you frankly there are some difficulties in my mind which prevent my believing the Bible, particularly the Old Testament.'

"Mr. Campbell replied, 'I acknowledge freely, Mr. Pardee, there are difficulties in the Bible—difficulties not easy to explain, and some, perhaps, which in our present state of information can not be cleared up.

But, my dear sir, when I consider the overwhelming testimony in its favor, so ample, complete and satisfactory, I can not resist the conviction of its divine origin. The field of prophetic inspiration is so varied and full, and the internal evidence so conclusive, that, with all the difficulties, the preponderance of evidence is overwhelming in its favor.' This reply, so fair and manly, and so different from the pulpit denunciations of 'skeptics,' 'infidels,' etc., to which he had been accustomed, quite disarmed him, and led him to hear the truth and its evidence in a much more rational state of mind. Within a year he became fully satisfied of the truthfulness of the Holy Scriptures, and apprehending clearly their testimony to the claims of Jesus of Nazareth as the anointed Son of God, he was prepared to yield to him the obedience of his life.''

My father was present with his uncle Aaron at that interview with Mr. Campbell, and he too was led by it to listen favorably to Mr. Campbell's clear and powerful presentation of divine truth. He followed Mr. Campbell to other meetings, and listened, read, and investigated until he, too, became convinced of the truth of the Bible.

His uncle Aaron, who is still living, said in a recent letter: "I remember going to meeting with Pardee sometime about a year before I was immersed, when he put some questions to me on the subject of religion, which were very difficult to answer."

In June, 1835, at a meeting held in Mr. Clark's new barn, my father and his uncle, Aaron Pardee, confessed their Saviour, and were baptized by Elder Newcomb, in a stream on Elder Newcomb's farm. A brother and sister of A. B. Green, and a sister of Holland Brown, were baptized at the same time. Holland Brown had been baptized the previous week. He walked down to the water with father, and remembers hearing him exclaim, on the way to the water, "Lord, I believe! Help thou mine unbelief." He also remembers hearing Elder Newcomb remark, "Now we can take everything; we have Bro. Butler and Bro. Pardee to fight the infidels, and the Browns to fight the Universalists." Holland Brown's brother, Leonard, and his wife—he had married my father's eldest sister, Ann Butler—had been baptized not far from that time.

Holland Brown relates the following incident, which occurred some time afterward:

"Bro. Butler was away from home, and driving a horse, which, though of fine appearance, was badly wind-broken. At times the horse appeared perfectly sound, and at one of those times Bro. Butler was offered a handsome sum for him.

"No,' said Bro. Butler, 'I can not take that sum for the horse, he is badly wind-broken.'

"Why didn't you take it? the man was a jockey, anyhow;' asked some one in my hearing.

" ' Because,' was the ringing answer, ' I think less of the price of a horse than of my own soul.' "

About that time father began teaching school in neighboring districts, which he followed for several years. But all of his spare time was spent in studying the Bible, church history, the writings of A. Campbell, and other religious books. It was at that time that he began committing the New Testament to memory.

Grandfather Butler and Samuel Green were the leaders of the new organization, as they had been of the Baptist Church, in Eld. Newcomb's absence—for he was away evangelizing much of the time. They called on the young people to take part in their social meetings on the Lord's day, at first only asking them to read a passage of Scripture, afterward to talk and pray, and, as they gained confidence in themselves, they were asked to lead the meetings. Thus there grew, in that church, one after the other, within a few years, eight preachers: A. B. Green, Wm. Moody, Holland Brown, Leonard Brown, Philander Green, B. F. Perky, Pardee Butler and L. L. Carpenter.

A. B. Green had been preaching a year or more before father was baptized, but I do not know which of the others began first, nor do I know the exact time when father began to preach, but it was about 1837 or 1838. He was not ordained at Wadsworth, for the church at that time doubted whether there was any Scriptural authority for ordination.   He was ordained some six or seven years afterward, in 1844, at Sullivan.

In such times of religious excitement it was not necessary for a man to have a college education, to become an acceptable preacher.   But father saw the advantages of a good education, and resolved to attend A. Campbell's school, then known as Buffalo Academy, but which was soon changed to Bethany College.   But the means to acquire an education must be obtained by his own exertions.

About the year 1839 grandfather sold his place in Wadsworth, and moved to the Sandusky Plains, a level, marshy prairie, in northwestern Ohio.   Part of the Plains belonged to the Wyandotte Indian Reservation, and was opened to settlement, a few years afterward, by the removal of the Indians to Wyandotte, Kansas.

Father and grandfather made sheep-raising their business while there.   Father herded sheep in summer and taught school in winter.   And, while herding sheep, he finished committing the New Testament to memory.   He could repeat it from beginning to end, and even in his later years he remembered it so well that he could repeat whole chapters at once.   I never saw the time that any one could repeat a verse in the New Testament to him, but that he could tell the book, and nearly always the chapter in which it was found.

He and his father's family put their membership

into the church at Letimberville, some miles distant ;
and there he occasionally preached.

He sometimes went back to Wadsworth, and on
the way back and forth stopped and preached for the
little church at Sullivan, Ashland Co.   There he made
the acquaintance of Sibjl S. Carleton, the daughter of
Joseph Carleton, one of the leading members of the
church.   They were married August 17, 1843 ; and
he never had cause to regret his choice, for she proved
to him a helpmeet indeed.

While living there, at the solicitation of his neighbors, he held a debate with a Universalist preacher, to
the satisfaction of his friends and the discomfiture of
his opponent.

Many parts of the Plains were covered with water,
and were musical with frogs in the spring, but in hot
weather they dried up, leaving here and there a stag-
nant pond.   I have heard father tell how one of his
neighbors tried to break a field by beginning on the
outside, and plowing farther in as the land dried up.
But the snakes and frogs grew thicker and thicker, as
he neared the center.   At length the grass seemed almost alive with snakes, and his big ox-team became
wild with fright, and ran away, and he could not get
them back there again.

Of course, such a country was unhealthful, and
father's family was much troubled with sickness.   His
parents both died ; my mother was nearly worn out

with the ague ; and he not only suffered from poor
general health, but from a sore throat, and had to quit
preaching.   He moved to Sullivan, but without any
permanent benefit to his health.   He did not at that
time attribute his sore throat entirely to the climate,
but thought it a chronic derangement that would utterly unfit him for a preacher.   Many years afterward
he wrote of that disappointment as follows :   " For
five years I saw myself sitting idly by the wayside,
hopeless and discouraged.   I felt somewhat like a
traveler, parched with thirst, on a wide and weary
desert, who sees the mirage of green trees and springs
of cool water that has mocked his vision, slowly fade
away out of his sight.   So seemed to perish my castles
in the air.   At that time making proclamation of the
ancient gospel was too vigorous a work, and too full
of hardship and exposure to be undertaken by any except those possessing stalwart good health.   If I had
been predestinated to the life I have actually lived, and
if it were necessary that I should be chastened to bear
with patience all its disabilities, then, I suppose, this
discipline I actually got might be considered good and
useful.   If I have been able to bear provocation with
patience, and to labor cheerfully without wages, and
at every personal sacrifice, this lesson was learned when
I saw all my hope dashed in pieces."

In the spring of 1850 father sold his property and
decided to go to Iowa.   Shortly before the time of

starting, my little sister and baby brother took the scarlet fever and, ere long, they were both laid in the old graveyard. Heart-broken as my parents were, they did not give up the long, lonely journey. Father bought a farm in Iowa, and built a log house on it, intending to become a farmer. He and mother united with the nearest church, at Long Grove, sixteen miles distant. Father did not tell them at first that he had been a preacher, but they questioned him and learned the facts. As his health improved he occasionally preached for them.

Eld. N. A. McConnell gives the following account of his preaching in Iowa:

"I first met him at his temporary home in Posten's Grove, in the fall of 1850. During that winter he taught a shool in Dewitt, Clinton Co., and preached occasionally at Long Grove. The next spring he attended a co-operation meeting at Walnut Grove, Jones Co., at which he was employed to labor with me in what was called District No. 2. His district included the counties of Scott, Clinton, Jackson, Jones, Cedar, Johnson, a part of Muscatine, Linn and Benton, and west to the Missouri river. He preached at LeClaire, Long Grove, Allen's Grove, Simpson's, Big Rock, Green's School-house, Walnut Grove, Marion, Dry Creek, Pleasant Grove, Burlison's, Maquoketa and Posten's Grove, as well as at numerous school-houses scattered over a large district of the country.

He did excellent work in preaching the word. He was not a revivalist, nor was his co-laborer, yet there were a goodly number added to the Lord during the year. I think not less than one hundred. The next year, 1852, the annual meeting of the co-operation was held at Dewitt, Clinton Co. At that meeting the district was divided into East and West No. 2. Your father was assigned to the eastern division and I took the western. His field included Davenport, Long Grove and Allen's Grove, in Scott Co.; Maquoketa and Burlison's in Jackson Co., and Dewitt in Clinton Co. He labored also in Cedar Co., and did a grand work, not so much in the numbers added as in the sowing the good seed of the Kingdom, and recommending our plea to the more intelligent and better informed of the various communities where he labored. You will remember that he held in mind nearly the entire New Testament, so that he could quote it most accurately. I think he had also the clearest and most minute details of the Old Testament history, of any man I ever knew. Nor was his reading and recollection limited to Bible details; for he was very familiar with other history, both sacred and profane.

"I call to mind two sermons that he delivered. One was based on the language of Christ addressed to the woman of Samaria, at Jacob's well—John iv.: 'Ye worship ye know not what. We know what we worship; for salvation is of the Jews.' In this sermon he detailed the history of Israel to the revolt under Jereboam, the history of Jereboam and his successors until the overthrow of the ten tribes, and the formation of the mongrel nation called Samaritans. In this he showed that God's promise—Ex. xx., 'In all places where I record my name, I will meet with you and bless you,' was fully realized by the people of God, and that a disregard of the law in harmony with this promise was followed by most disastrous results. And that the same is true under the Gospel—where his name is recorded, and only there, he now meets and blesses his people.

"The second sermon was on the subject of 'Justification by faith.' This was doubtless one of the very best efforts of his life. I will not trouble you with the details of this grand effort, since it was published in full in the *Evangelist* in 1852. The sermon was published, not by his request, but by the unanimous voice of the State Meeting held in Davenport that year.

"I am sorry that I can not give more of the details of his grand work in Iowa."

The winter of 1851–2 was very cold, but father did not stop for bad weather. I remember that when he started to his appointment one cold morning mother cried for fear he would freeze to death. The mail-carrier did freeze to death that day, but father kept from freezing by walking. The next summer was very rainy, and mother was always anxious when there were high waters, for there were no bridges, and father always swam his horse across streams, although he could not swim a stroke.

Then he preached for several years in Illinois, and was gone for months at a time.

In July, 1854, my little sister—for by that time I had another brother and sister—after a brief illness, closed her eyes in death. Fortunately father was at home, to mingle his tears with mother's, over the little coffin.

The next spring father sold his Iowa farm.

Before leaving there an incident occurred that I distinctly remember. The Iowa Legislature had passed some kind of temperance law, and the people were to vote on it at the spring election. Our country lyceum formed itself into a mock court, and tried King Alcohol for various crimes and misdemeanors. Father was appointed prosecuting attorney, and he went at it in earnest, as he always did at anything he undertook. He sent for every man in the vicinity who ever drank, or who had good opportunities to observe the effect of drink on others, to appear as a witness against King Alcohol The trial lasted three evenings, with increasing crowds. Father's adroitness in drawing facts from witnesses—often against their will—kept the audience laughing and applauding. I remember hearing people say that he had mistaken his calling; that he ought to have been a lawyer. On the last evening, when he addressed the jury, he became eloquent. He pictured the terrible effects of intemperance, the ruined homes, the weeping wives, the ragged children. He denounced King Alcohol as guilty of every known crime—of stealing the bread from the mouths of children, of robbing helpless women of everything they valued most, of brutally shedding the blood of thousands, and of filling the whole earth with violence, until the cries of widows and orphans reached to high heaven. When he finished, the house rang with applause. The attorney for the defense tried to reply, but the boys said Mr. Butler had spoiled his speech. The jury brought in a verdict of guilty. The election came off soon afterwards, and people said that it was strongly influenced, in that township, by father's speech.

The next May, mother, my little brother, and I, went to my uncle Gorham's, near Canton, Illinois; while father went to Kansas to buy land, intending, however, to live several years at Mt. Sterling, Illinois, before moving to Kansas.

MRS. ROSETTA B. HASTINGS.

PERSONAL RECOLLECTIONS.

CHAPTER I.

I came to Kansas in the spring of 1855, having been preaching in that part of Illinois known as the Military Tract, during the three preceding years ; but my residence was in Cedar County, Iowa, one hundred and fifty miles from my field of labor, and twenty-six miles to the northwest of the city of Davenport. I had been employed for one year in Iowa as a co-laborer with Bro. N. A. McConnell ; but the church at Davenport, which was the strongest and richest church in the Coöperation, determined to sustain a settled pastor, and this left the churches too poor to support two preachers, and I was left to find another field of labor.

When I first came to Cedar County I came simply as a farmer; and there were but nine families in the township in which we settled. But when the country came to be settled up the result was not favorable to the expectation that we should have prosperous churches in that region. Those who have watched the progress of the temperance reform in Iowa have noticed that, while the prohibitory law is enforced almost throughout the State, there are yet exceptions in the cities of Davenport and Muscatine and the adjacent counties. Here the law is set at defiance. This is owing to the presence of a German, lager-beer-drink-ing, law-defying population, Godless and Christless, and that turn the Lord's day into a holiday. This tendency had begun to be apparent before I left Iowa.

When it became manifest that I could not any longer find a field of labor in Southeastern Iowa, I was recommended to the churches in the counties of Schuyler and Brown, in the Military Tract, Illinois.

My first introduction among them was dramatic, if, indeed, we could give to an incident almost frivolous and laughable, the dignity of a dramatic incident ; and yet the matter had a serious side to it. I had been commended by Bro. Bates, editor of the *Iowa Chris-tian Evangelist*, to the church at Rushville, where I held a meeting of days. The meetings grew in inter-est, there were some important additions, and the church was greatly revived. Twelve miles from Rush-ville was the town of Ripley, a small village, where the people were engaged in the business of manufact-uring pottery ware. Here two Second Adventist preachers, a Mr. Chapman and his wife, were holding forth. This Mr. Chapman was a devout, pious, and earnest man, and a good exhorter, and had an unfalter-ing faith that the Lord was immediately to appear. But his wife was the smartest one in the family. She was fluent and voluble. She had an unabashed fore-head and a bitter and defiant tongue. It was her hobby to declaim against the popular idea of the exist-ence of the human spirit apart from the body. With her this was equivalent to a witch riding on a broom-stick or going to heaven on a moonbeam. Spirit is breath—so she dogmatically affirmed—and when a man breathes out his last breath his spirit leaves his body. But it was her especial delight to declaim against the Pagan notion of the immortality of the soul, and to affirm that the Bible says nothing of the immortality of the soul. A Bro. McPherson undertook to contest the matter with her, but, not finding the scripture he was looking for, she exclaimed with bitter and vixenish speech, "Ah! You can't find it! You can't find it! It isn't there! I told you so!" And thus this couple were fast demoralizing the church, Billy Greenwell, the richest man in the church, being wholly carried away with this fanaticism. John Brown lived half way between Ripley and Rushville, but was a member of the church at Rushville. Bro. Brown was a man of good sense, excellent character, and had been a member of the Legislature. He attended our meeting at Rushville, and, in the intervals of the meeting, was full of questions concerning this heresy that had been sprung on them at Ripley.

Our meeting at Rushville came to a close. It had been a good meeting ; the church had been revived, and there had been important additions. I took dinner with Bro. Brown, and in the afternoon we rode toward Ripley. On crossing the ferry at Crooked Creek, "Old Rob Burton," the ferryman, a tall, stalwart Kentuckian, looking down on me, asked, "Are you the man that's goin' to preach at Ripley to-night?"

"Yes."

"Wall, don't you know thar's a woman thar that's goin' to skin you?"

"Well, I don't know. We shall see how it will be?"

At Rushville I had done my best, and now, being withdrawn from the excitement of the meeting, felt exhausted ; and determined not to touch any debatable question that night. The house was crowded with eager and expectant listeners. My fame had gone before me, and the "woman preacher" was present, ready for a fight. But, alas! My sermon was a bucket of cold water poured on the heads of my brethren. At any other time it would have been accepted as a good and edifying exhortation ; but now, how untimely! The meeting was dismissed and the buzzing was as if a hive of bees had just been ready to swarm. The woman's disciples were jubilant ; and, above the din and hurly-burly, I heard a thin, squeaking voice say, "Give that woman a Bible, and she would say more in five minutes than that man has said in his whole dis-c-o-u-rse." This was Billy Greenwell.

Brother Brown said nothing that night; but the next morning he said to me :

"Bro. B., the people were disappointed with you last night."

"Why, Bro. B., was it not a good sermon ?"

"Yes ; but it was not what the people expected."

"Bro. B., did the people expect me, uninvited, to pitch into a quarrel with which I have nothing whatever to do ?"

"Oh, is that it? Well, wait a little and you shall have an invitation."

Bro. Brown went out, and soon returned with a request that I should discuss the question that Mr. Chapman and his wife had been debating. I sat down and wrote out a statement of the subjects on which I proposed to speak in all the evenings of the coming week. The first commanded universal attention : "Does the spirit die when the body dies ? " They had never thought of that. They had been thunderstruck when this woman told them that the Bible says nothing about the immortality of the soul, but beyond this they had never gone. There was probably more Bible reading that day in Ripley than any day before or since.

At night the house was jammed, and "the woman" was there, Bible in hand. I began: "The Bible speaks of a man as composed of body, soul and spirit. The body is that material tabernacle in which a man dwells, and which Paul hoped to put off that he might be clothed with a house not made with hands, eternal in the heavens. The soul is that animal life we have in common with all living and material things. Thus Jesus is said to have poured out his soul unto death. But what of the spirit? God is spirit, and God can not die. The angels are spirits, and the angels can not die; Jesus says so. Man has a spirit, and can man's spirit die? But spirit sometimes means breath. Yes, and heaven sometimes means the firmament above our heads, where the birds fly. But does it never mean more than this? Paradise sometimes means the happy garden where Adam and Eve dwelt; but does it never mean more than that? So, granting that spirit sometimes means breath, may it not also mean more than that?

"When Jesus said, 'Into thy hands I commend my spirit,' did he mean, 'Into thy hands I commend my breath'? So, when the disciples saw Jesus walking on the water and cried out, 'It is a spirit,' did Jesus say to them, 'This is an old wives' fable; there is no such thing as a spirit'? Did he not rather say to them, 'It is I; be not afraid.' So, also, when he appeared to them in a room, the doors being shut, and

and they cried out, 'It is a spirit,' he said to them, 'Handle me and see; for a spirit hath not flesh and bones, as ye see me have.' In all this Jesus encouraged the disciples to hold the idea which was then popular among the Jews, that the spirit may exist apart from the body, and after the body is dead."

I thus discoursed to them for one hour in development of the Bible teachings concerning human spirits; and in my turn ridiculed the persons that had ridiculed the ideas that had evidently been held by Jesus and the apostles.

Mrs. Chapman had always invited objections; but she was sure to make an endless talk over them. I said, "We will not have an endless confabulation to-night; but I will quote one passage of Scripture, and on that I will rest my case. Any other person may then quote one passage of Scripture and on that rest the case. I have preached one sermon; the other party has preached twenty. So far we will count ourselves even, and it only remains that I should quote my Scripture, and let the other party quote the one Scripture on the opposite side, and then we will be dismissed." I gave the views of the Pharisees and of the Sadducees as detailed by Josephus, and then quoted Luke in the Acts of Apostles: "The Sadducees say there is no resurrection, neither angel nor spirit; but the Pharisees confess both." And Paul says, "Men and brethren, I am a Pharisee, the son of a Pharisee." So I also say, I am a Pharisee, the son of a Pharisee, and hold to the existence of human and angelic spirits.

When I announced that I should call for objections, I saw Mrs. Chapman take up her Bible in a flutter and nervously turn over its leaves. When I sat down all eyes were turned on her, and there was a death-like stillness in the house.   Then she rose up, and in a moment was out of the house.   She left the town the next morning and never came back.   Then it was "Old Bob Burton's" turn to speak.   He said to Billy Greenwell: "Your chest is locked, and the key is lost in the bottom of the sea."

The brethren were gratified that the power of this "soul-sleeping" delusion was broken.   Billy Greenwell never recovered from his infatuation.   He afterwards built a house that, in the number of rooms it contained, was wholly beyond his necessities.   But he thought that when the Lord should come, and he should own all the land that joined him, and should have children to his heart's desire, then he would need all the room.

CHAPTER II.

From Ripley I went to Mt. Sterling, the county-seat of Brown County. This church had fallen into decay for want of the care of a competent evangelist. Here I remained some weeks; and the church was very much revived, and there was a large ingathering. This was originally the home of Bro. Archie Glenn, now conspicuous in building up the University at Wichita. From the first Bro. Glenn, though modest and unobtrusive, was known as a solid and helpful member of the church. He always had the confidence of the people of Brown County, and was by them elected to various public offices, at last becoming Lieutenant-Governor of the State. But his business not prospering to suit him, he removed to Wichita, which was at that time a straggling village of uncertain fortunes, situated on a river of doubtful reputation, and located in a country concerning which the public were debating whether it should be called "The Great American Desert," or a decent place, where civilized men could live and thrive.

But Bro. Glenn did not lose faith in the Lord nor in his country. He went to his new home to be a live man. Wichita has decided to be a city, and not a straggling village of doubtful and cow-boy reputation; the Arkansas River has agreed to behave itself and to co-operate with human hands in giving fertility to its valley, and the geographers have unanimously agreed to strike the "Great American Desert" from the map of the United States. Sister Shields has grown up since these old days to be a woman, then a widow, and now a true yoke-fellow with her father in these great undertakings.

Bro. Lewis Brockman was pointed out to me, when first I came to Mt. Sterling, as a disaffected member; but, on a better acquaintance, it became apparent that his disaffection was that the church members had made a solemn vow to keep the ordinances of the Lord's house, and did not do it. When better order was obtained, he was once more in harmony with the church ; came to Atchison County, Kansas, and died, a pattern of fidelity to his conscience and to every known duty.

During the period of three years in which I remained preaching in the Military Tract, I visited almost all its churches. The number of disciples was large. They had a large amount of wealth at their disposal, and were not averse to using it to promote the advancement of the cause. But the children of this world are, in their generation, wiser than the children of light, and there is a certain practical wisdom that has been abundantly learned by other religious communities that has only come to our churches through a sore and bitter experience; and it was through the fire of this experience they were passing at the time of which we write. "Billy Brown" had been a notable evangelist among them. Indeed, he had been the father in the gospel of the churches in Brown and Schuyler Counties. He was popularly described as having a head "as big as a half bushel," surmounted

by a great shock of hair.   He was an iconoclast, and
devoted his life to the business of image-breaking, and, of
course, the breaking in pieces of the idols of the people created a great tumult.   There was this difference,
and only this difference, between the work of Billy
Brown and Sam Jones; Sam Jones declaims against
sins already condemned by the popular conscience,
but Billy Brown assailed convictions enshrined in the
innermost sanctuary of the hearts of the people.   He
did so because these popular superstitions stood in the
way of the acceptance by the people of the apostolic
gospel.   Of course, the work of such a man carried
with it an inconceivable excitement.   At Mt. Sterling
a man in the audience made some objection.

"What is your name?" said Billy Brown.

"My name, sir, is Trotter."

"Well, come forward, and I will knock your *trot-
ters* out from under you."

But Billy himself sometimes found his match.   At
Ripley he had been preaching after his accustomed
style, and riding away from the place of meeting—it
was in the spring of the year when the mud was deep—
he saw an old man painfully and with difficulty making
his way through the mud.   Knowing that he was a
preacher from his white cravat, his broad-brimmed hat
and single-breasted coat, he said to him:

"Well, old Daddy, how did you like the preaching?"

"Have n't heard any," stiffly replied the old gentleman.

But when the tumult and excitement of this conflict
had passed away, and his converts were brought
face to face with the grave duties of a religious life,

and with the serious work of keeping the ordinances of the Lord's house, they did not know how; they had been born in a whirlwind and could only live in a tempest. Notwithstanding, they loved the Lord's cause, and they trembled for themselves and their children, if they should not be found faithful.

If these churches are not able at the present time to exhibit a growth adequate to their opportunities, it must be remembered, on their behalf, that they have sent to the West an incredibly large number of disciples to serve as the nuclei for other churches throughout that mighty empire that within the past thirty years has grown up between the Missouri River and the Pacific Ocean.

The days I spent in these churches are the golden days of my life. There has been no field in which my labor as an evangelist has yielded a richer harvest; none in which there have been bestowed on me more flattering or more kindly attentions. It was the bright and joyous sunshine of a spring morning, before the bursting of the storm.

Though each year increased my attachment to the people, and apparently added their good-will to myself, there had been coming to the front a difficulty that could not any longer be thrust aside or disregarded. I was one hundred and fifty miles away from home, and from my wife and children. On holding a council of war to consider our future tactics, in which Mrs. Butler, was commander-in-chief, and myself, second in command, she said to me, "Pardee, I am willing to go wherever you say, only when we go there we must go to stay. We must not put our house on wheels. We must not leave our children without settled employment, exposed to all the hazards of a city life, or a life without a permanent habitation."

Under such circumstances the settling on a home in reference to which it could be said, "Here we are to stay," was not an easy matter. The people of the Military Tract were, almost all of them, Kentuckians. There were evidently impending storms in the political horizon. I could not bend my sails to suit every favoring gale; and if, in the future, there should come a time that my conscience should lie in one direction, and my popularity and pecuniary interest in the other, I did not like to invite such a temptation. At any rate, I did not like to place myself in such a position that to bring down on my head popular odium would be to invite pecuniary ruin. These counties in the Military Tract were old settled counties, and land was high; and I was not rich. At this time the Kansas-Nebraska bill had been adopted by Congress, and Kansas had been opened for settlement. It was certain that Eastern Kansas, in the matter of fertility of soil, and all the elements of agricultural wealth, would be a desirable location.

"But there might be a political and social conflict." Yes, and there might be a political and social conflict in Illinois; or, for the matter of that, it might cover the West as with a blanket. It was certain that Eastern Kansas would be early settled from Missouri; and in no State was there a larger percentage of the people known as Disciples. I would, therefore, be among my brethren; and, if I had kept the peace for three years with Kentuckians in Illinois, could I not do the same thing with Missourians in Kansas? In any case, there was a fair prospect of gaining in Kansas a position of pecuniary independence ; and any man can see that such a position was worth all the world to Alexander Campbell, when he was constrained by his conscience to bring down on his own head the utmost wrath of his Baptist brethren.

I started in the spring of 1855 to ride on horseback through Missouri ; but was soon made to feel that there were more things in this world than were known in my philosophy. I had determined to remain over Sunday in Linnville, Linn County, Missouri, the county-seat of the county, as here was a congregation of Disciples ; and called on a merchant of the place, who had been mentioned as one of the leading members. He remarked that he had become acquainted with me through the *Christian Evangelist*, published by Bro. Bates, in Iowa ; but, on learning my destination, seemed strangely oblivious that anything more should be due from him to me. And so, having waited patiently about for a goodly time, I mounted my horse and rode on till dark ; then seeing a light, and having called at the house, I found an old man who kindly received and lodged me. In the morning it appeared that his house was surrounded by negro cabins. Having inquired my destination, he began to talk to me concerning the subject that seemed to be in every man's heart. I replied, submitting to him such views as were held by a majority of Northern men. To my surprise he flared up in anger, and said :

" If you talk that way when you get to Kansas you will never come back again ; they will hang you."

The thing was so absurd I only laughed in the old man's face, and said to him:

" Well, you can not teach an old dog new tricks.

I have spoken my mind so long that I shall continue to do it if they do hang me," and so bade him good-bye.

It was Sunday morning, and it was eighteen miles to Chillicothe. Arriving at the hotel, the people were getting ready for meeting. On questioning them where they were going, the landlord replied :

"To the Christian Church. Will you not go along with us ? "

On asking my name he said:

" O yes ; I have seen your name in the *Christian Evangelist*. You have been preaching in Illinois. I will introduce you to our preacher, and we will make an appointment for you this afternoon."

This landlord was a brother to that Congressman Graves that shot Cilley, a member of Congress from Maine, in a duel with rifles, at Washington. The people described "mine host" as one of "fighting stock" ; and spoke of him as being as thoughtful of the comfort, health and welfare of his slaves as of his own children. To me he seemed simply a genial, jovial, friendly and traditional "Boniface," chiefly intent on furnishing comfortable fare and an enjoyable place for his guest.

By the members of the Christian Church I was kindly received, and was invited to take dinner with the preacher. After dinner two brethren came in, to whom I had been introduced at the meeting-house. After some desultory talk, they asked me :

" *Are you an abolitionist ?* "

I was both angry and confounded. I had never in my life made myself conspicuous in this controversy that was going on between North and South, and why should I be insulted with such a question. I did not answer yes or no, but proceeded to give my views on the subject in general. They listened and remarked that they did not see anything offensive in such views; then made this apology for their seeming rudeness: An old man, a preacher, whom they called Father Clark, had come from Pennsylvania to Chillicothe to live with a married daughter, and had said something concerning slavery offensive to the people, and they had called a meeting of the citizens, and he had been driven out of town and ordered never to return. They had, furthermore, resolved that no abolitionist should thereafter be allowed to preach in the city. These brethren explained that, as I would be called on and interrogated by a committee, they thought it would be better that this should be done by friends, than that I should be questioned by strangers.

" Are You an Abolitionist ? "

I was angry with myself for having consented to preach a sermon after being met with such a question. But by mine host, Bro. Graves, I was treated with the most frank and manly courtesy, albeit that he was brother to the man that shot a brother congressman in a duel with rifles. He seemed to feel like the town clerk at Ephesus: " What man is there that knoweth not that the city of the Ephesians is a worshiper of the great goddess Diana, and of the image that fell down from Jupiter ? Seeing then that these things can not be spoken against, ye ought to be quiet and do nothing rashly."

The Hannibal & St. Joseph Railroad was just being located through the city, yet the town was a dead town, though it was surrounded by a fertile and prosperous country. Bro. Graves seemed awake to all its advantages, and pressed me to remain, pointing out the rapid advance that must take place in the value of its property. But I kept thinking of the question: " Are you an abolitionist?" and bade him farewell.

At nightfall I found myself beyond Gallatin, on the road to St. Joseph. As there were no hotels I called at a private house and was hospitably received. This man, on whom I had called, had come from the State of Pennsylvania, and had grown to a prosperous farmer. There seemed to be no books or newspapers about the house; but he was shrewd and sagacious to a proverb, and was eager to hear from the land of his fathers, and of what was the cause of all this din and clamor and excitement of the people about him. What was the meaning of the Kansas-Nebraska bill? What were the intentions of the Black Republicans? What was the *New York Tribune* doing, that it should raise such a tumult? And what were the purposes of the Emigrant Aid Society that it should be such an offense to the people in Missouri?

On my own part, I also had much to learn from this man, so shrewd and well-informed, and yet so ignorant. What did it mean that citizens of Missouri should go over in force and vote in the Territory of Kansas? We had heard something of this in Illinois, but supposed it was something done by that turbulent and somewhat lawless element that gathers along the borders of civilization; but now it was apparent that this movement was under control of leading citizens of Missouri, and had been participated in by conscientious men, members of the various churches of Missouri, who would in no wise knowingly do anything wrong. What did it mean?

The reader will not be surprised that we should sit up to a late hour of the night, nor that we should renew the subject again in the morning. When I had got ready to leave this man, who had so hospitably entertained me, he explained that he had business on the road on which I was traveling, and that he would accompany me a number of miles.

This emigrant from Pennsylvania, now a citizen of Missouri, who carried his library in his brain and read his books when he conversed with men, and kept his own counsel and lived in peace with his neighbors, was now about to say farewell. With some hesitation he said: " Mr. Butler, I thank you for all you have told me. I feel just as you do; but I must advise you to be careful how you talk to other men as you have talked to me. There are many in this country that would shoot such a man as you are. Good-bye."

CHAPTER III.

It is said, "There are two sides to every question." In my association with men in the free States I had learned one side of this question; now I was learning the other side, and began to be able to put in intelligible shape to myself those reasonings by which these men justified their action. They reasoned thus: "War is a state of violence and always involves a trenching upon what we call natural rights; and its decisions depend not so much on who is right or wrong, as on who wields the longest sword and commands the heaviest battalions. And if in carrying on a war some evil comes to innocent parties, this is only one of its necessary consequences, and is justified by the final result; provided always that the war, as a whole, is right and just. And in such a strained and unnatural condition of affairs men can not be governed by the same scrupulous regard for others' rights by which they are governed in time of peace. But the North and South are already practically in a state of war. This comes of the mistakes made at the formation of our government. Thomas Jefferson and the fathers of the Revolution were mistaken in holding slavery wrong. It is a rightful and natural relation, as between an inferior and superior race. The black race is far better off here in America, in slavery, than they would be in Africa, in freedom and in paganism; and if there is something of hardship in their lot, it is only because there is hardship in the lot of every human being."

These men also said: "Consequent on these erroneous views held by Thomas Jefferson and others, the settlement made as between the North and South has been wrong, from the beginning, It was wrong to close the Northwest Territory, embracing Indiana, Illinois, Michigan, and Wisconsin, against slavery. So also it was wrong to close Kansas against this institution by what was called the Missouri Compromise Line, agreed upon on the admission of Missouri into the Union."

So these men reasoned, and they said: "Now we propose to go and take by the strong hand those rights of which we have been wrongfully deprived since the beginning of the American Government. A little severity now—a resolute seizing on our rights now, in this golden opportunity—will be worth more than the shedding of rivers of blood by and by. Therefore the primary and rudimental legislation of this infant Territory will be worth everything to us in the final settlement of this question. It is certain that the law is against us; but the law itself is wrong, and has been wrong from the beginning. The right that belongs to us is the material and inalienable right of revolution."

We have no right to assume that a majority of the people of Missouri held the sentiments we have here indicated: probably they did not. But the dissent was generally unspoken. The men of this stamp commonly adopted the policy of the man with whom I had just parted. But there was dissent in some cases, bitter and vehement, followed sometimes by bloodshed.

Before I had gone to Iowa, and while I yet lived in Ohio, I had visited Kentucky. An Ohio colony had gone down into Kentucky and located in the counties of Wayne and Pulaski, on the Cumberland River. A brother of mine had gone with them, and I had made him a visit. I thought then, and think now, that there is no region on which the sun shines, more desirable to live in than the region of the Cumberland Mountains. At Crab Orchard I found a man that was born in the State of New York. He had been a soldier at Hull's surrender, at Detroit, in the war of 1812, with Great Britain. From Detroit he had made his way into Kentucky, had married a rich wife with many slaves, and had become a vehement partisan for slavery. But because he was born in the same State with myself, and because I could tell him much about that people that were once his people, he was glad to have me stop with him. Being old and choleric, he would go off into a fierce passion against the abolitionists. He would say: "These men are thieves! Our niggers are our property, and they steal our property. They might as well steal our horses." After awhile he would begin to talk about his children. He would say: "These niggers are ruining my children! My girls are good for nothing! They can not help themselves! They are so helpless they can not even pick up a needle. And my boys! These niggers are ruining my boys! My boys won't work!" And then he would go on to tell the nameless vices the young men of the city were drawn into through their intimacy with the blacks. I thought, but did not say, "My dear sir, if slavery is working such a ruin on your own children, would not the abolitionists be doing you a kindness if they would steal every nigger you have got?"

But there was a still graver aspect that this question was beginning to assume: A woman that is a slave has neither the motive nor the power to protect her own virtue; and the land was threatened to be filled with a nation of mulattoes. But this mixed race would possess all the pride, ambition and talent of the superior race; at the same time they would feel all that undying hatred that a subject people feel toward the men by whom they are subjugated. We would then be sleeping on a volcano, such as may at any hour engulf the empire of Russia.

All this I pondered in my heart as I slowly made my way toward St. Joseph, on the Missouri River, which flows along the western border of Kansas. And now this question was coming to the front and forcing a settlement, and in Kansas would be the first real conflict. In Congress they had only paltried with it; now the people were to try their hand. And what should I do? Had I any right as a Christian and as an American citizen, when providentially called to this work, to withdraw myself from aiding in its settlement? And should I turn my horse in the opposite direction, go back to my Bro. Graves at Chillicothe, and say to him: "You are a man of undoubted courage, but I am a paltroon and a coward, and I am going to hunt a hole and hide myself, where I will be out of danger when this battle is fought between freedom and slavery."

I did not turn back, but revolving all these matters in my mind, reached the city of St. Joseph. Here I had been commended by a friend to a merchant in the

city, a member of the Christian Church. He received
me kindly and treated me courteously, but his partner
in business did not seem to be of that mind. He was
all out of sorts, and gruffly said, ''Kansas is a hum-
bug. It will not be settled in thirty years.''

In revolutions men live fast. I had been ten days
on my journey, and the man that now crossed the
Missouri River at St. Joseph was not just the man that
ten days before crossed the Mississippi at Quincy.
He was a wiser and a sadder man.

On the Kansas side the first company I met was a
two-horse wagon load of men that had been exploring
the Territory and were returning. They seemed thoroughly disgusted, and said: ''The wind blows so hard
in Kansas, it would blow a chicken up against the side
of a barn and hold it there for twenty-four hours.''

''Kansas will not be settled in thirty years.'' So
said my not very amiable friend in St. Joseph. It is
now somewhat more than thirty years, and Kansas has
more than a million of inhabitants. But the State has
a higher boast to make than that it has so increased in
wealth and population. It has been the first State in
the Union—indeed, it has been the first government
in the world—to incorporate prohibition into its fundamental law; and this is the best possible criticism
by which to mark its comparative progress in a Christian civilization.

CHAPTER IV.

After crossing the Missouri River I visited some of the principal settlements in the Territory, such as Atchison, Leavenworth, Lawrence and Topeka. Lawrence, Topeka and Manhattan were settlements made by men from free States, and with an eye single to making Kansas a free State. There was no town located on the Missouri River, and no settlement made in the counties bordering on the Missouri River, that were properly free State settlements. I thought this was a mistake. These counties had by far the largest population, and as these counties would go, the Territory would go; and I thought that no considerations of personal danger ought to hinder, that these counties should have respectable settlements of avowed Free State men among them.

What is now the city of Atchison was then a small village that was being built among the cottonwood trees on the banks of the Missouri River, about twenty miles below St. Joseph, and the same distance above Fort Leavenworth. It had been named after the notable David R. Atchison, who had been a Senator from Missouri, and acting Vice-President of the United States. D. R. Atchison and Gen. B. F. Stringfellow had at this time won a national notoriety in this struggle now going on in Kansas; and both were leading members in the Atchison town company. Dr. Stringfellow was deputed to act as editor-in-chief of the *Squatter Sovereign*, a paper at that time started in Atchison; but the editor was Robert S. Kelly. Bob Kelly, as he was popularly called, was a born leader among such a population as at that time filled Western Missouri. The towns along the Missouri River were the outfitting points for that immense overland freighting business, that was at that time carried on across the western plains, to Santa Fe in Mexico and to Salt Lake, Oregon and California; and here congregated a multitude of that wild, lawless, law-defying and law-breaking mob of men, that accompanied these expeditions, and were the habitues of these western plains, or were among the gold seekers of California.

Bob Kelly was left an orphan at an early age, and was from his youth surrounded with such a population. In person he was handsome as an Apollo, broad-shouldered and muscular, with fair complexion and blue eyes, and was the natural chief of the dangerous men that were drawn to him by his personal magnetism. Moreover, he possessed so much native eloquence, and such an ability to make passionate appeals, as made him a fit person to fire the hearts of these men to deeds of violence.

I obtained a claim to 160 acres of land, twelve miles from Atchison, and on the banks of the Stranger Creek. This claim I would be at liberty to buy, at government price, if I should continue to live on it until it should come into market. My nearest neighbor was Caleb May, a Disciple, and a squatter, from the other side of the river. Bro. May was in his way as much a character as Bob Kelly. He gloried, like John Randolph, of Roanoke, in being descended from

Pocahontas, and that he therefore had Indian blood in his veins. Born and reared on the frontier, tall, muscular, and raw-boned, an utter stranger to fear, a dead shot with pistol or rifle, cool and self-possessed in danger, he had become known far and near as a desperate and dangerous man when meddled with. But he had been converted, and had become a member of the Christian Church, and according to the light that was in him he did his best to conform his life to the maxims of the New Testament, and conscientiously sought to confine all exhibition of "physical force" to such occasions as those in which he might be compelled to defend himself. Then it was not likely to be a healthy business for his antagonist.

After securing my claim, and commencing to build a cabin, I began to look around me. Fully three-fourths of the squatters of this whole region were from the border counties of Missouri. But in Western Missouri the percentage of Disciples was perhaps larger than in any other portion of the United States, consequently I had brethren on every side of me. These men certainly were not refined and educated men, as the phrase goes, still they had the qualities that our Lord found in the fisherman of Galilee.

One thought was in every man's heart, and on every man's tongue. The name *Squatter Sovereign*, that had been given to the Atchison newspaper, indicated the trend of public opinion. They had been flattered with the idea that if they would come to Kansas they should be "Squatter Sovereigns," that the domestic institutions of the infant Territory should be determined not by the nation, nor by Congress, but by themselves. And yet, when the election day came, every election precinct in the Territory, except one, was taken possession of by bodies of men from Missouri, and the elections had been carried, not by *bona fide* citizens, but by an outside invasion. With pain and shame, and bitter resentment, my neighbors told me how they had driven their wagons to the place of voting, on the prairie, and hitched their horses to their wagons, and were quietly going about their business, when with a great whoop and hurrah, which frightened their horses and made them break loose from their wagons, a company of men came in sight, and with swagger and bluster, took possession of the polls, and proceeded to do the voting. Meantime whisky flowed like water, and the men, far gone in liquor, turned the place into a bedlam. In utter humiliation and disgust many of the squatters went home. Caleb May did not get into the neighborhood till afternoon. Before he got to the place of voting, he met Joseph Potter, and on hearing what was done he threw his hat on the ground, and in a towering rage protested he would no longer vote with a party that would treat the people of the Territory in such a way as that. This was done in March, but so far as any public expression of sentiment was concerned, the people seemed dumb. No public meeting was called in the way of protest till the next September, and that meeting was held at Big Springs, sixty miles from Atchison.

But if there was no public protest, there was plenty of it in private. The men from the State of Missouri grew sick at heart. It was a deep, unspoken, bitter and shame-faced feeling, for it was their old neighbors that had done this.

I often asked myself, Can it be hoped that an elec-

tion can be held that shall fairly express the real senti.
ment of the people, if they allow themselves to be
held down under such a reign of terror?

The prevalent sentiment of the squatters from Missouri was, "We will make Kansas a free white State;
we will admit no negroes into it." These men regarded the negro as an enemy to themselves. They
said: "We were born to the lowly lot of toil, and
the negro has made labor a disgrace. Neither ourselves nor our children have had opportunity for education, and the negro is the cause of it. Moreover,
an aristocracy at the South has assumed control of
public affairs, and the negro is the cause of that.
Now we propose to make Kansas a free white State,
and shut out the negro, who has been the cause of all
our calamities."

There was, however, a class of men among them
that had pity for the negro. I will repeat one story,
as it was told me by Bro. Silas Kirkham. Bro. Kirkham belongs to that family of Kirkhams so well
known to our brethren in Southeastern Iowa. Bro.
Kirkham was raised in a slave State. He said:
"When I was a boy I had never thought of slavery
as being wrong. There was a black boy in the settlement named Jim. Jim was so good-natured, faithful
and well-behaved that we all liked him. Jim married
a black girl and they had twins—boys—bright, likely
little fellows, and Jim's wife and twin babies were all
the treasure he had in the world.

Bro. Kirkham said: "One day I found Jim in the
woods, where he had been sent to split rails. He was
sitting down with his face buried in his hands, apparently asleep. I thought I would crawl slyly up to

him, and spring suddenly on him, and frighten him. I did so, but Jim was not asleep at all, but lifted up his head with such a look of unutterable woe that I was frightened myself, and said: "Why, Jim, what is the matter?" Jim cried out: "O, my boys! my boys! Massa sold my boys!"

Bro. Kirkham said: "I have vowed everlasting enmity to an institution that will legalize such treatment of a human being."

But while these ominous mutterings were heard in so many of the Kansas squatter cabins, little did the high and mighty Atchison Town Company, or the editorial staff of the *Squatter Sovereign*, or the puissant Territorial Legislature, reck that so soon they must take up the sad refain of Cardinal Woolsey:

> Farewell, a long farewell, to all my greatness!
> This is the state of man: To-day he puts forth
> The tender leaves of hope, to-morrow blossoms,
> And bears his blushing honors thick upon him;
> The third day comes a frost, a killing frost,
> And—when he thinks, good easy man, full surely
> His greatness is a-ripening—nips his root;
> And then he falls, as I do.

The following extract, from an editorial that appeared at this time in the *Squatter Sovereign*, will show what a rose-colored view these gentlemen took of the situation:

SLAVERY IN KANSAS.

We receive letters, by nearly every mail, asking our opinion as regards the security of slave property in Kansas Territory. We can truly say that no Territory in Uncle Sam's dominion can be found where the slave can be made more secure, or his work command a higher price. Our slave population is gradually increasing by the arrival of emigrants and settlers from the slave States, who, having an eye to making a fortune, have wisely concluded to secure a farm in Kansas, and stock it well with valuable slaves. Situated as Missouri is, being surrounded by free States, we would advise the removal of negroes from the frontier counties to Kansas, where they will be comparatively safe. Abolitionists too well know the character of the Kansas squatter to attempt to carry out the nefarious schemes of the underground railroad companies.

CHAPTER V.

Immediately on obtaining my claim, brethren had
sought me out and made my acquaintance, and soon it
appeared that there were enough Disciples in the settlement to constitute a church.   But the times were
stormy, and we delayed making any movement in that
direction.   It had now come to be the month of June.
There had been refreshing showers.   The singing birds
had come, and the bright sunshine.   The prairie had
put on its royal robes, the forest its richest garments,
and the people had become impatient with their long
isolation from religious meetings.   The Lord's day was
almost ceasing to be the Lord's day to them, and they
demanded a sermon.   We, therefore, came together in
the timbered bottoms of Caleb May's claim, on the banks
of the Stranger Creek.   The gathering was primitive
and peculiar, like the gathering at a Western camp-
meeting—footmen, and men and women on horseback,
and whole families in two-horse lumber wagons.   Some
were dressed in Kentucky-jeans, and some in broad-
cloth ; there were smooth-shaven men and bearded
men ; there were hats and bonnets of every form and
fashion ; all were dressed in such ways as best suited their
convenience or necessities.   In this crowd were those
that, as the years should go by, were destined to grow
in wealth, in understanding, in popularity and high position, and they should be known as the first in the land.

The singing was nòt in the highest style of the musical art, but it was hearty and sincere.

Looking up at the thick branches of the spreading elms above our heads I said:

My Friends and Fellow Citizens:—I have never seen trees clothed with leaves of so rich a green as the trees above our heads. I have never seen prairies robed in richer verdure than the prairies around us.

Since the year of 1832, it has been known that what is called the "Platte Purchase," in Missouri, is the garden spot of the West; and now it is apparent that we have here on the west side of the Missouri River what is the exact counterpart of the Platte Purchase on the east side. It is the same in genial suns, refreshing rains, and unequalled fertility of soil. It is, moreover, true that, owing to the peculiar circumstances under which this Territory will be settled we shall have a population inferior to no population on the face of the earth.

After the deluge was past, God promised enlargement to the sons of Japheth. "God shall enlarge Japheth, and he shall dwell in the tents of Shem;" and more than 3,000 years the sons of Japheth have been fulfilling their destiny. They came originally from the mountain regions around Mount Ararat, and moving westward, they have filled all Europe; and these tribes coming from the east have created the modern European nations. The last and westernmost settlement was made on the island of Great Britain, and here they were stopped from further progress by the Atlantic Ocean; and here, after many generations of war, they coalesced and mingled their blood together, and thus became the British nation; and thus out of the commingling of the blood of the most enterprising races that came out of the loins of Japheth has grown that nation, that in all lands has vindicated its right to be known as the foremost nation of the world.

Christopher Columbus discovered America, and now new causes began to operate that called for the planting of new colonies here in America. Martin Luther asserted the right of a man to stand immediately in the presence of the Lord, to be answerable directly to the Lord, and to confess his sins to the Lord alone, and from the Lord to receive pardon, without the intervention of any pope, priest, or ghostly mediator. This was counted by the Catholic Church a horrible blasphemy, and the Diet of Worms was called, and Luther was commanded to appear before it and recant. Presiding over this Diet was Charles

V., Emperor of Germany; here were Electors, Princes and crowned heads, popish priests, bishops and cardinals, together with the principal nobility of Catholic Europe—these all came together to compel the recantation of Friar Martin Luther. But Luther said : " Unless I be convinced by Scripture and reason, I neither can nor dare retract anything, for my conscience is a captive to God's Word, and it is neither safe nor right to go against conscience," and a great multitude of men in Germany, France, Switzerland, and Great Britain stood beside Luther and protested that they were amenable to the Lord alone, and that they could do nothing against conscience. But these Protestant governments stopped midway between popery and Protestantism; for each of these nations, while renouncing the Pope of Rome, assumed that it was the business of the king to instruct the people what to believe ; and so instead of having one pope they had many popes, consequently many Protestant sects ; and these took the place of that one apostolic church originally established by the apostles. Notwithstanding, there were some in all lands that remained steadfast to the principle enunciated by Martin Luther : " Unless I be convinced by Scripture and reason, I neither can nor dare retract "; and so it came to pass that there were Protestant persecutions as well as Catholic persecutions ; and so also it came to pass that men became wearied with this intolerance, and determined to seek beyond the Atlantic Ocean a place where they could worship God according to the dictates of their own consciences, with none to molest them or make them afraid. It was for such cause that the Puritans settled in New England, the Quakers in New Jersey and Pennsylvania, the Scotch and Irish Presbyterians in North Carolina ; and it was for this cause that the French Huguenots, driven out of France by the French king, came to South Carolina. The most notable cause that induced the planting of the thirteen original colonies here in North America was religious persecution in the Old World. And as the oak grows out of the acorn, so out of these colonies has grown this nation of which we are so proud.

Great Britain became more Lutheran than Germany, the native land of Luther, and God lifted the British nation up to become the chiefest nation of the world ; the United States of North America became more Lutheran than Great Britain, and the eyes of the world are fixed on us in admiration and astonishment. God blessed the house of Obed-edom, and all that he had, because the ark of God was in it.

But there are spots on the sun, and there are exceeding blemishes in our Protestantism, notwithstanding the fact that the glory of the American people has grown out of it. The image that Nebuchadnezzar saw in his dream had feet and toes, part of iron and part of potter's clay, partly strong and partly broken. So it is with our Protestant sectarianism, and because of it we are partly strong and partly broken. Compare the Protestant United States with Catholic Mexico, or compare Protestant Great Britain with Catholic Spain, and compared with these nations we have the strength of iron, but judged by our sectarianism we have the weakness of miry clay.

My friends and fellow citizens, I have the honor to represent to you a people that have said we will go back to that order of things originally established by Jesus and the apostles—we will make no vow of loyalty to any but Jesus, and we will have no bond of union save the testimonies and commandments of the Lord as given to us by the Lord himself and the holy apostles. Out of this we hope may grow such a union of God's people as Jesus prayed for when he prayed that all Christians might be one. We are striving for such an order of things that Protestants may present a united front against the world, the flesh and the devil, and against all disloyalty to Jesus.

To this appeal men often make reply: "We can not break loose from our religious surroundings, dear to us through life-long and most tender associations." But, my friends, this objection can have no weight with this audience, assembled here on this glorious Lord's day, and on this our first religious meeting. Here we have already broken loose from these associations. These ties, how dear so ever to us, we have already sundered. The people with whom we once met, and with whom we once took sweet counsel, the churches in which we once worshiped, shall know us no more forever. Here we are free to act, and to correct the mistakes that have been unwittingly made by the churches with which we have formerly been connected, just as our American fathers were free to frame a better government than the government of the nations out of which they came.

May I not appeal to you, my friends, and say you owe it to yourselves, you owe it to Christians in every land, you owe it to your Lord, you owe it to the future State of Kansas, to so act as to free the Christian profession from the trammels that have hindered its progress and glory ever since the days when our divisions began. If Protestantism has done so much in spite of all its divisions, what will it not do if these hindrances are taken out of the way?

Kansas is certainly predestinated to be a great State. The fertility of its soil, the healthfulness of its atmosphere, and the fact that its population is to be made up from the bravest, most daring and most enterprising men in the nation, all look in this direction; you ought, then, my friends, to see to it that as far as your influence may go its religion shall be nothing less than primitive and apostolic Christianity.

In ascertaining what is primitive and apostolic Christianity, we shall pay supreme respect to the time when the old or Jewish dispensation came to an end, and when the new or Christian dispensation began. The first, or Jewish dispensation, Jesus took out of the way, nailing it to the cross. The second, or Christian dispensation, began after Jesus arose from the dead and ascended up on high, far above the thrones, dominions, principalities and powers of the world of light, and became the Head over all things to the church. This was the proposition with which Peter closed his sermon on the day of Pentecost: "Therefore let all the house of Israel know assuredly, that God hath made that same Jesus, whom ye have crucified, both Lord and Christ." To this agree the words of Jesus after his resurrection, as recorded in the close of Matthew's gospel: "All authority is given to me in heaven and in earth. Go ye, therefore, and disciple all nations, baptizing them into the name of the Father, and of the Son, and of the Holy Spirit."

Luke records some things which Matthew does not record: "Thus it is written, and thus it behooved the Messiah to suffer, and to rise from the dead the third day: and that repentance and remission of sins might be preached in his name among all nations, beginning at Jerusalem; and ye are witnesses of these things." But Mark records some things that neither Matthew nor Luke have recorded: "Go ye into all the world and preach the gospel to every creature. He that believeth and is baptized shall be saved; but he that believeth not shall be damned." In carrying out this commission, thus recorded by these three evangelists, if we find an ignorant pagan that knows nothing of Jesus we shall say to him, as Paul said to the Philippian jailer, ignorant pagan that he was: "Believe on the Lord Jesus Christ and thou shalt be saved and thy house."

But if we find men who already believe, as did the three thousand who were pierced in the heart on the day of Pentecost, we shall say to them, as Peter did: "Repent and be baptized every one of you in the name of Jesus Christ for remission of sins, and you shall receive the gift of the Holy Spirit." If, however, we find a man that not only believes, but is a penitent believer, such as Saul of Tarsus was when Ananias found him, we shall say, as Ananias said: "And now why tarriest thou? Arise and be baptized, and wash away thy sins, calling on the name of the Lord."

In all this there is nothing human, nothing schismatical. All can accept it who are willing to accept the Word of the Lord. In the baptism we administer, we will give no cause for schism: it shall be a burial, and this, so far as the action of baptism is concerned, will meet the conscience of the Greek Church, the Roman Catholic Church, and of all Protestant churches.

Do not, my friends, attempt to turn aside this appeal which I now make to you with a laugh or a sneer. This is the Lord's word, and the word of the Lord is not to be put aside with a sneer. Do not scoff at this as a water of salvation. You certainly will not scoff at the word of the Lord.

And now, my friends, will you not demean yourselves worthy of the high place that God has given you? Adam and Eve carried in their hands the weal or woe of the unnumbered millions of their children that should come after them. Abraham, because of his great faith and because of his high integrity, sent down a blessing upon his fleshly seed for fifty generations; and for the same cause was constituted the spiritual father of a spiritual seed as numerous as the stars of heaven or as the sand upon the seashore. A few Galileean fishermen have filled the world with the glory of the Lord. Luther drove back the darkness of the dark ages and has filled the world with the light of God's Word. And now, my friends, you are laying the foundations of many generations, and will you not take heed how these foundations are laid? Can you repent if you take God at his word and do as did the apostles and the primitive Christians?

CHAPTER VI.

That sermon was preached almost thirty-three years ago. It was an extemporaneous discourse, and no notes were preserved. Nevertheless, there were circumstances attending its delivery, that have indelibly impressed its leading points on the memory of the writer.

S. J. H. Snyder was a Lutheran from Pennsylvania, and at that time was a resident of Atchison county. He had traveled to see the world, and was a writer of books. He heard the sermon, and was greatly taken with it. He wrote out a report of it, and handed his report to me for criticism and correction. He intended to send it for publication to a paper in Pennsylvania. I said to him that his report left out the most essential and vital part of the sermon, and proposed myself to write out an abstract of it for his use. This I did, but my friend Mr. Snyder concluded: "This is a hard saying, who can hear it?" He was not willing to be counted unsound in the faith by his brethren in Pennsylvania, and forwarded the original manuscript.

There were also in the audience two young gentlemen, recently come from the New England States to seek their fortune. They were just of that age to think that what they did not know, or at least what the people of New England did not know, was not worth knowing. Such a meeting in the open air; such an audience, in which the dress of every man and woman was got up according to their own notions, and that, too, without consulting Mrs. Grundy.; *such a preacher! and such a sermon!* Certainly these all were new to them, and did not command their highest admiration. These young gentlemen kept up a sort of running commentary between themselves, on what they saw going on, until, becoming tired of their misbehavior, I turned and said to them in effect: "Young gentlemen, you profess to be men of good breeding, and it is understood that well-bred people will behave themselves in meeting." They were very angry, and one of them wrote me a saucy letter about it. But finding little sympathy in the settlement, they went to Atchison, and there they found abundant sympathy and open ears to hear. A man who was a preacher, and a pronounced free State man, had come from Illinois and had settled on the Stranger Creek; and who could tell the mischief he might do to his brethren who were squatters from Missouri? When these same New England gentlemen were in their turn stripped of all they were worth by the "Border Ruffians" it changed their feelings toward their free State brethren "mightily."

And now that feeling of dissatisfaction that had been all along festering in the hearts of the people, began to come to the surface. An inside view would have revealed a perpetual murmur of discontent. The Territorial Legislature was now in session, and doing its work, and copies of the laws they had enacted were coming into circulation. No legislature in America had ever been elected as they had been, and we have already learned what a thrill of horror and pain this caused in the hearts of the squatters. It would have been a dictate of the most obvious common sense that a body of men whose claim to be a Territorial Legislature rested on such a basis should proceed with the utmost moderation. But they were intoxicated with success. It is an old and a wise saw, that whom the gods wish to destroy they first deprive of their reason, and these men were smitten with judicial blindness. No slave State had ever enacted such savage and bloody laws—laws of such barbarous and inhuman severity, for the protection of slave property. And now the people were reading copies of these laws, and nothing could long suppress the evidences of discontent. The following editorial is also copied from the *Squatter Sovereign:*

WATCH THE ABOLITIONISTS.

Circumstances have transpired within a few weeks past, in this neigborhood, which place beyond a doubt the existence of an organized band of Abolitionists in our midst. We counsel our friends who have slave property to keep a sharp lookout, lest their valuable slaves may be induced to commit acts which might jeopardize their lives.

Mr. Grafton Thomasson lost a valuable negro a week ago, and we have not the least doubt that she was persuaded by one of this lawless gang to destroy herself rather than remain in slavery. In fact, one of this gang was heard to remark that she did perfectly right in drowning herself, and just what he would have done, or what every negro who is held in bondage should do. We ask, Shall a man expressing such sentiments be permitted to reside in our midst? Be permitted to run at large among our slaves, sowing the seeds of discord and discontent, jeopardizing our lives and property?

In another instance we hear of a servant being tampered with, and induced to believe that she was illegally held in bondage; since which time she has been unruly, and shows evidence of discontent. Such is the effect produced by permitting the *convicts* and *criminals* of the Eastern cities shipped out here by the aid societies to reside in our midst.

The depredations of this fanatical sect do not stop here. Their crimes are more numerous and their acts more bold. It is well known that on Independence and Walnut Creeks, within a few miles of this place, a great number of free slaves and Abolitionists are settled whose thieving propensities are well known. We honestly believe that an organized band of these outlaws exists, whose objects are pecuniary gain and spite, to rob us of our property, drive off our cattle and horses, incite our slaves to rebellion, and, when opportunity afford them facilities for escaping, to aid them.

Within a short time about one hundred and fifty head of cattle have been stolen from this neighborhood, driven off, and sold. Eight or nine horses and several mules have been taken out of the emigrants' camp, driven to parts unknown, and the money is now jingling in the pockets of the Abolitionists. Occurrences of this kind were never before known in this neighborhood, and prior to the shipment of the *filth* and *scum* of the Eastern cities our property was secure and our slaves were contented and happy.

The enormity of these offenses, and the great loss of property, should open the eyes of our citizens to their true situation. We can not feel safe while the air of Kansas is polluted with the breath of a single Free-soiler. We are not safe, and self-preservation requires the total extermination of this set. Let us act immediately, and with such decision as will convince these deperadoes that it is our fixed determination to keep their feet from polluting the soil of Kansas.

We published in a former chapter the letter of recommendation this same Robert S. Kelley had written, certifying to the good behavior of the people of the county, and the facts of the case were not altered now; save and only this, that a black woman, the slave of Grafton Thomasson, had drowned herself. This said Thomasson was a drinking man, and when in drink was desperate and dangerous. What passed between this man, when intoxicated, and this slave woman the public have never been informed. An altercation grew out of this between Thomasson and J. W. B. Kelly, Esq., a young lawyer from Cincinnati, in which Thomasson, a great big bully, flogged Kelly, who was a small man, of slender build, and weak in body. A public meeting was called, in which resolutions were adopted praising this big bully for flogging this weak and helpless man; and then this Kelly was ordered to leave, and was not seen in Kansas afterwards. Beyond this, if there was any of this high-handed stealing and robbery we never heard anything of it afterwards.

During the month of July, an event occurred destined to have lasting influence on the Christian cause in Northeastern Kansas. A church was organized at Mt. Pleasant. It is now known as the Round Prairie Church. This church, after passing through varied fortunes, has finally issued in being one of the best and most active churches in Kansas. The last act in his public ministry was the organizing of this church by Elder Duke Young, father of Judge William Young. Duke Young was one of the pioneer preachers of Western Missouri. When in his manhood's prime he was abundant in labors, and though he was without any scholastic attainments he had a keen mother wit, good sense, and good natural gifts as a public speaker; and, working in poverty, exposure, hardship, misrepresentation, and implacable opposition, he was one of the men that laid the foundations of the cause in Western Missouri. Becoming old, he came with his son, William Young, to Kansas, and after organizing the church at Mt. Pleasant, he failed in health, and ceased his work in the ministry.

Connected with this church was Numeris Humber. Bro. Humber and his wife were among the excellent of the earth. Sister Humber was a matronly woman, comely in person, greatly beloved, and a queen of song. When D. S. Burnett afterwards held a protracted meeting at this place, it was the songs of Sister Humber and Stephen Sales, as much as the preaching of D. S. Burnett, that made the meeting a wonderful success, and one long to be remembered. Bro. Humber and Bro. Young were slave-holders. Bro. Humber was also an emancipationist in his views of slave-holding, and often said that if a position could be secured suitable for emancipated slaves he would gladly set his slaves free. When at last they were made free by the results of the war, and went to Leavenworth to live, it was always a burden on Bro. Humber's heart to watch over them, and try and save them from the temptations that were laid for their feet in that wicked city.

It will be readily seen that no scandal would be created in Atchison by organizing a church at Mt. Pleasant with such men to take the lead in it.

CHAPTER VII.

It was now the middle of August. My cabin was completed, and I was ready to go back and bring Mrs. Butler and the children to Kansas. Bro. Elliott accompanied me to Atchison, where I intended to take a steamboat to St. Louis, thence going up the Illinois River to Fulton county, Illinois, where Mrs. Butler had been stopping with her sister.

The things that had been happening in the Territory had been so strange and unheard of, and the threats of the *Squatter Sovereign* had been so savage and barbarous, that I wanted to carry back to my friends in Illinois some evidence of what was going on. I went, therefore, with Bro. Elliott to the *Squatter Sovereign* printing office to purchase extra copies of that paper. I was waited on by Robert S. Kelley. After paying for my papers I said to him: "I should have become a subscriber to your paper some time ago only there is one thing I do not like about it." Mr. Kelley did not know me, and asked: "What is it?"

I replied: "I do not like the spirit of violence that characterizes it."

He said: "I consider all Free-soilers rogues, and they are to be treated as such."

I looked him for a moment steadily in the face, and then said to him: "Well, sir, I am a Free-soiler; and I intend to vote for Kansas to be a free State."

He fiercely replied: "You will not be allowed to vote."

When Bro. Elliott and myself had left the house, and were in the open air, he clutched me nervously by the arm and said: "Bro. Butler! Bro. Butler! You must not do such things; they will kill you!"

I replied: "If they do I can not help it."

Bro. E. was now to go home. But before going he besought me with earnest entreaty not to bring down on my own head the vengeance of these men. I thanked him for his regard for me, and we bade each other good-by.

Bro. E. had come to feel that my life was precious to the Christian brethren in Atchison county. Except myself they had no preacher, and they needed a preacher.

The steamboat bound for St. Louis that day had been detained, and would not arrive until the next day. I must, therefore, stay over night in Atchison. I conversed freely with the people that afternoon, and said to them: "Under the Kansas-Nebraska bill, we that are free State men have as good a right to come to Kansas as you have; and we have as good a right to speak our sentiments as you have."

A public meeting was called that night to consider my case, but I did not know it. The steamboat was expected about noon the next day. I had been sitting writing letters at the head of the stairs, in the chamber of the boarding-house where I had slept, and heard some one call my name, and rose up to go down stairs; but was met by six men, bristling with revolvers and bowie-knives, who came up stairs and into my room. The leader was Robert S. Kelley. They presented me a string of resolutions, denouncing free State men in unmeasured terms, and demanded that I should sign them. I felt my heart flutter, and knew if I should undertake to speak my voice would tremble, and determined to gain time. Sitting down I pretended to read the resolutions—they were familiar to me, having been already printed in the *Squatter Sovereign*—and finally I began to read them aloud. But these men were impatient, and said: "We just want to know will you sign these resolutions?" I had taken my seat by a window, and looking out and down into the street, had seen a great crowd assembled, and determined to get among them. Whatever should be done would better be done in the presence of witnesses. I said not a word, but going to the head of the stairs, where was my writing-stand and pen and ink, I laid the paper down and quickly walked down stairs and into the street. Here they caught me by the wrists, from behind, and demanded, "Will you sign?" I answered, "*No*," with emphasis. I had got my voice by that time. They dragged me down to the Missouri River, cursing me, and telling me they were going to drown me. But when we had got to the river they seemed to have got to the end of their programme, and there we stood. Then some little boys, anxious to see the fun go on, told me to get on a large cotton-wood stump close by and defend myself. I told the little fellows I did not know what I was accused of yet. This broke the silence, and the men that had me in charge asked:

"Did the Emigrant Aid Society send you here?"

"No; I have no connection with the Emigrant Aid Society"

"Well, what did you come for?"

"I came because I had a mind to come. What did you come for?"

"Did you come to make Kansas a free State?"

"No, not primarily; but I shall vote to make Kansas a free State."

"Are you a correspondent of the *New York Tribune?*"

"No; I have not written a line to the *Tribune* since I came to Kansas."

By this time a great crowd had gathered around, and each man took his turn in cross-questioning me, while I replied, as best I could, to this storm of questions, accusations and invectives. We went over the whole ground. We debated every issue that had been debated in Congress. They alleged the joint ownership the South had with the North in the common Territories of the nation; that slaves are property, and that they had a natural and inalienable right to take their property into any part of the national Territory, *and there to protect it by the strong right arm of power,* while I urged the terms of the Kansas-Nebraska bill; and that under it free State men have a right to come into the Territory, and by their votes to make it a free State, if their votes will make it so.

At length an old man came near to me, and dropping his voice to a half-whisper, said in a confidential tone: "N–e–ow, Mr. Butler, I want to advise you as a friend, and for your own good, *when you get away, just keep away.*"

I knew this man was a Yankee, for I am a Yankee myself. His name was Ira Norris. He had been given an office in Platte county, Mo., and must needs be a partisan for the peculiar institution. I gave my friend Norris to understand that I would try to attend to my own business.

Others sought to persuade me to promise to leave the country and not come back. Then when no good result seemed to come from our talk, I said to them: "Gentlemen, there is no use in keeping up this debate any longer; if I live anywhere, I shall live in Kansas. Now do your duty as you understand it, and I will do mine as I understand it. I ask no favors of you."

Then the leaders of this business went away by themselves and held a consultation. Of course I did not know what passed among them, but Dr. Stringfellow afterwards made the following statement to a gentleman who was getting up a history of Kansas:

A vote was taken upon the mode of punishment which ought to be accorded to him, and to this day it is probably known but to few persons that a decided verdict of death by hanging was rendered; and furthermore, that Mr. Kelley, the teller, by making false returns to the excited mob, saved Mr. Butler's life. Mr. Kelley is now a resident of Montana, and volunteered this information several years ago, while stopping at St. Joe with the former senior editor of the *Squatter Sovereign*, Dr. J. II. Stringfellow. At the time the pro-slavery party decided to send Mr. Butler down the Missouri River on a raft, Dr. Stringfellow was absent as a member of the Territorial Legislature.

The crowd had now to be pacified and won over to an arrangement that should give me a chance for my life. A Mr. Peebles, a dentist from Lexington, Mo., who was working at the business of dentistry in Atchison, and himself a slave-holder, was put forward to do this work. He said: "My friends, we must not hang this man; he is not an Abolitionist, he is what they call a Free-soiler. The Abolitionists steal our niggers, but the Free-soilers do not do this. They intend to make Kansas a free State by legal methods. But in the outcome of the business, there is not the value of a picayune of difference between a Free-soiler and an Abolitionist; for if the Free-soilers succeed in making Kansas a free State, and thus surround Missouri with a cordon of free States, our slaves in Missouri will not be worth a dime apiece. Still we must not hang this man; and I propose that we make a raft and send him down the river as an example."

And so to him they all agreed. Then the question came up, What kind of a raft shall it be?* Some said, "One log"; but the crowd decided it should be two logs fastened together. When the raft was completed I was ordered to take my place on it, after they had painted the letter R. on my forehead with black paint. This letter stood for *Rogue*. I had in my pocket a purse of gold, which I proffered to a merchant of the place, an upright business man, with the request that he would send it to my wife; but he declined to take it. He afterwards explained to me that he himself was afraid of the mob. They took a skiff and towed the raft out into the middle of the Mis-

---

* When they were making the raft father noticed that one of the logs was sound and the other rotten. They fastened them together by nailing shakes—split shingles—from one to the other. Some one remarked that the nails would pull out the first time the raft struck a snag. Then they said they would drive in long wooden pins. But father noticed that the long pins were driven into the sound log, while the ends on the rotten log were only fastened by the nails.

One of the logs of which the raft was made was much longer than the other, and on the end of the longer log they put the flag. And over the rough swift current father walked the dizzy length of that single log and took down the flag. Mother still keeps that flag as a precious relic. Several years ago one of the men engaged in that mob ran for office in Northern Kansas. His opponent borrowed the flag, to use in the campaign, and returned it in good order. But we have since learned that he had several copies of it painted, and that one of them is now in the rooms of the Kansas Historical Society, in the showcase with John Brown's cap, and is shown as the veritable flag that was on Pardee Butler's raft.

souri River. As we swung away from the bank, I rose up and said: "Gentlemen, if I am drowned I forgive you; but I have this to say to you: If you are not ashamed of your part in this transaction, I am not ashamed of mine. Good-by."

Floating down the river, alone and helpless, I had opportunity to look about me. I had noticed that they had put up a flag on my raft, but had paid no attention to it; now I looked at it and it charged me with stealing negroes; and it was thought by many to be no sin to shoot a "nigger thief." Down that flag must come; and then I remembered that they had said they would follow me down the river and shoot me if I did pull it down. The picture on the flag was that of a white man riding at full gallop, on horseback, with a negro behind him. The flag bore this inscription: "GREELEY TO THE RESCUE: I HAVE A NIGGER. THE REV. MR. BUTLER, AGENT FOR THE UNDERGROUND RAILROAD."

This flag I pulled down, cut off the flag with my pen-knife, and made a paddle of the flag staff, which was a small sapling which they had cut out of the brush, and was forked at the upper end. Between these forks they had carefully sewed this flag with twine, and this part of the canvas I left and made it serve as the blade of my paddle; and so in due time I paddled to the Kansas shore. The river was rapid, and there were in the river heaps of drift-wood, called "rack-heaps," dangerous places into which the water rushed with great violence; but from these I was mercifully saved, and though I could not swim, I landed a few miles below Atchison without harm or accident, and made my way to Port William, a small town about twelve miles down the river.

THE FLAG THAT WAS ON PARDEE BUTLER'S RAFT.

CHAPTER VIII.

At Port William I had already become acquainted
with a Bro. Hartman. He had leased a saw-mill, and
was running it, and I had bought lumber of him.
Having reached Port William, I went to Bro. H. and
said, "I want to obtain lodging of you to-night; but
as I do not want to betray any man into trouble, I
must first tell you what has befallen me." I then told
him my mishap at Atchison, and said: " Now if you
do not want to lodge such a man, please say so, and I
will go somewhere else." He replied: "You shall
lodge with me if it cost me every cent I am worth."
He then went on to say that he had leased that mill of
men who were very bitter, and very ultra in their
views, and that they might be angry with him, and
turn him out of the mill. But at last he said: "There
is Bro. Oliphant living in the bluffs; he is under no
such embarrassment," and Bro. Hartman took me
there. The next day was the Lord's day, and Oliver
Steele was to preach the first sermon in that little village on that day. Oliver Steele was a notable citizen
of Platte county, Missouri. His name appears in the
early days of the *Millennial Harbinger* as a citizen of
Madison county, Kentucky. Bro. Steele complains of
the Reformers of Kentucky, that they are too much
wedded to Old Baptist usages to be true to the primitive and apostolic order of things. Then Bro. Steele

came to Platte county, Missouri, and had become one of its most wealthy and influential citizens. He was an eminent example of a courtly and courteous " Old Virginia gentleman," and was loved by the rich and loved by the poor, he was loved by white folks and black; loved by the mothers and their babies; and the people patronized his preaching, not because he was a great preacher, for he certainly was not, but because they loved the man. He was an old Henry Clay Whig, and like that great Kentucky statesman was an Emancipationist. Bro. S. was to come over the river and preach the first sermon in this new town, and it was a great event to the people. On returning to Port William in the morning Bro. Hartman said that I must take dinner with him, and he would introduce me to Bro. Steele. It was not until twenty-five years after-wards, and only after Sister Hartman had died, that Bro. Hartman told me what so much altered his feelings. She was a sweet Christian woman, and when Bro. H. went to her she said to him: "Husband, do n't you know that in the last great day the Lord will say, 'I was a stranger and ye took me in'; and do n't you remember how the good Samaritan showed mercy to the man that fell among thieves? Now we believe that this man is an innocent man; and what will the Lord say to us if we turn him out of doors?"

At dinner, at the house of Bro. Hartman, was also Dr. Oliphant, father of the Bro. Oliphant with whom I had lodged. He was a brusque, blunt-spoken, honest, anti-slavery Northern Methodist preacher. He said bluntly at the table: " Well, Mr. Butler, they treated you rather roughly at At-Atchison, did they not?" I said, "Yes—" attempted to say more, broke down and left the table, and went out of the house. My heart was not as hard here, among sympathizing friends, as it had been the day before, when I had to face a raging mob. When I returned no mother could be more tender seeking out the hurt of her boy bruised in a rough encounter with his fellows, than was Oliver Steele. He would hear the whole story, sighed over these "evil days," and listened with approval to the vindication I made of the purposes of the free State men. How many men that, through a sense of bitter wrong, are in danger to become desperate, could be won to a better temper the world has never fully tried.

The news of what had been done at Atchison flew like wild-fire through the country. This proved the last feather that broke the camel's back. It became apparent that the country was full of men that were ready to fight. As for my friend Caleb May, he went into Atchison and said: "*I am a free State man: now raft me!*" As no one seemed inclined to undertake that job, he faithfully promised them that if there was any more of that business done he would go over into Missouri and raise a company of men and clean out the town.

Meantime my friends at Port William provided means to send me down to Weston, there to take the steamboat Polar Star, bound for St. Louis. "Boycotting" was a word unknown to the English language at that time; and yet I was "boycotted" on board the steamboat. I heard nothing—not a word; and yet I could feel it. I had hoped to be a total stranger, but it was evident I was not, and the most comfort I could find was to keep my state-room, and employ my time writing out the appeal I intended to make to the people, through the *Missouri Democrat*, published in St. Louis. At length my work was done, and yet we were only half way to St. Louis. The reader will believe that my reflections were not cheerful. What would become of myself?" What would become of my wife and children? What would become of Kansas, or of the United States?

At Jefferson City a man had come aboard of the boat who seemed almost as much alone as myself. Still the captain and officers of the boat paid him marked attention. One thing I noticed, he abounded in newspapers, and I wanted something to read that should save me from my own reflections. I ventured to ask him for the loan of some of his papers; then when I returned them he went to his trunk and took out a book of travels and gave it to me, saying: "Take that, please. It will amuse you." At length we could see the smoke of the city of St. Louis, and I gave back to this stranger the book he had loaned me. He said: "No, thank you." I was startled, and said with some surprise: "I do not know why you should do this to a stranger." He laughed and said: "You are not so much a stranger as you think. Your name is Butler, is it not?"

"Yes."

"And they mobbed you at Atchison?"

"Yes."

"Well, please call on me at the office of the *Missouri Democrat*."

"And what is your name?"

" *They call me B. Gratz Brown.*

And so Providence had prepared the way for making my appeal to the people.   B. Gratz Brown had the preceding winter, at Jefferson City, either given or accepted a challenge to fight a duel; but the public authorities had interfered, and some . business connected with this matter had called him to Jefferson City.   But whence had he his knowledge of the mobbing at Atchison?   The *Squatter Sovereign* had been issued immediately after they had put me on the raft, and had contained the following editorial:

On Thursday last [it was Friday], one Pardee Butler arrived in town with a view of starting for the East, probably with the purpose of getting a fresh supply of Free-soilers from the penitentiaries and pest-holes in the Northern States. Finding it inconvenient to depart before the morning, he took lodgings at the hotel and proceeded to visit numerous portions of our town, everywhere avowing himself a Free-soiler, and preaching Abolition heresies. He declared the recent action of our citizens in regard to J. W. B. Kelley the infamous proceedings of a mob, at the same time stating that many persons in Atchison who were Free-soilers at heart had been intimidated thereby, and prevented from avowing their true sentiments; but that he (Butler) would express his views in defiance of the whole community.

On the ensuing morning our townsmen assembled *en masse*, and, deeming the presence of such a person highly prejudicial to the safety of our slave population, appointed a committee to wait on Mr. Butler and request his signature to the resolutions passed at the late pro-slavery meeting. After perusing the resolutions, Mr. B. positively declined signing them, and was instantly arrested by the committee.

After various plans for his disposal had been considerd, it was finally decided to place him on a raft composed of two logs firmly lashed together, that his baggage and a loaf of bread be given him, and having attached a flag to his primitive bark, Mr. Butler was set adrift in the great Missouri, with the letter "R" legibly painted on his forehead.

He was escorted some distance down the river by several of our citizens, who, seeing him pass several rock-heaps in quite a skillful manner, bade him adieu and returned to Atchison.

Such treatment may be expected by all scoundrels visiting our town for the purpose of interfering with our time-honored institutions, and the same punishment we will be happy to award to all Free-soilers and Abolitionists.

The *Missouri Democrat* was what was known as the "Tom Benton" paper of Missouri, and was not ostensibly a *Free-soil* paper, yet it vehemently inveighed against the ruffianism with which free State men had been treated. Of course there was sympathy in the office of the *Missouri Democrat*, that made some amends for the rough treatment I had got at the hands of citizens of Missouri.

Having completed my business in St. Louis I turned my face toward my old field of labor in the " Military Tract," *via* the Illinois River. The reader will believe that my reflections were full of anxieties. What would the brethren say of me ? Were my prospects blighted from this time forward ?

CHAPTER IX.

The brethren in Illinois were at the first amazed at
what they heard, and did not know what to think or
say.   Before they could make up their minds, the following editorial appeared in the *Schuyler County Democrat*, published at Rushville:

ELDER PARDEE BUTLER,

The gentleman who was placed on a raft in the Missouri River, with a
proper uniform for a Northern fanatic, is in Rushville. We saw hand-
bills posted around town stating that he would hold a meeting in the
Christian Church. We are informed he will deliver a series of lectures,
in which, *of course*, he will give vent to his indignation toward the people of Kansas, Judge Douglas and the Administration. We thought
Schuyler county was the last place which a *Northern fanatic* would visit
for sympathy. We hope that those that go to hear his lectures, which
differ with him in their sentiments, will not interrupt him or give him
any pretext by which he could denounce our citizens.

To the above notice of myself I made the following reply:

[For the Prairie Telegraph.]

MESSRS. EDITORS: *Sirs*—I find the above notice of myself in the
last issue of the *Schuyler Democrat.*

While in Kansas I diligently worked six days of the week, and on
Lord's day spoke to my neighbors, not in reference to affairs in Kansas,
but in reference to our common interest in a better and heavenly country. I do not know that I indicated my political proclivities, in any
word or allusion, on any such occasion. But I did, in private conversa-
tions with my neighbors, avow my intention to vote for Kansas to be a
free State, and gave my reasons for so doing. *This was my only
offence.*

What must you think of yourself, sir, in this notice you take of this transaction? And you pretend to be a conservator of public morals! If there is in town a clergyman that will consent to teach you a few lessons upon the items of justice and gentlemanly behavior, I suggest it may be to your advantage to put yourself under his tuition. You may perhaps learn that it is neither just nor gentlemanly gratuitously to insult a man, because you have *surmised* that he will show some resentment at the ruffianism of a Kansas mob, with which you seem to sympathize.

Since I came into Illinois I have steadily declined to make any statement of this affair in any public address. Still it is perhaps due to the world to know some additional facts. How the mob deliberated among themselves. . . . .

I have never yet made war on Judge Douglas. It is true that the Missouri Compromise, being a time-honored covenant of peace between North and South, I would much rather it had been suffered to remain; but now I am rather indignant at the clear and palpable violation of the principles of the Kansas-Nebraska bill, in the attempt made by border ruffians to drive out peaceable citizens from the free States. I am still more indignant that a Northern editor can be found to wink at such flagrant and unquestionable wrong. Judge Douglas may well exclaim, " Save me from my friends!"

Perhaps, upon reflection, you may be convinced of three things: First, that I am not a fanatic, and have not deserved the treatment I have received; second, that your friends may be trusted not to create any disturbance at my meetings; and, third, that instead of seeking to stir up against me the prejudices of ignorant partisans, you may safely devote yourselves to the more honorable employment of seeking to restore in our unhappy country the supremacy of law. Very faithfully,

PARDEE BUTLER.

RUSHVILLE, Sept. 11, 1855.

The final result was much more favorable than could have been expected, and the brethren gave me an invitation to remain with them through the winter.

I tarried six weeks in Illinois, and then returned to Kansas with Mrs. Butler and our two children, of whom the eldest is now Mrs. Rosetta B. Hastings. Milo Carleton had already reached the Territory, direct from the Western Reserve, Ohio. He was Mrs. Butler's brother, and it was determined that the two families should spend the winter together, while I should return to Illinois.

We will now pause in our personal narrative and tell what had been going on the preceding summer in other parts of the Territory. A delegate convention had been called by the free State men to meet during the preceding September at a place called Big Springs, on the Santa Fe trail, midway between Lawrence and Topeka. Here the free State men agreed on a plan, to which they steadily adhered through all the sickening horrors that gave to "bleeding" Kansas a world-wide and thankless notoriety. They resolved that they would not in any way, shape or manner, recognize the legality of this so-called Territorial Legislature, nor the machinery it should call into being for the government of the Territory. They would bring no suits in its courts; they would attend no elections called by its authority; they would pay no attention to its county organizations; and yet, as far as in them lay, they would do no act that might make them liable to the penalty of its laws. In short, they would be like the Quaker, who, when drafted into the army, replies: "Thee must not expect me to fight with carnal weapons;" and when amerced in a fine for non-compliance with the laws, makes the reply, "Thee must not expect me to pay money for such carnal uses, but thee can take my property." Nevertheless, there was superadded to these peaceful resolutions an un-Quakerlike intimation that under certain contingencies they would fight.

Beyond the Wakarusa, and about eight miles from Lawrence, was a placed called Hickory point. Here

were some timber claims, and here resided Jacob Branson, a peaceful and harmless free State man. Beside
him lay a vacant timber claim, and he invited a young
man named Dow to take it. Dow boarded with Branson. When the Missourians came into Kansas the
preceding March, many of them staked out a claim
which they pretended to hold. One William White,
of Westport, Mo., pretended, in his way, to hold this
claim. There was not a particle of legality in his pro-
ceeding. Notwithstanding, certain pro-slavery men,
among whom were Coleman, Hargis and Buckley, de-
termed to drive off Branson and Dow. They sent
threatening letters to Branson, and cut timber on
Dow's claim; and this made bad blood. One day an
altercation took place between Dow and the above-
named pro-slavery men at a blacksmith shop, and Coleman followed Dow and shot him. Dow was unarmed,
and held up his hands and cried, "Don't shoot," but
Coleman lodged a load of buckshot in his breast, and
he fell dead, and his body lay in the road till sundown.
Then Branson came and took up the body and buried
it. This murder created a prodigious sensation; and
a public meeting was called, at which there was violent
and threatening talk by the free State men. The
three above-named pro-slavery men were all present
when the murder was committed. They fled, and
their dwellings were burned. Coleman went to Westport and gave himself up to "Sheriff Jones." This
introduces us to the man that was able to achieve an
infamous pre-eminence among that band of conspirators that put in motion a train of causes that issued in
the death of half a million of American citizens, and
which covered the land with mourning from Maine to

Florida, and from the Atlantic to the Pacific Ocean. This Jones is described by the free State men as a bully and a braggart, as only brave when he was not in danger, and as one of the most noisy and obstreperous of the pro-slavery leaders. Though living in Westport, Mo., he was made sheriff of Douglas county, fifty miles from his place of residence. Buckley swore out a peace warrant against Branson—he swore that his life was in danger. Sheriff Jones took with him these three men, who were parties in the murder of Dow, and arrested Branson, dragging him out of his bed at night. He had also associated with himself eleven other men. The news spread like wild-fire among the free State men. This Jones was supposed to be capable of any atrocity, however horrible, and a company of sixteen men was gathered up for the rescue of Branson. Of this company Sam Wood, of Lawrence, was the leader. They met Jones and his company at Blanton's Bridge, on the Wakarusa River, where Jones was crossing to go to Lecompte, and called a halt. Jones demanded: "What's up?"

Sam Wood replied: "That's what we want to know."

Wood asked: "Is Jacob Branson in this crowd?"

Branson replied: "Yes, I am here and a prisoner."

Wood replied: "Well, come out here among your friends."

Jones threatened with oaths and imprecations to shoot. The rescuing party leveled their guns and said: "Well, we can shoot, too." Nobody was hurt, no gun was fired, and Jacob Branson, coming out from among his captors, walked away.

It will be seen that this was a clear and palpable

violation of the plan of procedure which the free State
men had agreed upon among themselves, and this act
made Kansas for three years a dark and bloody ground,
and concentrated on this Territory the eyes of the
whole nation.   Of the rescuing party only three were
citizens of Lawrence.   Sam Wood was in his element.
He was a man overflowing with patriotism, yet succeeded in doing more harm to his friends than to his
enemies.   He possessed unmistakable talent; he was
a clown and a born actor, and as a public speaker was
sure to bring down the house; he was a pronounced
free State man ; yet in this act he made himself the
marplot of his party.

CHAPTER X.

Sheriff Jones went away, vowing that he would have revenge, and sent the following dispatch to Gov. Shannon:

DOUGLAS CO., K. T., Nov. 27, 1855.

SIR :—Last night I, with a posse of ten men, arrested one Jacob Branson, by virtue of a peace warrant regularly issued, who, on our return, was rescued by a party of *forty men*, who rushed upon us suddenly from behind a house by the roadside, all armed to the teeth with Sharpe's rifles.

You may consider an open rebellion as already having commenced, and I call upon you for THREE THOUSAND MEN to carry out the laws. Mr. Hargis, the bearer of this letter, will give you more particularly the circumstances.   Most respectfully,

SAMUEL J. JONES,
Sheriff Douglas County.

TO HIS EXCELLENCY, WILSON SHANNON, GOVERNOR KANSAS TERRITORY.

On receipt of the above dispatch, Gov. Shannon wrote to Major-General William P. Richardson, reciting the story told him by Sheriff Jones, together with additional stories (equally false), told him by Hargis, and closed his letter with the following order:

You are therefore hereby commanded to collect together as large a force as you can in your division, and repair, without delay, to Lecompton, and report to S. J. Jones, Sheriff of Douglas County, together with the number of your forces, and render him all the aid and assistance in your power in the execution of any legal process in his hands. The forces under your command are to be used for the sole purpose of aiding the Sheriff in executing the law, and for no other purpose. I have the honor to be   Your obedient servant,

WILSON SHANNON.

8

Gov. Shannon knew, as well as he knew his name was Wilson Shannon, that this meant another invasion of Kansas Territory. There was no organized militia in Kansas. Gen. Richardson did not live in Kansas; he lived in Missouri, and it meant Missouri militia and not Kansas militia. Moreover, the Governor knew, or at least ought to have known, what an unreliable man this Sheriff Jones was. Jones was Postmaster at West-port, and Shannon was living at Shawnee Mission, in the neighborhod of Westport. And yet, without one moment's inquiry, he placed the issues of life and death of this infant Territory in the hands of this lying scoundrel.

There was a rallying of the clans of the blue lodges of Missouri. The following appeal, sent by Brig. Gen. Eastin, editor of the *Leavenworth Herald*, and commander of the second brigade, Kansas militia, must serve as a sample of the dispatches that were scattered broadcast through the border Missouri counties :

"TO ARMS! TO ARMS!!"

It is expected that every lover of *law and order* will rally at Leavenworth on Saturday, December 1, 1855, prepared to march at once to *the scene of rebellion* to put down the outlaws of Douglas county, who are committing depredations upon persons and property, burning down houses and declaring open hostility to the laws, and have forcibly rescued a prisoner from the Sheriff. Come one, come all! The outlaws are armed to the teeth, and number 1,000 men. Every man should bring his rifle and ammunition, and it would be well to bring two or three days' provisions. Every man to his post and do his duty.   MANY CITIZENS.

In answer to the above appeal 1,500 men, mostly from Missouri, encamped around Lawrence, under such notabilities as Maj. Gens. Strickler and Richardson, Brig. Gen. Eastin, Col. Atchison, Col. Peter T. Abell, Robert S. Kelley, Stringfellow and Sheriff

Jones. They had broken into the United States Arsenal at Liberty, Clay County, Mo., and stolen guns, cutlasses and such munitions of war as they required.

But when this was known the free State men turned out from all the settlements of Kansas with equal alacrity, to defend Lawrence. They came singly, and in squads and in companies. They came by night and by day. Sam Wood, Tappin and Smith, the rescuers of Branson, and who were residents of Lawrence, left the city, and there were none there against whom Sheriff Jones had any writs to execute. Dr. Robinson was appointed Commander-in-Chief for the defense of the city, and James H. Lane was appointed second in command. But Lane was the principal figure in the enterprise. He alone had military experience, and he alone had the daring, the genius and the personal magnetism of a real leader.

The free State men, for the last year, had been passing through the furnace-fires of a vigorous discipline, and they would have fought as the Tennessee and Kentucky backwoodsmen of Andrew Jackson fought behind their cotton bales at the battle of New Orleans. They had seen their rights wrested out of their hands by a mob of ruffians, and now they were proposing to settle the matter in that court of last resort that is the final and ultimate appeal of the nations. Except Gen. Lane, they had small knowledge of military tactics, but they knew how to look along the barrel of a rifle; moreover, they would fight behind breastworks, and this to raw troops would have been an immense advantage.

It is probable that the first intimation that Gov. Shannon got of the real state of affairs at Lawrence

was conveyed to him in the following letter, written by
Brig. Gen. Eastin :

GOVERNOR SHANNON :—Information has been received direct from
Lawrence, which I consider reliable, that the outlaws are well fortified
with cannon and Sharpe' rifles, and number at least 1,000 mem. It will,
therefore, be difficult to dispossess them.

The militia in this portion of the State are entirely unorganized, and
mostly without arms. I suggest the propriety of calling upon the
military of Fort Leavenworth. If you have the power to call out the
government troops, I think it would be best to do so at once. It might
overawe these outlaws and prevent bloodshed.   S. J. EASTIN,
                        Brig. Gen. Northern Brigade, K. M.

Gen. Eastin is mistaken in putting their number
at 1,000, but whether many or few they certainly
would have fought a hard battle. They were picked
men from all the Kansas settlements. Our old friend,
Caleb May, was there, as grim and as self-possessed as
Andrew Jackson. So also Old John Brown was there
with his four sons, though they did not arrive until
Gov. Shannon had made overtures for peace.

The Governor telegraphed to Washington to obtain
authority to call out Col. Sumner with the United
States troops at Fort Leavenworth. He also wrote
to Col. Sumner to hold himself ready to march at a
moment's notice. And now this simple-minded Gov.
Shannon, Ex-Governor of Ohio, who had come to
Kansas to waste in a few short months the ripe honors
he had been so carefully hoarding up for a life-time,
bethought himself that it was time for him to go and
look with his own eyes after this rebellion he had so
foolishly and recklessly stirred up.

We have already remarked that Gen. James H.
Lane was the most conspicuous figure in the defense of
Lawrence. It is proper to pause and consider the

character of this man, who shone for a time like a brilliant meteor, and then had his light quenched in the blackness of darkness.

He had now been eight months in Kansas. He came out of the Mexican war with a good reputation as a brilliant and dashing officer, and a man of approved courage. As a politician he had been highly favored by the people of Indiana. He was in the convention that nominated President Pierce. He was in Congress at the time of the passage of the Kansas-Nebraska bill, and aided in its enactment. He was the friend of Stephen A. Douglas. Yet he came to Kansas a man of broken fortunes. He was bankrupt in reputation, bankrupt in property, and bankrupt in morals, and he came away from unhappy family relations. Notwithstanding, he brought with him boundless ambition, and a consciousness in his own heart that he possessed genius that might lift him up to the highest pinnacle of honor. His first effort was to reorganize that political party that was in control of the Government at Washington, and that he had so faithfully served in Indiana. As respects slavery, he probably would have said with Mr. Douglas that he did not care whether it was voted up or voted down. But his effort fell stillborn and dead. Dr. John H. Stringfellow was an old Whig, and so also were many of the Pro-slavery leaders, and they would not hear to it that there should be any parties known save the Pro-slavery and Free State parties. The Free State men were equally averse to making any division in their own ranks. Mr. Lane was to choose, and he did choose *with a vengeance.*

Bad men usually pay this compliment to a righteous life, that they seek to conceal their wicked deeds and wear the outside seeming of virtue. But this strange man never pretended to be anything else than just what he was. He displayed such audacious boldness as gave an air of respectability even to his wickedness.

His public speaking did not belong to any school of oratory known among men ; yet, if to sway the people as a tempest bends to its will a field of waving grain, be oratory, then was Mr. Lane, in the highest sense of the word, an orator. He spoke once in Chicago when the people were most excited over the Kansas troubles. A great crowd came to hear, and he swayed them to his will, as only such men as Henry Ward Beecher and Patrick Henry have been able to do. But this gospel was the gospel of hate. Implacable, unforgiving hate was his only gospel.

At last this man, at once both great and wicked, having attained the highest honors the people had to bestow, died by his own hand. The people believed that he had gone wrong and betrayed them, and they withdrew from him their favor. Mr. Lane loved popularity more than he loved heaven, and he shot himself through the brain.

The writer, unwilling alone to take the responsibility of expressing such a judgment as the above, appealed to a gentlemen whose high position in public life and kindly and conservative temper eminently qualify him to speak, and this is what he says :

No one can question the fact that Mr. Lane's career in Kansas exerted a great influence in shaping the affairs and controlling the destiny of the young State. During his life I was alternately swayed by feelings of admiration and distrust. I recognized fully the marvelous energy and equally marvelous influence of the man, but I distrusted his sincerity and lacked confidence in his integrity. When I met him, or listened to one of his impassioned speeches, ne swept me away with the contagion of his seeming enthusiasm, but when I went out from the influence of his personal magnetism I felt that something was lacking in the man to justify a well-grounded confidence.

This man that had in him such a commingling of good and evil was now the leading spirit in the defense of Lawrence.*

---

* The Thirteenth Kansas Regiment, which was raised in 1862, was composed of Atchison County men. They voted to request father to become their chaplain, and they sent him word, requesting him to apply to Gen. Lane for the appointment. He did so, and received a letter from Gen. Lane, asking, " How much will you pay for the place?" Father replied, " If the position of chaplain is sold for a price, I do not want it."

CHAPTER XI.

When Sheriff Jones saw that the control of this business was being taken out of the hands of himself and his fellow-conspirators he wrote the following letter to Gov. Shannon :

CAMP AT WAKARUSA, Dec. 6, 1855.

To His EXCELLENCY, GOV. SHANNON :

Sir: In reply to yours of yesterday I have to inform you that the volunteer forces now at this place and Lecompton are getting weary of inaction. They will not, I presume, remain but a short time longer, unless a demand for the prisoner is made. I think I shall have sufficient force to protect me by to-morrow morning. The force at Lawrence is not half so strong as reported. If I am to wait for Government troops, more than two-thirds of the men that are here will *go away very much dissatisfied.* They are leaving hourly as it is.

It is reported that the people of Lawrence have run off those offenders from town, and, indeed, it is said they are now all out of the way. I have writs for sixteen persons who were with the party that rescued my prisoner. S. N. Wood, P. R. Brooks and Samuel Tappan are of Lawrence, the balance from the country around. Warrants will be put into my hands to-day for the arrest of G. W. Brown, and probably others in Lecompton. They say that they are willing to obey the laws, but no confidence can be placed in any statements they may make.

Most respectfully yours,
SAMUEL J. JONES,
Sheriff of Douglas County.

From the above, three facts are apparent :

1. Sheriff Jones is not willing that the militia shall go home, and Col. Sumner and the United States troops take their places.

2. He has writs against the sixteen rescuers of Branson. But of these he has ascertained that thirteen live in the country, and he does not need to go to Lawrence to find them. The three that belong in Lawrence are gone to parts unknown, and he does not need to go to Lawrence to find them. *At this writing Sheriff Jones has not a single writ against any person in Lawrence.*

3. If he has such a warrant the Lawrence people profess themselves willing that he should serve it, but he does not believe them. "No confidence can be placed in any statements that they may make."

So far as Sheriff Jones is concerned, it is now manifest that this was a devilish conspiracy against the people of Lawrence, to cut their throats and burn up the town. How far the men that were with him were conscious partners in his guilt, or how far they were ignorant dupes of a man that had murder in his heart, does not appear.

The people of Lawrence now thought it was time for them to open communication with Gov. Shannon, and Messrs. G. P. Lowery and C. W. Babcock, after running the gauntlet of the patrols, robbers and guerillas that infested the road to Shawnee Mission, succeeded in putting in the hands of the Governor the following letter :

To His Excellency, Wilson Shannon, Governor Kansas Territory:

Sir: As citizens of Kansas Territory, we desire to call your attention to the fact that a large force of armed men from a foreign State have assembled in the vicinity of Lawrence, are now committing depredations upon our citizens, stopping them, opening and appropriating their loadings, arresting, detaining and threatening travelers upon the public road, and that they claim to do this by your authority. We desire to know

if they do appear by your authority, and if you will secure the peace
and quiet of the community by ordering their instant removal, or compel
us to resort to some other means or a higher authority.

SIGNED BY COMMITTEE.

The Governor began to think it was time for him
to go to the camp of Sheriff Jones' army on the Wakarusa ; and when he came he was frightened at his own
work, and became just as eager to get out of the scrape
as he had been forward to get into it. He wrote to
Col. Sumner, frantically begging him to come to the
rescue ; but he had got no orders, and would not move
without orders. Sheriff Jones and the rank and file of
his camp were furious that they were held back from
pitching into the Lawrence people ; but the officers had
become cognizant of the bloody job they would have
on hands, and were willing to be let off. And so the
Governor patched up a peace, and sent his militia home
again, with their curses diverted from the Lawrence
Abolitionists to Gov. Shannon. Cowardly, weak-
minded and infirm in purpose as this unhappy man was,
he was not wholly a fool; and we may justly believe
that he had in his heart a foreboding of that awful day
of reckoning that would surely come, when inquisition
would be made for the blood of these citizens, and the
Governor himself would be called to answer, "Why
were these men slain ?"

And now that peace—angelic peace—sat brooding
over Lawrence with her dove-like pinions, they made a
love-feast and invited the Governor to partake of it ;
and what with the ravishing music, and the blandish-
ment of flattering tongues, and the intoxication of fair
women's eyes and sweet voices, the Governor was
made to forget, for the time being, that he was the

property, body, soul, and spirit, of the "Law and Order" party ; and his soft and plastic nature was beguiled into signing a document constituting the army of defense of Lawrence a part of the Territorial Militia, and giving them authority, under his own hand and seal, to fight with teeth and toe-nails against the outside barbarians that he himself had invoked to cut their throats. When, however, he had come to himself, and had to front the frowns and ungrammatical curses of the "Border Ruffians," he was fain to lay the blame on the sparkling wine of the feast, and the more sparkling eyes and sparkling wit of beautiful women.

These felicitations of the people of Lawrence with Governor Shannon did, however, have a somber and awful background. While this had been going on a boy had been murdered in the vicinity of Lawrence. Some young men rode out to see about it, and one of them was shot and killed. But a still more ghastly crime threw its baleful shadow over the people. It was perpetrated two days before the Governor concluded his treaty of peace.

Thomas W. Barber and Robert F. Barber were farmers, living about seven miles from Lawrence ; and on December 6th started with a Mr. Pierson to go home to their families. These were two brothers and a brother-in-law. They were intercepted on their way by J. N. Burns, of Weston, Mo., and Major George W. Clarke, United States Agent for the Pottawatomie Indians. These two men shot Thomas W. Barber. It is hard to find an explanation of their act, unless it were that they came to Lawrence to shoot down Abolitionists as they would have shot wolves on the prairie. They had no provocation. They rode apart from their companions to intercept the Barbers, and called on them to halt. Thomas W. Barber was unarmed, and gave mild and truthful answers to their questions. After the shooting the brothers started to ride away, when the murdered man said, "That fellow hit me;" began to sway in his saddle, was supported for a little time by his brother, then fell to the ground dead. His horse also had been shot, and died the same night. Familiar as Kansas had become with cruel and devilish deeds, there were circumstances connected with this act that made it exceptionally a blood-curdling horror. Thomas W. Barber was a somewhat notable farmer, and had married a young wife, that loved her husband with a love so passionate that she was sometimes rallied about it by her sister-in-law. It had been with misgivings and forebodings she had consented for Barber to go to Lawrence. The news of her husband's death had been kept from her; they dared not tell her. A young man was sent to bring her into the city, whither her husband's body had been already carried, and he blurted out, "Thomas Barber is killed!" and she shrieked, "O, my husband! my husband! Have they killed my husband?" It has been said that so frantic were her struggles, that it was with main force they had to hold her in the carriage which conveyed her into the city. Much has been written of the pathetic and voiceless woe of this wretched and sorrow-stricken woman, but we will spare the reader the recital.

This question, however, we did often ask ourselves: "What had we done that we should be made to suffer thus?"

But now there was peace, and Sheriff Jones, breathing out curses against the Governor who had balked him of his anticipated revenge, disbanded his army and went back to his post-office at Westport. It was past the middle of December, but some lingered on their way, robbing and stealing. The cold grew intense. A driving snow came down from the North. It was one of the coldest winters Kansas had ever known, and there fell one of the deepest snows. And now, winding through the deep snow, benumbed with cold, and all unprovided with clothing suitable for such inclement weather, the rear guard of the ring-streaked, speckled and spotted regiment of Kansas and Missouri Militia passed out of the Territory.

Thirteen leaders of the "Law and Order" party had met with Lane and Robinson, acting on behalf of the people of Lawrence, and had agreed to the terms of the treaty. But Sheriff Jones is reported to have said: "Had not Shannon been a ―― fool I would have wiped out Lawrence." It is reported that Stringfellow said that "Shannon had sold himself and disgraced himself and the whole Pro-slavery party." Atchison accepted the terms, saying to his followers: "Boys, we can not fight now. The position that Lawrence has taken is such that it would not do to make an attack on them. But boys, we will fight some time ―― !"

The peace was to be broken at the earliest opportunity.

CHAPTER XII.

The winter of 1855–6 that I spent in Illinois was uneventful. My success was not such as to discourage an evangelist that desires to be useful, neither was it such as to fill him with vanity. The weather was intensely cold, and the snow was deep.

It is said that before the coming of an earthquake, the sea gives forth deep moanings, as if it felt the approaching convulsion; so at that time there seemed premonitions in the hearts of the people that the whole nation, North, South, East and West, would be swept by a political cyclone that should leave behind it the desolation that is sometimes, in the West India Islands, left in the track of a tropical hurricane. We had heard of the murder of Dow, the rescue of Branson, and the invasion of Lawrence, and these certainly did not give promise that Kansas would be a favorable field for evangelical work, at least for a time. The writer had not hitherto spent much of his time in Adams county; he now spent a considerable part of the winter there, and visited the churches of Quincy, Chambersburg, Camp Point, and many others. The brethren at Quincy were making that experiment of monthly preaching that has been found so hazardous, especially to city churches. They have since changed the plan with wonderfully good results. It was at the church at Chambersburg that Bro. Cottingham who has now won a national reputation, achieved some of his earliest successes.

The majority of the leading members of these churches had been men and women of full age when they left Kentucky. Some had tarried a little time in Indiana. The memory of some went back to the time when the Mississippi Valley was almost an unbroken wilderness, with here and there a scattered settlement, made up of a frontier and uneducated people. What are now its great cities were then insignificant hamlets, and its means of commerce were rude flat boats on its rivers, and pack-horses, or clumsy, heavy lumber wagons on its rough and often impassable roads. There were few schools, fewer churches and still fewer educated men. The country was perambulated by itinerant preachers. These were guided by visions and revelations. Signs, omens and impressions directed them to their field of labor and controlled their lives. Ecstatic joy, vivid impressions, voices in the air, or seeing the Lord in the tree-tops, were their evidences of pardon.

Once every year the people came together to a great camp-meeting. There was intense excitement and enthusiasm, and many got religion; and this was followed by spiritual lethargy, coldness and apostasy. It was a short, hot summer, followed by a long, cold winter of moral and spiritual death.

Among the Old Baptists there was preaching once a month. This was all. There were no prayer-meetings, no meeting together every first day of the week to break break and read the Holy Scriptures. Christian morality was at a low ebb, and Christian liberality down to zero.

At length there came a change. The fountains of the great deep were broken up, and men broke loose from the dominion of these old and man-made systems. John Smith took the lead, and was followed by old Jacob Creath, Samuel Rogers, John Rogers, John Allen Gano, P. S. Fall, and many others. Alex. Campbell once said:

If any man can read the Acts of Apostles through three times, chapter by chapter, pondering each chapter as he reads, and then can remain an advocate of these old systems of conversion, may the Lord have mercy on him!

But the old Baptists fiercely resisted the Reformers, and cast them out as heathen men and publicans. And now the Bible was a new revelation to the men that came into this movement. The veil was taken off their eyes, and they could read the Scriptures as they had never read them before. They could now see that the Bible was a simple and intelligible volume, written to be understood by the common people, and they were only amazed at their former blindness.   But they were made to know what persecution means. All the denominations combined against them, and they were compelled to read the Scriptures to defend themselves; and thus pressed by their enemies on every hand, they were made to feel how near they were to each other, and how much they loved each other, and it became an easy thing to meet togther every first day of the week to sing, to pray, to exhort, and to commemorate the death of their risen Lord. But many of them were poor, and had growing families, and they had heard that there was a large and good land in the Military Tract in Illinois, and with many a tearful adieu, and bidding farewell to the land they loved so well, like Abraham going out into the land that God had given him, into this land flowing with milk and honey they came—and prospered.

And here the writer of these "Personal Recollections" found them, growing strong, and rich, and influential, and more prosperous than any other religious body in Adams county. It is now after the lapse of thirty years, to be mentioned to their honor—and to the honor of the churches of the State—that they have made commendable progress in the direction of a Christian liberality, and of moral, intellectual, and religious growth; still they are not yet up to the mark.

For the purpose of the moral, intellectual and religious education of his people, the Lord has given us one day in seven, and in one year he has given us fifty-two such days. This in seven years is one whole year, and in seventy-five years it is ten years, leaving out five years as the period of babyhood; and this as fitting men for the highest style of religious life, and of American citizenship is, if well employed, the best school on the face of the earth. Needs it to be said, that to do this work well, the teachers in this school of the prophets have need to be well qualified? There are certain Scriptures bearing on this point we will do well to ponder:

Meditate on these things; give thyself *wholly* to them, that thy profitting may appear unto all.

No man that warreth entangleth himself with the affairs of this life, that he may please him who hath called him to be a soldier. The Lord give thee understanding in all things.

We have no churches in this nation to whom these admonitions apply with greater weight of impressive authority than to the churches of Illinois. Where much is given, there much is required, and to no State in the Union has more been given in the way of worldly wealth than to the Disciples of that commonwealth. There is not such another body of rich land in this great nation, perhaps not in the world. Water is an element essential to the highest productiveness, even of fertile soil, and the vapors rising on the Gulf of Mexico have not a hillock three hundred feet high to obstruct their flow up the Mississippi eastward and northward, until they reach the State of Illinois. And the men that do business in the cities of this prosperous State, or till its fertile and alluvial soil, that was lifted up, not many geologic ages ago, from beneath the bottom of the sea, are so rich they do not know how rich they are. But it is a peril to be rich. Jesus, Paul and Solomon unite in saying so, and it is especially a peril when wealth comes suddenly. When a man starts poor, and has felt the sting of contempt because of his poverty, and then finds himself rich and prosperous and flattered, and tempted to indulge in every luxury, then this man is in great peril; and there is no security against this danger like using the wealth that God has given him for the glory of God and the good of men.

But there were brethren thirty years ago that needed no admonition as touching the disposition they should make of their world goods. I could give a goodly number of examples, but the reader will pardon me if, because of the narrow limits of these "Recollections," I confine myself to one.

Peter B. Garrett, of Camp Point, Adams county, had set himself, with honest purpose, to bring his Kentucky brethren up to the level of the demands of primitive and apostolic Christianity. Every man has his hobby, and Bro. G. had his hobby. When the writer first visited Camp Point, he was demanded of to know if it was not a fixed part of the apostolic order that each disciple should, on the first day of the week, lay by him in store, of money or goods, as the Lord had prospered him, putting it into the Lord's treasury? I could not quite affirm this, but Bro. G. stuck to his hobby.

Bro. Garrett knew the value of a full treasury, and was ready to do his part towards settling a preacher in the church, and paying him. But he could not bring his brethren up to the level of his own aspirations.

Bro. G. came from Kentucky a poor man, but he got hold of a considerable body of good land, when it was cheap, and cultivated it skillfully. Then the Quincy, Galesburg and Chicago Railroad was build in front of his farm, and the town of Camp Point grew up adjoining his premises. He also built a flouring mill, and this added to his gains; and thus he grew rich and influential, but he never thought of himself only as plain Peter Garrett. The writer in fifty years has known many excellent Christian families, but he has never known one family that, with saint and sinner, among persons outside and inside of the church, have had a more honorable fame than this Christian family. His wife was a motherly woman. She did not assume to know much, but what she did know she knew well, and translated her little store of knowledge into an abundance of good deeds. She knew how to guide the house, take good care of her children, live in peace with her neighbors, love the church and attend its meetings, fear God and entertain strangers; and so this house, like the house of the Vicar of Wakefield, became a resort for

"All the vagrant train,"

whether of tramps or preachers. His children, from the time they were able to toddle, were taught to do something useful. His little boys were made to bring in wood, and run on errands, and his girls to wash the dishes ; and thus this house became a hive of industry, and it came to pass that in process of time, when our beloved Bro. Garrison, of the *Christian-Evangelist*, went out to seek a woman to take care of his house, he very properly sought this favor at the hands of Peter Garrett's daughter. It is a good thing to follow a good example, and our devoted Bro. Smart, hitherto of the *Witness*, now co-editor of the *Evangelist*, went and did likewise.*

Bro. Garret loaned the writer a light spring wagon for the purpose of bringing his family back from Kansas, and thus equipped, he started a second time on the journey he had made one year before.

One thought filled his heart: Will this tumult pass away, and will the American people go forward and fulfill that glorious destiny to which God in his providence has called them?

---

* Bro. Garrett not only gave freely of his money to the church, but he gave freely of time, and trouble, and anxious watching. He also gave liberally and constantly of provisions and other necessaries to his poorer neighbors. His brother-in-law, Dr. Moore, complained that he was spoiling the church by taking such constant care of it. " O well," said Bro. Garrett one day, " every church has to have a wheel-horse, and I might as well be the wheel-horse as any body."

CHAPTER XIII.

The news of the coming of the South Carolinians had not reached Illinois when I started for Kansas, but when I had reached Western Missouri the country was alive with excitement. Maj. Jefferson Buford had arrived with 350 soldiers, and a part of them were quartered in Atchison. Some persons whose acquaintance I had made, and who were my friends, besought me not to go on.

The last night I stayed in Missouri was at De Kalb. A gentleman who had come from St. Joseph stayed over night at the hotel where I put up. He was tall of stature, with a flowing beard sprinkled with gray, and was of a remarkably dignified and impressive presence. We conversed during the evening on general topics, but no allusion was made to the one exciting topic, on which almost all seemed ready to talk *instanter*.

The next morning he overtook me. He was on horseback, and mentioned that he was going to Atchison, and for some distance rode beside my buggy, continuing the conversation. Then, as he could travel faster than myself, he rode on.

The reader will recognize this gentleman again in Atchison. An account of my adventures * on the other

---

* When father took this letter to Lawrence, he met Mr. Redpath, the *Tribune* reporter, who requested permission to copy it for the *New York Tribune*.

side of the river will be found in a letter addressed by myself to the *Herald of Freedom:*

[For the Herald of Freedom.]

STRANGER CREEK, Ocena P. O., May 6, 1856.

MR. EDITOR—*Dear Sir:* The bar of public opinion seems to be the only tribunal to which the free State men of Kansas can appeal for redress. I must, therefore, ask your indulgence while I make a statement of facts.

One year ago I came to Kansas and bought a claim on Stranger Creek, Atchison county. On the 17th of August, the Border Ruffians of the town of Atchison sent me down the Missouri River on a raft. We parted under a mutual pledge: I pledged myself that if my life was spared I would come back to Atchison, and they pledged themselves that if I did come back they would hang me. Faithful to my promise, in November last I returned to Kansas, and visited Atchison in open day, announced myself on hand, and returned without molestation. Kansas being sparsely settled, without churches or meeting-houses, it was determined that Mrs. Butler should live on our claim with her brother and her brother's wife, while I should return to Illinois, and resume my labors as a preacher.

April 30th I returned to Kansas, crossing the Missouri River into Atchison. I spoke with no one in the town, save with two merchants of the place, with whom I have had business transactions since my first arrival in the Territory. Having remained only a few moments, I went to my buggy to resume my journey, when I was assaulted by Robert S. Kelley, co-editor of the *Squatter Sovereign*, and others, was dragged into a saloon, and there surrounded by a company of South Carolinians, who are reported to have been sent out by a Southern Emigrant Aid Society. In this last mob I recognized only two that were citizens of Atchison or engaged in the former mob. It is not reported that these emigrants from the Palmetto State seek out a claim, and make for themselves a home, neither do they enter into any legitimate business. They very expressively describe themselves as having *come out to see Kansas through.* They yelled, "Kill him! Kill him! Hang the —— Abo-

---

Before Mr. Redpath had completed his copy, the editor of the *Herald of Freedom* demanded the manuscript to put in type. The edition of the *Herald of Freedom* containing it was destroyed, and father only obtained a mutilated copy of it. But from that portion printed in the *Tribune*, and what was left of the *Herald of Freedom*, he secured a complete copy of the letter.

litionist." One of their number bristled up to me and said, " Have you got a revolver?" I answered, "No." He handed me a pistol and said, "There, take that, and stand off ten steps; and ——, I will blow you through in an instant." I replied, "I have no use for your weapon." I afterwards heard them congratulating themselves in reference to this, that they had acted in an honorable manner with me. The fellow was furious; but his companions dissuaded him from shooting me, saying they were going to hang me.

They pinioned my arms behind my back, obtained a rope, but were interrupted by the entrance of a stranger—a gentleman from Missouri, since ascertained to be Judge Tutt, a lawyer from St. Joseph. He said: " My friends, hear me. I am an old man, and it is right you should hear me. I was born in Virginia, and have lived many years in Missouri. I am a slaveholder, and desire Kansas to be made a slave State, if it can be done by honorable means. But you will destroy the cause you are seeking to build up. You have taken this man, who was peaceably passing through your streets and along the public highway, and doing no person any harm. We profess to be 'Law and Order' men, and ought to be the last to commit violence. If this man has broken the law, let him be judged according to law; but for the sake of Missouri, for the sake of Kansas, for the sake of the pro-slavery cause, do not act in this way." They dragged me into another building, and appointed a moderator, and got up a kind of lynch law trial. Kelley told his story. I rose to my feet, and calmly and in respectful language began to tell mine; but I was jerked to my seat and so roughly handled that I was compelled to desist. My friend from Missouri again earnestly besought them to set me at liberty. Kelley turned short on him and said: "Do you belong to Kansas? Judge Tutt replied: "No; but I expect to live here in Atchison next fall, and in this matter the interests of Kansas and Missouri are identical." Chester Lamb, a lawyer in Atchison, and Samuel Dickson, a merchant of the place, both pro-slavery men, also united with Judge Tutt in pleading that I might be set at liberty. While these gentlemen were speaking, I heard my keepers mutter, "——. If you do n't hush up, we will tar and feather you." But when Kelley saw how matters stood, he came forward and said he " did not take Butler to have him hung, but only tarred and feathered," Yet in the saloon he had sa'd to the mob: " *You shall do as you please.*" He dared not take the responsibility of taking my life, but when these unfortunate men, whose one-idea-ism on the subject of slavery and Southern rights has become insanity—when these irresponsible South Carolinians, sent out to be bull dogs and blood hounds for Atchison and

Stringfellow—when they could be used as tools to take my life, he was ready to do it.

Our gunpowder moderator cut the matter short by saying, "It is moved that Butler be tarred and feathered and receive thirty-nine lashes." A majority said "Aye," though a number of voices said "No." The moderator said, "The affirmative has it; Butler has to be tarred and feathered and whipped." I began to speculate how that sort of thing would work as far north as the latitude of Kansas. There was a good deal of whispering about the house. I saw dark, threatening and ominous looks in the crowd. The moderator again came forward, and, in an altered voice, said: "*It is moved that the last part of the sentence be rescinded.*" It was rescinded, and I was given into the hands of my South Carolina overseers to be tarred and feathered. They muttered and growled at this issue of the matter. They said, "If we had known it would come out in this way, we would have let —— —— shoot Butler at the first. He would have done it quicker than a flash." One little, sharp-visaged, dark-featured South Carolinian, who seemed to be the leader of the gang, was particularly displeased. With bitter curses he said, "I am not come all the way from South Carolina, spending so much money to do things up in such milk-and-water style as this."

They stripped me naked to my waist, covered my body with tar, and for the want of feathers applied cotton. Having appointed a committee of seven to certainly hang me the next time I should come into Atchison, they tossed my clothes into my buggy, put me therein, accompanied me to the outskirts of the town, and sent me naked out upon the prairie. It was a cold, bleak day. I adjusted my attire about me as best I could, and hastened to rejoin my wife and little ones on the banks of the Stranger Creek. It was a sorrowful meeting after so long a parting, still we were very thankful that, under the favor of a good Providence, it had fared no worse with us all.

Many will ask now, as they have asked already, what is the true and proper cause of all these troubles I have had in Atchison? I have told the world already; I can only repeat my own words. I have said, The head and front of my offending hath this extent, no more: I had spoken among my neighbors favorably to making Kansas a free State, and said in the office of the *Squatter Sovereign*, "I am a Free-soiler, and intend to vote for Kansas to be a free State."

Still it will be regarded as incredible that a man should receive such treatment for uttering such words as I report myself to have uttered. The matter is plain enough when the facts are understood.

Prior to August 17, 1855, there was no Free-soil party organized in

Atchison county—perhaps not in the whole Territory of Kansas. Free-soilers did not know their own strength, and were disposed to be pru dent—some were timid. Here in Atchison county we determined that if the Border Ruffians were resolved to drive matters to a bloody issue, the responsibility of doing so should rest wholly with themselves. There are many Free-soilers in this county—brave men—who have no conscientious scruples to hinder them from arming themselves, and preparing to repel force with force. The Border Ruffians sought by a system of terrorism so to intimidate the Free-soilers as to prevent them from organizing a Free-soil party, or even discussing the subject of freedom and slavery in Kansas. They carried this to such an extent of outrageous violence that it came to be currently reported that it was as much as a man's life was worth to say in the town of Atchison, "I am a Free-soiler." We deprecated violence, and wished a peaceful discussion of the subject. It was therefore most fitting that a man whose profession forbade him to go armed should put to the test of actual experiment whether an American citizen of blameless life could be permitted to enjoy the right of free speech—the privilege of expressing views favorable to making Kansas a free State—such views being uttered without anything of angry, abusive or insulting language. It was for this purpose the above words were spoken, and which have been the cause of all my troubles in Atchison.

If there is any class of men who stand behind the curtain and pull the wires, we would respectfully represent to them that it will do no good to urge these understrappers on to these deeds of violence and ruffianism. We are not a class of men to utter childish complaints at any wrongs we may suffer, *but we know our rights and intend to have them.*

Subscribing myself the friend of all good and civil men, whether North or South, I am very truly, PARDEE BUTLER.

CHAPTER XIV.

We have already told how Sheriff Jones failed to
wipe out Lawrence ; how Gov. Shannon patched up a
peace, and how that, in no good temper, the "Law
and Order" party returned to the border. But immediately the Free State party gave evidence that its
spirit had not been broken. A convention had been
called to meet at Topeka, in November, 1855, to frame
a free State Constitution, and this was ratified at an
election called December 15 following, 1,731 votes being cast in its favor, the election having been held only
one week after the treaty of peace had been made.
Then in less than two weeks a second convention was
called to meet at Lawrence, at which a full board of
State officers was nominated, the election having been
set to be held on the 15th of January.

At Leavenworth, the attempt to hold the election resulted in such mobs and tumult that it was forbidden
to be held by a faint-hearted Free State mayor, and was
consequently adjourned to Easton. The Free State
printing press of Mark Delahay was, during these
troubles, destroyed. At Easton, a mob undertook to
break up the election, but was driven off, and in the
affray one of the attacking party named Cook was mor-
tally wounded. Then the *Kansas Pioneer*, published
at Kickapoo, made an inflammatory appeal to the
"Law and Order" party to rally and avenge Cook's

death, and in an answer to this appeal the "Kickapoo Rangers" and Captain Dunn's company, from Leavenworth, in all about fifty men, turned out to go to Easton on this errand. A number of gentlemen had gone from Leavenworth to Easton to attend the election, and had stayed over night, among whom were Captain R. P. Brown, a resident of Salt Creek Valley, near Leavenworth. Captain B. was a man well esteemed in his neighborhood, and was a member-elect of the Legislature. Captain Dunn and his company met these men returning to Leavenworth, and took them prisoners, carrying them back to Easton. Here they got up a sort of Lynch-law trial for Captain Brown, but the rabble composing Dunn's company, having maddened themselves with drink, broke into the room where the trial was going on, seized Captain Brown, who was unarmed and helpless, and tortured him with barbarity that has been supposed to be only possible among savages, and then threw the wounded and dying man into an open lumber wagon, in which they hauled him home to his wife, over the rough, frozen roads, in one of the coldest nights of that bitter cold January; stopping meantime at the drinking-houses by the way, they consumed seven hours in making the journey. His wife became insane at the sight of her butchered and dying husband, thrown into the door by these brutal wretches, and was, in that condition, taken to her brother in Michigan. All this was testified to, with every *minutia* of detail, before the Investigating Committee.

The border papers were aflame with appeals to the "Law and Order" party to go over into Kansas and wipe out the pestiferous Free State men, who set at naught the Territorial Legislature. The following sample of these appeals we extract from a speech made by David R. Atchison, at Platte City:

> They held an election on the 15th of last month, and they intend to put the machinery of a State in motion on the 4th of March, *I say, prepare yourselves; go over there.* And if they attempt to drive you out, then —— drive them out. Fifty of you with your shot-guns are worth two hundred and fifty of them with their Sharpe's rifles.

Meanwhile a great cry of wrongs and outrages against the Free State men had filled the whole North, and Congress could not choose, but had to pay attention to it. Ex-Governor Reeder came forward and contested the seat of Mr. Whitfield as Territorial delegate to Congress, alleging that Mr. W. owed his election to the votes of men not residents of the Territory. As a result, a Committee of Investigation was appointed to go to Kansas to take testimony, this committee being composed of Sherman of Ohio, Howard, of Michigan, and Oliver, of Missouri. These took an immense number of depositions, which were published in a volume of more than 1,200 octavo pages, and of which 20,000 were ordered to be printed. This investigating committee made a majority report signed by Howard and Sherman, in which they summed up their conclusions under eight heads. Of these we shall copy four:

MAJORITY REPORT.

> 1. That each election held in the Territory under the organic or Territorial law has been carried by organized invasion from the State of Missouri, by which the people of the Territory have been prevented from exercising the rights secured to them by the organic law.
>
> 2. That the alleged Territorial Legislature was an illegally constituted body, and had no power to pass valid laws, and their enactments are therefore null and void.
>
> 3. That Andrew H. Reeder received a greater number of votes of resident citizens than John W. Whitfield for delegate,

4. That in the present condition of the Territory a fair election can not be held without a new census, a stringent and well-guarded election law, the selection of impartial judges, and the presence of United States troops at every election. (*Signed*) WM. A. HOWARD,
JOHN SHERMAN.

Mr. Oliver made a minority report, summing up his conclusions under seven heads.   From this we shall copy three:

MINORITY REPORT.

1. That the Territorial Legislature was a legally constituted body, and had power to pass valid laws, and their enactments were therefore valid.

2. That the election under which the sitting delegate, John W. Whitfield, holds his seat was held in pursuance of valid law, and should be regarded as a valid election.

3. That the election under which the contesting delegate, Andrew H. Reeder, claims his seat, was not held under any law, and should be wholly disregarded by the House. (*Signed*) M. OLIVER.

As a result, Congress permanently unseated Mr. Whitfield, and ordered a new election, thus affirming the conclusions of Howard and Sherman.   This committee began its work in April and ended in June.

The " Law and Order " party did not, however, wait for the conclusion of these proceedings at Washington.   Col. Buford, as we have told in a former chapter, arrived early in the spring with his company of South Carolinians, and Gen. David R. Atchison had gathered, along the borders, several hundred men to make a second raid on Lawrence.   These all marched to Lecompton, where they held themselves in readiness to act, as soon as a pretext could be found invoking their help.

And now the inevitable Samuel J. Jones, Sheriff of Douglas County, again put in an appearance.   This time it was to arrest Sam Wood for the rescue of Branson. Jones arrested Wood on the streets of Lawrence. A crowd gathered around, and in the jostling and pushing Jones and Wood were separated, and Wood walked away. No threats were made, and no violence used. The next day was Sunday, and Jones again appeared, but Sam Wood was missing. He had stayed that night at the house of the writer, in Atchison County, being then on his way to the free States. Jones, however, had writs for the arrest of those who had been the occasion of Wood's escape, and the Sheriff called on some of the church-going people to act as his *posse* in making his arrests. But these were of "the most straitest sect" of the Puritans, and it was contrary to their consciences to do any manner of carnal work on the Sabbath day, and in their estimation this was exceedingly carnal work, and they kept their faces set as if they would go to the synagogue. Samuel F. Tappan was one of the Branson rescuers, and Jones seized Tappan by the collar, and Tappan struck Jones in the face. This was enough ; Jones had been resisted, and he went to the Governor and demanded a *posse* of United States soldiers to aid him in making his arrest. Thus reinforced with a detachment of United States troops, our valorous Sheriff Jones went a third time and arrested without resistance six respectable citizens of Lawrence, on a charge of contempt of court, because they had declined to break the Sabbath in aiding him to make arrests on the Lord's day. In due course of law, it should have been his duty to take his prisoners before a magistrate, and allowed them to give bail to appear at a given time to answer for this alleged contempt. But Jones elected to keep his prisoners without bail, and to act as his own jailer, and so he encamped in a tent on the prairie, using these United States soldiers as his guard. This was a manifest bait to the people of Lawrence to attempt a rescue, but they did not walk into the trap, and so these prisoners slept on the prairie, and their wives slept at home bereaved of their husbands. Somebody shot Jones. It is presumed that somebody thought he ought to be shot, but it was as great a calamity to Lawrence as was the rescue of Branson. The people of Lawrence removed Jones to the Free State hotel, showed every sympathy they could show, and offered a reward of $500 for the apprehension of the assassin. Notwithstanding, all Western Missouri was immediately aflame with appeals to the people to come to the rescue, and avenge the death of the murdered Jones. But the papers making these appeals did not publish the proceedings of the indignation meeting held at Lawrence, nor did they tell that a reward had been offered for the apprehension of the assassin, nor did they tell that Jones' wound was so slight that he was able to be removed the next day to Franklin.

Meanwhile a conspiracy was hatched at Lecompton, in which Chief Justice Lecompte was the chief conspirator, to arrest the leading Free State men on a charge of treason, and keep them prisoners without bail, and thus smother out the Free State movement. James F. Legati was one of the United States grand jurors, and violated his oath of secrecy and made a night journey to give warning to the men that were to be made victims to this conspiracy. Gov. Charles Robinson fled down the Missouri River, but was detained at Lexington, was brought back under charge of treason, and placed in confinement at Lecompton ; others fled the Territory, and Lawrence was left to fight its battles with its old leaders gone.   According to the purpose of this conspiracy a large number of Free State men were indicted for high treason ; and the Free State hotel and the two printing presses were returned by the Grand Jury as *nuisances*, and as such were by Judge Lecompte ordered to be destroyed.   Immediately following Legati's nocturnal visit, Ex-Governor Reeder received a summons at the hands of Deputy Marshal Fain to appear at Lecompton *as a witness*.   Mr. Reeder declined to obey the summons.   The next day a writ was served on him to appear on a charge of "contempt of court" for not having appeared as a witness.   Mr. Reeder refused to submit to the arrest for two reasons—first, that his life would be in danger; second, he plead his privilege of exemption from arrest because he was a member-elect of Congress.   Then United States Marshal Donaldson issued the following

PROCLAMATION.

WHEREAS, Certain judicial arrests have been directed to me by the First District Court of the United States, etc., to be executed within the county of Douglas, and

WHEREAS, The attempt to execute them by the United States Deputy Marshal was evidently resisted by a large number of people of Lawrence, and as there is every reason to believe that any attempt to execute these writs will be resisted by a large body of armed men ; now, therefore, the law-abiding citizens of the Territory are commanded to be and appear at Lecompton as soon as practicable, and in numbers sufficient to execute the law.

Given under my hand this 11th day of May, 1856.

J. B. DONALDSON,
U. S. Marshal of the Territory of Kansas.

On receipt of this proclamation the citizens of Lawrence called a public meeting and adopted the following preamble and resolution :

WHEREAS, By a proclamation to the people of Kansas Territory, by J. B. Donaldson, it is alleged that certain judicial writs of arrest have been directed to him by the First District Court of the United States, etc., to be executed within the county of Douglas, and that an attempt to execute them was evidently resisted by a large number of the citizens of Lawrence, and that there is every reason to believe that an attempt to execute said writs will be resisted by a large body of armed men ; therefore,

Resolved, By this public meeting of the citizens of Lawrence, that the allegations and charges against us, contained in the aforesaid proclamation, are wholly untrue in fact and in the conclusion which is drawn from them. The aforesaid Marshal was resisted in no manner whatever, nor by any person whatever, in the execution of said writs, except by him whose arrest the Deputy Marshal was seeking to make. And that we now, as we have done heretofore, declare our willingness and determination, without resistance, to acquiesce in the service upon us of any judicial writs against us by the United States Deputy Marshal, *and will furnish him with a posse for that purpose*, if so requested ; but that we are ready to resist, if need be, unto death, the ravages and desolation of an invading mob.

CHAPTER XV.

Before Marshal Donaldson had issued the proclamation copied in our last chapter, the citizens of Lawrence had forwarded to Gov. Shannon the following:

WHEREAS, We have most reliable information of the organization of guerrilla bands, who threaten the destruction of our town and its citizens; therefore

Resolved, That Messrs. Topliff, Hutchingson and Roberts constitute a committee to inform His Excellency of these facts, and to call upon him, in the name of the people of Lawrence, for protection against such bands by the United States troops at his disposal.

To this the Governor made the following reply:

EXECUTIVE OFFICE, May 12, 1856.

GENTLEMEN: Your note of the 11th inst. is received, and in reply I have to state that there is no force around or approaching Lawrence, except the largely constituted *posse* of the United States Marshal and Sheriff of Douglas county, each of whom, I am informed, has a number of writs in his hands for execution against persons in Lawrence. I shall in no way interfere with these officers in the discharge of their official duties.

If the citizens of Lawrence submit themselves to the Territorial laws, and aid and assist the Marshal and the Sheriff in the execution of processes in their hands, as all good citizens are bound to do when called upon, they will entitle themselves to the protection of the law. But so long as they keep up a military or armed organization to resist the Territorial laws and the officers charged with their execution, I shall not interpose to save them from the legitimate consequences of their illegal acts.

The following is a list of the notabilities that were in command of the army that was to serve as the *posse* of Marshal Donaldson, David R. Atchison in command of the Platte county riflemen of Missouri; Capt. Dunn, of the Kickapoo Rangers; Gen. B. F. Stringfellow, Robert S. Kelley and Peter T. Abell having charge of the recruits from Atchison; Col. Wilkes, of South Carolina; Col. Titus, of Florida; Col. Boone, of Westport, Mo., and Col. Buford, of South Carolina. More than three-fourths of this army was composed of non-residents of Kansas.

A third time the citizens of Lawrence called a public meeting, and this time they appeal to Marshal Donaldson. They say, "We beg leave to ask respectfully, what are the demands against us?" They repeat their oft-repeated assurance that they will submit to arrests, and demand protection against the gathering mob from the men representing the authority of the General Government. Marshal Donaldson only replied with jeers and insults. The people of Lawrence were indeed in evil case.

The beleagured citizens saw themselves shut in by armed bands, engaged in murder, robbery, and plunder; and this time they appealed to the Investigating Committee, now gone to Leavenworth; but that committee had no power to help them. Col. Sumner could not help them, unless the Governor should speak the word; and Shannon was dumb.

Lane had gone East; Robinson was a prisoner; Ex-Gov. Reeder had fled, disguised as a common laborer; and others were in hiding; and perforce the management of affairs had to be given into the hands of new men. A Committee of Public Safety was chosen, and this committee determined on a policy of abject submission and non-resistance. A committee of volunteers from Topeka offered their assistance, but were told: "We do not want you." Pusillanimous as Gov. Shannon was, he found he had a man to deal with more pusillanimous than himself, in the person of S. C. Pomeroy, chairman of the Committee of Public Safety. Citizens of Lawrence left in unspeakable disgust. The people of the Territory looked on in amazement. The boys jeeringly called the Committee of Public Safety "The Committee of the Public Safety Valve."

The writer had given his testimony before the Investigating Committee while they were yet in Lawrence. A number of South Carolinians had been present while this testimony was being given, and they had protested in a towering rage, "We will shoot Butler on sight." It was evident the town had to be given up to the tender mercies of this mob of ruffians. There was nothing to be gained by remaining, and the writer, sick at heart, went back to Atchison county; but he afterwards returned to see the blackened ruins of the desolated town.

On May 21st the monster *posse*, led on by Marshal Donaldson and Deputy Marshal Fain, gathered around the doomed city. The town was quiet—unusually so. Deputy Marshal Fain went into the city and arrested G. W. Deitzler, G. W. Smith and Gains Jenkins, on the charge of treason. The Marshal went to the Free State hotel, that they were soon to batter down, and got his dinner, *and went away without paying for it.* And now the opportune moment had arrived for the final *denouement.* Sheriff Jones — the mourned and lost and murdered and much-lamented Sheriff Jones— whose tragic death had fired the hearts of all the Missouri border, now put in an appearance and showed himself a mighty lively corpse, and led his *posse* into the town. The flag of the lone star of South Carolina, blood-red, and on which was inscribed the motto, ''Southern Rights,'' floated beside the Stars and Stripes. The monster *posse*, with loaded cannon, marched into the city and in front of the Free State hotel, and the ''Committee of the Public Safety Valve'' was called for. Mr. Pomeroy came forward and shook hands with Sheriff Jones—should not *gentlemen* shake hands when they meet? Sheriff Jones demanded the arms of the people, otherwise he would bombard the town. Mr. Pomeroy went and dug up the cannon that had been buried, and surrendered it to Jones. But further than this he could not go: *the people had their arms, and intended to keep them.* Then they tried to batter down the Free State hotel with cannon. Failing in this, they tried to blow it up with powder; and, failing in that, they burned it down. They also destroyed the two printing presses, burning the buildings, and then sacked the town.

Sheriff Jones was beside himself with joy. In frantic excitement he said, ''I have done it! I have done it! This is the happiest moment of my life! I determined to make the fanatics bow before me in the dust and kiss the Territorial laws, and I have done it! The writs have been executed. Boys, you are dismissed.'' It will be doing Senator David R. Atchison, Ex-Vice-President of the United States, a kindness to conclude simply that he was drunk, otherwise he displayed utter savagery and barbarism. He inculcated gallantry to ladies, but said: ''If you find any woman with arms in her hands, tread her under foot as you would a snake." The Caucassian white woman of Lawrence had no more rights of self-protection than the slaves of a South Carolina rice plantation—they were wholly and absolutely at the mercy of their masters!

We have no comments to make on the work of this drunken rabble; but there is one man that must be held to a terrible responsibility before the judgment-seat of posterity. Gov. Wilson Shannon was not drunk: and it is to be presumed he had read that Constitution of the United States which he had so often sworn to support. He knew, therefore, that this document stipulates:

1. "That the right of the people to *keep* and bear arms shall not be infringed;" yet he showed a fixed purpose to deprive the Lawrence people of their arms.

2. The Governor knew that the Constitution guarantees "freedom of speech and of the press" to the American people; yet the burning of these printing presses was an attack on the freedom of the press.

3. The Constitution guarantees that "in all criminal prosecutions the accused shall enjoy the right to a speedy and public trial." Property of large value was destroyed because its owners were charged with high crimes and misdemeanors; yet the owners of this property had never been given a trial.

4. Gov. Shannon alleged that it was treasonable for the people of Kansas Territory to frame a State Constitution without an enabling act from Congress; yet California had done this very thing, and under that Constitution had been admitted as a State.

5. He treated the Free State men as traitors, because they would not admit the legality of the Lecomp-

ton Territorial Legislature. But the majority of the Investigating Committee held the same view with the Lawrence people, and Congress affirmed the same judgment in permanently unseating Mr. Whitfield as Territorial delegate to Congress.

Would that men could remember that there is a *hereafter*; that *to-morrow* forever sits in judgment on *to-day*. There are three men most conspicuous in the sacking of Lawrence. Let us look at them in the electric light of the awful *to-morrow*. Since the Kansas struggle had begun David R. Atchison had made himself the most conspicuous figure. He was the representative of the John C. Calhoun school of Southern politics, and from the hour of the destruction of Lawrence he was to disappear from public view, as absolutely as that Free State hotel which was burned by his orders; yet he did not die—he was simply *buried alive* out of the public sight. He was done with the nation, and the nation was done with him. He went back and lived on his plantation in Western Missouri, where he was forgotten. It is said he loved his slaves so well, and petted them so much, that they became masters on the plantation, and not himself. He lived to see Kansas a free State, with almost a million of inhabitants, and fairly taking the lead of Missouri in the elements of education, enterprise, and the highest civilization.

We have seen the crawling servility with which Gov. Shannon served the "Law and Order" party; yet in less than three months he was to see his office as Governor go up in smoke, as these burning buildings had gone up in smoke. Mr. S. became frantic when he saw the carnival of bloodshed and murder, of riot and robbery, that had been brought about by his means.   Dr. Gihon, the incoming Gov. Geary's private secretary, reported that Mr. Shannon fled the Territory in fear of his life.   When the troubles were over he came to Kansas and sought the pity and forgiveness of that city he had turned over to the tender mercies of a mob of ruffians.   It need not be said that he could have done no better, for his successor, Gov. Geary, had only to speak a word and this tumult of disorder was instantly hushed.

As the years went by the people could not believe that a man that displayed so many good and amiable qualities could have been a party to such outrages as characterized his administration.   He died in Lawrence very much respected.

Sheriff Samuel J. Jones strutted his brief hour on this stage in which the play had been both a blood-curdling tragedy and a comedy; and now he was to step down and out.   In the last act he had said, "*I have done it!*"   *And he had done it!*   He and his fellow conspirators, whether of high or low degree, had set in operation a train of causes that should issue in abolishing throughout the United States that institution of slavery they had so frantically sought to establish in Kansas.

Joseph said to his brethren, "You meant it for evil, but the Lord meant it for good."   *Sheriff Jones and his fellow conspirators were in the Lord's hands, but they did not know it.*

CHAPTER XVI.

When the news came of the sacking of Lawrence, the great mass of the squatters had not yet lost faith in the nation, nor had they lost hope that justice would be done, tardy though it might be; but the utmost limits of human endurance were fast being reached. There were, however, many that had already gone beyond this point, and they returned an answer that made the hearts of the people stand still with horror. It was the answer of a wild beast that had been hunted to its lair, and that turns with savage ferocity on its pursuers. It was an answer framed not in words, but in deeds. It said, "We have come to an end. We have been robbed of the rights guaranteed to us by the Kansas-Nebraska bill. We have been robbed of the rights of American citizens. We have been given the alternative of abject and degrading submission or of extermination. And now we make our answer. We will return blow for blow, wound for wound, stripe for stripe, and burning for burning. Murder shall be paid back with murder, robbery with robbery; and every act of aggression shall be paid back with swift and terrible retaliation." It must be remembered that at that time news traveled slow, and that it was slow work to take men from their ordinary farm life and organize them into bands of soldiers, and it was some days before "Old John Brown, of Osawatomie," appeared on the scene of conflict with a company of men. Of this company his son, John Brown, Jr., was captain. But the "old man " had come too late. He was terribly excited, and denounced as a set of cowards the "Committee of the Public Safety Valve " that had dug up the hidden cannon and had surrendered it to Sheriff Jones. Captain Brown and his company determined to return. Old John Brown selected a squad of six men to go on a secret expedition. Of these, four were his own sons, and one was his son-in-law. His son, Captain Brown, was unwilling that his father should go, and when the old man would not be persuaded, he cautioned him, " Father, do n't do anything rash." "Old John Brown" took old man Doyle and two sons and two other men in the dead hour of night and put them to death. The facts of this awful deed have never been made public—there has never been a judicial investigation. It is said that Doyle and his sons were desperate characters, and were in the act of driving off Free State men ; but nothing is certainly known.

And now it appeared that the whole country south of the Kaw River was full of armed Free State guerrilla bands. They rose up out of the earth as if they had been specters—their blows were swift, terrible and remorseless. They visited and robbed the houses of Pro-slavery men, as the houses of the Free State men had been visited and robbed. They stole the Pro-slavery men's horses, stopped them on the public highways, and repeated in every detail and in every act of violence the cruel atrocities that had been so long perpetrated on themselves. They showed no partiality—if they stole the horses of Pro-slavery men, they also stole Gov. Shannon's horses, and the Governor posted over the country with a squad of soldiers to find them. The town of Franklin, six miles from Lawrence, that had been a rendezvous for the "Law and Order" robbers, and out of which they issued to visit Free State settlers' houses, rob Free State men on the public highway and make raids on Lawrence, was cleaned out. H. Clay Pate, leader of a "Law and Order" company of militia, went to hunt John Brown and put him to death as he would go to hunt a wild beast. An African lion hunter, when questioned, "Is it not fine sport to hunt lions?" replied, "Yes, it is fine sport to hunt lions, but if the lion hunts you it is not so fine." H. Clay Pate went to hunt the lion, and found the lion was hunting him. John Brown attacked Pate with an inferior force, dispersed his command, and took him prisoner, together with twenty-eight of his men, and kept them in an inaccessible fastness which he made his hiding place. A number of Pro-slavery men fled from the Territory, telling everywhere a blood-curdling story of hard and cruel treatment. The people of the State of Missouri were filled with rage and horror, and its presses groaned with frantic appeals to the people to rise in their might and avenge the blood of their murdered brethren. Hitherto they had witnessed with perfect composure the savage butchery of the Free State men, and the outrage of Free State families; but now the case was bravely altered. It was their ox that was being gored.

Gov. Shannon passed as usual from the extreme of insolence to the extreme of helpless imbecility, and called on Col. Sumner to come forward and put a stop

to this riot of confusion, blood-shedding and violence.
The Governor really wanted Col. S. to disarm only the
Pree State guerrillas ; but Mr. S. made a more liberal
interpretation of his orders, and proceeded to disarm all
armed bands in the Territory. He visited Old John
Brown's hiding place, told him he must consider himself under arrest, and intimated to Deputy Marshal
Fain that he was at liberty to arrest these men, who
were under charge of murder. But the Marshal replied
that he had no arrests to make. Marshal Fain had no
stomach for the business of lion hunting. It is said
that Col. S. gave Marshal Fain a piece of his mind
that was more explicit than polite.

Col. Sumner ordered John Brown to give up his
prisoners, and disband his men. John Brown expostu-
lated with him, that it was not right to require him to
do this, while the country was full of armed bands of
Pro-slavery militia and guerrillas. Col. S. agreed to
disband and disarm all companies of persons armed,
and then John Brown agreed to comply with his re-
quests. Gen. Whitfield was in the vicinity, and at the
request of Col. S. agreed to remove his men from the
Territory; but while doing this they continued the
business of riot, robbery and murder.

Thus wearily passed the month of June of 1856,
on the south bank of the Kaw River. The coming
Fourth of July was looked forward to with intense interest by both parties, and on the north side of the
Kaw River, as well as on its south side. The Fourth
of July was the day on which the Legislature, elected
under the Free State Constitution, was to meet at Topeka; and on that day, and at that place, a mass convention of all the Free State men in Kansas had also

been called to meet and agree on their future policy. Col. Sumner had at least done this good service, that the highways were clear, and traveling was safe; but not knowing what might happen, the men generally carried their muskets hidden in their wagons. The writer of these "Recollections" went to Topeka with the Free State men of Atchison county. At this convention it appeared that there was the greatest possible divergence of judgment as to the best policy for the Free State party to pursue. There was nothing of the noise and bluster that characterizes a drunken mob; they were sober and quiet men; nevertheless, they evidently labored under an intense and burning excitement. Some were for war, bloody, relentless and unforgiving war; others advised a more pacific policy. If the reader can imagine the savage determination with which the old Scotch Covenanters turned at bay when hunted into their mountain fastnesses by their bloody persecutors, then he will have some idea of the spirit that animated a great part of that assembly. Two companies of soldiers, handsomely equipped, armed and drilled, one from Topeka and one from Lawrence, were drawn up in front of the Topeka House, where the Free State Legislature was to meet. It is probable that this crowd of men assembled at this convention could have laid their hands on five hundred muskets hidden away in their wagons, in ten minutes.

Meanwhile Col. Sumner had quietly drawn up his company of dragoons just outside of the crowd. In front of the dragoons were two loaded cannon, and by them grimly stood soldiers with burning fuse. While the members of the convention were discussing among themselves their proper policy, United States Marshal Donaldson came forward, accompanied by Judge Elmore, and taking possession of the stand from which the speakers were addressing the people, Judge Elmore read a proclamation from the President and from acting Gov. Woodson, commanding the Legislature to disperse.

To this Col. Sumner had appended the following note: "The proclamation of the President and the orders under it require me to sustain the Executive of the Territory in executing the laws and preserving the peace. I therefore hereby announce that I shall maintain the proclamation at all hazards."

This act of Marshal Donaldson was fiercely denounced as an impertinent intermedding with other men's business. The general drift of the reasoning was as follows : "Our act in framing a constitution and in electing a legislature is not treasonable nor revolutionary. There is no law against it : consequently we are breaking no law. It is, moreover, something that has to be done at some time by the majority of the citizens of this Territory, and we hope to be able to convince Congress and the President that we are that majority. If we had undertaken to set in operation a government in contravention to the one now recognized by the President, then might there have been some apology for this interference ; but we have done nothing of the kind."

The writer will say to the reader that Gov. Walker, an ex-Senator from Mississippi, and the ablest Governor Kansas ever had, admitted afterwards that this reasoning of the Kansas squatters was perfectly correct. But however this might be, here was a patent fact.   Here was Col. Sumner with his United States dragoons, and he was a man to obey orders ; and what were we going to do about it?   Should we fight, or should we not fight?   The writer submitted the fol-lowing resolution :

Resolved, That this Convention expresses its determination not to resist the United States troops.

The resolution was carried, and a committee was sent to Col. Sumner to inform him of its adoption. His answer was one to draw the hearts of the people to himself: "I knew," said he, "that you were loyal to the old flag."

Our readers will be incredulous that such a resolu-tion should be needed, or that there should be any division of sentiment as touching its adoption.   It is for this reason we call this incident up.   It is that the reader may understand how strained was the state of feeling of many of the Free State men.   They had spent the past months fighting, and they, in their own minds, associated the United States troops with the oppressors of Kansas Free State men.

When Mr. Sumner went into the Legislative hall to disperse the Legislature, he spoke as tenderly as a woman.   He said: "Gentlemen, this is the most painful act of my life.   But I must obey orders, and you must disperse."   When he wheeled his dragoons to march away the boys cheered Col. Sumner.   They cheered the old flag and the United States soldiers, but they gave such groans for the Lecompton Legislature as, it was said, frightened the dragoons' horses.

There was now no further cause that the writer

should tarry longer, and he immediately mounted his horse and rode towards home, with a heart heavy with the thought of all the distempers that had come on unhappy Kansas.

CHAPTER XVII.

We have already told how the campaign was opened, in the spring of 1856, in Atchison county, in a letter which we at that time addressed to the editor of the *Herald of Freedom.* This paper was printed at Lawrence, on the printing press destroyed by the " Law and Order " mob. The weekly issue in which this letter was published was passing through the press on the day the town was sacked, one side having been printed, the other side being yet blank. Then the Border Ruffians came into the town, broke up the press and threw it into the river, and tumbled the half printed weekly issue into the street. The above-named article was on the printed side, and was read by the whole crowd, and they were terribly angry. If the writer had been in town he certainly would not have escaped alive, if this mob could have found him. As it was, their curses would not be edifying reading in a Christian newspaper. Lecompton could not give its friends food or lodging. It had been located in an out-of-the-way and inaccessible place ; its proprietors were Sheriff Jones, Judge Lecompton, and men of that *ilk*, and business men avoided the place as if it had been smitten with a pestilence. The people of the surrounding country were generally Free State men, and the South Carolinians could not choose, but were forced to return to Atchison. They had been angry and impatient when their friends in Atchison had constrained them to do things up in such "milk and water" style, and in Lawrence they had been held back in the same manner, and they returned in a savage temper. Should a cowardly Yankee be allowed to defy them, and scoff at them, and call them "bull-dogs and blood-hounds," with impunity? and now, with this man they had to have a settlement.

We have already seen how the contending factions spread murder and violence south of the Kaw River; but from May till September Leavenworth county became a "dark and bloody ground." Immediately after the Fourth of July, Col. Sumner had been, because of his too great leniency to Free State men, superseded in command at Fort Leavenworth by Persifer F. Smith, a man whose heart was hard as a rock of adamant toward the Free State people, and under his eyes Leavenworth city and county were given up to blood and robbery.

In Atchison county, from the beginning of these border troubles to the end of them, not one man's life was taken, and yet David R. Atchison, Gen. B. F. Stringfellow, and his law partner, Peter T. Abell, were the leading members of the Atchison town company. Robert S. Kelley and Dr. John H. Stringfellow also maintained unchanged their bloody purposes. We find in the *Squatter Sovereign*, under date of June 10th, the following editorial, and this displays its uniform temper:

The Abolitionists shoot down our men, without provocation, wherever they meet them; let us retaliate in the same manner. A free fight is all we desire. If murder and assassination is the programme of the day, we are in favor of filling the bill. Let not the knives of the Pro-slavery men be sheated while there is one Abolitionist in the Territory. As they have shown no quarters to our men, they deserve none from us. Let our motto be written in blood on our flags, " *Death to all Yankees and traitors in Kansas.*"

Why, then, were not these bloody counsels made good by deeds? Our circumstances were peculiar. It will be seen above that it was only the Yankees and Abolitionists in whose bodies the knives of the "Law and Order" party were to be sheated; and the Yankees in the country were only a handful of men, and were therefore powerless; but between them and these bloody-minded chieftains was interposed a barrier that proved insurmountable. The great mass of the squatters were just from the other side of the river. Sometimes a son had left a father, and crossed the river to get a claim; or a brother had left his brother, or a girl had married a young man in the neighborhood, and as the young folks were poor, they had left the old folks and had gone to seek their fortune in the new Territory. Of course the old folks would still have a care for the young couple. They were in easy reach of each other, and would still visit back and forth. Now who does not see that to touch any one of these was to touch all? It was like touching a nest of hornets. The reader will observe that these people had no quarrel with the people of the South: they were bone of their bone and flesh of their flesh. Neither had they any special quarrel with Southern institutions; only this, that they would rather live in a free State. They did feel that way, and they could not help it. But in one thing they had been sorely wounded. In the invasion of Kansas, and in the carrying the elections by violence, their personal rights had been invaded, and

they did resent that. And now here were some
Yankee neighbors whom they knew to be kindly and
peaceable people, and whose help they needed in
building up their churches; and yet these were to be
murdered or driven out of the Territory *for nothing!*
and it touched their Southern blood. It was neither
just nor right, and they would not allow it; and in
such an issue there would be a common bond of sympathy on both sides of the river. Moreover, such men
as Oliver Steele, Judge Tutt and the Irvings and Harts
and Christophers had grave misgivings what would be
the final issue of this system of murder and violence
that had been adopted to make Kansas a slave State.

And so it was that the leaders in this conspiracy,
right here in this city and county of Atchison, which
was their headquarters, found themselves strangely
embarrassed and handicapped. Their will was good
enough, but how to carry out their purpose?—that
was the pinch. A private assassination was a thing
that looked easy enough at the first sight, but it might
turn out that they had undertaken an ugly job for
themselves.

A meeting of the Disciples was held at the house
of Archibald Elliott in the month of June. It was
called quietly, and no noise made about it. There
was a large attendance, and it was evident that if we
could hold regular meetings great good would be done.
But the neighborhood was soon filled with alarming
rumors. It was said that a company of South Carolinians were seen to go into a grove of bushes, about
nightfall, where the writer would be expected to pass,
and that they were seen to emerge from the same place
the next morning. One event, however, adjourned our

meetings without date. There was a man living in the western part of the county named Barnett, who was a man of considerable attainment, and had been a member of the Christian Church. But he was given to drink. His wife, however, who was an excellent Christian woman, remained steadfast to the church, and Barnett, as he saw his hold on the church and his hope of heaven slipping away from him, clung the more loyally to his wife, as though her Christian excellencies would save them both. At her request he invited me to preach a sermon at his house, and I consented. But when the South Carolinians in Atchison heard of it, they sent an insulting message to Barnett that they would come and shoot me. Barnett's Southern blood was all on fire. Who were these men that had come to Atchison county to ride rough-shod over him in his own house? He sent a message equally defiant back to them, that if they did come he and his neighbors would shoot them. But there was one man in the county that needed to have no nervousness as touching his reputation for personal bravery. That man was Caleb May; and he interposed and said: "Let us wait patiently for more peaceful times. The Son of man did not come to destroy men's lives, but to save them." But this adjourned without date our meetings.

One incident must illustrate the strained and peculiar condition of affairs in Atchison county. Archimedes Speck lived on the Stranger Creek, several miles below the residence of the writer. He was a man of magnificent physical development, and was a pronounced Free State man. His wife's people originally came from North Carolina, and she was proud of her

Southern blood ; and the husband and wife did not come to Kansas to be run over by anybody.   Yet they were eminently peaceable people, if let alone.   These gentlemen in Atchison had determined to disarm the Free State people living in the country; and Mr. Speck, being a Free State man, open and avowed, they called on him, but he was not at home.   They therefore asked his wife : "Has your husband a rifle, musket, or fire-arms of any kind?"   She brought out an old Queen Anne's musket, as rusty and worn as if it had been in service ever since the Revolutionary war. But while they were inspecting the rusty old thing, whether it was worth carrying away, she took from a closet a bran span new double-barrel fowling-piece, and, putting her finger on the trigger, she said, "Now, sir, if you do not lay down that musket and leave the house, I will shoot you."   If this gentleman had suddenly roused up a female tiger, he would not have been more terror-stricken than when he found himself facing this woman, blazing with scorn and irrepressible resentment, and he concluded he did not want the rusty old musket, *and did not ask to examine the other one.*

Mr. S. had threatened to flog one of his Proslavery neighbors who had insulted him, as he alleged, and the man went to Atchison and made oath that he was in fear of his life, and the Sheriff was sent out with a warrant to arrest Mr. Speck.   But at this time Leavenworth county was full of murder and bloodshed ; guerrilla parties, both Free State and Pro-slavery, were fighting in many parts of the Territory, and Lane had returned, and was leading the Free State men in this warfare, and had threatened with many oaths to wipe out Atchison, and there were rumors that he was already near at hand. And so, to provide against all contingencies, the Sheriff was accompanied by a *posse* of forty armed men, who took with them a cannon which had been loaned to Atchison by the people of Missouri.

Mrs. Speck received the Sheriff graciously, explained to him that her husband was absent, but would soon return, but to all questions as touching his present whereabouts, she shook her head mysteriously and refused to explain. The thing looked suspicious. Was it possible that Lane was even now in the neighborhood? and the Sheriff went back to his *posse* to hold a council of war. He had stationed them on a high bluff on the north bank of the Stranger Creek, and, looking across the wide timbered bottom to the opposite bluff, they could dimly see a large number of objects approaching through the brush-wood. What could it be? Was it Lane coming to attack him? And now two horsemen emerged from the brush and rode on a full gallop down the bluff.

"It is Lane! It is Lane!" they cried. "Let us ride back to Atchison and get ready to defend the town," and on a gallop they skedaddled back to Atchison.

Mr. Speck had been with some of his neighbors to bring home a herd of cattle. An old cow had broken from the herd, intending to get back to her former grazing-ground, and Mr. Speck and his neighbors had ridden full gallop to head her off. On reaching home, and learning of the visit of the Sheriff, he went at once to Atchison to give bonds to keep the peace; and to make all things square, he took with him the rusty old musket and proffered it to the gentleman that had been so solicitous to get it. Mr. Speck assured him that Mrs. S. was now willing he should have it, and *would not shoot him if he took it.*

These gentlemen had been making money out of pocket. They had been frightened out of their wits by a spunky woman ; and forty armed men, with a loaded cannon, had been stampeded and made to run pell-mell into Atchison by a herd of cattle and two or three men on horseback, riding at full gallop after an old cow.

These men had undertaken to do a wicked thing, and had been made ridiculous in doing so ; and this contributed largely to that revolution in the public opinion of the county, which had been going on for eighteen months, and which at the last compelled a radical change in the policy of these '' Border Ruffian '' leaders. But this again gave the chiefs of this conspiracy abundant experience that it pays to do right, and that a good Providence had brought them prosperity and honor by defeating their original counsels and turning them into foolishness.

But first we must tell of the carnival of riot, ruin, and robbing that had been going on in other parts of the Territory.

CHAPTER XVIII.

The *Squatter Sovereign*, in its issue of July 1st, made the following announcement:

The steamer, Star of the West, having on board seventy-eight Chicago Abolitionists, was overhauled at Lexington, Mo., and the company disarmed. A large number of rifles and pistols were taken at Lexington, and a guard sent upon the boat, to prevent them from landing in the Territory. After leaving Lexington, it was ascertained that they had not given up all arms, but still held possession of a great number of bowie knives and pistols, which were probably secreted while the search was going on at Lexington. At Leavenworth City, Captain Clarkson, with twenty-five men, went on board of the boat and demanded the surrender of all the arms in the possession of the Abolitionists. Like whipped dogs they sneaked up to Clarkson and laid down their weapons to him.

The men thus robbed of their arms give the following version of the matter: They say that at Lexington they were taken by surprise; that their arms were not accessible to them, and that there was nothing to do but to yield. But that a pledge was made to them, that if they would give up their arms, they should be allowed to proceed peaceably to Kansas. They furthermore state that at Kansas City Col. Buford came aboard the boat, accompanied by a company of soldiers; that David R. Atchison and Gen. B. F. Stringfellow came on board, and that after the boat had left the landing these gentlemen informed them that they would in no wise be allowed to enter the

Territory; that after the boat had stopped at Weston, they should be taken back to Alton; but that if they would not accept this arrangement, "they should be hung, every mother's son of them."

At various times the *Squatter Sovereign* and *Leavenworth Herald* report similar outrages. The latter paper reports, July 5th, the sending back seventy-five emigrants that had come upon the steamer Sultan. In reference to this occurrence, the *Squatter Sovereign* makes the following remark:

We do not fully approve of sending these criminals back to the East, to be reshipped to Kansas—if not through Missouri, through Iowa and Nebraska. We think they should meet a traitor's death; and the world could not censure us if we, in self-protection, have to resort to such ultra measures. We are of the opinion that if the citizens of Leavenworth city, or Weston, would *hang* one or two boat-loads of Abolitionists, it would do more towards establishing peace in Kansas than all the speeches that have been delivered in Congress during the present session. *Let the experiment be tried.*

The Missouri River was thus blockaded against the incoming of emigrants from the free States, and this created intense excitement throughout the North. The result was, that the immigration to Kansas, instead of being diminished, was largely increased; but it changed its direction, and Iowa City became the *entrepôt* for the incoming tide of free State settlers, which now sought an overland route through Iowa and Nebraska, and began to reach Kansas about the 1st of August.

The leaders of the Pro-slavery party made a pathetic appeal to the people of the South to send a corresponding class of emigrants; but the appeal was feebly responded to. Slave-holders would not come, because their slaves would be insecure; and now slaveholders felt that they had small cause to come to fight a battle that was not theirs.

Gov. Shannon held the scepter of power with a more and more feeble hand. He was going to resign, and he was not going to resign. But whether he did or did not resign, the substance of power had already passed into the hands of his secretary, Mr. Woodson, who was hand and glove with his fellows in this conspiracy to make Kansas a slave State.

Meantime Col. Sumner had been superseded in command at Fort Leavenworth by Persifer F. Smith. Col. Sumner had obeyed orders like the brave soldier that he was, but he had shown too much sympathy for these victims of oppression in the discharge of his shameful duties.* He did his appointed work, but he did not do it with an appetite, and he had been succeeded by a man that felt no more pity toward the Free State people than the wolf feels for the lamb out of which he makes his breakfast. The consequences of this state of affairs began soon to appear. The Missouri River had been blockaded. Trains sent to Leavenworth from Lawrence and Topeka were robbed on the public highway of the merchandise and provisions with which they were loaded, and these interior Free State settlements began to feel the sharp pressure of hard necessities, while they a third time saw companies of so-called "Law and Order" militia occupying various points in the Territory which these men proceeded to fortify, and from which they could overawe the inhabitants and make raids on the citizens;

---

* When Col. Sumner's soldiers were asked what they would do if they were ordered to fire on the Free State men, they replied, "We would aim above their heads."

and thus the old business of robbery, murder, spolia-
tion and oppression was again begun.

And now this new immigration of a squatter sol-
diery, who came bearing their muskets in one hand
and their implements of husbandry in the other, and
were perfectly indifferent whether it should be work
or fight, came pouring over the Nebraska line and into
Kansas Territory. A feeble attempt was made to stop
them, but it amounted to nothing. They were not now
on a Missouri River steamboat. Jim Lane came with
them. He remained *incognito* a few days, and then threw
off his disguise, and Capt. Joe Cook was Jim Lane. And
now the old, hard rule of the law of Moses, "An eye for
an eye, and a tooth for a tooth," was again the law of
Kansas. It was, " You have robbed us, and we will rob
you; you have subsisted yourselves upon us, and we
will subsist ourselves on you; you have blockaded the
Missouri River, and waylaid our freighting trains,
and pillaged them of their freight, with intent to starve
out the Free State people, and all that belongs to you
and yours shall be free plunder to us."

The places that had been fortified by this "Law
and Order" militia were one by one stormed and the
garrisons driven off. Franklin was a second time attacked and its occupants taken prisoners. Col. Titus
had fortified his residence in the suburbs of Lecompton, and here he kept a company of men that made
raids on the surrounding Free State inhabitants. This
fort was taken by assault, and Col. Titus and his men
were taken prisoners, while Major Sedjwick, with a
company of United States troops, was encamped only
two miles away. The citizens of Lecompton were
frightened out of their wits, and Gov. Shannon was

found under the bank of the Kansas River, badly demoralized, and trying to get across the river on an old scow, and thus escape the danger. He came the next day to Lawrence, accompanied by Maj. Sedjwick, to make peace and negotiate an exchange of prisoners. He announced this as his last official act, and exhorted the people in a speech he made to them, to live in peace with each other, while they shouted in angry retort, "Give us back Barber and the men that have been murdered under your rule."

But in spite of all these reverses that had come upon the "Law and Order" party, they still had faith that Providence is on the side of the heaviest battalions, and that they would yet succeed in driving out these Free State rebels; and they proceeded to raise, along the Missouri border, a larger army than it would be possible for the Free State people to raise. Did they not have on their side the President and his Cabinet? Was not Congress on their side? Was not Persifer F. Smith, Commandant at Fort Leavenworth, at least indifferent to all their deeds of violence? And more and better, Woodson had succeeded Shannon as acting Governor, and it would be a bad day that should not see the full fruition of their hopes.

But there was one thought to mar their otherwise perfect joy, just as Providence always pours a drop of bitterness into every cup. A Governor unfriendly to their purposess might be appointed, and it became them, therefore, to make hay while the sun was shining. They, therefore, addressed the following pathetic appeal to the people of the South:

We have asked the appointment of a successor who was acquainted with our condition; who, a citizen of our Territory, identified with its interests, familiar with its history, would not be prejudiced or misled by the falsehoods which have been so systematically fabricated against us.

In his stead we have one appointed who is ignorant of our condition, a stranger to our people; who we have too much cause to fear will, if no worse, prove no more efficient to protect us than his predecessors.

With, then, a government which has proved imbecile, has failed to enforce the laws for our protection, with our army of lawless banditti overturning our country—what shall we do?

Though we have full confidence in the integrity and fidelity of Mr. Woodson, now acting as Governor, we know not at what moment his authority will be suspended. We can not await the convenience of the incoming of the newly appointed Governor. We can not hazard a second edition of imbecility or corruption.

We must act at once, and effectively. These traitors, assassins, and robbers must be punished; must now be taught a lesson they will remember.

It is, then, not only the right, but the duty of all good citizens of Missouri and every other State to come to our assistance, and enable us to expel these invaders.

Mr. Woodson, since the resignation of Governor Shannon, has fearlessly met the responsibilities of the trust forced upon him, has proclaimed the existence of the rebellion, and called on the militia of the Territory to assemble for its suppression.

We call on you to come, to furnish us assistance in men, provisions, and munitions, that we may drive out the army of the North, who would subvert our government and expel us from our homes.

CHAPTER XIX.

Gov. Shannon left the Territory a disgraced and ruined man. He had proved himself, both to the Free State party and the Law and Order party, a broken staff that pierces the hand of him that leans on it. ' Mr. Woodson, who took his place as acting Governor, showed himself hale fellow well met with such spirits as Sheriff Jones and Judge Lecompte ; and this faction made piteous appeals to the Great Father at Washington to give them a man after their own heart, and this they found in John Calhoun, Surveyor-General of Kansas and Nebraska, whose official patronage made him a man of considerable influence, and whose freighting outfit, kept for his peculiar business, would have made him eminently useful to this party in the transportation of military stores. But their appeal had been denied them, and instead of Surveyor-General Calhoun, Mr. Geary, of Pennsylvania, had been appointed.

That great party, of which the President was the official head, was convulsed with such internal feuds and contentions, consequent on these very Kansas troubles, as threatened its existence. A Presidential election was pending, and attention must be paid to this fact, rather than to the desperate schemes of this Kansas faction. John W. Geary was, therefore, announced as the appointee of the President. Mr. G.

came with high claims to public favor.   He had passed through the Mexican war with honor ; he had discharged high public trust in California with such fidelity and skill as won for him a distinguished reputation.   He was the friend, and almost the neighbor, of the incoming President, James Buchanan, and he enjoyed the confidence of the outgoing President, Franklin Pierce ; and was closeted with him and with his Secretary of State, Mr. Marcy, before leaving Washington.   That nothing might be wanting to his success, he spent a day at Jefferson City, Mo., with Gov. Sterling Price, and with him arranged to have the blockade removed from the Missouri River.

Mr. Geary met at Glasgow, Mo., the retiring ex-Governor, and Dr. Gihon reports that he was fleeing in terror that his life would be taken by the men for whom he had been such an abject tool.

While these parting ceremonies were being performed a steamboat bound down the river, and directly from Kansas, came along side the Keystone.   Ex-Governor Shannon was a passenger, who, upon learning the close proximity of Gov. Geary, sought an immediate interview with him.   The ex-Governor was greatly agitated.   He had fled in haste and terror from the Territory, and still seemed laboring under an apprehension for his personal safety.   His description of Kansas was suggestive of everything that is frightful and horrible.   Its condition was deplorable in the extreme.   The whole Territory was in a state of insurrection, and a destructive civil war was devastating the country.   Murder ran rampant, and the roads were everywhere strewn with the bodies of slaughtered men.

Dr. Gihon afterwards published a small volume of 348 pages, from which the preceding extract has been taken.   The work is entitled ''Governor Geary's Administration in Kansas.''   This work does not bear the sign manual of Gov. Geary, but as it was written by the Governor's private secretary, it must be taken as an authentic statement of what these gentlemen saw with their own eyes, and heard with their own ears, as touching the condition of things in the Territory. Dr. Gihon gives the following testimony concerning the troubles in and around Leavenworth and their cause:

After the removal of Shannon on the 21st of August, when Secretary Woodson became acting Governor until the arrival of Gov. Geary in September, the belligerents had matters pretty much their own way, and the ruffians improved the time, under pretense of authority from Woodson, to perpetrate with impunity the most shocking barbarities.

During this time Gen. Smith received much censure from the Free State people. Emory, Wilkes, Stringfellow and others were driving these from their homes in Leavenworth, and many of them fled in terror for protection within the enclosures of the fort; when the General caused hand-bills to be posted over the grounds commanding them to leave before a certain specified time, and gave orders to his subordinates to enforce this command. These unfortunate people, among whom were men of the highest respectability, and even women and children, were compelled, some of them without money or suitable clothing, to take to the prairies, exposed at every step to the danger of being murdered by scouting or marauding parties, or at the risk of their lives effect their escape upon the downward-bound boats. Some of these were shot in the attempt upon the river banks, whilst others were seized at Kansas City and other Missouri towns, brought back as prisoners, and disposed of in such a manner as will only be made known at that great day when all human mysteries will be revealed.

Captain Frederick Emory, a United States Mail Contractor, rendered himself conspicuous in Leavenworth at the head of a band of ruffians mostly from Western Missouri. They entered houses, stores and dwellings of Free State people, and in the name of "Law and Order" abused and robbed the occupants, and drove them out into the roads, irrespective of age, sex or condition. Under pretense of searching for arms, they approached the house of William Phillips, the lawyer who had been previously tarred and feathered and carried to Missouri. Phillips, supposing he was to be subjected to a similar outrage, and resolved not to submit to the indignity, stood upon his defense. In repelling the assaults of the mob, he killed two of them, when the others burst into the house, and poured a volley of balls into his body, killing him instantly in the presence of his wife and another lady. His brother, who was also present, had an arm broken with bullets, and was compelled to submit to an amputation. Fifty of the Free State prisoners were then driven on board the Polar Star, bound for St. Louis. On the next day a hundred more were embarked by Emory and his men on the steamboat Emma.

At this time civil war raged in all the populous districts. Women and children had fled from the Territory. No man's life was safe, and every person, when he lay down to rest at night, bolted and barred his doors, and fell asleep grasping firmly his pistol, gun or knife.

Emory's company were all mounted on "pressed" horses, the owners of some of which were present to point out and claim them; but as there existed no courts or judges from whom the necessary legal process could be obtained, and as Gen. Smith would not listen to their complaints, they had no means by which to recover their property.

Emory and his company held their headquarters at Leavenworth City, whence they sallied into the surrounding country to "press," *not steal*, the horses, cattle, wagons and other property of Free State men. It was during these excursions that Major Sackett, of the United States Army, found in the road near Leavenworth City a number of the bodies of men who had been seized, robbed, murdered and mutilated, and left unburied by the wayside.

On the 17th of August, 1856, a shocking affair occurred in the neighborhood of Leavenworth. Two ruffians sat at a table in a low groggery, imbibing potations of bad whisky. One of them, named Fugert, bet his companion six dollars against a pair of boots that he would go out and in less than two hours bring in the scalp of an Abolitionist. He went into the road, and, meeting a Mr. Hoppe, who was in his carriage just returning to Leavenworth from a visit to Lawrence, where he had conveyed his wife, Fugert deliberately shot him; then, taking out his bowie knife, whilst his victim was still alive, he cut and tore off his scalp from his quivering head. Leaving the body of Hoppe lying in the road, he elevated his bloody trophy upon a pole, and paraded it through the streets of Leavenworth. On the same day a teamster, who was approaching Leavenworth, was murdered and scalped by another human monster.

A poor German, when the scalp of Hoppe was brought into Leavenworth, was impudent enough to express his horror of the shocking deed, when he was ordered to run for his life—in attempting which a number of bullets sped after him, and he fell dead in the street.

CHAPTER XX.

In the month of August, 1856, a company of so-called Territorial Militia established themselves at Hickory Point, Jefferson county, about twenty miles north of Lawrence, and proceeded to make raids on the Free State settlements. In one of these raids they pillaged the village of Grasshopper Falls, robbing the stores of their contents. Gen. Lane and Captains Harvey and Bickerton determined to attack and dislodge these marauders. But on the 11th of September Gov. Geary, having arrived at Lecompton, issued a proclamation ordering all armed bands of men, whether known as Territorial Militia or Free State Guerrillas, to disperse and retire to their homes. Gen. Lane determined at once to leave the Territory, and sent a message to that effect to Capt. Harvey, who had arranged to unite his command with that of Gen. Lane in an attack on Hickory Point; but the messenger failed to meet Harvey, who made the attack alone and captured these robbers. But Harvey's men were in their turn taken prisoners by a company of United States troops and were conveyed to Lecompton and kept during the winter as treason prisoners. But while the Free State forces were thus being scattered, disbanded and taken prisoners, by virtue of Gov. Geary's proclamation, an army of 3,000 men had been enlisted in Missouri and along the border towns, and were marching to destroy Lawrence and wipe out the Free State settlements. Delilah bound Samson with cords, then said, "The Philistines be upon thee, Samson"; and so these "Law and Order" leaders saw the Free State forces dispersed by the Governor's proclamation, and then thought to bring on the helpless settlements the whole power of this Missouri invasion. But we will let Mr. Geary's private secretary tell the story in his own way:

But the most reprehensible character in the drama being enacted was the Secretary of the Territory, then acting Governor. More than three weeks after Gov. Geary had received his commission and Secretary Woodson had every reason to believe that he was on his way to the Territory, that weak-minded, if not criminally defective, officer issued the following proclamation :

WHEREAS, Satisfactory evidence exists that the Territory of Kansas is infested with large bodies of armed men :

Now, therefore, I, Daniel Woodson, Acting Governor of the Territory of Kansas, do issue my proclamation declaring the said Territory to be in a state of open insurrection and rebellion, and I do hereby call upon all law-abiding citizens of the Territory to rally to the support of the country and its laws.

Not satisfied with the proclamation, which of itself was sufficiently mischievous, he wrote private letters to parties in Missouri calling for men, money and munitions of war. This proclamation and these letters called together thousands of men, mostly from Missouri, with passions inflamed to the highest degree, and whose only thought was wholesale slaughter and destruction.

It was the fixed purpose of Secretary Woodson to keep Gov. Geary in ignorance of the extensive preparations that were being made to attack and destroy the Free State settlements. As yet the Governor had not seen Woodson's proclamation. Governor Geary issued the following orders:

ADJT. GEN. H. J. STRICKLER :—You will proceed without a moments's delay to disarm and disband the present organized militia of the Territory.

Notwithstanding the positive character of these orders they were utterly disregarded. Suspecting that treachery was somewhere at work he forthwith dispatched confidential messengers on the road to Westport to ascertain, if possible, what operations were going forward in that vicinity.

Messengers were constantly arriving from Lawrence bringing in-telligence that a large army from Missouri was encamped on the Waka-rusa River and was hourly expected to attack the town. As these men were styled Territorial Militia and were called into service by the late acting Governor Woodson, Gov. Geary commanded that officer to take with him Adjutant-General Strickler with an escort of United States troops and disband, in accordance with the proclamation issued, the forces that had so unwisely been assembled. Woodson and Strickler left Lecompton in the afternoon, and reached the Missouri camp early in the evening.

Here Woodson found it impossible to accomplish the object of his mission. No attention or respect was paid to him by those having command of the forces. The army he had gathered refused to acknowl-edge his authority. He had raised a storm, the elements of which he was powerless to control; neither could the officers be assembled to re-ceive the Governor's orders from the Adjutant-General. The militia had resolved not to disband, the officers refused to listen to the reading of the proclamation—they were determined upon accomplishing the bloody work they had entered the Territory to perform. Nothing but the destruction of Lawrence and the other Free State towns, the massa-cre of the Free State residents, and the appropriation of their lands and other property, could satisfy them.

Mr. Adams, who accompanied Secretary Woodson to the Missouri camp, dispatched the following:

LAWRENCE, 12 o'clock Midnight, Sept. 14, 1856.

To His EXCELLENCY, GOV. GEARY:

SIR:—*Secretary Woodson thought you had better come to the camp of the militia as soon as you can.* THEODORE ADAMS.

Before this dispatch reached Lecompton the Governor had de-parted with three hundred United States mounted troops and a battery of light artillery, and arrived in Lawrence early in the morning, where he found matters precisely as described. Skillfully stationing his troops outside the town, in commanding positions, to prevent a collision be-tween the invading forces from Missouri and the citizens, he entered Lawrence alone, and there he beheld a sight which would have aroused the manhood of the most stolid mortal. About three hundred persons were found in arms, determined to sell their lives at the dearest price to their ruffian enemies. Among these were many women, and children of both sexes, armed with guns and otherwise accoutered for battle. They had been goaded to this by the courage of despair.

Gov. Geary addressed the armed citizens of Lawrence, and when he assured them of his and the law's protection they offered to deposit their arms at his feet and return to their respective habitations. He bade them go to their homes in confidence, and to carry their arms with them, as the constitution guarantees that right, but to use them only in the last resort to protect their lives and property and the chastity of their females.

Early in the morning of the 15th, having left the troops to protect the town, the Governor proceeded alone to the camp of the invading forces, then within three miles and drawn up in line of battle. Before reaching Franklin, he met the advance guard, and upon inquiring who they were and what were their objects, received for answer that they were the Territorial Militia, and called into service by the Governor of Kansas, and that they were marching to wipe out Lawrence and every —— Abolitionist in the country.

Mr. Geary informed them that he was now Governor of Kansas, and Commander-in-chief of the Territorial Militia, and ordered the officer in command to countermarch his troops back to the main line, and conduct him to the center, which order, after some hesitation, was reluctantly obeyed.

The red face of the rising sun was just peering over the top of Blue Mound, as the Governor, with his strange escort of three hundred mounted men, with red shirts and odd-shaped hats, descended upon the Wakarusa plain, where in battle array were ranged at least three thousand armed and desperate men. They were not dressed in the usual habiliments of soldiers, but in every imaginable costume that could be obtained in the western region. Most of them were mounted, and manifested an unmistakable disposition to be at their bloody work. In the back-ground stood at least three hundred army tents and as many wagons, while here and there a cannon was planted ready to aid in the anticipated destruction. Among the banners floated black flags, to indicate the design that neither age, sex nor condition would be spared in the slaughter that was to ensue.

In passing along the lines murmurs of discontent and savage threats of assassination fell upon the Governor's ears, but heedless of these and regardless, in fact, of everything but a desire to avert the terrible calamity that was impending, he fearlessly proceeded to the quarters of their leader.

This threatening army was under the command of John W. Reed, then and now a member of the Missouri Legislature, assisted by ex-Senator Atchison, Gen. B. F. Stringfellow, Gen. L. A. Maclean, Gen. J. W. Whitfield, Gen. George W. Clarke, Gens. William A. Heiskell,

Wm. H. Richardson and F. A. Marshal, Col. H. T. Titus, Capt. Frederick Emory and others.

Gov. Geary at once summoned the officers together, and addressed them at length and with great feeling. He depicted in a forcible manner the improper position they occupied and the untold horrors that would result from a consummation of their cruel designs; that if they persisted in their mad career the entire Union would be involved in a civil war, and thousands and tens of thousands of innocent lives be sacrificed. To Atchison he particularly addressed himself, telling him that when he last saw him he was acting as Vice-President of the nation and President of the most dignified body of men in the world, the Senate of the United States, but now with sorrow and pain he saw him leading on to a civil and disastrous war an army of men with uncontrollable passions, and determined upon wholesale slaughter and destruction. He concluded his remarks by directing attention to his proclamation, and ordered the army to be disbanded and dispersed. Some of the more judicious of the officers were not only willing but anxious to obey this order, while others, resolved upon mischief, yielded a reluctant assent.

CHAPTER XXI.

It is now one-third of a century since Kansas began to be settled. Great as has been the progress of the States of this Union within this period, the progress of Kansas has been exceptionally and peculiarly so. Its chief glory is not in its large agricultural and mineral resources; it is not in its railroads and lines of telegraph; it is not in the rapidly increasing population of educated men and women, but it is in this, that it was not only the first State in the nation, but the first Commonwealth in the world, to solve the problem of the drink evil, the giant curse of Christendom, by incorporating prohibition into its fundamental law.

In union there is strength. Jesus said so. He said, "Every kingdom divided against itself is brought to desolation." And so evidently does this principle commend itself to the common sense of men, that we have engraved on our national ensign the motto, "*E Pluribus Unum*"—one out of many.

How did such growth in Kansas come to be? Not in division, but in union. We have thought it would do us good to look squarely in the face that hard, cruel, and bloody period when it seemed the business of the people to cut each other's throats. But cutting each other's throats does not create such growth as we have had in Kansas.

Two peoples came together in Kansas, one from

the South and one from the North. They were of one original stock, but circumstances had intervened and made them two peoples. For two years this bloody strife had been going on. It is said that in revolutions men live fast. It was two years, if we count the time by the revolutions of the earth around the sun, but if we count by the experience men had gained, it was many years.

Dr. Gihon tells that when Gov. Geary disbanded this Missouri army on the Wakarusa, there grew up a marked antagonism of sentiment among its leaders. He says: "Some of the more judicious of the officers were not only willing but anxious to obey this order, whilst others, resolved upon mischief, yielded a very reluctant assent." There was really a large majority that accepted the result with hearty good will, but there was also a small and malcontent minority determined on mischief.

Gen. B. F. Stringfellow, because of the vehement zeal with which he had addicted himself to the enterprise of making Kansas a slave State, had won for himself a national notoriety. He had staked life and good fame and everything on the final issue of his work, yet himself and his law partner, Peter T. Abell, went back from the Wakarusa never to lift a finger again in that business. Mr. S. is a high-spirited, hot-blooded, proud-spirited Virginian. His law partner, Col. Abell, had a temper as unbending as Andrew Jackson, and did to the day of his death hold a faith in the institution of slavery as abiding as John C. Calhoun. But he was a wise and a just man, and both himself and Mr. Stringfellow recognized the fact that, with such a population as had come into Kansas, its becoming a free State was only a question of time; and both these men were too sagacious to be found fighting against fate. Mr. S. had always relished a joke, and, when rallied by his friends on his sudden abandonment of this enterprise, he facetiously replied: "Yes, I did try to make Kansas a slave State; but I could not do it without slaves, and the South would not send slaves, and so I had to give it up." From the time these gentlemen returned from the Wakarusa there was a general softening of the asperities of feeling of the people of Atchison and vicinity, and one year after they were prepared to announce to the Free State people, "You deal fairly with us, and we will deal fairly with you"—and they made their words good by deeds, for they took Free State men into partnership with themselves in the management of the Atchison Town Company.

But by this change Robert S. Kelley found "Othello's occupation gone," and the control of the *Squatter Sovereign* passed into the hands of John A. Martin, now Governor of Kansas, and "Bob Kelley" shook off the dust of his feet and walked away, respected for his bravery and for his outspoken honesty and sincerity, even by those that did not love him.

The writer will tell of his last interview with the South Carolinians in a future chapter of these Recollections.

Peter T. Abell and Gen. B. F. Stringfellow were State's rights men in their political opinions, and, therefore, according to the light that was in them, owed their allegiance to the State of Kansas; and from that allegiance they never swerved to the breadth of a hair. Still, the people of the South were their brethren, and they gave to them their profoundest sympathy during that bloody struggle that was to decide whether the South should be an independent nation. Let us admit that this did put these gentlemen in a strait betwixt two, like Paul, the Apostle, but they never swerved to the right hand nor to the left.

We have, with some particularity, drawn out the history of the two most distinguished of the Southern leaders, because that, with slight change, it would be the biography of a great number of citizens of Kansas that came from the South. Now, who does not see that here is the basis of hearty co-operation, whether in the church or in the world, of men from the South or from the North? provided always we can take into our hearts the law of love: "All things whatsoever ye would that men should do to you, do ye even so to them; for this is the law and the prophets."

In further illustration of this remark we will relate an incident concerning a Disciple, who will come prominently before us in the formation of our first missionary society. Spartan Rhea was from Missouri, and belonged to a family intensely Southern in their convictions. He was commissioned a justice of the peace by the Territorial authorities. A horse had been stolen by the Kickapoo Rangers from Gains Jenkins, of Lawrence. Gov. Geary requested Bro. Rhea to recover the horse, and he did so with some peril to himself, and made a journey to Lawrence to restore the animal to its proper owner. He sought to make it evident that the men of his party wanted justice done.

But Dr. Gihon also tells us that there was at the Wakarusa a small faction of irreconcilables, who, if they could do nothing else, could at least curse.

"Gen. Clarke said he was for pitching into the United States troops rather than abandon the objects of the expedition. Gen. Maclean didn't see any use of going back until they had whipped the —— Abolitionists. Sheriff Jones was in favor, now that they had sufficient force, of wiping out Lawrence and all the Free State towns. And these and others cursed Gov. Geary for his interference in their well-laid plans.

"The broad ground assumed by these rabid leaders of the Pro-slavery party in Kansas was, that an equilibrium of the slave power must be maintained at any sacrifice in the American Union, and this could only be effected by increasing the slave States in proportion with the free. Whilst, therefore, the South was willing to give Nebraska to the North, they demanded that Kansas should be ceded to the South. It was of little consequence what number of Northern men located in Kansas—they had no right to come unless with the intention to make it a slave State."

This malcontent minority did, therefore, become a dangerous and revolutionary faction, entertaining criminal purposes, which they were ready to carry out by desperate methods. They were also in possession of dangerous elements of power. They controlled the Territorial Legislature, and all the Territorial judges were parties in this conspiracy. Dr. Gihon testifies that "every federal officer in the Territory, and every Territorial officer from the supreme judges to the deputy marshals, sheriffs and clerks, were wedded to the slave power, and pledged at all hazards to its extension."

But daylight had already begun to dawn. Some

of the wisest Pro-slavery men in the Territory were beginning to call a halt, and to say: "We will travel no further in this road in which we are being led by these desperate and scheming adventurers."

CHAPTER XXII.

Gov. Geary had won ripe and rich honors from the people of this nation in the official positions he had heretofore held, and which he had discharged with such eminent ability. The position of the Governor of Kansas, as seen from afar, and under the *glamour* that surrounded it, was a position of high honor.

Every child has heard the story of old "Blue Beard," how that, having married a number of wives who had mysteriously disappeared, he courted and married a beautiful young lady, possessing every accomplishment that can give grace and attractiveness to a woman, and had carried her to his castle, where she should have at her disposal an unlimited amount of money and be served by obsequious servants, and stand on a level with all the fine ladies and gentlemen in the land. Old Blue Beard gave to her the keys un-. locking all the rooms in his castle, but said to her, "There is one key, unlocking one door, into one room, and into that room you must in nowise enter." But, overcome by her woman's curiosity, she did unlock that door and enter that room, and there she beheld the horrid sight of all the murdered wives of the wicked old Blue Beard, hanging and rotting on its walls, and now this was also to be her sad fate.

Kansas was becoming the graveyard of Territorial Governors. Reeder and Shannon had already lost their official heads. Within six months Gov. Geary's head was also to drop into the basket. Three more governors were to succeed him, each one of whom should in his turn lose his official head. Gov. Geary's position was indeed very like that of the wife of the wicked Blue Beard, only that she had certainly some advantages over the Governor. She had a great and fine castle, rich and costly dresses, many servants ready to come and go at her beck and call, and the company of great lords and fine ladies; but when Gov. Geary came to his castle, his private Secretary shall tell us what he found:

Lecompton is situated on the south side of the Kansas River, upon as inconvenient and inappropriate a site for a town as any in the Territory. It was chosen simply for speculative purposes. It contained, at the time of Gov. Geary's arrival, some twenty or more houses, the majority of which were employed as groggeries of the lowest description. It was the residence of the celebrated Sheriff Jones, who is one of the leading members of this town association, and was the resort of horse-thieves and ruffians of the most desperate character. Its drinking saloons were infested by these characters, whose drunkenness, gambling, fighting, and all sorts of crime, were indulged in with impunity.

Here was congregated, and here was the head-quarters of, that band of desperate men, who were in a conspiracy to make Kansas a slave State at whatever cost of blood, of fraud, or violence. Here the Terri-torial Legislature met to enact their bloody code of laws, and here the Territorial Judges held their courts, which were a burlesque on the very name of a civilized and Christian jurisprudence ; and here, also, were kept the treason prisoners, while atrocious murderers were not molested, because they were ''sound on the goose question.''

We have already told how Harvey's men, that had

attacked and taken prisoners the "Law and Order" robbers that pillaged the defenseless village of Grass-hopper Falls, were themselves taken prisoners by the United States troops.   These were tried for treason in the Pro-slavery courts, and were condemned to various terms of imprisonment, varying from six months to six years.   They were kept in a wretched, old, tumble-down house, without doors or windows, during the bit-ter cold of a Kansas winter, guarded by "Law and Order" militia, exposed to every insult, wallowing in filth, and eaten up with lice.   But there was one circumstance to mitigate their hapless condition—their jailer was a good-hearted, honest Kentuckian, who had humanity enough to pity them, and bravery enough to do what he could to mitigate the hardships of their lot.   Their hard-hearted judges had condemned them to wear a ball and chain; but Gov. Geary refused to provide balls and chains for them, and the honest Capt. Hampton refused to fasten these symbols of degrada-tion on the limbs of men he knew to be decent Amer-ican citizens ; and thereat Sheriff Jones became furious. The facts of the case were just these: All the people were, so to speak, fighting.   The Governor issued his proclamation.   These Hickory Point "Law and Or-der" militia were simply robber banditti, and Captain Harvey and his company thought they ought to be "cleaned out," and proceeded to do so, and this act, though intrinsically it was a righteous act, yet techni-cally, laid them open to the law.   This happened on the 12th of September, but up to the 14th of September 3,000 "Law and Order" militia, coming into Kansas as outside invaders, refused to be disbanded by the Governor's proclamation, and both before and after

contiued the business of murder and robbery. Yet
this was nothing, because these were "Law and Order" men. The other was treason, for these were
Free State men fighting for their homes and firesides.
But Capt. Hampton saw the matter just as it was, and
acted accordingly. Dr. Gihon testified of these treason
prisoners, "These prisoners were not all rough and
desperate adventurers. Some of them were gentlemen of polished education."

The sunlight may sparkle and shimmer on the surface of the foul and putrid marsh, noxious with offensive and poisonous exhalations—so Dr. Gihon throws
a kind of grim and ghastly humor over his narrative
of the repulsive and brutal surroundings of himself
and Governor Geary during the winter they were im-
prisoned at Lecompton. The Doctor tells the following story at the expense of a Southern gentleman:

A good anecdote is told by a gentleman from one of the Southern
States, in regard to these Free State prisoners, when under the charge of
Captain Hampton. Having expressed a desire to see these robbers and
murderers, as he styled them, the Governor directed him to the prison.

He immediately started, and looking in vain for anything that re-
sembled a prison, he approached two men who were enjoying themselves
with a game of quoits.

"Can you tell me," he inquired, where the prison is where these
robbers and murderers are confined?"

"That's it," said one of the men, pointing to a house near at
hand.

"What! that old building, falling to pieces, without either doors
or windows?"

"That is the only prison we have here," replied the man, deliberately pitching his quoit.

"Well," said the Southern gentleman, "I want to see these prisoners."

"I am one of them," said the quoit-player, "and that is another,"
pointing to his companion.

"What! you convicted felons? You the terrible murderers about whom I have heard so much?"

"Yes, we are certainly two of them. The others are gone over to the House of Representatives, to hear the members abuse the Governor."

"But," says the old gentleman, "they do n't allow convicted murderers to go about in this way, without a guard to watch them?"

"O! yes," says the man interrogated; "they used to send a guard with us when we went over to the Legislative Halls, to protect us against violence from the members, but they found that too troublesome, so they gave each of us a revolver and bowie-knife, and told us we should hereafter be required to protect ourselves."

"But why do n't you run away? There is nothing to prevent you."

"Why, to tell the truth, we have often been persuaded to do that, but then these rascally legislators have been threatening to assassinate the Governor, and we have determined to remain here to watch them and protect him."

The old gentleman had no desire to see any more of these thieves, murderers and assassins.

There are those who find a Spanish bull fight or a civilized American boxing match very enjoyable events. Such men would have found great enjoyment in one incident that served to enliven the monotony of the winter's residence of the Governor at Lecompton. There was one Sherrard who came from Virginia. He was of a good family, but strong drink had been his ruin. He had been appointed by the Legislature Sheriff of Douglas county in place of S. T. Jones, who for some reason was to go out of office. The Governor refused to commission this Sherrard because he was a drunkard, a brawler, and a cursing, swearing, gambling ruffian and bully. This made Sherrard furious, and Sheriff Zones and all his crowd of bullies were furious with him. Then Sherrard tried to raise a row by insulting individuals in the personal service of the Governor. This failing, Sherrard spit in the Governor's face; but Mr. Geary, mindful of the dignity of his office, and that it did not become the Governor of Kansas to get into a brawl with a common blackguard, walked straight on. Afterwards Sherrard, who kept himself crazy drunk, provoked a general affray in a large company of men, in which pistols were fired in every direction; when John A. W. Jones, the young man on Gov. Geary's staff whom Sherrard had assaulted a few days before, shot him in the forehead.

CHAPTER XXIII.

One circumstance at last brought to a sudden close
Gov. Geary's term of office. When he had disbanded
the three thousand "Law and Order" militia that
were to attack Lawrence, that part of them known as
the Kickapoo Rangers were returning home by way of
Lecompton. One of this number went into a field
where "a poor, inoffensive, lame young man" named
David C. Buffum was plowing, and demanded his
horses. Buffum protested against this robbery, but the
wretch shot Buffum and took the horses. The unhappy
man gave the following account of the matter:

> They asked me for my horses. I told them I was a cripple—a poor
> lame man—that I had an aged father, a deaf and dumb brother, and
> two sisters, all depending on me for a living, and my horses were all I
> had. One of them said I was a —— —— Abolitionist, and, taking me
> by the shoulder, he shot me.

Gov. Geary was returning to Lecompton, and hearing of what had been done, he called with Judge Cato
at Buffum's house, and by the Governor's direction
Judge Cato took the dying man's deposition. Gov.
Geary was terribly shocked, and said to himself, "I
never witnessed a scene that filled me with so much
horror." Mr. Geary sent a detective on the track of
the Kickapoo Rangers, and found that the murderer
was one Charley Hayes, living in Atchison county.
He had the horses still in his possession. The Gov-

ernor ordered his arrest, and the Grand Jury found a bill against him of murder in the first degree. Meantime the Free State men came to the Governor making a bitter complaint of the persecutions they were suffering. They said, "Our relatives and friends are arrested and confined for weeks and months in a filthy prison, not fit for dogs to live in, and are kept without proper food or clothing, and are not allowed to give bail even for bailable offenses; while murderers of the other party are allowed to go at large and no attention is paid to them." They said, ' The murderers of Dow, Barber, Brown, Phillips, Hoppe and Buffum, have not even been arrested or examined."

The Governor replied that he had already ordered the arrest of Hayes, and that a grand jury of Pro-slavery men had found a true bill against him, and that Hayes should be tried for his life. But while he was yet speaking a messenger brought word that Judge Lecompte had released Hayes on bail, and that Sheriff Jones had gone on his bail bond, a man notoriously not worth a dollar; and this when the crime of murder in the first degree, for which Hayes had been indicted, was not a bailable offense. The Governor was terribly indignant, and ordered Hayes to be re-arrested. But while he was absent at the land sales at Fort Leavenworth, Judge Lecompte a second time set this wretch at liberty. Mr. Geary was provoked beyond endurance, and wrote to the President that he would not remain in office and allow such a scoundrel to be kept in a position to pervert the ways of justice. President Pierce nominated C. O. Harrison, of Kentucky, to take Lecompte's place, but for some unexplained cause the appointment was not confirmed in the Senate, and

Judge Lecompte retained his place, and in unspeak
able disgust Gov. Geary resigned, making his resignation take effect on March 20, 1857. Thus he had
spent a winter in the chamber of death of the wicked
old Blue Beard, but did not lose his official head till
spring.

The writer was acquainted with the family of this
Charley Hayes. They were decent sort of people ;
but when a young boy Charley went on the plains,
where he became a brutal ruffian. A good many
years ago there was a story current in Atchison county,
that when this Hayes was acting as wagon-boss on the
plains, in a train owned by Russell, Majors & Waddell,
that one of the teamsters having offended him he tied
him up to a wheel of one of the train wagons, and,
holding a pistol in one hand, he cowhided him with
his black-snake whip with the other. And this teamster was a white man.

But there are avenging furies that follow a man,
even though the law does not reach him. There is a
man now living in Atchison county whose truthfulness
has never been questioned, and he stated that he spent
a winter in the Missouri River bottoms, sleeping in the
same cabin with Charley Hayes, and that it seemed as
if the devil had a mortgage on the ruffian's soul, and
tormented him in his sleep with images of the horrors
that awaited him in the future world. That it seemed
as if he was wrestling in mortal struggle with the men
he had maltreated and murdered, and that they were
choking him to death. Hayes afterwards died of a
consumption presumably brought on by his dissipated
habits and by his debaucheries.

Meantime the writer had started for Illinois the preceding summer, had been prostrated for four weeks with a fever, and late in the autumn of 1856 had returned to Kansas, there to remain. The times were becoming quiet, the peaceful counsels of such leaders as Stringfellow and Abell were beginning to take effect, and it evidently would be safe for the writer to go to work on his claim. But he needed a supply of corn, and had to go over into the Missouri River bottoms to buy it. A heavy snow had fallen. I had a heavy, well-trained yoke of oxen, and my faithful riding horse was obedient in every place. Myself and brother-in-law had made a heavy Yankee sled that would hold all the load that was put on it. I borrowed from my neighbor, Caleb May, two additional yoke of oxen, but they only knew how to pull in a big freighting team, and were not leaders. But putting my own heavy oxen behind, my wild steers in the middle, and my horse in the lead, I made out a good freighting team. But I had to pass through Atchison. The business men of the place had already made this overture to me. They had said: " You can come to Atchison during the day time and we will guarantee that you shall not be molested, but we would rather you should not be here in the night. The South Carolinians are here, and there are other desperate characters here, and in the night we do not know what might happen." And so, on the strength of such an agreement, I had done business in Atchison, and to get my corn across the river had gone over one day and back the next.

I had yet one more load of corn to haul. There had been a thaw, and then the snow had frozen again, making it in many places slippery traveling. The

river bank, from the top of the bank down to the ice
of the river, was about twenty feet, and very steep;
and this by much traveling had become a perfect glare
of ice, so that teams could not hold their footing at
all. I had gone over for my last load one day, intending to return the next day, but I had found unex-
pected hindrances, and when I got to the east bank of
the river opposite Atchison, it was sometime after
dark. I got down as best I could and crossed over on
the ice to the Atchison side of the river, and I was
now to get up that bank of glare ice.* I placed my
sled load of corn at the bottom of the bank, and taking my team up in an unfrequented place, I stationed
them on the top of the bank directly above my load
of corn at the bottom. Before coming over I had cut
a long, slender pole in the timbered bottoms, and in
view of this contingency had also brought extra chains
from home, and by means of the chains and this long
pole I hitched my team on the top of the hill to my
load of corn at the bottom. The thing worked well,
and I had my load well on the top of the bank on the
level ground; but here the road turned suddenly to
the left close along the river bank, and my horse, too
eager to get home, turned too soon, and this brought
my sled with a sudden crash against a rock, and down
went my load to the bottom of the bank again. A
chain had broken, and now my load of corn was left
in such a position that I evidently could not get it up
again without help. In the hindrances to which I had
been subjected it had come to be 9 o'clock. I looked

---

* When father reached the east bank it was so slippery that the oxen would
not go down. So he hitched them to the back of the sled, and, with a handspike,
pried it to the edge of the bank, and started it down. Of course it slid down the
hill, and pulled the oxen with it.

about and saw no light save in a saloon that had been built under the bluff to catch custom, for this was the ferry landing. I do not usually visit saloons, but "necessity knows no law," and I walked in; and whom should I find but Grafton Thomassen, the man that made the raft on which they sent me down the river, sitting and playing cards with a number of South Carolinians! They were thunderstruck, and I have to confess that I was almost as much taken aback as they were. But I spoke to them and said, "Gentlemen, good evening." Then I explained, as well as I could, what had befallen me, and that I had come in for assistance. But they were dumb—they never spoke a word. I waited till my position became embarrassing, then said, "Well, gentlemen, you seem to be busy, and I do n't want to interrupt; I will go somewhere else." I had already opened the door when Grafton Thomassen found his voice and said, "Boys, it is not right to leave Butler without help. Let us go and help him." "Yes! yes! yes!" they all cried at once, "we will go and help him." And, springing to their feet, and hastily putting on their overcoats, hats and gloves, they came rushing to the door, saying, "Yes! yes! We will help you. What is it we can do for you?"

I went with them to the river bank, pointed out my sled loaded with corn on the ice, and explained to them it had to be brought up the bank. They asked incredulously, "An' kin ye haul that thar slide up that slippery bank?"

"I said, "Yes, I have done it once" then I explained how the chain had broken, and how my load of corn had gone down onto the ice again.

They exclaimed, " O ! Well now ! We have come all the way from South *Carliny* to see a Yankee trick an' haint we got it ?"

They were eager to help, so as to see the fun. When everything was ready I gave my horse in charge of one of them, saying to him he must in nowise let the horse turn till the load of corn was well up and in the traveled road, then gave the word to start. My team was eager to pull, for they were getting impatient; and in fine style they brought the load up on the level ground, and then immediately were in front of the saloon, and I called a halt. When we got everything fixed I said to them, " Gentlemen, I thank you. You have done me a real kindness. But the night is cold" —and handing one of them a piece of silver, I said, "Please take that and get something to warm you."

He took it and with something of hesitation said, " Won't you come in and drink with us ?"

I replied, " Please excuse me. You know me ; you know I do n't drink. But all the same I want you to take it."

He said rather proudly, " We did not work for you for pay. We did it to oblige you."

But I insisted. I said, " You did me a real kindness, and I want to do you a kindness in return. I want you to take it." Then they bade me good night and went into the saloon.

The wind had been rising, and the snow was drifting ; and it was evident that in many places the road would be obliterated, and I had a long stretch of prairie to travel over on which there was not a human habitation. It was dangerous to undertake it, and I had to stay in Atchison. I found an empty corral, where my teams would be decently sheltered, and went to the only hotel in town. The sleeping room they assigned me was separated from the bar-room only by a thin board partition, and I could hear every word that was said. This hotel was the boarding-place of the South Carolinians, and they soon began to drop in from about town, and word was passed among them that Butler was in the house. Then one fellow, who was decidedly drunk, got turbulent, and protested, with terrible oaths, that such a man should not stay in the house, but that he would go in and drag him out of bed. Then another company came in and demanded: "What's all this fussing about?" These were my friends, the South Carolinians from under the bluff. They heard what this fellow had to say, then said: "This thing has to be dried up." They then told what had happened down at the river, and concluded: "Butler is a gentleman. He talks like a gentleman; *he treats like a gentleman;* he came into this house like a gentleman, and we will show him that we are gentlemen." And when the drunken fellow became uproarious they hustled him off to bed.

I was evidently among friends, and slept soundly and without apprehension till morning. I never saw my South Carolina friends again. They returned home at an early day.

They had not made Kansas a slave state, but they had seen a Yankee trick.

CHAPTER XXIV.

Gov. Geary, sick in body and sick at heart, had left the Territory in fear of private assassination, his best friends at Lecompton being the treason prisoners. These, with something of bitterness, remarked that the Governor went away in such haste that he had forgotten to pardon them as he had promised; and thus while he got had out of prison, they still stayed in.

The party in power at Lecompton had said to the President at Washington: "We are sick of Northern Governors. They won't do to tie to. For pity's sake give us a man from the South." And so a Southern Governor was given them in the person of Robert J. Walker. Rehoboam, the son of Solomon, said to the Jews: "My little finger shall be thicker than my father's loins." So this Lecompton party found the little finger of this Southern Governor to be thicker than the loins of Gov. Geary.

Mr. W. stood so high in public position that no man stood higher than himself, save alone the President. He had been a Senator from Mississippi, and had been Secretary of the Treasury in Mr. Pierce's Cabinet. The complications of this Kansas question had become such as to call for a man of the highest rank and ability. The main object of Mr. Walker's mission to Kansas was to induce the Free State people to vote at the Territorial elections, which alone were appointed by the government at Washington, and recognized by it. Until he could accomplish this, nothing was done toward the pacification of the Territory. To induce them to do this, he pledged to the Free State men a fair election. But he found that he was speaking to ears that could not hear. He had said in his inaugural address with all apparent fairness:

I can not doubt that the Convention, after having framed a State constitution, will submit it for ratification or rejection by a majority of the actual *bona fide*, resident settlers of Kansas.

With these views well known to the President and Cabinet, and approved by them, I accepted the appointment of Governor of Kansas; my instructions from the President, through the Secretary of State, under date of the 30th of March last, sustain the regular Legislature of the Territory in assembling a convention to form a constitution, and they express the opinion of the President that when such a constitution shall be submitted to the people of the Territory, they must be protected in their right of voting for or against that instrument; and the fair expression of the popular will must not be interrupted by fraud or violence.

This seemed very fair, but what did it amount to! The people knew that the Governor must consent to be a mere cat's paw and convenience of these conspirators, or else be unceremoniously thrust aside; and that the authorities at Washington would sustain them and not him. This had been the fate of Reeder, of Shannon and of Geary, and this also would be the fate of the present Governor. Dr. Gihon, on behalf of Mr. Geary, had bitterly complained that there was not a single officer in the Territory responsible either to the people or to the Governor; that all were the appointees of the Legislature, and responsible to it alone. The Lecompton Legislature had passed a bill calling a convention to frame a State constitution; and Gov. Geary had vetoed the bill because it made no provision for submitting the constitution, when framed, to a vote of

the people ; and the Legislature had passed the bill
over his veto, and now what power had Gov. Walker
in the matter more that Gov. Geary?

An event happened at that time that was a nine
days' wonder, and a nine days' talk among the people ;
and yet it does not seem to have been put on record
in any extant history of the period. The Governor
had sought the privilege of addressing the Free State
people on this question of voting, which he made his
hobby. It was at a meeting at Big Springs. Gen.
Lane was present, as also were a large number of Free
State men, and the Governor had pressed on them, as
the only road out of their difficulties, the necessity of
voting at those Territorial elections, which alone were
recognized by the government at Washington.

Gen. Lane arose to reply, and in a speech of terrible energy and power he arraigned the Lecompton
party for all their wrongs and outrages ; then, when
he had reached the climax of his argument, he leaned
forward, and, looking at Mr. Walker from beneath his
shaggy eyebrows with his deepset, piercing black eyes,
and shaking at him his long bony finger, his whole
frame quivering with passion, he said in his deep gut-
tural tones, which seemed more like the growl of a
savage wild beast than the voice of a human being:
"*Gov–er–nor Wal–ker, y–o–u c–a–n–'t con–t–r–ol your
allies !*"

The effect was prodigious ; and the Free State men
were swept away as with a whirlwind. Even Gov.
Walker felt the force of the appeal. But he showed
himself a brave man ; and came back resolutely to the
battle. He said: "*I am your Governor!* You must
admit that I have at least a *legal* right to control my

allies, so far as to give you a fair election; and I pledge you my word and honor that I will do it. Now try me! and see if I do not keep my word!"

The Free State men began to falter and to ask each other, "Is it not best to try the Governor, and see if he will be as good as his word?" And from this time forward there began to appear a division in the Free State ranks; which sometimes grew to be bitter and acrimonious. This division had indeed begun to appear one year before, when on the Fourth of July Col. Sumner had dispersed the Free State Legislature at Topeka. Gov. Robinson was at that time a prisoner, and was, therefore, not present; but he said in his next annual message as Free State Governor:

When your bodies met, pursuant to adjournment, in July last, your assembly was interfered with and broken up by a large force of United States troops in battle array, who drove you hence, in gross violation of those constitutianal rights *which it was your duty to have protected.*

Wm. A. Phillips, correspondent of the *New York Tribune*, and afterwards a member of Congress, was a man terribly in earnest, and he did, on the above-named Fourth of July, in a speech, take the position that we ought to fight for our rights and defy Col. Sumner and his dragoons. The men that demanded that we should fight said: "We can take possession of the houses and fire out of the windows, and thus avoid the onset of Col. Sumner's cavalry." But the majority said: "We are loyal to the old flag, and in no case, and under no circumstances will be found fighting against it." It was this more conservative majority that began to demand that the Free State men should listen to Gov. Walker's overtures and vote at the coming election.

Gen. Lane had been uncompromising in defying the Territorial laws. He had said: "Gov. Walker has said, 'Vote next week.' What for? Have we not made our constitution? And do not the people of freedom like it? Can't we submit this to the people, and who wants another?" But now he had become at the first reticent, and finally said: "Vote." This singular man that constantly kept on exhibiting his desperate determination to resist the bogus laws, really kept in his heart the one supreme purpose to make himself the oracle of the prevailing sentiment among the Free State men. When, therefore, Gen. Lane said, "Let us vote," it was good evidence that this had become the prevailing sentiment among the Free State party.

A convention was held at Grasshopper Falls, August 26, 1857, at which this was the main question, and it was decided in favor of voting at the coming election of Territorial officers. The Hon. Henry Wilson had recently visited Kansas from Massachusetts, and he had earnestly entreated the Free State men to vote. Phillips, Conway and Redpath still protested against it. Gov. Robinson, however, gave his voice in favor of voting.

An election had already been held June 15th to elect delegates to the Lecompton Constitutional Convention, at which the Free State men had taken no part. Fifteen Free State counties had in this election been disfranchished, no election having been ordered in them.

At the election of Territorial officers, held October 6, 1857, both parties turned out. The Free State men cast 7,887 votes for the Territorial Legislature. The

Lecompton party was reported to have cast 6,466 votes. But though the Free State men had a numerical majority of votes, yet the districts had been so arranged that the above returns gave a majority in the Legislature to the Lecompton party. Johnson county, bordering on Missouri, had been united in one district with Douglas county, in which Lawrence is situated, and this district had been given eight members. Oxford precinct, in Johnson county, was a place of not over a dozen houses, and polled 124 votes for township officers, yet it reported 1,628 votes for the Lecompton party. When, however, Gov. Walker and Mr. Stanton came to canvass the votes they threw out this Oxford vote. They also set aside 1,200 fraudulent votes in McGee county. The vote at Kickapoo, equally fraudulent, was also set aside. This gave a majority to the Free State party in the Lecompton Territorial Legislature, and thus Gov. Walker redeemed his pledge that the people should have a fair election.

Judge Cato felt that it was time to come to the rescue of his friends, and issued a writ directed to "Robert J. Walker, Governor of Kansas Territory, and Frederick P. Stanton, secretary of the same," commanding these gentlemen to issue certificates of election to the men who appeared to be elected according to the original returns. Gov. Walker good-naturedly refused to obey the order of the court, offering to submit to arrest for contempt of court, and tendering the judge a *posse* of United States troops to aid in making the arrest. The judge began to see that he had been making a fool of himself, and dropped the subject. These Territorial judges had shown themselves capable of any excess of villainy, and had been

a sure refuge in every time of trouble to this Lecompton party; but even the courts had now failed them,
and these "border ruffian" judges were only laughed
at by this Southern Governor.   One year before, these
conspirators had assembled an army to drive out the
Free State settlers, and to give the Territory into the
hands of the South; but Gov. Geary had interfered to
thwart their purpose, and, what was worse, a majority
of the leaders of that army, men of note along the
Missouri border, had declared themselves in sympathy with Mr. Geary.   Then they had asked for a
Southern Governor, for would not he be true to the
South?   And now even this man had failed them, and
had given the control of the Territorial Legislature into
the hands of the Philistines!   They were indeed in
evil case.   It seemed as if heaven and earth had combined against them, and that only hell was on their
side.   One last chance remained.   If this was a desperate chance, it must be remembered they were playing a desperate game—they would make Kansas a slave
State in spite of the Governor, in spite of the Territorial Legislature, and in spite of the people of Kansas.

CHAPTER XXV.

The Convention that had been called to frame a State Constitution, and in which election the Free State men had taken no part, had met to do its work in September of 1857, and finished in November; but to the last it refused to make provision to submit the Constitution, when framed, to a vote of the people, for acceptance or rejection. But in place of this thing, had virtually said to them: "You must accept this Constitution whether you like it or not. We will allow you to vote *for* the Constitution with slavery; or, *for* the Constitution without slavery; but you must vote in every contingency *for* the Constitution."

But admitting the people had voted for the Constitution *without* slavery, still a trap was set for them in the following proviso, which would still remain an integral part of the Constitution.

"If, upon such examination of such poll-books it shall appear that a majority of the legal votes cast at said election be in favor of the 'Constitution with no slavery,' then the article providing for slavery shall be stricken from this Constitution, and slavery shall no longer exist in the State of Kansas; *except that the right of property in slaves now in this Territory shall in no manner be interfered with.*"

Thus, which ever way they should vote, Kansas would still remain a slave State. Of course the Free

State men did not walk into the trap, but staid away from the election, which was ordered for December 21, 1857; and the Constitution was adopted by a strictly one-sided vote. And now Gov. Walker began to realize in the bitterness of his heart that "uneasy lies the head of him that wears a crown." He had staked his manhood, his veracity, his honor, his everything, that this Constitution, when framed, should be submitted to a vote of the people for acceptance or rejection, and now he was to be put to shame in the eyes of the whole world; and Gen. Lane was proved a true prophet when he had said to the Governor with such withering power: " Gov. Walker, you can't control your allies." Mr. Walker was able to show a private letter from President Buchanan, assuring him in the most positive terms, that this Constitution, when framed, should be submitted to a vote of the people; but of what avail was such a promise? There was a power behind the throne at Washington stronger than the throne itself; and Gov. W. was able to see what a hollow mockery was that power which he supposed himself to possess.

The Governor made known to the people that he would be absent on business for three or four weeks; and he went away to Washington, never more to return. There was neither pity nor justice for him there; and in unspeakable disgust he resigned; and Mr. Stanton took the oath of office and reigned as Governor *for one month*. Then he also was removed, and Gov. Denver took his place. Thus, five Kansas Governors had each in their turn been officially decapitated. Stanton had been superseded by Denver because he had called a special session of the now Free State

Legislature, and it had ordered an immediate election to vote for or against the Lecompton Constitution, and at this election 10,226 votes were polled against it.

It had been intended that under whip and spur Kansas should be admitted by Congress as a slave State before the time should arrive for the regular assembling of the Territorial Legislature, which had now passed into the hands of the Free State men; but by calling a special session of the Legislature, he had enabled that body to order an immediate election, that should give official evidence that an overwhelming majority of the people were opposed to the Lecompton Constitution.

And now Stephen A. Douglas, at Washington, came forward as State Senator from Illinois and made it impossible that Kansas should be admitted as a State unless that document should first be submitted to the people for acceptance or rejection. A bill to this effect was finally passed by Congress. It was called the English bill. It proffered a magnificent bribe if the people would accept the Lecompton Constitution —five million five hundred thousand acres of public land should be given to Kansas; besides other munificent donations. But the English bill also contained a menace as well as a bribe. It threatened that if the people rejected this offer they should be remanded back for an indefinite period, to all the miseries of a Territorial life.

In the face of such a menace, and tempted by such a bribe, the whole voting population of the Territory turned out at the election, which was ordered to be held August 2, 1858. At this election, 1,788 votes were cast for the Constitution, and 9,512 against it.

From whence then came this overwhelming majority? The majority of the Free State party was about two to one. "Wilder's Annals," the best extant Free State authority, puts it at this. "The Free State or Republican party has carried every election in Kansas since this date (1857), usually by two to one." But here is a majority of six to one; and we must go outside of the Free State or Republican party to find it. Dr. John H. Stringfellow wrote at this time to the Washington Union against the admission of Kansas under the Lecompton Constitution. He says: "To do so will break down the Democratic party at the North, and seriously endanger the interests and peace of Missouri and Kansas, if not of the whole Union."

Judge Tutt, of St. Joseph, Mo., had said to the South Carolinians: "I was born in Virginia, and have lived forty years in Missouri. I am a slave-holder, and a Pro-slavery man; and I desire Kansas to be made a slave State, *if it can be done by honorable means*. But you will break down the cause you are seeking to build up." And Judge Tutt voiced the sentiments of a large number of Pro-slavery men and slave-holders in Kansas.

The city of Atchison gave a majority of votes against the Lecompton Constitution; and Atchison county gave a majority of almost three to one against it; and Leavenworth city, which two years before had been the theater of such murders, riots and robberies, gave a majority against the proposition of the English bill of more than ten to one, notwithstanding the huge bribe offered if the people would accept it.

We are writing these "Recollections" for posterity as well as for the present generation. It is only the verdict of posterity that will justly estimate the men and the influences that went to make up the final result of the early Kansas struggle. Up to the present time the writers that have written on this subject have been too near the battle, and themselves too much a party in it, to write with perfect impartiality. Southern and Pro-slavery writers and speakers have not been able to admit that Southern men were the original wrong-doers; while Northern and Free State writers have not been able to rise to the level of such fair dealing, as to admit that when the decisive vote was cast that determined the question of freedom and slavery in Kansas, as absolutely as it had already been determined in Ohio, Indiana and Illinois, the Free State people were indebted to the nobility of heart and elevation of mind, displayed by Southern and Pro-slavery men in making the vote so overwhelming as to put the question beyond the possibility of controversy forever; yet this was done in the unprecedented vote of six to one, cast in condemnation of the Lecompton Constitution.

From this time forward the two parties that had been struggling with each other for four years in such fierce antagonism were dead; and in their place have appeared the two political parties that are found throughout the United States; and the lines of difference between the men of the South and the men of the North have been as completely obliterated in thirty years, as they were obliterated in Old England, between Saxon and Norman, after 500 years of savage strife and turmoil.

And now, if the superior races of the world have been formed by the amalgamation of the kindred stocks, may we not believe that Providence has been preparing in this central State a people that shall bear a distinguished part in that mighty battle that is so swiftly coming to the American nation, in which we will be called to fight against a Christian barbarism and a paganized Christianity, for all that is precious in our Christian civilization, and for all that is true and good in our American form of government?

Rome fell under an invasion by foreign barbarians; so an inundation of the barbarians of the world is pouring in on us, and threatens to swallow us up; it is like the flood the dragon poured out of his mouth. Of our duties growing out of this catastrophe we shall write hereafter.

The writer of these "Recollections" is a fallible man, like other fallible man. He has shown at least this, that he is ready to stand by his convictions, living and dying; and he holds this conviction fixed and immutable, that there is a crisis coming on us of over-topping and overwhelming magnitude, and demanding the American people should come together and look each other honestly in the face, that they may take into their hearts this weight and extent of the reasons that call that they should join in united effort for the salvation of the nation and the conversion of the world; and that this does not allow that there shall be anything of flimsy, shallow, or hypocritical conceal-ment of the facts of our history.

The world has had abundant experience of these border feuds. Scotland had her feuds between her Highlands and Lowlands. In Ireland there has been unceasing enmity for 250 years between her Protestant and Catholic populations. The French and English peoples of Canada are never at peace with each other; and now there is a feud that can not be healed between

England and Ireland. In some of the mountain regions of the Southern States, where the people yet retain the clannish temper of their Scotch and Irish ancestors, there are neighborhood enmities that go down from father to son, from generation to generation; and that issue in such fist-fights, brawls, and mobs, as sometimes to tax the whole energy of the public authorities to suppress them. And now, with such foundation laid for the indefinite perpetuation of similar feuds in Kansas, we do argue that it has manifested on the part of our population no ordinary qualities of heart and soul, that they were so soon able to eliminate from among themselves their turbulent and dangerous elements.

CHAPTER XXVI.

The men that had settled in Kansas were generally
poor, and few had any reserved fund from which to
draw their support, but were literally dependent for
their daily bread on their labor day by day; and to
take away the horses of such a man was literally to
take the bread out of the mouths of his children.
Free State men and Pro-slavery men had each in turn
been thus despoiled and compelled to flee the Territory; or if they remained they were paralyzed and
unfitted for work.

But the spring and summer of 1857 had brought
a new order of things. Gov. Geary had put an end
to these disorders, and the presence of S. C. Pomeroy
and other Free State men in Atchison was an additional guarantee of peace and security. As a result
the Kansas squatters had gone to work with a will.
Old things had passed away, and all things had become
new. There did indeed remain a chronic state of disorder in Southeastern Kansas; but this was local and
exceptional.

But religious and thoughtful men looked far beyond this question of what shall we eat and what
shall we drink, and wherewithal shall we be
clothed? Intemperate habits were growing fast on
the people. Coarse profanity and ribald speech
were becoming so common as to be the rule

and not the exception. Fathers and mothers began to tremble when they thought what their boys were coming to; and this turned their thoughts to the question of schools and churches. Then all the denominations simultaneously began their work. A church was organized at Leavenworth by our brethren, in which S. A. Marshall and W. S. Yohe were the leading members. Dr. Marshall had formerly been a resident of Pennsylvania, and W. S. Yohe was from the South, a slave-holder, a man of considerable wealth, and of eminent personal excellence.

The church that had been built up in 1855 at Mt. Pleasant had fallen to pieces in the troublous times, and was now reorganized at what has come to be known as "The Old Union School House," a place that has been hallowed to precious memories, because of the great revival that took place under the labors of D. S. Burnett in the year 1858.

The brethren that lived along the valley of the Stranger Creek and its tributaries, and that had met to worship two years before under the spreading elms that lined its bottoms, now organized themselves into a church at a village called Pardee. This ambitious little town was located on the high prairie; but it shared the fate of many other Kansas towns, equally aspiring and equally ill-fated. When the railroads were built they followed the courses of the streams, and it was left out in the cold; but for a time it was the center of social, political and religious influence in the county outside of Atchison.

Among the brethren that had been in Kansas from its first settlement, and whom we have not mentioned, were John and Jacob Graves, brothers from Tennessee, who have since grown rich in worldly goods, and richer still in good works. There were also Brethren Landrum and Schell, and many others whom we can not name. In the fall of 1857 came Lewis Brockman, who loved the church more than he loved his own life. He was brother to that Col. Thomas Brockman conspicuous in the Mormon war in Illinois, which resulted in the exodus of the Mormons to Salt Lake, there to build up a kingdom that cherishes a deadly and undying hatred to the United States, its people, and its institutions. Norman Dunshee, now Professor in Drake University, Des Moines, Iowa, also came to Kansas from the Western Reserve Eclectic Institute at Hiram, O., in the fall of 1859, and settled at Pardee. Dr. S. G. Moore, of Camp Point, Ill., who came in the spring of 1857, was brother-in-law to Peter Garrett; and these two men were of one heart and one soul in their aspirations for a larger liberality on the part of Disciples and a better order of things in our churches; but they had to take up the sad refrain so oft repeated: "We have found the Old Adam too strong for the young Melancthon." Dr. Moore was a man that, when he knew he was in the right, pushed his enterprises with such a rigorous purpose as sometimes to alienate from himself men who might have been won by a more complaisant temper. His stay in Kansas was limited. The dwelling in which he lived was struck by lightning, and Bro. and Sister Moore were seriously injured. From these injuries Sister Moore has never fully recovered. With broken health she became homesick, and pined to be among her kindred. Moreover, a valuable farm that Dr. Moore had sold at Camp Point fell back into his hands, and he felt constrained to return to Illinois in 1861. With such elements of power the reader will not think it strange that we should go to work with a will to recover the ground we had lost in this social and political turmoil and religious inaction.

The writer did not travel much abroad this summer; he found too much to do at home. We had meetings every Lord's day, and had frequent additions by letter and by baptism. One day, as my manner was, I gave an invitation to sinners to obey the gospel. There had been no indication, however remote, that any would desire baptism; but my daughter, Rosetta, now thirteen years of age, came forward and demanded to be baptized. Two years before I had brought her, then eleven years of age, with her mother, to Kansas. Some part of this time we had spent in the very presence of death; and Rosetta and her mother would not have thought it strange if a company of men had come into the house at night with murderous intent. I have not told in these "Recollections" how many times I felt it expedient to be away from home; and then Rosetta was her mother's only companion. Of young company such as girls usually have at her age, she had almost none. We had talked of these daily occurring tragedies until they had lost both their terror and their novelty. These certainly were not fitting surroundings for a little girl, intelligent and thoughtful beyond her years, and of an unduly sensitive and nervous organization. But she was her mother's only girl, this was our only home, and, coming out of the furnace fires of such a life, we could not think it strange that she should feel the need of a Heavenly Father in whom she could trust, of a

Savior's arm on which she could lean, and of a home in the church where she could find help and sympathy.

One thought was ever present in my heart, how far could brethren co-operate together who had been on opposite sides? To learn what could be done I made the acquaintance of brethren everywhere. The brilliant and erratic Dr. Cox, of Missouri, had sent an appointment to "Old Union," and Oliver Steele came with him. I attended his meeting, and Bro. Steele, Cox and myself accepted the hospitality of Bro. Humber. Bro. Cox, being now in the presence of a man reported to be a live Abolitionist, opened a discussion on the question of slavery.

I had been brought up on the Western Reserve, Ohio, and inherited intense anti-slavery convictions. But I had learned from the writings of A. Campbell to judge slave-holders with a charitable judgment. They had inherited the institution of slavery from their fathers, and like the aristocratic institutions of the old world, it had come down to them without any fault of their own. My experiences in Kansas certainly had not made me love slavery any better; still, all this, how bitter soever it might be to me, had revealed so much of real nobility in the hearts of many slave-holders that it had not impaired my feeling of good will to them. If I were to grant that they had been associated sometimes with men of desperate morals, had I not also been associated with Jim Lane, and had I not been compelled to hide myself behind the old maxims, that "Politics, like poverty, makes us acquainted with strange bedfellows?"

And so I argued with Bro. Cox the views I held, stoutly asserting them, when, for a wonder to him,

Bro. Steele and Bro. Humber expressed themselves as coinciding with my views much more than with the views of Bro. Cox, who held the ultra Southern, John C. Calhoun theory of slavery. It appeared that these brethren held that if Providence has given to the Caucasian descendants of Japheth, a fairer skin, a higher style of intellectual power, and greater force of will, that the same divine Providence has given to the sons of Ham a darker color to their skin; but that all are alike the children of the love of one common Father; that Jesus died for all, and that he will not suffer with impunity any indignity to be offered even to one of the least of these his brethren. To the inquiry why these brethren did not give that freedom to their colored servants which they asserted was their natural right, they made reply, alleging the unfriendly legislation not only of the slave States, but of the free States; and that had interposed grave difficulties in the way of such a step. The Big Springs Convention had framed the first Free State platform for Kansas, August 15, 1855, and this, with hard-hearted inhumanity, had avowed the purpose to drive out of Kansas the free blacks as well as the slaves. The same principle was also incorporated in the Topeka Free State Constitution.

It will throw additional light on this subject if I mention that, in 1858, one year after this conversation with Bro. Cox, when the Free State men had obtained control of the Territorial Legislature, Bro. Humber went to Lawrence and laid before Judge Crosier, a leading member of the Legislature, from Leavenworth, the following proposition. He said: "I will emancipate my slaves, and will sell them land. I want them to remain where I can look after their welfare. I do not want them to be driven out of Kansas." Judge Crosier, while greatly sympathizing with Bro. Humber, had to tell him the thing was impossible. It is comforting to know that "The world do move;" that colored people do freely enjoy in Kansas now the rights Bro. Humber in vain sought of a Free State Legislature then on behalf of his slaves.

CHAPTER XXVII.

The reader has already heard of Big Springs as a locality where Free State Conventions were wont to be held. Lawrence and Topeka were twenty-five miles apart, and both were on the south bank of the Kansas River. Big Springs is midway between these towns, and is situated on the high divide, lying between the Kansas River and the Wakarusa.

Here, at Big Springs, were located four brethren, L. R. Campbell, C. M. Mock, A. T. Byler and Jack Reeves. Bro. Campbell was a Disciple from Indiana, of much more than average attainments, and of great force of character. In his immediate neighborhood, and as he had opportunity, he was a preacher, and when a church was organized he naturally became its leader and elder. His early death seemed the greatest calamity that ever befell the church, though he raised a family of boys that in process of time have taken his place, and make his loss seem not irreparable.

C. M. Mock was not a preacher, yet there is many a preacher that might well be proud to make himself as widely and as favorable known as "Charley Mock," and to be remembered with as much affection. He only remained in Kansas a few years, and then returned to his original home in Rushville, Rush county, Indiana. We may truthfully say, "What was our loss was their gain."

Bro. Byler was simply a large-hearted and kind-natured farmer from Missouri, who was too full of brotherly love to have anything of sectional prejudice about him. George W. Hutchinson, whom we will hereafter introduce to our readers, used to call him his " Big *Boiler*." His death after a few years was sad and pathetic ; he had been to Lecompton and driving a spirited horse ; the horse took fright, and threw him from his buggy and killed him.

Jack Reeves was the son of B. F. Reeves, of Flat Rock, Ind., so long the venerated elder of that church, and a sort of patriarch over all the churches. And the above-named brethren, as well as a number of others, hearing that I was preaching near the Missouri River, sent for me to come and make them a visit. I accordingly did so, and now, for thirty-one years I have not forgotten to visit them, and they have not forgotten me. From this time forward I preached for them as I had opportunity, and thus began to make the acquaint· ance of brethren south of the Kansas River. The church grew apace. At their organization they had twenty-five members. Two years afterwards they were able to report a membership of seventy-two persons.

The year 1857 passed rapidly away. My time was divided between working on my claim on Stranger Creek, preaching for the churches that had been organized, and making the acquaintance of brethren wherever I was able to find them.

And now the year 1858 was upon us, predestinated to bring with it consequences far-reaching, as touching the future of Kansas. In this year should be settled the question that had filled the Territory with agitation, tumult, and war for four years ; and it was in this year that our Kansas missionary work was begun, and in which was organized the first missionary society. The time was the early spring of 1858. The place was "Old Union," a little, log school-house situated in a ravine opening into Stranger Creek bottoms. The *personnel* were, first, Numeris Humber, with his tender heart and quenchless love for missionary work. Then there was his sister wife, that with saintly presence and sacred song made us feel that this was the very house of God and gate of heaven. Judge William Young was also present, who had neither song nor sentimentality about him, but in his unpoetic way looked at everything in the light of cold, hard fact. And yet Bro. Young is neither cold nor hard, only on the outside. There also was Spartan Rhea (these brethren were all from Missouri), whose fine sense of honor and upright conduct we have already had occasion to commend while acting as justice of the peace during our former troubles. Joseph Potter was also there, and so, also, was Joseph McBride, a notable preacher of Tennessee, that many years ago was one of the pioneers that planted the Christian cause in Oregon. All told, we had a crowd large enough to fill a little, log school-house. Brethren Yohe and Marshall, of Leavenworth City, also gave us assurances of their hearty help and sympathy. This Dr. S. A. Marshall was a brother-in-law to Isaac Errett, and always deeply interested himself in this work of building up the churches. The church at Pardee was also represented. And this constituted the make-up of our first missionary society. Three churches represented, and enough persons decently to fill a little seven-by-nine log school-house. Let us learn not to despise the day of

small things.   As for the amount of money pledged—
well, it would not have frightened even one of those
little ones, that are scared out of their wits at the
thought of an over-paid, over-fed, proud, luxurious
and domineering priesthood.   As for the missionary
chosen to go on this forlorn hope—to explore this
Africa of spiritual darkness, it was Hobson's choice; it
was this or none.   Except myself, there was no man
to be thought of that would or could go on this errand,
and so there was no contest over the choice of a
missionary.

Conspicuous among these early churches were the
churches that were formed in Doniphan county.   This
is the most northeastern county in the State, and is in
a great bend of the Missouri River, having the river on
three sides of it.   It is a body of the best land in Kansas, and no county had at its first settlement as many
Disciples.   Their first beginning was unfortunate.   A
man named Winters, calling himself a preacher, came
among them and made a great stir.   But he brought
with him a woman that was not his wife.   With a
character unblemished this man would have won an
honorable fame; but when questioned he equivocated,
but was finally compelled to confess the shameful
truth, and in their grief and shame the newly-organized
church seemed broken up.   Jacob I. Scott was a man
of spotless life and dauntless purpose, and feeling that
it would be an unspeakable humiliation to allow everything to go to wreck because of the frailty of one unfortunate man, and learning that I had taken the field
in the counties further south, he besought me to come
over and help them.   In no counties in this State have
there been more churches than in Doniphan county,

but in no county in the State have the churches been more evanescent and unstable, and yet it is not because these brethren have apostatized, but it is that the men that have settled in Doniphan county are men that keep on the borders of civilization, and the opening of a great empire for settlement to the west of them tempted them to move onward. Indeed, this has been the case in all the churches in Eastern Kansas. Just as soon as we would gather up a strong church it would straightway melt out of our hands, and its members would be scattered from Montana to Florida, and from the Missouri River to Oregon.

Some twenty-five miles to the northwest of my place of residence, in what is now Jackson county, on the waters of the Cedar Creek, was a settlement mainly from Platte county, Mo. The best known of these was Bro. John Gardiner, whose heart now for thirty years has held one single thought, the interest and prosperity of the Christian Church. He has sacrificed much, has labored much, and has done a great deal of preaching without fee or reward. Bro. J. W. Williams, from Southeastern Ohio, a man of saintly character and indefatigable purpose, was also of this settlement. There also we organized a church.

The places for holding meetings were of the most primitive kind. A log school-house was a luxury; the squatter cabins were too small; but we had to use them during the winter. The groves of timber along the streams were always waiting; but we only could use them in fair and pleasant weather, and for six months in the year. As for hearers, we were never lacking an audience, we were never lacking for a crowd that were ready to listen with honest good-will to the message which we brought them.

It was an eventful summer. More rain fell than in any season I have known. The streams were always full, the bottoms were often flooded, and crossing was sometimes dangerous; but I had a good horse and was not afraid.

In religious matters everything was broken up, and men were drifting. But this good came of it, that they were ready to listen to this strange and new thing that was brought to their ears, in which so much was made of the Lord's authority, of apostolic teaching and apostolic example, and so little of traditions, theories, and time-honored observances, of which the Bible knows nothing, but which have been sanctified by universal acceptance.

As for myself, there had been romances enough about my life to make the people wish to see me, and I was proud to know that the boys could remember my sermons and repeat them. The men with whom I was immediately associated in this work, and who had sent me on this errand, were of inestimable advantage to me. They were well and favorably known as men of unblemished reputation in Eastern Kansas and Western Missouri. "Old Duke Young," as the father of Judge William Young had been affectionately called in Western Missouri, had been an eminently popular frontier and pioneer preacher, and Judge Young had inherited an honorable distinction as being the son of such a father; and when it was known that I was acting with the concurrence and under the approval of such men, the arrangement was generally accepted as satisfactory.

And now I had my heart's best desire. I was in the field as an evangelist; the harvest was abundant and the grain was already ripe and waiting for the sickle. But above all, and beyond all these, was peace in the land. We all had had a lover's quarrel, but we had made it up and were the better friends. Everywhere they had their joke with me, as to my method of navigating the Missouri River, and to the attire I sometimes put on; but I had come out the upper dog in the fight, and could afford to stand their bantering. There is a warmth, freshness, and enthusiasm in the friendships formed under such conditions that can never be transferred to associations of older and more orderly communities. As a result of this summer's work, here were seven churches full of zeal and rapidly growing, and occupying a field that had been almost absolutely fallow, for outside of the towns there was no religious movement except our own.

But at one point we were put at a very great disadvantage. Older and better established denominations were able to plant missionaries in such cities as Atchison, Topeka and Lawrence, while we were not; and yet in each of these cities there were from the first a small number of brethren, who might have served as the nucleus of a church. Speaking in general terms, monthly preaching never built up a church in any city, and the reader will see that in the very nature of things I could not set myself down to the care of a single congregation.

CHAPTER XXVIII.

The same causes that have made me a preacher, have also made me an abundant contributor to our periodical literature. As I wish to present a living picture of these early days, I will, from time to time, furnish extracts from the contributions I have made to our religious journals:

[Written for the Christian Luminary.]

OCENA P. O., Atchison Co.,
Kansas Ter., May, 1858.

Having myself had a very full experience of the advantages and disadvantages, the trials, pleasures and perils of a pioneer life, I propose to write a series of essays on the matter of emigrating to the West.

While a grave necessity demands that many shall emigrate to the West, it is not to be denied that it is an enterprise fraught with many dangers to the moral and spiritual well-being of the emigrant. We have here men from the four quarters of the civilized world, and have thus congregated together all the vices found in Europe and America. The semi-barbarism of the Irish Catholicism of Tipperary and Clare is now fairly inaugurated in Leavenworth city. All the horses of the livery stables are hired to attend an Irish funeral, and as the mourners take a *"wee bit of a dhrap"* before starting, they are lucky if they get the corpse well under ground without a fight. By this time, having become over-joyful, they raise a shout, and with a whoop and hurrah they start for home, and the man that has the fastest horse gets into the city first. The unlucky traveler, whose horse gets mixed up with theirs in this stampede, and who thus involuntarily becomes one of the company at an Irish wake, has need to be a good rider.

German infidelity has been nurtured in Germany by a thousand years of priestly domination and oppression, and is now translated into our Kansas towns by Germans, who have no Lord's day in their week.

Corresponding with our Lord's day, they have a holiday—a day to hunt, to fish, to do up odd jobs, to congregate together and listen to fine music, dance, sing, feast, drink lager beer, and have a good time generally. Under the best *regimen* it is hard for men to keep their hearts from evil; but here, it is a fearful thing for young men, released from all the restraints of their native land, to find the house of revelry and dancing so near the house of God, and the gates of hell, alluring by all the fascinating and seductive attractions of harmonious sounds, so near the gate of heaven.

I am appalled at the amount of drinking and gambling that has existed in Kansas, especially in the Missouri River towns, for the last three years. Under the shade of every green tree, on the streets, in every shop, store, grocery and hotel, it has seemed as if the chief business of the people was to gamble and drink.

There are other causes full of evil, and fearfully potent to work apostasy and ruin in the West. Men come here, not to plead the cause of a suffering and dying Saviour; not to give to the people a more pure and self-denying morality, and a higher civilization; but to get rich. They have had a dream, and are come to realize that dream. They have dreamed of one thousand acres of land, bought at one dollar and a quarter per acre, that by the magic growth of some Western town becomes worth fifty thousand dollars. They have dreamed of money invested in mythical towns, which towns are to rival in their growth Toledo, Chicago or St. Louis. The dream is to do nothing and get rich. Land sharks, speculators, usurers and politicians who aspire to a notoriety they will never win—a station they will never occupy—swarm over the West thicker than frogs in Egypt, and more intrusive than were these squatting, crawling, jumping pests, when evoked from the river's slime by the rod of Moses.

Some men are too old when they come to the West. They are like a vine whose tendrils are rudely torn from a branch around which they have wound themselves, and are so hardened by time that they can not entwine themselves around another support. Such men forever worship, looking to the East. They form no new friendships; engage in no new enterprises; they care for nobody, and nobody cares for them. They live and die alone.

But there are more sad and gentle notes of sorrow that fall upon our ears. The children mourn for the peach tree and the apple tree, with their luscious fruit. The mother-wife asks who will watch the little grave, or tend the rose tree growing at its head, or who will train the woodbine, or care for the pinks and violets. Then sadly she sings of home—"Home, sweet home!" The father, too, remembers his pasture for his pigs, his calves, and sheep, and cows. He remembers that on one poor forty acres of land he had a house, a barn, an orchard, woodland, maple trees for making maple sugar, a meadow, room for corn, wheat, oats and potatoes, besides pasture for one horse, two oxen, three cows, together with a number of sheep and pigs. Then there was the three months' school in winter, and four months in summer. There was the Sunday-school and the church, where serious and honest men uttered manly and religious counsel to sincere hearts, which nurtured good and holy purposes. All this he has bartered away for the privilege of being rich—of having more land than he knows what to do with; more corn than he can tend, and pigs till they are a pest to him.

Having glanced at some of the evils attendant on Western life, I must hasten to indicate what class of men should come to the West. The poor of our cities, whose poverty becomes the more haggard by being placed in immediate proximity to measureless profusion, luxury and extravagance—respectable people, whose whole life is a lifelong struggle to keep up appearances, and in whom the securing of affluence is like putting on a corpse the frippery and finery of the ball-room ; young men with brave hearts and willing hands—these are the classes that may come, and should come, to the West. And if Adam, realizing that the world is all before him, where to choose, looks to the West to find his Eden, I would respectfully suggest that he has an infirmity in his left side, and that his best security against the perils of a pioneer life is to take to himself the rib that is wanting.

The tenant, living on the farm of another man, should come to the West. He can not plant a tree and call it his own. God gave the whole world to Adam and his sons, and the true dignity of every son of Adam requires that he should be able to stand in the midst of his own Eden and say: "This, under God, is mine."

There is yet another class of men that may always go to the West, or to any other place. Whether young, or old, or middle-aged— whether rich or poor—they may go, and the blessings of God go with them. These are the men whose hearts are full of faith, and hope, and love—who sympathize with all, and who, consequently, will find friends among all—who are willing to be missionaries of the cross, and to be pillars in the churches they have helped to nurture into life.

Kansas is full of men who were once members of our churches, but who are stranded on the rocks of apostasy, on whom the storms of life will beat yet a little while, and then they will sink down into everlasting ruin. Strong drink, the love of money, or, perhaps, the inadequacy of their former teaching, is the occasion of their fall. Others, scattered over this great wilderness of sin, remain faithful amidst abounding wickedness, and stretch out their hands and utter the Macedonian cry, " Come over and help us."

The apostolic age was pre-eminently an age of missionary effort. What will the world say of us, and of our confident, and, as some would say, arrogant, pretense to have restored primitive and apostolic Christianity, when our Israel in so large a part of the great West is such a moral wreck—such a spectacle of scattered, abandoned, and, too often, ruined church members, unknown, untaught and uncared for.

The peerless glory of our Lord Jesus Christ—his measureless, boundless and quenchless love—this is the great center of attraction around which the affections of the Christian do continually gather. The Lord is the center of the moral universe, and all its light is but the emanation of his glory. He dwells in the human heart, and fills it with his love; he dwells in the family, and becomes its ornament as when he dwelt in the house of Lazarus; he dwells in the church, and makes it a fold in which he nurtures his lambs.

Chistians wandering over the earth like sheep having no shepherd, isolated from their brethren, dwelling alone—however frequent this spectacle now—is not often witnessed in the New Testament. There they congregated in churches. But this experiment of isolation is most perilous to the individual, and a prodigal expenditure of the wealth of the church, which has souls for her hire. It is true that a few persons become centers of attraction to new churches that grow up around them; but very many are lost in the great whirlpool of this world's strife.

What, then, is the remedy? Evidently this: Jesus accepts no divided empire in the human heart. He will have all or nothing. The Church of Christ, the cause of Christ, the people of Christ—these must be the centers of attraction to which the heart of the Christian turns with all the enthusiasm with which an Eastern idolater bows before the shrine of his idol. In return for such devotion Jesus gives to his people every imaginable blessing. Wealth, power, dominion, science, civilization, genius, learning, power over the elements of nature, and insight into its magnitude, do now belong to the Lord's people in Europe and America as they never belonged to any people before. Yet all these must be laid at Jesus' feet before he will make the returning prodigal the recipient of his love. Everything must be subordinated to our religion.

Since the almighty dollar has become the touch-stone by which everything is to be decided, I assert that this is a good speculation: secure a neighborhood homogeneous and not heterogeneous. Let its tendencies be favorable to temperance, education and religion, and in doing so a man will have added fifty per cent. to the selling value of his property. The present thrift, wealth, genius, enterprise and intelligence of the people of the New England States is the legitimate outworking of the training bestowed on their sons by the stern, old Puritans that first peopled these inhospitable shores.

But all temporal and earthly considerations disappear, as fade the stars at the approach of day, when we consider that measureless ruin, that gulf of everlasting despair, that voiceless woe, into which the emigrant may sink himself and family by locating in a profligate, dissipated or irreligious neighborhood, or in a community wholly swallowed up in the love of money, or absorbed in the questions, What shall we eat, or what shall we drink, or wherewithal shall we be clothed? What home on the beautiful prairies, what treasures of fine water and good timber, what corner lots, what property in town or country, can equal in value the guardianship of our Lord, the indwelling of God's good Spirit, the approval of a good conscience, the smiles of angels and the inheritance of a home in heaven? Let no man, therefore, fall into the folly— the unspeakable folly—of subordinating his spiritual and eternal interests to his temporal welfare. "Seek ye God and his righteousness, and all these things shall be added."

To teach, to discipline and perfect the churches we have already organized; to gather into churches the lost sheep of the house of our Israel, scattered over this great wilderness of sin; to try and help those who are still purposing to tempt its dangers; and to lay broad and deep the foundations of a future operation and co-operation that shall ultimate in spreading the gospel from pole to pole, and across the great sea to the farthest domicile of man—this is the purpose which we set before us, and which should be pursued with the zeal and enthusiasm displayed by the followers of the false prophet of Mecca; and with the patience of the coral workers, who build for ages and cycles of ages their marble battlements in the waters of the Pacific Ocean.

CHAPTER XXIX.

In 1859 I only spent part of the year preaching in
Kansas. At the earnest solicitation of Ovid Butler,
the founder and munificent patron of Butler University,
I spent six months preaching in the State of Indiana.
A missionary society had been organized in Indianapolis, in which Ovid Butler was the leading spirit,
and such men as Joseph Bryant, and Matthew
McKeever, brothers-in-law to Alexander Campbell,
together with Jonas Hartzell, Cyrus McNeely, of
Hopedale, Ohio, and Eld. John Boggs, of Cincinnati,
and many others, were associated with him in the
movement. By these brethren I was for some time
partially sustained as a missionary in Kansas. The
formation of this society had grown out of a difference
existing between these brethren and the General Missonary Society, touching what had become the over-
topping and absorbing question, both to the churches
and the people of the United States. As this question
has ceased to be of any practical interest to the American people, I shall spend no time in its discussion,
only to narrate, briefly, what happened to us in Kansas
growing out of the existence of these two societies.

Ovid Butler had set his heart on this, that the brethren
in Indiana should have personal knowledge of the man
that himself and others were sustaining in Kansas. I
found myself greatly misunderstood, and was often

hurt at the slights that grew out of these misunderstandings ; and I tried hard to make these brethren know just what was in my heart, and what were the objects I was seeking to accomplish.

In the early spring of 1860 I returned to Kansas and resumed my work. Geo. W. Hutchinson had been a preacher in what was known as the "Christian Connection" in the New England States, and had been eminently successful in winning converts. But these churches were poor, and he having married a wife, his compensation did not meet his necessities, and like many others he went to California with a hope of bettering his fortunes. Afterwards he came to Lawrence, in Kansas, under the auspices of the Emigrant Aid Society. But his freighting teams having been plundered of a stock of goods, which they were bringing for him from Leavenworth to Lawrence, he was left to fight his battle as best he might. It was at this conjuncture that he made the acquaintance of the brethren at Big Springs, and became impressed with the simplicity and scriptural authority of our plea. It is well known that there never was more than a paper wall between ourselves and "The Old Christian Order," and there seemed nothing in the way of Bro. Hutchison. He had in his heart no theory of a regeneration wrought by a miracle, and which gives to a convert a supernatural evidence of pardon before baptism, and that should, therefore, compel him to reject the words of Jesus: "He that believeth and is baptized shall be saved."

The Christian Brethren have been supposed to have some leaning to Unitarianism, but he betrayed no such leaning. But while he had no love for the barbarous language in which Trinitarians have sometimes spoken of the divine relation subsisting between the Father, Son and Holy Spirit, yet he was willing to ascribe to our Lord all that is ascribed to him in the Holy Scriptures. Thus joyfully he accepted this new brotherhood he had found in Kansas, and our churches just as joyfully set him to preaching. We needed preachers, and here was one already made to our hand.

Early in the spring of 1860 the weather came off exquisitely fine. It was like a hectic flush—the deceptive seeming of health on the cheek of the consumptive. It was a spring without rain, in which the sun was shining beautiful and bright, in which the evenings were balmy and pleasant, and the road good; but to be followed by a summer of scorching heat, of hot winds that burned the vegetation like the breath of a furnace, leaving the people to starve. The inhabitants of Kansas will never forget the year 1860, the drought and the famine.

It was in the springtime, in the midst of this beautiful weather, we called Bro. Hutchinson to come to Pardee and help us. This protracted meeting resulted in a great ingathering. It was largely made up of young men, who, for the time being, were located on the eastern border of Kansas, but that in the stirring and stormy times that were to follow were to be scattered over every part of the Great West. And now Bro. Hutchinson's fame as a revivalist began to spread abroad, and many neighborhoods where there were a few Disciples, and who were anxious to build themselves into a congregation, sent for him to come and help them; and thus our churches rapidly grew in number, and our acquaintance with the brethren was greatly extended. As a result, there came to be a common feeling among them that we ought to come together in a State, or rather a Territorial, meeting. Pursuant to such a purpose, a general meeting was called at Big Springs, Aug. 9, 1860, C. M. Mock having been called to the chair, and W. O. Ferguson, of Emporia, having been made secretary.

The following churches reported themselves as having been organized in the Territory:

	No. of Members.
Pardee, Atchison Co	92
Union Church, Atchison Co	60
Leavenworth City	70
Big Springs, Douglas Co	72
Prairie City, Douglas Co	44
Peoria City, Lykins Co	23
Leroy, Coffey Co	108
Emporia	80
Stanton, Lykins Co	91
Iola, Allen Co	21
Humbolt, Allen Co	12
Burlington, Coffey Co	9
Wolf Creek, Doniphan Co	70
Rock Creek, Doniphan Co	30
Independence Creek, Doniphan Co	12
Cedar Creek, Doniphan Co	16
Olathe, Johnson Co	10
McCarnish, Johnson Co	40
Oskaloosa, Jefferson Co	10
Cedar Creek, Jackson Co	30

Thus of organized churches there were reported 900 members, and of unorganized members it was ascertained there were enough to make the number more than one thousand.

We find on record, as having been adopted at this meeting, the following resolutions:

Resolved, That the thanks of this Convention be tendered to the Christian Missionary Society, at Indianapolis, for the service of Bro. Butler as a missionary in Kansas, and that the Society be requested to sustain him until the churches in Kansas shall be able to sustain their preachers.

Resolved, That Brethren G. W. Hutchinson, Pardee Butler, Ephraim Philips, S. G. Brown, W. E. Evans, and N. Dunshee be recommended to the confidence and support of the brethren as able and faithful preachers of the gospel.

WHEREAS, The brethren of Southern Kansas are in destitute circumstances; and

WHEREAS, Bro. E. Philips, having spent much of his time preaching, without fee, or reward, needs pecuniary support; and

WHEREAS, Bro. Crocker is about to visit the East; therefore,

Resolved, That we commend Bro. Crocker as worthy to receive contributions made on behalf of Bro. Philips.

Resolved, That we will encourage and, so far as we have ability, sustain by our prayers and means those who labor for us in word and doctrine.

Resolved, That we are in favor of Sunday-schools and Bible classes, and that we will use our influence to sustain social meetings in all our churches.

Resolved, That when we adjourn, we adjourn to meet at Prairie City, on Wednesday before the second Lord's day in September, 1861.

Resolved, That the thanks of this Convention be tendered to the brethren of Big Springs for their kindness and liberality during the sessions of this Convention.

On motion, the Convention adjourned to the time and place appointed. C. W. MOCK, Chairman.

W. O. FERGUSON, Secretary.

The convention in its results was full of encouragement and joy. Insignificant as had been our beginning two years before, here were twenty churches and more than one thousand members ready to coöperate together and plant the cause in this infant Territory. This meeting also introduced us to many new acquaintances. Eld. S. G. Brown, of Emporia, had been diligently employed planting churches along the Neosho

River from Emporia to Leroy. Bro. Ephraim Philips, at Leroy, also at that time became known to us. Bro. Philips, after some years, returned to Pennsylvania, and there went into the oil business with his brother; the brothers were successful, and afterwards distinguished themselves by a generous and Christian liberality. Bro. Crocker also, before his death, had won a large place in the hearts of his brethren. Elder Wm. Gans, at that time of Lanesfield, but afterwards of Olathe, will long be remembered with earnest affection; and it was at this time that he became known to us.

For reasons that we have already mentioned, the General Missionary Society had done nothing for us, but seeing that we were fighting a brave battle, and that we were keeping the peace with each other, they felt themselves moved to help us. Eld. D. S. Burnett was at this time employed preaching in Western Missouri, and was deputed by the Missionary Board to visit G. W. Hutchinson at Lawrence, who was winning golden opinions as an eminently successful evangelist. Bro. H. was not at home, but was away holding a protracted meeting, and Bro. Burnett therefore called on his wife. Mrs. Hutchinson was a pious, refined, and educated New England woman, who had married her husband after he had become known as the most successful evangelist in the "Old Christian Order" in the New England States. She had with pain seen him turned aside from his chosen work by hard necessities, and was now greatly rejoiced to see him once more a preacher. Bro. B. was an accomplished gentleman, whose polished and cultivated manners sometimes laid him open to the charge of a proud and aristocratic exclusiveness; but this Yankee lady herself knew how to queen it, and stood before him with no sense of inferiority. She frankly said to him that herself and husband were abolitionists, but that they knew the value of peace, and would do what could be done, in good conscience, to make peace and keep it. Bro. Burnett evidently went away from Lawrence with a good opinion of this family of Yankee abolitionists, and Bro. H. was immediately accepted as a missonary of the General Missionary Society. He used quietly to indicate to me that, as touching this interview, his wife was a better general than himself, and that it was lucky for him that he was not at home.

And so we two became missionaries, sustained by two different, and, in one particular, antagonistic missionary societies. Of course we did not quarrel; why should we? If I was sometimes charged with abolitionism, was not this man blacker than myself? We often traveled together, and held protracted meetings under the same tent. I had for a lifetime studied this plea which we make for a return to primitive and apostolic Christianity, and it was, therefore, my business to press upon the people the duty to yield a loyal obedience to the Lord Jesus Christ as our only Lawgiver and King, and thus to renounce all human leadership and the authority of all human opinions; and it became the business of Bro. Hutchinson to win the people by his magnetic power, and fill them with his own enthusiasm, and thus induce them to act on the convictions that had been already formed in their hearts.

I take on myself to say there never have been two more diligent evangelists than were Bro. Hutchinson and myself in the year that followed the Big Springs

Convention.   Looking over the whole ground, I am able to see that in that year was laid the foundation for that abiding prosperity that has distinguished our effort down to the present time.

CHAPTER XXX.

There had come to the Big Springs Convention two brethren—Father Gillespie and his son, William Gillespie, living at St. George, on the Kansas River, fifty miles above Topeka and about eight miles below Manhattan. These brethren came to tell us that here were two settlements of brethren waiting to be organized into churches; and Bro. Hutchinson and myself both visited them during the ensuing autumn. A military road ran up the Kansas River from Fort Leavenworth to Fort Riley, passing through the village of St. George. But if I were to go to St. George by this route, I would lose thirty miles of travel, and I therefore determined to start directly west from my place of residence. But, in doing so, I would have to cross the Pottawatomie Indian Reserve, on which for forty miles there was not the habitation of a white man. Stopping over night with Bro. J. W. Williams, on the eastern border of the Reserve, I started betimes to St. George, traveling to the west. But night came on, and I had not reached the line of white settlements. I picketed my horse on the prairie, made a pillow of my saddle, and slept until morning. The night was warm and pleasant, and I did not suffer with the cold, and in the morning I was ready betimes to ride on to the residence of Bro. Gillespie. He was so glad to see me. It was worth a journey of one hundred miles to get such a welcome. And then there was Sister Gillespie, and a house full of young Gillespies, and they were all so glad to see me.

"Have you had your breakfast?"

"No."

"Well, where did you lodge?"

This was a poser. I attempted to pass the question by; but nothing would do, and I had to confess I slept under the canopy of heaven.

"O, dear! O, dear!" And had it come to this that their preacher had to sleep on the prairie! This was a family of hospitable Kentuckians, who were born to a love of music, and the old gentleman was a fiddler, and next to his Bible he loved his fiddle. Of course, we had a grand, good time, and were all filled with joy; and this was the beginning of the churches on the upper waters of the Kansas River. Twelve miles above St. George was Ashland, where we found Bro. N. B. White, father to A. J. White, who has hitherto been pastor of the church at Leavenworth City; but since has been acting as district evangelist. Bro. N. B. White came from Carthage, Ky., and long remained a faithful and indefatigable preacher. In my experience as an evangelist, I have known many men of superior Christian excellence; but never one man of more singleness and integrity of heart; never one man that had a clearer conception of the ultimate pur-poses and results of Christianity; never a man whose life was more unselfish and self-sacrificing. Being of an intensely nervous and high-strung organization, and doing his work in a mixed population that would have taxed the patience of Job in its management, it is no wonder that Bro. White was sometimes misunderstood, and, like all reformers, was made to feel that he was living before his time.

Thus passed in abundant labors the year 1860, and the time drew on for our yearly meeting, which had been appointed to be held at Prairie City in September, 1861. The brethren came together with real enthusiasm. During the past year the number of Disciples had been multiplied, and the cause had been greatly strengthened. It had been a year of constant ingathering. New churches reported themselves at this meeting, and brethren whom we had never known before. As evidence of what was being accomplished I will copy a note which I find appended to the minutes of the Prairie City meeting:

The following letter was received from a church meeting in Monroe township, Anderson County, said church being of the "Old Christian Order":

To the Elders of the State Meeting at Prairie City:

We, the Church of God meeting at North Pottawatomie, do recommend to your honorable body, Bro. Samuel Anderson, as our pastor. We also represent our church as in good standing and in full fellowship, numbering twenty-eight members.

Bro. Anderson, the bearer of the above letter, came before the Convention and said: "It does yet appear to me that a man's sins are forgiven as soon as he believes; but I do not think that for this cause there ought to be a schism between us. I am willing to unite with you in exhorting men to obey all the commands of the gospel, and in seeking to unite all Christians on the one foundation.

But there appeared one cloud in our horizon, one cause to hinder the perfect success of this, our second yearly meeting. The country was full of rumors of war, and there seemed impending a great national conflict. Bro. Hutchinson had been for one year an eminently successful evangelist; but now he went into the Union army as an army chaplain, and thus his work among us ceased. And now the war was upon us; we were predestined to see dark days, and the hearts of the people were full of forebodings of evil. Many of our young men went into the army, and for two years the produce raised by the farmers brought almost nothing, and many of our preachers retired from their work. And then there appeared in the land wolves in sheep's clothing—thieves wearing the disguise of loyalty to the "old flag," and who held themselves self-elected to punish "rebel sympathizers," and in the estimation of this gentry the best evidence that could be had that a man was a rebel sympathizer was, that he owned a good span of horses. It is said, "There is no great loss without some small gain," and these evil days gave opportunity to some of us who owed a debt of gratitude for kindness rendered to us when we were in sore straits, to pay back this debt by demanding justice on behalf of loyal citizens of Kansas, whose only offense was that they had been born in the South.

It is the purpose of this series of articles to tell how two peoples, the one from the South and the other from the North—the one the sons of the Puritans, and the other the children of the younger sons of the old English cavaliers—came together and settled in one Territory; how they were divided by the question of American slavery, and how they strove in an antagonism as fierce as that which once subsisted between the Saxon and Norman in Old England; how they peacefully settled their controversy, and in one-third of a century have grown into an eminently peaceful, prosperous, enterprising and well-ordered commonwealth, that stands conspicuous as an illustration and proof of the excellence of our national institutions. We are also to tell how that, out of the furnace fires of such a strife, a community of churches grew up that have for their purpose a restoration of primitive and apostolic Christianity, and the unity of all Christians under a supreme loyalty to the Lord Jesus Christ as our only Leader and Lawgiver, and as the great Author of our American civilization. We are also to tell how the discipline of such a strife has created a people of such heroic temper, that this has been the first government among the nations to grapple with the saloon power in a final and decisive battle, which has banished it beyond the boundaries of the State, and has branded it as an enemy to Christian homes, an enemy to our Christian civilization, and an enemy to the welfare of the whole human race. Other States have paltered with the evil by means of feeble and frivolous legislation, but Kansas has grappled the monster by the throat by incorporating Prohibition into its fundamental law.

But, above all, we are to press upon the attention of the people the imminence of that danger that is threatening us, and that embodies within itself all other perils that hang over the nation. We are threatened to be overwhelmed by a foreign and alien emigration that brings with it the anarchy of atheism and the un-American and the anti-American traditions of a paganized Christianity. We have now fifteen millions of foreign-born citizens and of their children of the first generation in the United States. The Rev. Josiah Strong estimates that in twelve years their number will be forty-three millions; and a great part of this population is now, and shall hereafter be, under the control of Jesuit priests, that seek to maintain in the hearts of these millions loyalty to a foreign prince, resident in Rome, as superior to and more binding on their consciences than is that allegiance which they owe to the United States.

The city of New York has eighty persons in every one hundred of its population that are either foreign born or else the children of foreign born parents. Boston has sixty-three; Chicago has eighty-seven; St. Louis has seventy-eight; Cincinnati, sixty; San Francisco, seventy-eight, and Detroit and Milwaukee have each eighty-four citizens in every one hundred of their population that are either foreign born or else the children of foreign born parents. A nation is dominated by its cities, as England is dominated by London; as France is dominated by Paris, and Germany by Berlin; and our great cities have already become foreign cities, controlled by a foreign vote, and dominated by a foreign public opinion. Here in Kansas, in cities where there is a dominant element of foreign born citizens, we have to invoke the power of the State to compel obedience to our temperance laws on the part of this alien and un-American population; otherwise they overawe the city government and rebel against the laws. Self-evident it is that the presence of such a population is a threat against our social and domestic life, against our government, and against the Christian religion. But the presence of such an evil calls for union among ourselves. Poland was dismembered and ceased to exist among the nations, because of intestine strifes and divisions among its nobility, who were its governing class; and in the presence of such a danger menacing the American people it would be a madness unspeakable in us to keep up among ourselves either our religious feuds and bickerings, or the animosities heretofore existing between the North and South.

We must be one people, or this nation will surely perish. And this oneness is not to be brought about by the utterance of feeble platitudes, nor by the hypocritical profession of a good-will we do not feel; we must follow the guidance of that Book of all books that God has given us, by exhibiting that robust and manly courage that looks the truth and the whole truth squarely in the face. After making all necessary discount and rebate because of faults and infirmities, there is enough yet remaining of solid and essential excellence in the citizens of every State in this nation that they can afford to have the honest truth told about themselves. Is the sun less glorious because there are spots on the sun? Is the moon less beautiful because the man in the moon does not wear a handsome face?

On the late Fourth of July there was a rallying of the clans of the veterans—the men in blue and the men in gray—on the field of Gettysburg, to commemorate the battle they fought twenty-five years before, and to do honor to the bravery displayed by each man in fighting for what he honestly thought to be the right. This was as it should be. But there ought to be the celebration of another battle—it ought to be, even though it may never occur—that should never be forgotten. In that battle there was no dreadful carnage as on the battlefield of Gettysburg; there were no desperate charges made by cavalry and infantry; there was no heroic courage displayed under the pitiless peltings of a deadly hail of shot and shell; there were no great generals of national reputation in command, but humble men unknown to fame, in the final result came together, and with honest speech said, '' We will shake hands and be friends. We will let bygones be by gones, and see what can be done by a united effort to promote the welfare of all.''

Now we insist that Kansas is worthy of more honor than Gettysburg. But as in this wicked world the best men do not get the highest honor, nor the best deeds the highest praise, we will be content to bide our time, knowing that the Lord does not forget, and that he will speak a good word for us at the great judgment day.

Kansas led the nation in the abolition of American slavery ; Kansas ought a second time to lead the nation in a universal amnesty, so that there shall be nothing to hinder that we shall preach the gospel to the devotees of the mother of Babylon, and to the millions of godless, Christless heathen that are thrown upon our hands, thus making them good Christians that they may be good American citizens.

CHAPTER XXXI.

In 1862 our yearly meeting was held at Emporia, and in 1863 at Ottumwa. These meetings were little better than failures. Yearly district meetings were kept up in Northeastern Kansas, in which more vigor was manifested.

And now the writer began to feel the pressure of hard necessities. For five years I had kept myself in the field on a salary utterly inadequate to my needs, and had been gradually running into debt, and these debts had to be paid. In anticipation of the future wants of my children, I had invested my available means in land; but as this land was not improved, it yielded me no return. In the distress that came on the people in those days, one means of making money presented itself, and many availed themselves of it. Gold had been discovered at Pike's Peak, and thitherward had flocked a great multitude of people. There were no railroads, and all supplies had to be carried across the plains in freighting wagons. This business was carried on by the roughest class of a rough and frontier population; still, it was an honest business, and honest men might lawfully engage in it, provided they had the hardihood to face the dangers and exposures of such a life.

During the years 1862, 1863 and 1864, I went into this business with a small freighting outfit. This certainly was not just the thing for a preacher to do, but necessity knows no law. In the spring of 1862, Bro. James Butcher was going to Denver with a freighting train, and he with myself agreed to go in the same train for mutual convenience.

The President, Abraham Lincoln, had ordered a draft, and many young men in Missouri had found themselves in a sore strait. In the South were their kindred, and they felt that they could not and would not fight against their own flesh and blood ; and to avoid this they determined to flee to the gold mines in the mountains, where every man did what was right in his own eyes—and so they came to Atchison or Leavenworth and engaged to drive these freighting teams to Denver. Many of them were sons of rich fathers, well educated, and had never engaged in manual labor, much less in such menial work as this, and when these proud and high-spirited fellows felt what an ignoble life they had been reduced to, the reader may well believe they did not feel good-natured over it. And now, when these young gentlemen came to understand that they were to be associated with a man that was reported to be the representative of the hated Yankees, who had made war on the people of the South, and set free their slaves, they bitterly attacked me in wordy warfare. Of course I defended myself. And so day after day, in the intervals while our cattle were grazing, we debated every question relative to slavery that has been debated within the last fifty years. Their hearts were bitter ; they were passionately excited, and would often end the talk, which they themselves had begun, with noisy profanity. They seemed to think they had

this advantage of me, that they could swear and I
could not.

We were now traveling up the valley of the Platte
River.   It was the month of June.   The weather had
become rainy and there were frequent showers.   One
night we had corralled our train on an almost dead level
bottom, and I was sure, from the appearance of the
heavens, that we should have a storm.   Bro. Butcher
had been taken sick and had returned home, and, except myself, there were none to think or care what was
coming ; and yet it was plain to be seen that the air
was thick and sultry, and the heavens overcast with
clouds, and that everything betokened a tempest.   Our
canvas-covered wagons had been so crowded with merchandise that we could not get into them, and we had
slept on blankets on the ground ; but here on this dead
level bottom, in case of a heavy rain, we would be
drowned out by the flooding of the ground.   I dragged
under my wagon a number of ox-yokes, and with these
and some strips of boards I made a platform, and on
this I laid a narrow pallet, and crept under the wagon,
where I would be sheltered from the rain by the wagon-
bed above me.   During the night there fell frequent
showers, and the boys were soon drowned out from
their pallets on the ground.   They were tired and
sleepy ; they were homesick and in bad temper at their
mean and unaccustomed surroundings, and were inclined to hold the Yankees responsible for it all, and
they began to curse and swear in rough and bitter
speech.   Then there came on the most awful thunder
storm I ever witnessed.   Vivid flashes of lightning kept
the whole heavens illuminated with a blaze of light,
while a thousand electric lights would not so have

turned night into day around our corral of train-wagons. Crashing peals of thunder were in the air, and the bolts seemed to descend to the earth around us.   Then there came down a flood of rain that was as if a water spout had burst above our heads.   I looked out from my narrow bed, and could see the boys gathered in groups, standing leaning against their wagons, soaked to the skin, and their faces white with ghastly paleness; but not a word was spoken.   They had forgotten to swear. Then there was a lull in the storm, which subsided into a drizzling cold rain, and I went to sleep.

When morning came we were a sorry looking lot. The boys were soaked, and chilled, and *blue*, and dreadfully homesick.   Words would not tell what these poor fellows would have given if they could have been where they could have been coddled and petted by their mothers and sisters.   I saw that a warm cup of coffee and a substantial breakfast would do them good, and I hastened to have it provided.   They came with alacrity at the call for breakfast, for they were hungry. When a good square meal had somewhat thawed them out, I said, ''Boys, what made you quit swearing last night?''   The one who was usually their spokesman, and who knew how to be a gentleman if he had a mind to be, said reverently, ''We were afraid.''   From this time forward our debates over slavery and the Southern Confederacy were at an end, or if we had them it was in a friendly way.   Given a fair chance, these boys were not so bad as they seemed.

In the summer of 1864 we had reached the '' Cutoff,'' and were within eighty miles of Denver.   It was late on Saturday afternoon when we got to the Bijou Ranch.   We were tired and our teams were tired, and we debated for some time whether we should drive ten miles further, where we would find better feed for our oxen. We did so, though it took us till midnight; and there we rested on Sunday. This was providential; for it was on this Sunday that the Cheyenne Indians made their memorable raid and plundered the trains, burned the ranches and stole the horses for three hundred miles along the Platte River. They attacked the Bijou Station that we had left on Saturday, but they did not venture any nearer Denver; consequently we were safe. On our return we saw how the people had been murdered, the trains plundered and the ranches burned along our route; and it presented a terrible spectacle. A man named Butler was killed and scalped on the Little Blue River, and the people in Kansas got the word that it was myself. Immediately on my return home I rode up to the church at Wolf Creek, in Doniphan county, where we had a district meeting appointed. It was to them as if I had come from the dead. I went home for dinner with my old friend, Bro. John Beeler. I noticed his little boy peering attentively at me; he climbed upon a bedstead close behind me, then, jumping down, he ran to his mother and, pulling Sister Beeler by the apron, said, "Ma! Ma! The Indians did scalp Bro. Butler; I can see it on the top of his head." The reader must know that, like "Old Uncle Ned," I have no hair on the top of my head.

But, in spite of disasters and hardships, and dark and stormy days, our churches continued to grow and prosper, and we kept up a vigorous and aggressive church organization. On Sept. 27, 1864, the churches of the State came together at their fifth annual State meeting at Tecumseh, Shawnee county. Here the brethren organized a missionary society, fashioned after the plan of our General Missionary Society, and in which life directorships, life memberships and annual memberships were obtained by the payment of a sum of money.

The writer of these Recollections will explain that the formation of this Society was not his work. He doubted whether the brethren were prepared for it. Nevertheless, he was willing to be governed by the majority. By resolution of the State meeting, the writer was requested to prepare for publication with the minutes of the meeting an address, of which the following is a copy :

ADDRESS TO THE CHRISTIAN BRETHREN OF THE STATE OF KANSAS.

Beloved Brethren : We present to you in these pages the details of the organization of the Christian Missionary Society of the State of Kansas. We hope for your approval and ask for your contributions.

The warrior may fight for his country on the battle field : the statesman may seek to develop its resources and improve its laws; the husbandman may make its fields heavy with their weight of golden grain ; and those who love domestic life may seek to create in that place they call home a second paradise ; but broader, deeper, more comprehensive and sweeter far, is the work of Christianity. It underlies all good, and is the only sure basis of progress.

For two thousand years China and Japan have been without the Bible, and what they were then, that they are now. For two thousand years the millions of India have been left without God and without hope in the world, and they have only progressed into infinite degradations. The aboriginal inhabitants of America, left without the Bible, have only gone down deeper and deeper into a night as black as that which brooded over old chaos.

No Herschel counts the stars, numbers the planets, measures the length of their years and computes the number of their days, unless his observatory is illuminated by the rays of the Sun of Righteousness. No Luther thunders against priestcraft, shakes the thrones of tyrants, and wakes the nations to a new life and a new progress, save that Luther that finds a Bible in his cell. No Franklin calls down electricity from the clouds to carry messages across a continent swift as the lightning flashes through the sky, save that Franklin whose fathers brought the Bible with them from their native land, and prized it more than all the gold of Ophir. No mother country has had such reason to be proud of any colony that was ever planted on the face of this green earth, as Great Britain has had reason to be proud of her colonies in North America, and no colonies ever so loved the Bible. Judson, Howard, Wilberforce, and Florence Nightingale drew the inspiration of their benevolence from a dying Saviour's cross, and learned of him who, "though he was rich, yet for our sakes become poor, that we through his poverty might be rich."

Christianity, as it was given by Jesus to the apostles, and by the apostles to mankind, was as perfect as the God who gave it. Our whole duty then is this, that we should restore primitive and apostolic Christianity again to the world. Many reformers have sought to do this; but they have only reformed in part. Though they fled from Babylon they stopped short of Jerusalem.

We can not pause in this work which we have begun. We can not allow ourselves to grow cold and our churches to die. We must go forward in that path in which the rays of our glorious sun—the Sun of Righteousness—grow brighter and brighter unto the perfect day.

God does not make Christians as he created Adam out of the dust of the earth. He works by *means:* "How shall they believe in him of whom they have not heard?" God works through the voice of the Bible scattered over the world. If any doubt this, let them reflect that among all the millions of men that inhabit the whole earth not one becomes a Christian save him who either hears or reads of a crucified Saviour.

Money is the sinews of this war. True, there is peril in money. It is not safe to be rich; and it is admitted that by wealth preachers may be corrupted. But this is not the present danger. The present peril is, that haggard want, stalking in at the preacher's door, will paralyze his tongue, make his knees feeble and his hands heavy, and turn away his heart from his proper work to the question, What shall I eat? and what shall I drink? and wherewithal shall I be clothed? The preacher is told to put his trust in the Lord. But when, after long waiting, no ravens come to feed him, he sometimes loses his heart, and says, "I go a fishing." Surely the brethren will not have a controversy with the Lord. They will not deny that he has appointed that "they that preach the gospel shall live of the gospel."

It is by no weak, sickly, faint-hearted, lukewarm, languid, and spas-
modic efforts that the cause is to be kept alive. God will have all or
nothing. This is an age in which, if never before, both good men and
bad men are truly in earnest. The devil is fearfully and terribly in
earnest. "Therefore rejoice you heavens, and you that dwell in them.
Woe to the inhabitants of the earth and of the sea! for the devil is come
down to you, having great wrath, because he knoweth he hath but a
short time."

*We must give till we feel it. The widow's mite was most precious in
the eyes of Jesus, because it was her all.*

The objects we aim at are unquestionably scriptural. "Go disciple
all nations." This was the Saviour's last command. To sustain our
missionaries by the free-will offering of our brethren—this is also
scriptural.

CHAPTER XXXII.

In the year 1865 the State meeting was held at Prairie City. Meantime, however, a vigorous local district organization had been maintained from the first in Northeastern Kansas. This year its annual meeting was held at Leavenworth City, continuing from the first till the 4th of June. In addition to the ordinary purposes for which this meeting was held, it undertook to perfect the Missionary Society that had been organized the preceding year at Tecumseh.

Among all the conventions held in Kansas, whether of State or District, this must be regarded as the most notable:

1. It offers devout thanksgiving to the Lord for the return of peace to the nation : "*Resolved*, That with hearts full of gratitude to Almighty God, we hail the return of peace to our long distracted country."

2. After seven years of labor, beginning in 1858, and ending in 1865, notwithstanding the disorders of the period, this Convention is able to give a tabulated report of seventy-nine churches organized in the State with their bishops, deacons and evangelists, and having an aggregate of 3,020.

3. It is able to report a missionary society, that in the eight months intervening between the Tecumseh State meeting and the present Convention, has collected and paid over to its four evangelists—J. H.

Bauserman, Pardee Butler, S G. Brown and J. J. Trott —the sum of $827.

4. The Convention was able to adjourn, full of hope and enthusiasm, and to promise itself that it would do a still better work in the time to come.

The names of the following persons appear as the accredited messengers of the churches: Leavenworth —J. C. Stone, G. H. Field, S. A. Marshal, H. Allen, J. T. Gardiner, Calvin Reasoner. Ottumwa—J. T. Cox, Wm. Gans, J. Jenks, Peter Smith. Tecumseh— J. J. Driver, M. Driver, A. J. Alderman. Americus —W. C. Butler, S. S. Chapman. Le Roy—S. G. Brown, Allen Crocker. Little Stranger—J. H. Bauserman, S. A. Lacefield, J. Adams, J. P. Bauserman. Iola—S. Brown. Nine Mile—N. D. Tyler, J. T. Goode, H. Dickson. Garnett—J. Ramsey, H. Cavender. Holton—E. Cope, J. P. Nichols, T. G. Walters, A. B. Scholes. Pardee—Pardee Butler, N. Dunshee. Belmont—J. J. Trott. Monrovia—J. N. Holliday, John Graves, Caleb May. Mt. Pleasant—Joseph Potter, Thomas Miller, Joseph McBride, N. Humber. Olathe P. E. Henderson, John Elston, Martin Davenport, Addison Bowen. Lanesfield—O. S. Laws, Wm. Maxwell, H. C. Maxwell. Prairie City—H. H. Johnson. Buck Creek—C. M. Short, Thomas Finch, Martin Stoddard. Grasshopper Falls—James Ritter, S. Smith. Winchester—Cyrus Taylor, A. R. Cantwell.

But we wait for a period of seventeen years, then Eld S. T. Dodd, of Topeka, is appointed by the Kansas Christian Missionary Society to write a history of the work of the Christian Church in Kansas, which he does in a tract of thirty-eight pages; and Bro. D., writing under date of 1882, makes the following summary of the work done :

From 1856 to 1865 anything like church work was as good as thrown away, except as affording temporary privileges.

Finally a time came when the clatter of arms and the clatter of raiders were ended; railroads were built, and emigration poured in from all States and nations, among which were many Disciples of Christ, who should have been builded into existing churches, or collected into new ones; but many were permitted to drift along in carelessness and irresponsibility until their identity as members has been lost.

During the past five years there has been a general awakening among our brethren, which has resulted in very many new organizations and the possession of Atchison, Topeka, Wichita, and several other strongholds.

Bro. Dodd makes report of the following State meetings as having been held in Kansas:

In 1869, Grantville; in 1870, Le Roy; in 1871, St. George; in 1872, Emporia; in 1873, Topeka; in 1874, Olathe; in 1875, Ottawa, in 1876, Manhattan; in 1877, Emporia; in 1878, Gates Center; in 1879, Emporia; in 1880, Manhattan; in 1881, Salina; in 1882, Emporia.

To the above summary the writer will add the following list of the earlier Territorial and State meetings :

In 1860, Big Springs; in 1861, Prairie City; in 1862, Emporia; in 1863, Ottawa; in 1864, Tecumseh; in 1865, Prairie City; in 1866, Ottawa; in 1867, Olathe.

To the above statistics we will append the following reflections :

1. Among the preachers that prominently appear in the first seven years of our work, there are none remaining, save the writer of these Recollections. Some are fallen out by the way. Elders S. G. Brown, Wm. Gans, N. B. White, S. A. Marshal and Allen

Crocker have died in the faith and hope of the gospel. The name of J. H. Bauserman does, indeed, appear, but he had only just begun his work ; but having put the armor on, he has never laid it off. The name of J. B. McCleery does not yet appear on the minutes of our yearly meetings, still he was already an evangelist. He had been in Ohio the friend and companion of James A. Garfield, and soon came to be known as one of the first pulpit orators of the State. The government, like death, '' loves a shining mark,'' and claimed Bro. McCleery for its service, and he is now an army chaplain. The churches will never cease to regret his choice, and yet he had a right to make it.

2. The facts do not bear out the remark of Bro. S. T. Dodd, that ''from 1856 to 1865 anything like church work was as good as thrown away.'' With seventy-nine churches organized, and with upwards of three thousand church members in the State, work could scarcely be said to be '' as good as thrown away.''

3. Notwithstanding, the facts bear witness that there were grave imperfections in our work. After a heroic battle, fought under insuperable difficulties, and when there was every promise of still more brilliant triumphs, the cause went into an eclipse, from which it emerged only after many years of disaster.

From and after the year 1875, the churches spread themselves over a territory of two hundred miles in width and four hundred miles in length, and a great number of men became responsible for the good or the evil that should come on the cause of primitive and apostolic Christianity. It is probable that since the period of which we are speaking, 100,000 Disciples have located somewhere in these Western Territories.

If the church should now undertake to make inquisition for these church members, and make inquiry into their present condition, temporal and spiritual, the story of their wants and woes would be full of pathetic eloquence.

Since the days of the apostles an enthusiasm never has been known greater than that which was felt by the men who, under God, are responsible for this Reformation. In the beginning of the present century the missionary spirit among Christians was dead, and their zeal was wasted in disgraceful squabbles over inoperative and metaphysical opinions, or over modes of church government of which the Bible knows nothing.

The Protestant sects were divided into two hostile camps, known as Calvinists and Arminians. The Calvinist dogma was that Jesus died only for the elect, who were chosen in a by-gone eternity; that all men are spiritually as dead and helpless as was the cold dead dust of the earth out of which Adam was created, but that God will quicken into a new life dead sinners who are of the elect, and will give them evidence of their acceptance by the joyful emotions which he will create in their hearts. And so the supreme interest of men centered in this, that they were to seek in their own hearts those raptures and ecstasies that were evidence that they had experienced this spiritual change. The Arminians gloried in a free salvation. Christ died for all. But they demanded identically the same evidence of pardon demanded by the Calvinists, and men-found it just as hard to get this Arminian evidence of pardon as to get the experience that assured them that they were of the elect, according to the gospel of Calvinism; and so it came to pass that this lethargy of Christians over missionary work, and these wranglings over human opinions, had, before the Revolutionary War, covered the American colonies like a blanket with the spirit of infidelity. The corruption of Christianity by the Roman Catholic Church issued in the atheism of the French Revolution, and has created the infidelity of modern European nations; so like causes had precipitated a similar result in America. Men were groping as the blind grope in darkness, and then came, during the first half of the present century, the proclamation of primitive and apostolic Christianity. Alexander Campbell, John Smith, Jacob Creath and Samuel Rogers in Virginia and Kentucky, and Walter Scott, the Haydens and John Henry in Northeastern Ohio, made the people understand that the plan of salvation is as simple as the primer of our childhood; that it is all comprehended in this, that we must bow to the authority of Jesus, that we must believe in him and keep his commandments, and that the whole story is told in the four gospels and in the Acts of the Apostles with such simplicity that he that runs may read, that he that reads may understand, and that he that understands may act.

Alexander Campbell has said that a persecution made up of defamation, proscription and slander may be as hard to bear as that which issues in bonds and imprisonments; and this these early Disciples had to bear. But the world was ripe for reformation, and the cause spread like fire on the prairies.

Those who originally planted these churches in Kansas were, in large part, men and women who had drawn their inspiration directly from the founders and leaders of this Reformation. To some of them it had been given to sit at the feet of Alexander Campbell. Others had listened to John Smith, and had been magnetized by the inimitable wit and wisdom of that marvelous man, and their hearts had drawn heroic courage from his heart. Others still had been captivated by the boyish and unstudied drollery of Walter Scott, only to be swept away by a whirlwind of passionate appeal and terrible invective, or to be melted with the tenderness of his portrayal of the love of Jesus. And all these came to Kansas bearing a great cause in their hearts, and determined to build up here such churches as they had left behind them. But this was not all. Here were not only people among the most refined, well informed, and pious in the nation, but here were those who had been born in a storm of religious fanaticism, and could only live in a whirlwind of excite ment. These were the "big-meeting" Christians. There were also those whose truthfulness was doubtful, whose business methods were questionable, who could, on occasion, indulge in coarse and vulgar jokes and smutty jests, and whose religion scarce kept them outside the grog-shop. Added to all this, there were many whose hearts were yet bleeding with wounds they had received in that terrible struggle out of which the nation had just emerged. And now, afflicted with poverty, drouth, grasshoppers and starvation, we were left an agglomeration of heterogeneous materials, to fight our own battle as best we might. We might hope for help from the Lord, but not from our brethren in the older States. They were too busy debating the divine plan of missionary operations to help us.

The reader may well believe that the writer of these Recollections did not find himself carried to the skies on flowery beds of ease while this was going on, nor did he find himself reposing on a couch soft as downy pillows.

CHAPTER XXXIII.

Whatever may have been thought by a certain class of men, when the writer began his work in Kansas, it is now universally admitted among the Disciples that temperance work is legitimate church work—that the saloon being an enemy to our homes and our families, and the greatest peril that confronts the church and nation, its extinction is a legitimate object of Christian endeavor.

There was a young evangelist prominently engaged with us in our early work whose history is so sad, and whose relations, who are of the excellent of the earth, have already had their hearts so wounded because of him, that I have not been able to bring myself to write his name. He was of Irish descent, and before he became a preacher, or even a disciple, and while learning his trade, he had formed the drinking habit. He was not a young man of brilliant gifts, but they were solid. Moreover, he was humble, patient, industrious and persevering, and, having excellent health and a good physical organization, he gave promise of enduring usefulness. In short, he belonged to that class of young men that, while the people do not spoil them with flattery, yet the church set a great store by them. I can not write the history of his fall, for it was not made known even to his friends ; only this, that the time came that he seemed hesitating whether he should continue a preacher, and finally he wholly abandoned the ministry. His wife, who was a most estimable and Christian lady, was paralyzed with grief. At length the shameful truth came out—he was a drunkard! A brother undertook to admonish him of the awful fate that awaited him in the future world, but this apostate and disgraced preacher turned fiercely around and said : *" Don't talk to me of hell! I am in hell now !"*

There was living in the neighborhood of the writer a Christian family—though not of the Disciples—who had a boy that they regarded as of great promise, and they did what they could to give him a good education. After he had been for a while a school teacher, he became a lawyer, resident in Atchison, and finally became a politician. He was talented, social, companionable and ambitious, and soon made himself a man of mark, and was petted and courted by the people, and was the idol of his father and mother. All this brought him much into company. But at that time the brewers and saloonkeepers exercised a despotism over the politicians and public men of the city as absolute as is the despotism of the Czar over the Russians. But there was this difference : instead of being slaves to a great monarch, these politicians were tools and lick-spittles to a set of coarse, brutal, low-bred liquor dealers, who were exceptionally ignorant, degraded and vile. These wretched and vicious corrupters of the public morals insisted on controlling every caucus, and that the candidates, of whatever party, should be men well pleasing in their sight. If not, then the fat was in the fire, and the candidate was forthwith slaughtered. The writer of these Recollections has been a Republican as long as there has been a Republican

party, and has probably loved the party as well as it
has deserved. This party, as is well known, has assumed to be "the party of moral and religious ideas."
Now I have known, in cases not a few, men to be
nominated for office by this party—men who were respectable and Christian men, and they have told me,
and they have made the confession with shame and
humiliation—that the party managers have come to
them and said, "You are assessed so much for campaign expenses." The pretext was, that this was for
legitimate campaign work; and yet they knew that
the pretext was a lie, and that it was to constitute a
corruption fund, to be put into the saloons. And
these men were thus made candidates, to give respectability to the saloonkeepers' party, and, though they
did not go into the saloons themselves, they must pay
toll to the devil all the same.

It was under such circumstances that this boy, who
had been raised in our neighborhood, but had grown
to be a man, and had entered upon public life, now
became a center of attraction to the hale-fellows-well-
met of the saloon and the caucus. The reader need
not be told that this gifted young lawyer was walking
into the very jaws of death. There were soon alarming rumors that he was becoming dangerously addicted
to drink, and his friends entreated him to save himself
while he could, and he made promise to his mother
and wife to reform. But, alas! it was too late!

I was traveling home from Topeka, and on the railroad train I met a gentleman from Atchison—an inti-
mate friend of this young lawyer—and I was congratulating him on the reformation of our mutual friend.
He shook his head, and said: "Don't deceive your-

self. He tells me that he can remain sober two or three months, but that then he can hold out no longer, and, not wishing to make a public spectacle of himself, he buys a bottle of liquor, locks himself up in his room, and goes into a regular debauch. Then, after three or four days, he is able to appear on the streets again."

After a while the friends of this young man buried him. The doctors gave his sickness a respectable name, and reported that he had died of such a disease as decent people may die of, but his friends, with heart-breaking sorrow, knew they were burying a man who had died of a drunken debauch.

I have spoken freely of the evils wrought by our border troubles ; but now we had to realize that, taking all the men murdered in our early feuds, and comparing them with the men murdered by strong drink in the city of Atchison, counting man for man, there have been more men murdered by strong drink than by all our border troubles. There have been more women that have had their hearts broken, more children turned into the streets, more fortunes squandered, in the single city of Atchison than in all the Kansas war. But there is another point of comparison. The men who wrestled with each other in that early conflict verily thought they were right. They may have been mistaken, but they thought they were in the right; they therefore maintained their own self-respect. But those who have died in this battle of the bottles and the beer glasses have lost everything—self-respect, reputation, honor, everything ; and they went to the dogs and their souls went to perdition.

I have been a somewhat voluminous writer on many subjects now for forty years, but all this would scarce exceed in amount what I have written in Kansas newspapers, during a series of years, on the single subject of temperance. Besides, I spent much time in lecturing, for the welfare of the church and of the nation was at stake; and yet, what was done by myself was only a drop in the bucket compared with what went to make up, year after year, a great agitation. At length the people became so aroused that the law-makers at Topeka came to understand that something must be done in the way of temperance legislation; and they gave us a local option law. But crafty politicians obtained that cities of the first and second class should be exempted. This was nothing but mockery. The cities were the very places where the law was most needed, for men from the country went into the city and there they encountered their old enemy, the saloon. And so we kept up the agitation, and demanded that the saloon should be prohibited throughout the State. At length the pressure became so great that the politicians understood a second time that something must be yielded to the popular demand, and they tried another dodge. They said: ''We will give you the privilege to vote an amendment to the constitution incorporating prohibition into the constitution of the State.'' This would at least put off the evil day for two years, for it would take two years before such an amendment could go into operation. But here again was seen the usual treachery. The amendment to be voted on read as follows: ''The manufacture and sale of intoxicating liquors shall be forever prohibited in this State, except for medical, scientific and mechanical purposes.'' This was a stumbling-block laid in the way of feeble-minded Christians, for was not this an attack on their Christian liberty to use intoxicating wine at the Lord's table, and would not this be awful? Moreover, it forbade a farmer to manufacture *hard* cider from his own orchard, and would not this be a *hard* and tyrannical law? This was vexatious, for we were fighting the saloon, and were not seeking to palter with such frivolous and inter-meddling legislation. Nevertheless, in spite of these crafty attempts to excite popular odium against the amendment, it was adopted by a majority of more than eight thousand, and it became the duty of the next Legis-lature to enact a law enforcing the amendment. Then some of us waited on these "conscript fathers" at Topeka, and entreated them, and supplicated them, and almost got down on our knees to them, beseech-ing them to use a little courage and common sense. The House of Representatives was largely made up of farmers and men from the country, and was over-whelmingly in favor of an honest temperance law; but the Senate was largely made up of lawyers and men from the city, and was full of treachery and open and secret enmity. And so the Senate took the lead in making the law, and got up a bill that they pur-posely made as full of imperfections as a sieve is full of holes, and sent it down to the lower house. It was manifestly the duty of the House of Representatives to amend the bill, but now a great scare was got up. The cry was raised: "There is treachery! treachery! You must adopt this Senate bill without amending it, to the extent of changing the dot of an *i* or the cross-ing of a *t;* for if it goes back to the Senate it will certainly be killed." *And yet the Senate had adopted it by an almost four-fifths majority!*

The fact was, that these Senators, with all their bluster and bravado, were trembling in their boots, and dared not face their constituents at home while voting against any temperance law, however stringent, and this gave the friends of the law good warrant to make just such a law as was needed. And so the bill became a law; and then there followed such a farce in the courts as might make us lose faith in our Christian civilization and in our civilized jurisprudence. And it came to be understood that a coach-and-four could be driven through the loopholes that had been left in the law, and saloonkeepers began to remark, "Prohibition do n't prohibit." But from this evil we had what must be regarded a providential deliverance. A judge was found who made up in his own integrity and courage whatever was imperfect in the provisions of the law, and his good example was followed throughout the State.

John Martin, a lawyer, resident in Topeka, is a solid, sensible and honest man. His brethren of the Democratic persuasion wanted to make him a candidate for Governor, but because they would not insert in their platform a plank affirming that the law—because it was the law—ought to be enforced, he declined to accept the nomination, and Geo. W. Glick was nominated and elected. Then Mr. Glick, to reciprocate this courtesy, appointed Martin to a vacant judgeship in the Topeka judicial district; and a whisky case came before Judge Martin. The principal witness undertook to play the usual dodge of perjury and equivocation, but Judge Martin stopped the witness and said: "Sir, you are to tell whether the liquor you bought was whisky."

The witness again began to repeat his story of

equivocation: "Well, I called for *cold tea*, and I suppose I got what I called for."

"Stop!" said the Judge in a voice of thunder. "This witness is lying! Sheriff, take the witness and lock him up in jail."

The Sheriff had got as far as the door when the witness called out: "Judge, are you going to lock me up?"

"Yes, and I will keep you there till you rot unless you tell the truth."

"Well, I will tell."

The witness was placed again in the witness box. "Now," said the Judge, "was it whisky you bought of this saloonkeeper?"

"*Yes, it was whisky.*"

The example of Judge Martin was imitated by all the courts, and incredible sums of money have been collected as fines from the saloonkeepers, who, with the brewers, fought the battle to the bitter end, and appealed their cases to the Supreme Court of the United States. But it has ended in their absolute defeat, and even these gentlemen do now admit that prohibition does prohibit—in Kansas. Since that time the law has been greatly amended, and the saloons have been driven out of the State.

One evil yet remains. Just across the Missouri River from Atchison is East Atchison, and here whisky and beer are as free as water. Of course, this is a great calamity to us, but we wait in expectation and hope that prohibition will yet be achieved in Missouri.

John A. Brooks lives in Missouri; we live in Kansas. This man was once a rebel; we were loyal men.

Yet we pray the Father of Mercies to spare the life of this man, to prosper him and keep him, until he shall achieve this great good, not only to Missouri, but to ourselves.

CHAPTER XXXIV.

This reformation in the rapidity of its growth is
without parallel in the history of Protestant parties.
Those acquainted with its history need not be told
that a large number of its members were at first drawn
from the Baptists. It is indeed a matter of wonder
that a Presbyterian minister, but a short time identified
with the Baptists, should exert such an influence over
them as to induce a great multitude of churches and
church members to resolve that when he was driven
out of the Baptist Church they also would share his
fortune, and accept loss of reputation and exclusion
from their former brotherhood for the sake of the
principles they had learned from him. Now, when we
reflect that this embraced not only young men, but old
men—men already arrived at that period of life at which
it is most difficult to change our habits of thinking and
acting, it becomes a question of profoundest interest;
were these men able to make a change so radical as to
plant themselves completely on reformation principles,
and to abandon everything in their old Baptist order
incompatible therewith?

When we remember that this movement embraced
gray-haired Baptist ministers, who all their lifetime had
been accustomed to lead and not to follow, we
curiously inquire, Did they do this, or did they locate
themselves on a sort of half-way ground which was a

compromise between reformation principles and old Baptistism ?

Let us briefly notice wherein they changed, and wherein they did not change.

1. They laid aside the name Baptist and took the name Christian.

2. They built upon the Bible alone, instead of the Philadelphia Confession of Faith.

3. They taught that the church began at Pentecost, rather than with the preaching of John the Baptist.

4. They baptized men into a profession of faith in the Lord Jesus, that he is the Messiah, rather than into a Christian experience, made up of voices in the air, marvelous and strange sights, trances and rapturous feelings.

5. They taught that in conversion and sanctification, the Holy Spirit operates through the truth.

Thus far the change was radical, but here a large minority paused and brought with them into the reformation their old Baptist Church usages. The Baptists in the Great West and South are known as " Missionary Baptists," and " Old Baptists," or " Hardshell Baptists." Adoniram Judson and Luther Rice, who had been sent to Burmah by a Congregational Missionary Society, made known to the Baptists that they themselves had become Baptists, and had been repudiated by their own society, and asked for help. The Missionary Baptists are by far the most enterprising in all that pertains to the spread of Christianity. They are the most numerous, most wealthy, best educated, and most liberal. In translating the Bible into all languages, in carrying it into all lands, and in sending the gospel to all nations, they have made some amends for that unrelenting bitterness which they have shown toward our brethren from the first day till now. We shall glance at what has hitherto been their order by making certain extracts from the *Central Baptist*, published in the year 1870. The reader must bear in mind that we are writing of those old days:

In Arkansas there are but four Missionary Baptist Churches that sustain a regular pastor, or sustain preaching more than once a month. In North Alabama, two; in the whole of Alabama, twelve ; in Missouri, twenty-seven. Missouri has six hundred white churches, with a membership of fifty thousand, which have preaching once a month. Once a month preaching by secularized ministry! Is it any wonder that the cause does not go forward faster? Not more than two dozen out of seven hundred churches in Missouri have service every Sunday.

Let us pause a moment over this picture of Southern and Western Baptist Churches, drawn by themselves. In Arkansas but four churches had at this time preaching every Lord's day; in Alabama, twelve, and in Missouri twenty-four out of seven hundred ! Well may the writer ask, "Is it any wonder that the cause does not go forward faster?"

But if this was the order of the Missionary Baptists in the year 1870, what must have been the order of the Old Baptists seventy years before, when "Raccoon" John Smith was groping his way out of darkness into the light of the gospel, all unconscious of his utter blindness, that the reading of the Scriptures would conduce, either directly or indirectly, to his regeneration or sanctification.

The people known as "Hardshell" Baptists do not wish to be called by that name. They wish to be known as Old Baptists, or United Baptists, for they allege that they are the lineal descendants of the

United Baptists, and that the Missionary Baptists have apostatized, and gone away after strange gods.   The Old Baptists had long been declaiming against college-bred preachers and a hireling ministry.   They had certain pet theories concerning man's inability and God's sovereignty concerning a certain special, super-natural, immediate and efficacious work of grace on the heart of the sinners.   They said, "If God wants a missionary, he can send him, and maintain him, too. He needs no human help in the conversion of sinners, whether at home or abroad. We can find no Scripture for Sunday-schools, Bible classes, prayer-meetings, weekly meetings, hireling preachers, missionaries or missionary societies."   So they kept to their monthly meetings and monthly preaching.

They have no schools of learning, few educated men, no well-educated men, no missionaries, no con-tributions for missionary purposes, no weekly meetings, no weekly preaching, no weekly breaking of the loaf, no Sunday-schools, no Bible classes, no prayer-meet-ings.   But they have monthly preaching, by a man who is reputed a pastor over four churches, and who, in the nature of things, can not reside in three of the four churches over which he professes to preside.   He obtains but meager pecuniary reward for his preaching. He therefore provides for his own sustenance and that of his family by the labor of his own hands.   For this reason he must needs go to his appointments on Sat-urday, and return on Monday morning, and is therefore comparatively a stranger to the greater part of his four several flocks.   He can not know their daily life.   A few preachers among the old Baptists preëminently godly, self-sacrificing, and devoted to the Lord's cause, have left their families to suffer poverty and want, and have spent their lives in looking after the stray lambs of the flock; but this is not the general rule. This Baptist bishop has no authority whatever in any matter of discipline, his function being that of a moderator in a Saturday business monthly meeting. The sitting in judgment on the alleged acts of disorderly members belongs to the whole church, men and women, boys and girls.

We are now prepared to take the measure of the means of spiritual culture enjoyed by this people. It is just one sermon a month ; or, if they are peculiarly favored, it is three sermons a month. The children are left at home. They run wild like so many young apes, and wander along the streams or through the forests; or, if they are brought by their parents to the meeting, there is nothing especially for them.

It will be well for us to ponder well the inevitable consumption and slow decay that is surely wearing out these Old Baptist churches. Like the house of Saul, they are growing weaker and weaker. What a contrast between their condition now and seventy years ago. Then the United Baptists were the most powerful religious body in the great West. Then Jacob Creath and Jeremiah Vardeman could, if they had been so disposed, have elected the Governor of Kentucky. Then the Baptists were strong in the affections of the people, and strong in the memory of those men who had, through incredible toil, obloquy, poverty and loss of goods, planted the Baptist cause in the American wilderness. Alexander Campbell, with his eminent gifts of eloquence and learning, was welcomed among the Baptists almost as an angel from heaven. But his well-meant efforts to work a reformation in the Baptist churches were despised, and he was thrust out as a heathen man and publican.

What treasures untold reside in the Lord's house, the Lord's day, the Lord's book, and the ordinances of the Lord? It is the glory of Christianity. Now let the members of a Christian Church fail to meet at the Lord's house for Christian worship on the Lord's day, and to what snares and temptations do they not subject themselves and their children? What temptations to idleness and to wasting the Lord's day in visiting and gossiping, or in drowsy lethargy!

The sanctification of the Lord's day by meeting in honor of the resurrection of the Saviour, and especially with a reference to the celebration of the Lord's supper, is essential to the edification, spirituality, holiness, usefulness and happiness of the Christian community. It is not designed to throw into the shade any other duties of the Christian Church while contending for those above stated; but because no society save the Disciples of Christ so regard, observe and celebrate the Lord's day. We endeavor to arrest the attention of our fellow professors to the great design of it and of the coming together of the members of Christ's family on that day. When assembled for this chief purpose, the reading of the Scriptures, teaching, exhortation, prayer, praise, contributions for the poor, and discipline when called for, are all in order and necessary to the growth of the Christian Church in all the graces of the Spirit, and in all the fruits of holiness.—ALEX. CAMPBELL, in *Millennial Harbinger*, Vol. I., p. 534, New Series.

And what an audacious wrong and unutterable blunder would it be for God's chosen people to adopt an order that should defraud themselves, their children, their neighbors and their neighbor's children of such a glorious privilege.

If we could imagine two communities, one of which should, with their children and their children's children, diligently devote the Lord's day to purposes of moral, religious and intellectual improvement, while the other community should waste the day in idle and frivolous dissipation, what unmeasured progress would ultimately be made by one beyond that made by the other. And to which of these two classes will that favored people belong to whom will be awarded the high privilege of introducing among jarring sects and parties the true millennial church?

And do not these considerations go far to explain the contrast that is everywhere seen to exist between Protestant and Catholic countries? Among Protestants the day is a day to be sanctified to purposes of religious worship, among Catholics it is a holiday.

The peculiarity of our position creates an invincible necessity that we shall make the largest possible provision for the moral, intellectual and religious training and development of our people. This provision is largely found in keeping the ordinances of the Lord's house and the Lord's day. We have made a vow, and that vow is recorded in heaven, that we will meet together every first day of the week to break bread. To do otherwise—to show a good-natured imbecility of purpose—to drift helplessly along in the usages of the Old Baptists, conscious in our own hearts that this is not the ancient order of things, and having sternly demanded conformity to the apostolic order, at whatever sacrifice of peace, now to suffer our own brethren to travel on in the old ruts, rather than hazard the pain and trouble that will be the price of reform, would be a folly so inexcusable, a shame so unutterable, that the very stones might well cry out against us.

CHAPTER XXXV.

Professor William H. Whitsitt, of the Southern Baptist Theological Seminary, at Louisville, Ky., has written a book that has for its leading feature to make it appear that the Disciples are an "offshoot from the Sandemanians."

The Sandemanians, like the Baptists, had both faults and virtues. They were one of the earliest sects of the Scotch Presbyterians to protest against a union of Church and State; they practiced a weekly breaking of the loaf; held to a plurality ot elders in every church, and were exceptionally helpful to the poor; and surely, even Dr. Whitsitt will not call these damnable heresies. But they were also rigid separatists. They were Calvinists of the straitest sect, and made all their opinions a bond of union. In this they were like the Baptists, but essentially dissimilar to the Disciples. They exalted feet washing and the holy kiss into church ordinances, and excluded all who did not agree with them in these opinions, just as the Baptists exclude from the Lord's table all who are not of "our faith and order," though they admit that those persons thus excluded are regenerated, accepted of the Lord, and enjoy the indwelling of the Holy Spirit. Differing from the Sandemanians in the most essential element of our plea, we hold a very remote relationship to them—that of fortieth cousin, perhaps. The

Disciples are just as evidently an offshoot from the Baptists, as children are an offshoot from the parental stock.

Twenty years after the writer had begun his work in Kansas, he was able to count among fifty churches which had been organized within his knowledge, twenty-five that were dead; and there were six meeting-houses that were left unoccupied or sold for debt. And the church members would say to me: "We can neither preach, nor pray, nor read the Scriptures, nor break the loaf to edification, and we are too poor to hire a preacher. What shall we do?" They had no training, save that training they had obtained in the old Baptist churches, or one similar in our own, and now that they were scattered over the great West, and were poor in this world's goods, they were indeed in a pitiably helpless condition.

I sometimes said, "Get up a Sunday-school." But the old heads would get together and begin to debate where Cain got his wife, or who was the father of Melchisedec, or what was the thorn in the flesh that afflicted Paul; or they would dispute over the mode of baptism, or the operation of the Holy Spirit, and the boys, verifying the old adage that the devil always finds work for idle hands to do, and not appreciating this sort of thing, would shoot paper balls at each other and at the old folks, and the girls would do naughty things and grieve their mothers, and the whole thing would go up in smoke.

Nothing seemed to be left to these brethren, only the protracted meeting and monthly preaching. To many of them "pastorating" was one of the sorceries which, with the mother of Babylon, had bewitched the world.   These brethren seemed to have forgotten that Paul gives highest praise to that elder that not only rules well, but so addicts himself to the ministry of the Word and teaching as to require that he shall be sustained by the freewill offerings of the brethren.   And when we sought an arrangement by which all should give—each man, according to his ability—we were alarmed with fearful prognostications of evil : " Beware ! beware ! "   These brethren said, " You are making a veritable Popish bull, and he will gore you to death. Beware of missionary societies ! "   And when we turned to these men and besought them, "Tell us, dear brethren, how we shall obtain, without offense, the means to send help to those perishing churches ? " they were silent.   This was not their function.   Their vocation was to warn the people against Popish bulls and human missionary societies, for which there can not be found a thus saith the Lord, in express terms or by an approved precedent.

Meantime the churches in the older States had contributed one hundred thousand Disciples—this has sometimes been the estimated number—as emigrants to the great West, and these were scattered over its wide extended Territories, and it was to be shown how far this contribution, more precious than gold or silver or costliest gems, should be as water spilled on the ground, or as treasure cast into the bottom of the sea, or how far it should be as precious seed bearing fruit, some thirty fold, some sixty, and some one hundred fold.

When our first churches were organized in Kansas, Alexander Campbell had become old and well-stricken in years.   I have already written of the missionary society that was created in 1864, and of the great convention held in Leavenworth City in 1865, in which we sought to perfect the workings of that society. Within the following year Mr. Campbell died, and the always welcome *Millennial Harbinger* ceased its monthly visits. The voice of Mr. C. had been a bugle blast calling men to heroic deeds, and his overshadowing influence had restrained from that tendency to division, for opinion's sake, which is our inheritance from our common Protestantism. But now a great emigration had come into Kansas from every part of the United States, and among these were many who looked with no favor on any innovation on the traditions of the fathers.

Mr. C. had said in his notable debate with the Rev. N. L. Rice, at Lexington, Ky.: "Men formerly of all persuasions, and of all denominations and prejudices, have been baptized on this good confession, and have united in one community. Among them are found those who had been Romanists, Episcopalians, Presbyterians, Methodists, Baptists, Restorationists, Quakers, Arians, Unitarians, etc., etc. We have one Lord, one faith, one baptism, but various opinions. All these persons, of so many and contradictory opinions, weekly meet around our Lord's table in hundreds of churches all over the land. Our bond of union is faith in the slain Messiah, in his death for our sins and his resurrection for our justification."

It is perfectly apparent that to harmonize these elements—often opposite and conflicting—thus brought together in one body was no easy task, but we had more than this to do; we were also to harmonize the fierce antagonisms growing out of our early contests, and then to make those brethren who had been heretofore averse to any combination whatever for religious work other than that of the single congregation—to make them feel the absolute necessity of united action and coöperation. This was indeed a task most difficult. And if the final good results have only slowly become apparent we are entitled to the judgment of charity.

It is admitted that every liberty that God has given to men may be abused, and has been abused. Marriage, religion, civil government, the rights of property, eating and drinking—in short, all liberty, of whatever kind, may be and has been abused. Still we must use our liberty, our very existence depends upon it. I have said it already, and I say again, if sixty millions of the American people can unite together to promote the public tranquillity, and all citizens enjoy more of personal liberty than they could enjoy if every county were an independent principality, then our whole brotherhood, from the Atlantic to the Pacific, may be trusted to meet together, by their messengers or in person, to promote necessary Christian work without endangering our Christian liberties. If all the churches of Macedonia could unite together to send relief to the poor saints at Jerusalem, then, surely, the brethren everywhere may combine together to send relief to people perishing for want of the word of life.

And so with much weariness and painfulness, and often with gratuitous and unrequited labor, with long rides by day and by night, and much exposure to heat and cold, to floods and storms, and to rough treatment by wicked men—in short, with that relentless and persistent toil which makes a man old before his time, and in which one man has carried on the work of two men year after year, I have labered on, never doubting, but always hoping for that good time coming, when churches will be just, and give honest pay to honest men who do honest work. My hope has been that if I can not live to profit by that better order of things, it will at least be better for the men that come after me.

The wife of a traveling evangelist will always be the proper object of pity and sympathy, if pity and sympathy are to be given. She is not cheered by the smiles of admiring crowds, nor does she feel the intoxication of flattering tongues. She dwells at home in the desolation and loneliness of a practical widowhood, and often ekes out a meager support from a stingy and starveling salary.

But somebody has to do this frontier and pioneer work; and might it not as well be me and my wife as any other man and his wife?

I have given a wide range to these "Recollections." In doing so, I have not followed the example of a cowardly, corrupted and compromising Christianity, but rather have imitated the robust and manly courage of the writers of the Old and New Testament, who tell of the deeds of good men and bad men, and who also use the same freedom in speaking of the evil deeds of wicked rulers that they use in speaking of the things that more immediately concern the spiritual and eternal interests of men.

I have made the briefest possible mention of the hapless condition our churches were in twenty years ago. The picture is neither flattering nor cheering; but right royally are the churches now redeeming themselves from the reproach they were under then. A pastor is now being settled in each church as fast as the pecuniary circumstances of the congregation will permit, and a grand enthusiasm in Sunday-school work, simplifying and illustrating all its details, has made it possible for the weakest and poorest church to keep itself alive. Wherever there are children with their young enthusiasm—and the children, like the poor, are always with us—and wherever there are parents ready to lead their children in the way in which they should go, there the permanency of a church is assured.

And now, with many misgivings as touching our immediate future, but with an abiding hope of triumph in the end, I bid the reader farewell.

CHAPTER XXXVI.

REMINISCENCES.

By Mrs. Rosetta B. Hastings.

When father went back to Illinois, after he was rafted, we visited for several weeks among the churches where he had preached. Then we returned with him to Kansas, to visit my uncle, and to stay on our claim awhile, lest some person should jump it. We left our goods at Mt. Sterling, for father had promised to preach there that winter; but he told us that he had determined to move to Kansas sooner than he had first expected. We ferried the Missouri River near Jefferson City, and crossed the Kansas River in the woods, where Kansas City, Kansas, now stands. There was little of Kansas City then, except a few warehouses where freight was landed for Independence, which was the starting point of the Santa Fe trail.

Claims were being taken so rapidly that we remained to hold ours, while father returned to Illinois to preach. Two families in one room made it rather crowded, but we had a comfortable cabin. It contained a twelve-paned window—the only one in the settlement; cabins usually had no windows, or very small ones. Mr. May's folks had oiled paper over a narrow opening, which they closed with a board shutter. I asked their little girl why they did not have a larger window, and she said the Indians might get in. But no Indians troubled us.

When father came home, April 30th, we all ran out to meet him. But mother's quick eye detected something wrong. "Why, I look all right, don't I?" he asked, smiling. When we reached the house she again questioned him, and he sat down, rolled up his sleeve, and showed us his arm, brown with tar, and fuzzy with cotton. Then he told us his story. They had not tarred his face, except a spot on his forehead, where, he said, they had stuck a bunch of cotton as large as his two fists. The road to Ocena, as our post-office was called, ran up the bluff now known to Atchison people as Sam Kingstown. On the top of that ridge he had stopped, and pulled off his coat of tar and cotton, put on his clothes and come home.

A few evenings after that, we heard that a company of South Carolinians had camped near Mr. May's house. Father said they had probably come after either himself or Caleb May. So he went up to Mr. May's, to see what to do about it. After he left, uncle nailed shakes over the window, and cleaned up his old flint-lock musket, and loaded it carefully. Aunt moulded bullets, while mother got the ax and butcher knife, and then stuffed rags in the cracks, and brought in the half-bushel to turn over the light, so that they could not see where to shoot. Then we all took turns standing out in the darkness at the corner of the house, to keep watch, and listen for the sound of guns from Mr. May's. Father came home at eleven. He said the South Carolinians had asked permission to sleep in an empty cabin. He and Mr. May had followed them, and he had crept under the cabin floor and listened, and they had seemed to be sleeping soundly. So we all went to bed, but father slept with a revolver under his head, which Mr. May had insisted on lending him. The next morning the South Carolinians went quietly on their journey. We learned afterwards that they were on their way to lay out the town of Marysville, in Marshall County, and did not know that they were in the same neighborhood with Pardee Butler and Caleb May.

Father wrote an account of the Atchison mob, and took it to Lawrence to be published in the *Herald of Freedom*. The Congressional Committee summoned him to give his testimony. While there, the Lawrence people gave him a pistol, and insisted that he must carry it. Father told us how the Carolinians had sworn to kill him, when they heard his testimony before the Committee ; and as soon as he heard they were coming back, after the destruction of Lawrence, he knew that he was in danger. Brave as he might be, he saw no good in allowing himself to be butchered by those infuriated men, and resolved to keep out of their way. He kept his horse picketed on the grass near where he was at work, with saddle and bridle close by. One day as I was helping him drop sod corn on uncle's claim—two miles from our own—while uncle worked at his new cabin, we saw some horsemen coming over the hill.

"They are South Carolinians," said father, and saddling his horse, he rode in the opposite direction. In the afternoon he came back, saying that they had followed him all day, and he had circled here and there over the hills, and he had happened to meet two of them, one at a time, and recognized them as some of the men who had mobbed him; and they knew him too, but they had not dared to attack him single-handed. He thought they were trying to get together, to attack him the next time they saw him. He wanted uncle to change coats and hats with him, so that, if they saw him in the distance, they would not know him. He wore a black coat and hat, and uncle wore a white palmleaf hat, and had with him, in case of rain, an old-fashioned, light gray overcoat. These father put on, and throwing a white cloth over his horse, rode away, telling us that he would not be at home that night, and that we need not look for him until we saw him. Day after day those men followed him, like hounds after a wolf. Through the day he rode here and there, spending the night with first one neighbor, then another. One day, when uncle was working at his cabin, some South Carolinians rode up, and not seeing father, they searched the woods and ravine near by, and rode away. Father spent one night with Mr. Duncan, and had just gone out of sight in the morning, when the South Carolinians rode up.

"Does Pardee Butler ride a bay horse?" they asked.

"No, sir," replied Mr. Duncan.

"We saw a man ride into the woods just now," said they, "that looked like Pardee Butler, but he was riding a bay horse."

"Pardee Butler never rides a bay horse." And so they went the other way. Father rode a spirited young "copper-bottom" horse, named Copper, that looked either bay or gray at a distance, as the light happened to shine.

One day, father went to the post-office after his mail, and two young neighbors riding up, and seeing his horse hitched there, thought to have some fun. With loud shouts they galloped up, and hearing them, he stepped to the door, sprang on his horse, and dashed off over the hill, with them after him. But when they reached the top of the hill they found that he was standing on the ground behind his horse, with his pistol levelled at them across his saddle. They were glad to make themselves known, and own up to the joke.

Father slipped home a few minutes almost every day, to let us know that he was yet alive, and to see if we were safe. Every night we fastened up the house, expecting that before morning the Ruffians would try to burst in to search for father. Those were days of terrible anxiety for mother, for she thought every time father rode away that it was probably their last parting. Yet she was brave and quiet, and said little.

But father grew tired of being dogged, and told us that he was going to Lawrence. He was gone some time and we did not know where he was.

My little four year old brother George heard much talk of Border Ruffians, and he went around flourishing a long thorn for a dagger, and boasting in childish accent: "Bad Border 'uffians s'an't get my pa. I hit 'em in 'e eye wid my dagger." One day I was helping uncle drop corn, when George came running to us, much excited. "I foun' a Border 'uffian! I foun' a Border 'uffian! I hit 'em in 'e eye! I hit 'em in 'e eye!" We ran to see what he had found, and he ran ahead, picking up pebbles as he ran, "to fro at 'e bad Border 'uffian." What do you think he

had found ?   A mud turtle !   And that was his idea of
a Border Ruffian.   But he had a chance to see one.
One day, while father was away, two men rode up to
the house, whom we knew to be Border Ruffians by their
red shirts and the revolvers in their belts.   Mother told
George and me to hide behind the door, while she
talked to them.   They asked for a drink of water, but
while they waited for it, one of them rode almost into
the door, and looked around the room—we had only one
room—evidently looking for father.   George became
impatient, and kept whispering " Let me out, let me
see a Border 'uffian.   I *will* see a Border 'uffian."   And
he pulled loose from me and peeped around the edge
of the door.

When father came home he brought some type,
and some half-printed papers, blackened with powder,
that he had picked up in the sand on the river bank at
Lawrence, where the Border Ruffians had thrown the
Herald of Freedom press and papers into the river.   On
the printed side of the papers was the article he had
written about his last mob.

Years afterwards I asked father what he was doing
when he was gone from home in May and June, 1856.
He replied : " I was organizing the Republican party
in northern Kansas.   I first went to Lawrence, and
there the leaders insisted that I ought to visit various
points in the northern part of the State, and organize
the new party, and I did so."

Soon after father's return, in June, some of the
neighbors announced a meeting for him at Bro. Elliott's,
four miles from our house, of which he speaks in
Chapter XVII.   To that meeting the people came
armed, for the report of the appointment had reached

Atchison.   They left their guns in their wagons, or set them in convenient corners, while they listened to the preaching ; for they were determined to defend father in case of attack.

Mr. John Quiett, who is yet one of our neighbors, was one of three men who stood guard at the fence, watching for approaching enemies, while father preached.   But no attack was made.

Uncle Milo had taken us to the meeting ; and mother asked father to go home with us, and he replied, "Yes, I am going home once more."

Mother told him she would be glad to have him go with us, but she was afraid to have him stay all night.

"I am going to stay at home for one night, for I have some letters to write," was his reply.

Mother was very uneasy on the road home, for she said the Border Ruffians would be watching for us in the woods.   But we reached home without molestation. Father sat up until after midnight, writing letters, and then went to bed and slept safely.   The next day one of our neighbors told us that just at dark that evening she saw a band of men ride into the woods between her house and ours, but she was afraid to come over and tell us.   Other neighbors saw them go out on Monday morning, and ride toward town.   A few days afterwards, a neighbor, who stood "on both sides of the fence" in regard to politics, went to Atchison, and he told us that nine South Carolinians hid in our woods to take father that night, but they had seen his light burning so late that they were afraid, and went back and told that he had forty armed men, who stood guard all night, and they could not take him.

But father was not by any means the only one whom the Border Ruffians molested. They were continually riding around the country, frightening the people, and "pressing" horses—which was another name for stealing them. And the Free State man who made himself prominent was liable to be shot any time they could catch him. The Free State men kept their horses hidden in the brush, and often hid there themselves. Every time any of the neighbors saw several horsemen riding over the prairie, they thought it was the Border Ruffians.

One day Caleb May saw quite a company of men riding toward his place. He and his son and hired man stationed themselves under the bank, where both the house and the ford would be within range of their guns. Mrs. May was to talk to the horsemen as they rode past the house, and, if they were Border Ruffians, she was to shut the door, as a signal to the husband to to be ready for attack. When they rode up, however, they proved to be Mr. Speck, and about twenty other neighbors from the lower neighborhood, who had brought their horses up to Mr. May's to guard them from the Ruffians, who stood in great fear of Caleb May.

When the Ruffians returned to Missouri, after one of their raids, some of them told in De Kalb, where Mr. May lived before coming to Kansas, that they had killed him. One of his old neighbors, named Jones, rode into De Kalb one day, and was accosted by one of the returned Border Ruffians with "We've got Caleb May this time; got his head on a ten-foot pole."

"Anybody killed?" queried Mr. Jones.

"Oh, no."

"Anybody hurt ?"

" No."

" Then it 's a lie !" responded Mr. Jones.   " I know Caleb May well enough to know that when you get him somebody 's going to get hurt."

Mr. May had for years been a temperance man, in the midst of a drinking population of the frontiers of Arkansas and Missouri, and made the first temperance speech ever made in De Kalb. His oldest son, when fifteen, had never tasted whisky. One day, when Mr. May had gone on a journey, the boy was in town, and loafers, seeing him pass a saloon, shouted, " Cale May 's gone; let 's have some fun with his boy." So they dragged him into the saloon, and poured whisky down his throat, and sent him home drunk to his mother. When Mr. May returned home they told him what had happened.

At that time there was a local option temperance law in Missouri, under which a majority of the people in a township, by signing a petition to the court, could have the saloons abolished as public nuisances. De Kalb was full of saloons, and there was one on almost every road corner in the county.

Years afterwards I heard Mr. May tell the incident, and his eyes flashed, as he said with his slow, strong emphasis, " When I came home and heard what had happened, *you bet I* WAS *wrathy !*   I just jumped on my horse, and I rode that township up and down, and I never stopped until I had signers enough to my petition, and I cleaned every saloon out of that township."

Doubtless many a man signed that petition because he dared not refuse ; for, although usually kind and quiet, few dared to face his anger.

When Lawrence was besieged, in May, a company of Free State men was raised around here, and they sent John Quiett to Lawrence to offer their services for the defense of the town, but were refused by Mr. Pomeroy. Soon after the return of the South Carolinians from Lawrence they found Mr. Quiett in the Atchison postoffice. They at once seized him as a Free State leader, and began to debate whether to shoot or hang him. But one of the Pro-slavery merchants of Atchison interfered, and begged them to let him go. He got out, mounted his horse, and started for home, twelve miles away. But the Carolinians, like Pharaoh of old, repented that they had let him go, and soon started in pursuit. It was a hot race, for as Mr. Quiett reached the top of each hill he could see his pursuers coming behind him. But he reached home; and when they came to the creek near his home, they were afraid to pass through the woods— probably fearing an ambush—and returned to town. But parties were sent out to take him when he was unprepared; and, finding that he was hunted, he was afraid to stay at home nights. I have heard Mrs. Quiett say, that one day, when her husband had been away several days, he came home for a little while, and she gave him something to eat. After eating he lay down to sleep on a lounge that stood along the front side of the bed. She was rocking her baby in the middle of the cabin, when the Border Ruffians rode up to the house, and one of them, riding so close that his horse's head was inside of the door, leaned forward and looked around the cabin. The door was at the foot of the bed, and it so happened that the lounge on which Mr. Quiett lay was so close to the bed, and so low, that the edge of the bed just hid his body. The Ruffian said not a word, but looked until he seemed satisfied that there was no one in the room but Mrs. Quiett, and then they both rode away. She said that she could not speak, but felt as though she was frozen to her chair, for she was sure that, if they had seen Mr. Quiett, they would have shot him before her eyes. Not until they were out of sight did she speak or stir.

Mr. Quiett and Mr. Ross went with father to Topeka, when the Free State Legislature and Convention met, July 4, 1856, of which father speaks in chapter XVI. Mr. Quiett says that the Free State men went there determined to defend the Legislature. There were several large companies of well-armed men stationed near, awaiting orders from the Convention; and one company armed with Sharp's rifles lay behind a board fence by the side of the road. Several speakers made excited speeches, urging the members of the Convention to be men, and defend their lawful rights, even at the risk of their lives. The Free State men were wrought up to the verge of desperation. The vote was about to be taken, whether or not to resist the troops. There was much suppressed excitement; and, had the vote been taken then, it would undoubtedly have been in favor of resistance. Father, in the meanwhile, was on a committee, in a back room. Mr. Quiett began calling for Pardee Butler. Others took up the call, and, hearing it in the committee room, he came out. They demanded a speech on the question in debate. He begged them to bear their wrongs patiently, and to allow no provocation to cause them to resist the United States authorities. He besought them to be loyal to their country, and never fire on the old stars and stripes. Mr. Quiett said it was a powerful speech, timely and eloquent. When he sat down the tide had turned. The vote was taken, and it was decided not to resist the troops. Mr. Quiett says that without a doubt that speech not only saved them from a bloody battle that day, but that it saved the Territory from a long, fierce war.

After they disbanded, the members of the Convention went out and sat down on the prairie grass to eat their dinner, which each took from his pocket, or his wagon. Mr. Quiett and Mr. Ross took theirs from the wagon, in which they had ridden to Topeka; but father had gone on horseback, as he usually did, and took his dinner from the capacious pocket of his preacher's saddle-bags. Mr. Quiett said that in getting out his dinner, father took a pistol out of his saddle-bags. This created much merriment for them, as they thought it would have been of little use to him in case of attack. They told him that if that was where he carried it, the South Carolinians would shoot him some day before he could unbuckle his saddle-bags.

But father disliked very much to carry arms, and I think he never did in his life, except for about two months during that dreadful summer.

About two weeks afterwards we started to Illinois, in the buggy. We crossed the River at Iowa Point. About nine miles northeast of Savannah, in Gentry county, Missouri, father was taken very sick, and we were obliged to stop at the nearest house. The man at whose house we happened to stop was a Mr. Brown, from Maine; and he and his family were very kind to us. There, for four weeks, father lay sick of a fever.

One day, while mother was in father's room, Mrs. Brown questioned me about living in Kansas, and whether the Border Ruffians ever troubled us. So I told her how father had been treated. Father called me into the bed-room, and said that I ought not to have told that, under the circumstances; that it would be a dreadful thing for us to be attacked, with him flat on his back, and we among strangers. I replied that I thought it would do no harm, because Mr. Brown's folks were from the North, and our friends. But he said it might bring trouble on Mr. Brown if his neighbors should learn that he had harbored Pardee Butler. When Mr. Brown came in at noon, his wife told him the news. He went right in, and told father that Butler was such a common name, that he had no idea that he had the honor of sheltering Pardee Butler. ''Now,'' said he, ''you need not be uneasy while you are here. Yonder hang four good Sharp's rifles, and I and my boys know how to use them; and nobody shall touch you unless they walk over our dead bodies.''

As soon as father was able to travel we finished our journey in safety. We visited our old friends in Illinois, and father preached on Sundays. While we were at Mt. Sterling, he lectured on temperance one night, and the bad fellows made a little disturbance. The previous afternoon I had visited a little girl in the village, and we had found and thrown away a nest full of rotten eggs. The next time I saw her she said that her big brother was mad at us, for he was saving those eggs, and he and some other big boys had intended to throw them at Pardee Butler while he was making that temperance speech; but when they went to the barn, their eggs were gone. The truth was, that her big brother was one of many boys who were fast being made drunkards by the village saloons.

Mother went to Ohio on a visit, and father went to Iowa to attend to some business. On his return he met one of the State Republican Committee, who insisted on making arrangements for him to stay in Illinois until the presidential election, and speak for Fremont.

It was raw November weather when we started back to Kansas, with a one-horse wagon, drawn by Copper, and a heavily loaded mule team, driven by a boy named Henry Whitaker, who is now one of the merchants of Atchison. Mother was sick, and we had to stop a week. Then the mud became so deep that father had to buy a yoke of oxen and hitch on behind the mules. Then it froze up, rough and hard, and we stopped for a blacksmith to make shoes for the oxen, and were directed to stay with a widow who had an empty house. She had built a new house of hewed logs, with a window in it, and we were allowed to stay in the old cabin. She could not keep from talking about that window.

"I 've lived all my days without ary winder, an' got along mighty well," said she. "For my part, I den't like winders ; they make a house look so glarin', like. We uns never had ary one where I had my raisin'. But the childern is gettin' a heap o' stuck up notions these days, an' they jes' set up that we had to have a winder in our new house."

The weather was very cold the rest of the way, and father suffered severely from a felon on his hand. When we reached St. Joseph the Missouri River was frozen, and our teams were the first to cross on the ice. Father took the teams to the top of the icy banks, and hitched them to the ends of the wagon-tongues by means of long chains. We traveled all day over unsettled prairie, hoping to reach Mr. Wy-mer's house, on Independence Creek. We reached the place at nine o'clock, but no house; it had been burned. It was very dark, and bitter cold, but we traveled on. At eleven o'clock we found Mr. Snyder's cabin, where Lancaster is now built. A little later and we should have seen no light. A party of belated surveyors had found the house before the family went to bed; and they were just lying down when we drove up. In those days no one thought of refusing a trav-eler lodging. The cabin was about fourteen feet square. The family had crowded into one bed, part of the surveyors occupied the other, and the rest were on the floor. We had not eaten a bite since morning. The cooking stove was in a little, cold, floorless shed, and there mother baked some corn griddle-cakes for our supper. The surveyors gave their bed to mother and me, and the men all crowded down on the floor—nineteen in one room. The next morning we drove on to our own house before getting breakfast, glad to find it had not been burned.

On Sunday, May 10, 1857, a meeting was held at our house, at which it was agreed that a Sunday-school should be organized the next Sunday, in Mr. Cobb's grove, near Pardee. There we met nearly every Sun-day that summer, and father usually preached.

Much of his time that summer was spent in improv-ing forty acres of his farm, on which he raised some sod corn and vegetables. Our corn for bread was ground in Mr. Wigglesworth's treadmill, turned by oxen. We had no fruit for many years, but a few wild sorts, and the vegetables were a welcome variation in our diet of meat and molasses.

August, 29, 1857, the Pardee church was organized, at the house of Bro. A. Elliott, with twenty-seven members. In October a frame school-house was finished at Pardee, which was thereafter used for church purposes. During father's absence the meetings were led by our elders, Dr. Moore, Bro. Elliott, and Bro. Brockman. We often rode to meeting in the ox-wagon, as did some of our neighbors.

CHAPTER XXXVII.

Father again preached in Illinois from October,
1857, until New Year. He preached in Pardee the
rest of the winter ; but in the spring he began traveling and preaching in various parts of the Territory.
It was the wettest summer I ever knew, and he was
continually swimming streams. Mother often told
him that a man who could not swim ought not to swim
a horse. But he continued to do so until the streams
were bridged, many years later. The last time he did
so was in the spring of 1871. He was riding a little
Indian pony, and carried some bundles. The Stranger
Creek was full, and very cold, and when his heavy
overcoat became water-soaked, he saw that the pony
was about to be swept down the current. Sliding off
from its back, he kept his arm about its neck, thinking the water would hold part of his weight. But he
soon saw that he was pulling it down stream, so that
it was likely to be tangled in some willows, and he
reached back and caught hold of its tail, and it pulled
him safely to shore. He reached home very wet, but
with bundles and overcoat all safe.

He then determined to have a bridge on the road
along his boundary line. But every man, up and
down the creek, wanted a bridge on his own line, and

so there was much opposition. But he at length succeeded in obtaining a bridge. This was the only one
of father's many contests in which he contended for a
personal benefit: his other contests were all for the
good of the public.

From this deviation I will now return to the year
1858. Father was so busy preaching in other places,
that he only preached occasionally in Pardee.

He has sometimes been accused of preaching politics. A good brother who formerly lived in Missouri,
said, not long before father's death: "They used to
tell me before I came to Kansas that Pardee Butler
preached politics, and I said that if ever I heard him
begin to preach politics, I was going to get right up
in meeting, and ask him to show his Scripture for
preaching politics. Now I've been hearing him
preach, off and on, for twenty years, and I've never
got up in meeting yet, for I've never heard him preach
any politics."

The only sermon that I can remember as containing any allusion to politics, was one that he preached
at Pardee that summer of 1858. It was from the
text, "Woe unto you scribes and Pharisees, hypo-
crites! for ye pay tithe of mint and anise and cum-
min, and have omitted the weightier matters of the
law, judgment, mercy, and faith: these ought ye to
have done, and not to leave the other undone." After
speaking in a general manner of Christian duties that
are left undone by those who are precise about certain theological points, he spoke plainly of the injustice and unmercifulness of slavery, and besought
Christians to be careful how they upheld it in any
manner, lest they be condemned by the words of the text.

Another sermon that he preached at Pardee, August 1, 1858, was from I. Kings xviii. 21 : "If the Lord be God, follow him: but if Baal, then follow him." After delineating very graphically the terrible drouth, and the long contest of Elijah with Ahab and Jezebel, he told of the final triumph of religion, and the merited defeat and punishment of wickedness. He finished with an eloquent appeal from the text, "If the Lord be God, then serve him." At the close two boys confessed their Savior. One of them was an orphan boy, then making his home at my father's house, and since known as Judge J. J. Locker, of Atchison, who died last September.

But winter came, and the co-operation that had engaged father that summer felt that they had paid all they could raise. It had not been enough to pay a hired man, and meet our frugal expenses. Yet that was the first money he had made for three and a half years, except by his two trips to Illinois. He had appealed to the General Missionary Society, and they had declined to support him, unless he would promise not to say a word about slavery. But the people were calling to him from every direction to come and organize churches. He decided to appeal personally to the churches in the older States. From December, 1858, until May, 1859, he preached constantly in Illinois, Indiana, Michigan and Ohio, collecting what money he could. He reported $365 as the amount received, expenses $110, leaving a balance of $255. He received enough more during the summer to make his salary $297.42.

The next summer he preached in Kansas ; but was not gone all the time, as when in other States. When preaching in distant counties he was sometimes gone four or five weeks, but he was sometimes at home a part of every week. When at home he worked very hard on the farm, to accomplish what he saw must be done, that he might go back to his preaching as soon as possible. Mother looked after the work in his absence, and was a good manager, but there was much to which she could not attend. Father was nervously energetic, always working and walking rapidly. Even after he was sixty years old, although he was a slender man, only five feet nine inches in height, with his right arm trembling with palsy, I have known robust young men to complain that they did not like to work for Pardee Butler, because he would work with them, and they were ashamed to have such an old man do more than they did, and he worked so hard that he wore them out. He scarcely spent an idle moment. Other men could be content to pass their time in careless conversation, but he never could. Unless he had some subject that he thought especially worthy of conversation, he said little. He seldom spoke of what he had done, and scarcely ever related any of the many experiences of his trips away from home. In his backwoods boyhood experiences he had learned to make or mend almost every article used by a farmer. He was full of projects, always improving something on the place. Every spare moment was used, either in fixing something about the farm, or in reading or writing. He sometimes complained that the days were not half long enough to suit him. He once told his sister that the Border Ruffians never knew what a service they did him when they rafted him, for he had leisure to think while he was going down the river. My brother

Charley once said that father was so greedy of time he
was afraid he might lose a minute.   Often in the evening we had to make room by the cooking stove for his
shaving-horse, or his leather and harness tools, while
he worked until ten or eleven o'clock making or mend-
ing some implement or harness.   And often, after
laboring all day, he read or wrote until eleven or twelve
o'clock at night.   He read a great variety of books
and newspapers, but was particularly fond of church
history and religious books of a doctrinal nature.

He wrote much for various papers, and was a pains-
taking writer.   He usually wrote his articles two or
three times, and the account of his second mob that
was written for the *Herald of Freedom* he re-wrote
seven times.   He could write best in the morning,
and frequently read and wrote half of the forenoon;
and then worked and chored until nine or ten at night,
to make up lost time.

Few ever knew the strong desire that he constantly
felt for a life devoted wholly to study and preaching.
Living, as we did in those days, in a log house with
only one room, he had no private place for study, but
read or wrote in the midst of the family.   Yet neither
crying babies nor the noisy play of older children distracted him.   Often he sat, with a look of abstraction,
in the midst of our conversation; and we frequently
had to speak to him several times before we could attract his attention.

We have several hundred of his newspaper articles
saved in scrap-books.   He preached altogether without notes, and never seemed to make any especial
preparation for preaching a sermon.   I once asked him
how long it took him to prepare a sermon, and he

replied, "Sometimes longer, sometimes shorter, generally two or three years. Of course I do not think of it all that time, but I seldom preach on a subject when it first enters my mind, but let it mature. I always have several subjects on hand at once, and when I am reading I retain whatever strikes me as pertaining to any one of my subjects." "When do you do most of your thinking?" I asked. "Whenever I can; mostly on horseback."

His education was never finished; he was a student to the day of his death. Even during his last sickness he asked me to return a volume of Macaulay's "History of England" that I had borrowed, so that some one could read to him from it.

In July, 1859, he was sick for some time; but in September reports thus: "Since I recovered from my sickness I have held a series of meetings,—one near Atchison, which resulted in eight additions; one at Big Springs, at which four were added by baptism; and one at Pardee, where there was one baptized.

November 1, 1859, the Northwestern Christian Missionary Society was organized at Indianapolis. Father attended it, and remained preaching and collecting money until February. He collected about the same amount as the previous year.

In March, 1860, father and Bro. Hutchinson held the meeting at Pardee, of which he speaks in Chapter XXIX., at which there were forty-five additions. Father preached on Sunday night. The school-house was closely seated with planks, and crowded almost to suffocation, while a crowd stood outside at doors and windows. Father preached on the life of Paul, although he did not mention Paul's name until near

the close of the sermon.   He spoke of him as a talented young nobleman, brought up in ease and luxury
in a great city, to whom were open the highest positions in his nation.   There were but few Christians in
the land, and they were poor and despised.   But at
length he felt the power of God, and learned to love
the Savior.   He told how he gave up wealth and position, and became poor and despised, and went everywhere preaching Christ and his mighty power to save.
He told of his wonderful zeal and energy, as he traveled from country to country, preaching Christ to eager
thousands.   He vividly depicted the courage with
which he endured trials, hardships, and persecutions.
Then he told of his last days—a feeble, gray-haired
old man, ending his days in a prison, his few faithful
friends far away, enemies on every hand, and a painful,
violent death in store for him.   Did he see the folly of
his course?   And then he quoted Paul's triumphant
words: "I count all things but loss for the excellency
of the knowledge of Jesus Christ my Lord, for whom
I have suffered the loss of all things.   .   .   .   For I am
now ready to be offered, and the time of my departure
is at hand.   I have fought a good fight, I have finished
my course, I have kept the faith: henceforth there is
laid up for me a crown of righteousness, which the
Lord, the righteous Judge, shall give me at that day,
and not to me only, but unto all them also that love his
appearing."   After speaking of the powerful effect of
Paul's life and teachings, in helping to transform the
world, he eloquently appealed to the young men and
women to turn their ambition to life's highest object,
to follow the example of that grand old hero, and live

a life of true heroism in this world, and win honor and immortality in the world to come.

The house rang with that rousing old hymn, "Come, you sinners, poor and needy," and eleven young men and women rose to their feet and confessed their Savior.

No sermon to which I have ever listened has impressed itself so deeply on my memory as that sermon twenty-nine years ago.

CHAPTER XXXVIII.

In the spring of 1860 father rented his farm, so that he could devote his whole time to preaching. He built a house in Pardee, that we might live near school and meeting until George should be old enough to do the work on the farm. There was plenty of open prairie to pasture the cows, and George and I tended them, while mother made cheese to help support the family.

Father traveled and preached almost constantly that summer, sometimes alone, sometimes in company with Bro. Hutchinson.

At many of the points at which he organized churches, the old members are now either dead or scattered. But Bro. John A. Campbell, of Big Springs, where he built up a strong church, writes as follows of his work there:

He told me that his first visit to Big Springs was in May, 1858. My first recollection of him was that he preached there on the 4th day of July, of that year, when he organized the church with twenty-eight members, my father (L. R. Campbell) and C. M. Mock being appointed elders. His subject on that occasion was the "Unity of all Christians," and he spoke with great power. He again preached there on the 29th day of August, 1858, and his subject was "Faith." On that day the first addition to the church was made by baptism. He continued to preach for the church about once each month through 1858-9, and a part of 1860. During that time very many were added, but I have no means of knowing the number. In the fall of 1859 he held a successful protracted meeting, and another in the winter with Bro. G. W. Hutchinson. In 1860, he was at the State meeting at Big Springs, at which the ground plan of our present co-operative plan of missionary work was laid. There was also raised at that meeting money to buy a large tent, with which Bro. Butler was to travel and preach as State evangelist. Again, in the year 1877 or 1878, he preached once per month at Big Springs and some adjacent points—once on the Waukarusa, on the subject of the Seventh-day Sabbath, out of which grew a correspondence for a debate, but it was not held, owing to a failure to get a suitable house.

In the forepart of December past our church held a memorial service for him, and many pleasant things about his relation to dear brethren and sisters were spoken of. The relation between him and myself was always very pleasant, and I delight to bear testimony to his great ability and grand life and character. I regarded him as my father in the gospel, and he was a source of great help and strength to me.

The tent of which Bro. Campbell speaks was made by the ladies in the Pardee school-house. In size it was forty by sixty feet, the roof being shaped like the roof of a house. The second State meeting, and many district meetings, were held in it; and father used it in his meetings for nearly ten years, when it was finally torn up by a storm.

In the fall of 1860 the Missionary Society wished him to visit Indiana again, to stir up an interest, and collect his salary. I find no report of his work that winter, except this item from one of his letters: "There have been seventeen additions at meetings which I have recently attended—six at Brownsburg, Hendricks county, and eleven at Springville, Lawrence county, Ind."

I have found the note-book which he kept from November, 1860, to November, 1861, in which I find this account: He received $368.50; traveling expenses, $72.55, leaving for his year's work, $295.95.

That was the year of the "drouth," and he apprised the brethren where he preached of the destitution in Kansas. Dr. S. G. Moore and my uncle, Prof. N. Dunshee, of Pardee, had been appointed to receive contributions for destitute brethren ; and they reported the receipt and distribution of $670.96, besides boxes of clothing.

After father's return, in March, 1861, he traveled almost constantly. I have found, in the note-book mentioned above, the time and place, and either the subject or text of each sermon he preached that year, one hundred and fifty-three in all. Here are some of the subjects named: "The Gospel;" "Christian Union;" "Kings of Israel;" "Noah and the Deluge;" "Types of the Law;" "For What Did Jesus Die?" "Baptism, its Authority and Design;" "From Whence Am I? and Whither Am I Going?" "The Material Results of Christianity;" and "The Kingdom of Heaven."

Father had spent all of the money that was due him from property sold in Iowa, except a thousand dollars, with which he intended to pay his debts, and finish paying for land in Kansas. While he was in Indiana that spring that amount was forwarded in a draft to mother. The war was just breaking out, and by the time she could write to father and receive his instructions as to its disposal, the bank broke, and he lost a large part of it. He had already been running in debt for necessary expenses, hoping each year that his support would be increased, and the loss in the bank threw him so much in debt that he felt it would be impossible for him to preach much longer.

In September, 1861, he attended the State meeting

in Prairie City.   On Thursday the meeting was held in an empty store-room, for the poles had not yet been cut to raise the tent.   After some preliminary business father made a short speech, telling them that he must soon quit preaching for them.   He told them how necessary it was that churches should be planted at once in this new State, and how he had tried in vain to arouse the brethren at the East to their responsibility in the matter, but that he was at last obliged to give up and go to work, like an honest man, and pay his debts.   He told them how he had loved the work, and how willingly he had toiled and suffered hardships, and begged them to hold out faithfully and do what they could; and when his debts were paid, he would return again to the work.   When he closed his hearers were nearly all in tears.

Many went long distances to that meeting, the brethren and sisters from Emporia going in a covered wagon, and camping out on the road.

Father continued to preach, however, much of the time that winter.   That part of his farm that was improved was rented for five years, and he had no money to improve the rest.   The renter proved an indifferent farmer, and the rent scarcely sufficed to pay the taxes and winter the cattle.   So father entered the only paying business, that of freighting, as he relates in Chap-XXXI.   Perhaps some may think from reading that chapter that he only took one trip, but he crossed the plains five times.   He first went in the spring of 1862, in Bro. Butcher's train, taking George, who was only ten years old, along to drive one of his teams, because he could not afford to hire a driver.   It was a hard, monotonous life, driving all day and camping at night through all weather; but the hardest part of it was that men and boys all had to take their turn standing guard over their cattle at night. After Bro. Butcher was taken sick on that first trip, father acted as his boss, and on all his later trips he went as wagon-boss of some large train owned by Atchison freighters, also taking along two teams of his own.

The wagon-bosses were frequently rough, overbearing men, who not only went armed, but who often treated their drivers tyrannically. They not only cowed the boys with abusive language, but with frequent threats of whipping, or shooting, which they sometimes fulfilled.

Father never carried arms about his person in any of his trips across the plains. But there was something in his quiet, determined manner that enabled him to rule even the most headstrong of the wild young fellows who usually drove the freighting teams. He was once traveling along, for a short time, in company with a train much larger than his own, whose wagon-boss was a big, burly, swaggering fellow, who was drunk much of the time. Each train was driving along behind it such oxen as were unfit for work, and some of the other cattle became accidentally mixed with father's drove. The boss, who was already partially drunk, had ridden on to a ranch to get more whisky. Father called on his own boys, and the boys of the other train—on the plains the drivers were often called boys, even though they were middle aged men—to help separate them. But those of the other train refused to help. They tried in vain to separate them, until they were tired out. As they neared the ranch father walked up to the well to get a drink, and there sat the drunken boss on his horse. When he saw father, he exclaimed, with a great oath, "—— —— ——, what you driving my cattle off for?"

"I asked your boys to help separate them," replied father, "but they refused, and I and my boys have worried ourselves out at it. If you will order your boys to help we will try again."

"—— —— you, go back and get them cattle out, or I'll send you to ——!"

Father looked him steadily in the face. and said quietly, "I would like to see the irons you would do it with."

"—— —— go back and get them cattle out, or I'll shoot you as sure as ——!" shouted the fellow, jerking out a revolver with a great flourish.

The frightened boys stood back, expecting to see him shoot, but father, without moving, coolly replied, "If you want your cattle out, you will get them out yourself; I will do nothing more about it."

The fellow, cowed by father's cool, determined gaze, put his revolver back in his belt, rode off, called his men, and they drove the cattle out themselves.

In October, 1862, father decided to make a winter trip, because he could earn more money than in the summer. The owners of the train intended wintering their cattle on the buffalo grass in the Colorado valleys, which they found cheaper than wintering them on corn in Kansas. The drivers were mostly Ohio boys, who drove teams because they wanted to reach the Pike's Peak gold mines. The oxen were a lot of wild Texas steers, and it took about half a day to get them yoked up the first time, so that they only traveled about eight miles out from Atchison the first day. George did not go that trip, but father took him to town to help them start—because he said that if George was only ten, he knew more about handling wild oxen than all those green Ohio boys—and sent him home the second day out. It had been a very pleasant fall; but I never saw it turn cold so suddenly as it did that day. I remember that I spent several hours gathering in squashes and covering up potatoes; and when I returned to the house at 3 P. M. every leaf on the trees and every flower in the garden was frozen stiff, pointing straight out to the southeast. It was the only time I ever saw a frozen flower garden in full bloom. It sleeted nearly all night, and the Texas cattle, frightened and chilled by wind and sleet, were so wild that father and all the boys had to herd them all night to keep them from stampeding. Their clothes were wet and frozen, for they were not very warmly dressed, and George said he never suffered so much with the cold in his life as he did that night.

It was a hard and stormy winter, and the Ohio boys, unused to such a life, suffered badly, many of them freezing their hands and feet. When they reached Denver the cattle were taken to the valleys, and father traded his own cattle for mules. Loading his two wagons with hides, so as to make money both ways, he and the two boys who had driven his teams started for home. I have heard him say that he never saw weather so cold, but that he could keep from freezing by walking. So by dint of much walking he succeeded in reaching home without being frozen. Their wagons were so full of hides that they had to sleep on the ground, and he said that on waking in the morning he often found himself buried in snow.

Wood was scarce, and they sometimes had to haul it quite a distance to build their camp fires at night, and it was sometimes so stormy that they could scarcely cook.

During the journey one wagon-load after another of returning Pike's Peak adventurers had fallen in with them, and kept together for the sake of company and protection against the Indians, until they made quite a train. By common consent—accordin' to the human nature of the thing, as they say on the plains—father came to be considered the boss of the train. There was a ranch near the road, kept by a Frenchman, who had an Indian wife. He had grown rich selling whisky and provisions, and wood and hay. When the half-frozen men, with their hungry teams, came by, he charged them extravagant prices; if they objected he blustered and threatened until he usually scared them into paying what he asked. Father and his train camped there one cold night, and some of the men went up to buy wood and hay; but he asked such high prices for them that they went back and asked father to go up. He was busy, and knowing the Frenchman's reputation, told them to go back and tell him that the boss said he could not pay such exorbitant prices, but to let them have the wood and hay, and he would come after awhile and pay a good round price for them. The men returned, and told what he said, but the Frenchman ordered them to clear out, and threatened to shoot them if they came back again without the money he demanded. He would not even allow them to draw water from the well. Again they begged father to go up, but he said he was too busy, and told them to go right back and take the wood, hay and water, and if the Frenchman said anything, to tell him that Pardee Butler told them to do it, and he would settle the bill. They went back, the one drawing water, the others getting wood and hay. Out ran the Frenchman, very wrathy, leveling his gun at them. "The boss told us to take them, and he'd settle," they said.

"Who's your boss?" he asked in surprise.

"Pardee Butler."

"Pardee Butler! Oh! Oh! Pardee Butler? Take 'em! Take 'em!" he exclaimed, dropping his gun and throwing up his hands. "Oh! Pardee Butler! Take 'em! Take 'em!" he continued, fairly dancing around, white with fright, and gesticulating as only a Frenchman can.

"Why, what's the matter? He wont hurt you," said one of the boys.

"Oh! Pardee Butler! He bad man. Oh! Oh!" he answered, still dancing and gesticulating.

"Oh, no; he is not a bad man; he never hurt anybody in his life."

"Oh, yees, Pardee Butler one veree bad man! He must be one bad man, 'cause they put heem down the river on one raft, down in Kansas. Pardee Butler must be one veree bad man!"

Father made no more winter trips, but spent his winters at lumbering. When he first came to Kansas he had bought eighty acres of timber land in the river bottoms, in Missouri, two miles below Atchison. Mills had been erected along the river, and lumber was at last in good demand. So he found profitable use for his teams, and large freighting wagons, in working that timber into lumber.

He crossed the plains twice more in the springs of 1863 and 1864.

The Indians often visited their camps, begging for bread, or for sugar or tobacco. Father said that on his winter trip it made his heart ache to see the pitiable condition of the women and children, chilling around in the loose wigwams during the winter storms. He often saw the women out in the snow gathering up and carrying great loads of wood on their shoulders. But he said the most pitiable sight he ever saw was little half-starved, half-naked children, too small to walk, creeping around under his mule's heels, eagerly eating the grains of corn that they had dropped.

But the Indians were every year growing more restless, and often attacked the trains, to obtain provisions, and cattle and mules. Father often saw them peering around the bluffs, or along the river banks, watching his movements. But he was very careful, never allowing the boys or stock to wander off alone, and keeping guards out at night. Knowing that the Indians were growing dangerous, Bro. Butcher had insisted on lending him a rifle for his later trips. One day they were traveling along the Platte River bottoms, the river half a mile to one side, the bluffs a mile or two back on the other. It seemed impossible for anything to hide in the low grass around them; but father knew that here and there in the grass were wet-weather gullies, deep enough for an Indian to lie in; and his watchful eye detected the grass moving, occasionally, here and there. He halted, telling the men there were Indians in the grass. At first they made light of it, saying they knew no Indian could hide in that low grass. But he told them that he had been watching for some time, and thought the Indians were creeping up on them from the river.   He took Bro. Butcher's rifle out of the wagon, saying, "I am going down there to see; who will go with me?"   But none of them offered to go, except a boy of sixteen, who, seeing the rest would not go, shouldered another gun, saying, "For shame! I wont see the old man go alone!"   The two went down through the grass, and when they reached the river, they saw a number of Indians running away under shelter of the bank.   The Indians seldom attack determined men, who are on their guard—unless they are on the war-path with a large force—and they saw that father was such a man, and gave him no more trouble.   It was on his last trip, in 1864, that the Indian raid occurred, which he men-tioned in Chapter XXXI.   On their return they found that armed bands of Indians were still riding about the country.   One afternoon, when they were within a little over a day's drive of Fort Kearney, they saw a band of Indians prowling about, first in one direction, then in another.   The boys were badly frightened, and wanted to run their teams all night, in order to reach the Fort.   The weather was hot, and the oxen already tired, and father feared that such a forced drive would kill them.   So he ordered the boys to camp for the night.   They kept out a strong guard, and were not attacked; but reached the fort in safety the next day.

The District Missionary Society of Northeastern Kansas had held two yearly meetings in the tent at Pardee, in August, 1862, and August, 1863, just after father's return each year from his summer trips across the plains.   In August, 1864, soon after his return from his last trip, another district meeting was held at Wolf Creek, Doniphan county, which was the home of Bro. Beeler, and of Brethren Jonathan and Nathan Springer. Father had held a number of good meetings there, and built up quite a church. But when the railroads went through there the town of Severance was built up on one side; and Highland, seven or eight miles on the other side, which was already a Presbyterian stronghold, received a new impetus. So the church at Wolf Creek was broken up, and one was organized at Severance, and one has since been built up at Highland, of which Bro. Beeler is the leading member.

Bro. Jonathan Springer—who has moved to Goffs, where he still maintains his old-time zeal—relates an incident which occurred a year or two before that district meeting. Father was holding a protracted meeting, when there came into the neighborhood a young preaching brother from one of the Southern States, running away from the Union soldiers. Upon learnwho he was, father invited him to preach, and they continued preaching together for a week, holding an excellent meeting, and father said not a word to him about the questions dividing North and South. Bro. Springer said, "I always thought that Bro. Butler was a peculiar, a wonderful, and a powerful preacher." Speaking of his ability to attract and hold the attention of an audience, Bro. Springer said, "I once heard him begin a sermon with the question, "Are we dogs, or are we men?'" At the district meeting his sermon was on his favorite theme, "Christian Union;" and it was two hours in length, yet he held the close attention of the audience to the end. Although he often preached on that subject, he always had something fresh to say. He could not crowd all that he had to say about it into one sermon. He was constantly reading of the change of sentiment on Christian union among other denominations, and referring to it in his sermons.

A few years ago he preached a series of discourses on that subject at Pardee, closing as follows: "The Protestant denominations will all become one yet, not by other churches coming to any one church, but their differences will almost imperceptibly disappear, and they will all melt into one, and no one will be able to tell how it was done."

In the spring of 1865 he moved back to the farm, and spent much of the summer in preaching. For the next four years his winters were spent in lumbering, and his summers in preaching, and improving his farm. Even while lumbering he preached somewhere nearly every Sunday; sometimes at home, sometimes in the schoolhouse near his timber, and sometimes he landed a raft at Port William on Saturday, and went across and preached for the church at Pleasant Ridge, Leavenworth county. And other Sundays he preached at various points easy to reach on Saturday evening, and return to his work on Monday morning.

He rafted many of his logs to Port William or Leavenworth, and usually helped to take them down; and there was much joking about where he learned the rafting business. It was dangerous, however, for rafts sometimes struck snags, or became unmanageable in the swift current, and went to pieces.

When the Central Branch Railroad was built, the company took corn of settlers in payment for lands, cribbing it by the road. Instead of shipping off the corn, they shipped Texas cattle to the cribs, to eat it up. They soon came to father in great perplexity. Their cattle broke every fence they could build, and they did not know what to do with them. So he told them how to build a fence the cattle could not break, and he had a quantity of extra strong lumber sawed for that purpose. When he called at the railroad office to receive pay for his lumber, the clerk paid him in rolls of bills sealed up in paper, with the value marked on the outside. After leaving the office he counted his money, and found that one of the rolls that was marked $100, really contained $1,000. Returning, he told the clerk he had made a mistake. "We correct no mistakes," was the gruff reply. "Young man, you are not doing business for yourself, but for the railroad company; come here and help me count the money." The label had been misplaced.

The greater part of father's lumber was sawed at Winthrop, now called East Atchison, and he did much hauling across the river on the ice. His teams were usually the first to cross when the river froze up, and the last to quit crossing in the spring; but as he was a good judge of the condition of the ice, he never lost a team. I have heard my brother George say that four or five times, when father or himself had, by careful driving, crossed in safety with large double teams and heavy loads, others, trying to cross behind them with light wagons, had broken through, and either lost their teams or been saved with difficulty. One spring the ice was thawing rapidly, and had become quite rotten; but father wanted to take one more heavy load across, and he drove it himself. It was drawn by several yoke of oxen, and their weight sunk the ice so that the water spouted through the air-holes, and frightened them. He knew that the beaten track, where the teams had trodden the ice solid, and the accumulated mud had shaded it, had not thawed as fast as the surrounding ice, and that to allow his wagon to swerve a foot, one way or the other, was to risk breaking in. He ran along by the lead yoke, watching them so closely that he did not notice where he was walking, and several times he stepped off, knee-deep in little air-holes; but he took his load safely over. As he went up the bank some half-drunken Germans in a sleigh dashed down on the ice and broke through, but were so near the shore that they easily got out. But one of father's wagons ever broke through, and it was driven by a careless hired man. Father was ahead with another team. He called back to the man to unhitch quickly and hitch on to the end of the tongue, for fear the team would break through, ,too, and running back, he put lumber under the wheels, and they pulled the wagon out.

Father gave away a great deal of wood over there. In those days coal was scarce and high, and, consequently, wood was high also. Many families were so glad to receive the wood as a gift, that they were willing to haul it twelve or fourteen miles. And, winter after winter, he also kept two or three poor families supplied with wood from his timber at home, allowing them to come and help themselves.

Father and mother were always very generous, giving freely of money, wood, fruits, vegetables, milk, or whatever they had to spare, to those more needy than themselves. I can not remember of ever seeing them charge any one for a night's lodging, or turn any one away.

When father had anything to sell, he often refused to accept its market value, because he thought it was not really worth the price. A friend once noticed him selling seed potatoes much below the market price, and told him that his generous habit of selling to his neighbors so cheaply would keep him poor. He replied that the market price was extortionate, and that his conscience would not allow him to accept it.

In his later years he gave freely to help build various churches; and to State and General Missionary Societies, and to the many calls for money.

He could never stand by and order men around, but always took hold and did the hardest of the work himself; and the excessively heavy work of logging injured his health. He had several severe spells of nervous rheumatism, and from that time his right arm was troubled with the trembling palsy, which grew worse until his death. He had not been able to write with a pen for several years, and his '' Recollections'' were all written by holding a pencil in his right hand, and steadying that with the left hand.

Once, while he was lumbering, mother remonstrated with him for wearing himself out so fast. He replied that he saw so much needing to be done, and done at once, he felt compelled to push his work off his hands as fast as possible. If it shortened his life, he said it made no difference to him, provided he could accomplish more than in a long life of easy work. I heard him say once that we ought to make our life-work of so much importance, that neither cold, nor storm, nor any other hindrance should be allowed to interfere with the performance of duty. And I seldom knew him to stop for bad weather of any kind.

In December, 1865, I had concluded to go to school a term at Manhattan, and asked father to take me there, for it was a hundred miles, and there was not a railroad in the State. He sent an appointment to hold a meeting there at that time. The morning that we were to start the thermometer was eighteen degrees below zero, and the wind blowing keenly from the northwest. But if we postponed our journey he would miss an appointment, and so we started. There was no snow, the roads were rough, and we had to travel in a lumber wagon, and were three days on the way. I was well wrapped in blankets, and did not suffer severely, but father, on account of driving, could not wrap up so much, and had to walk nearly half of the time to keep from freezing. His nose and cheeks were slightly frozen the second day, for it did not begin to moderate until the third day.

He held a good meeting of eight or ten days. There were about a dozen baptisms, the ice being cut in the river for that purpose.

CHAPTER XXXIX.

In May, 1867, my two-year-old brother, Ernest, was accidentally scalded. He lingered a week, then death claimed the youngest of the flock.

When the Central Branch Railroad was built the little town of Farmington was laid out, a mile to the northwest of father's house—Pardee being two miles to the southeast. Many of the original members of the Pardee Church had helped to organize the Pleasant Grove Church, six miles west. Father thought it would be wise to break up at Pardee, and move church and village to the railroad town, but some objected. Thinking that the rest would soon follow, he left Pardee, and organized a church of twenty-three members at Farmington, October 6, 1867. Bro. McCleery held a successful meeting here the next December, and preached once a month during the following year.

For several years much of father's time was given (gratuitously), in caring for this church and Sunday-school, and the church soon numbered a hundred members.

After the war many colored people came to Kansas, and a number of them settled in the neighborhood. They had heard of father, as a friend to the colored people, and some of them wanted to work for

him.   He frequently employed them, and usually
found them faithful and efficient.   They liked to work
for him because he treated them as he treated white
men.   As there were not enough of them in the country places to form churches of their own, they attended
our Sunday-schools and meetings.   We were much
surprised to find that some of our brethren objected to
colored children being in the classes.   One good old
colored man, who had been a member of the church in
Missouri, was much respected by the community.   A
white brother requested our deacon, W. J. May, a son
of Caleb May, to ask this colored brother to take a
back seat, and to pass the bread and wine to him last.
Bro. May replied: "I shall do no such thing; as
long as I am deacon in this church there shall be no
respect of persons."

A colored man, who had been a servant in the family of one of the governors of Virginia, presented himself for membership.   He was a neat, good-looking
man, with pleasant manners, and had been a member
of Col. Shaw's colored regiment, when they so val-
iantly stormed Fort Wagner.   A white sister borrowed
a pair of gloves, when she went up to give him the
hand of fellowship, so that she "would n't have to
touch a nigger's hand."

Father wanted to teach them, without giving un-
due offense, their Christian duty to the colored people.   He preached a sermon on the parable of the
Good Samaritan, telling how the Jews and Samaritans
hated each other, and how Jesus taught in that parable
that even the most despised of earth's races are our
neighbors.   He also told the story of Peter's vision at
the house of Simon, and how God taught him not to

call any man or nation of men common or unclean, but to carry the gospel to all nations. The nearest that he came to modern times, in that sermon, was the remark that the Jews despised the Samaritans as much as the Americans despised the Africans. He left them to make their own applications of the Bible teachings.

What an excitement it raised ! Many said the colored people had to be turned out of the Sunday-school, or they would leave ; and some did leave. In nearly all our churches father had to meet this prejudice, but he remained firm in his position, that in church and Sunday-school there should be neither white nor black, but all should have equal rights.

In the spring of 1869 father sold his timber land in Missouri, and paid the last of his debts. He had some money left, and the first thing he did was to go into a book store, and spend forty dollars for "Barnes' Notes," and "Motley's United Netherlands, and "History of the Dutch Republic." He remarked as he did so, "I have felt the need of these books for years, and this is the first money I could spare for them."

Men who had seen father working with tireless energy on his farm, or the plains, or "logging" in the timber, sometimes said: "He is craving to get rich."

He has often been misunderstood, but in no point more than this. I never knew a man who cared less for wealth than he. The one all-absorbing object of his life was to preach the gospel. But he had also resolved to have the means to pay his debts, and to have a home for his family.

About that time he spoke to me, in substance, as

follows : The one great anxiety of my life has
been to preach.   I had intended to go to Bethany,
and devote my life entirely to preaching.   My sore
throat caused me to give that up, but going to Iowa
improved my health, and I began to preach again.
When I took my claim in Kansas it was with the intention of holding on to the land, while I preached in
Illinois, until Kansas should be thickly enough settled to furnish me preaching here.   But you know how
necessity has driven me, and how preaching for a meager salary, and neglecting my farm, ran me in debt ;
and what a hard necessity has been laid on me to pay
those debts, and to improve my farm, so that you and
your mother and the boys can make a living from it.
You have no idea what a sore and bitter trial it has
been to me the last six or eight years to see the old
churches going to pieces before my eyes, and so many
opportunities for planting new churches being lost to
us.   There is only one thing more I must do, and then
I am determined to give myself wholly to preaching.
As for myself, I would live in a log house all my days
before I would take from my preaching the time necessary to earn and build a better house.   But Sybil has
been a good and faithful wife, and has borne with commendable patience all the trials of the hard life through
which I have led her ; and it worries her to entertain so
much company as we have in her log house.   With the
lumber and saleable stock I have on hand, I can build it
without incurring any further debt.   And then I will
be ready to preach without being dependent on any
man.

The house was built ; but before it was finished a
series of misfortunes befell him, that threw him in debt

nearly as badly as before. From snake-bites, disease, and accidents, he lost four or five horses, and several head of cattle, and the cholera killed nearly a thousand dollars' worth of his hogs.

He went to work again, but somewhat discouraged, for he saw that his long-deferred hope of devoting his entire time to study and preaching, could never be realized. He was nearly sixty, and had broken his constitution by hard work, and could not much longer have endured the incessant riding and preaching of a traveling evangelist, even could he have been supported. The boys were then old enough to do much of the farm work, and from that time he preached more constantly, but spent more or less time at hard labor.

For several years he was employed, for a small salary, at monthly preaching, by churches at Big Springs, Valley Falls, Round Prairie, and other points.

In the fall of 1875 he concluded to visit once more the churches for which he had preached before coming to Kansas, and bid farewell to his old friends. He accordingly spent the following winter in a preaching tour throughout Iowa and Illinois.

The State Meeting at Emporia, in 1877, in his absence, elected him President of the Society. Unable to find a State evangelist who would undertake the difficult task of reviving the old churches that had perished —which he thought was the work most needed at that time—he took the field himself. At the State meeting held at Yates Center the next year, he made the following report: "Time spent, five months; sermons preached, one hundred and fifty; churches organized, two ; compensation received, $186.36." He also revived many scattered churches and Sunday-schools,

and obtained regular preaching for some of them.   He
was greatly worried over the churches of this part of
the State.   They had been much weakened, and some
of them nearly broken up by the tide of emigration
that set into the southern and western counties.   Attempts at co-operative State and district work were im-
peded by conservative papers, which prejudiced the
brethren against missionary societies, and hireling pas-
tors.   He spent much time, both with tongue and pen,
in answering these sophistries, and teaching the
churches their duties.   Many of the churches were
really too poor to support regular preaching, and many
that were able, thought themselves unable to do so.
Yet someone must care for them, or they would perish.   He resolved for the rest of his life to preach,
without remuneration, where such preaching was
most needed.   And so the last eight or nine years of his
life were spent in preaching on Saturdays and Sundays for
weak churches, and the remainder of the time in working
and writing. If a church was building a meeting house,
and felt unable to support a preacher while doing so,
he preached for it until it was built. If a church had
already built, and felt oppressed with debt, he preached
for it until the debt was paid. If, from any cause, a
church was weak or disorderly, he preached for it until
it was again in good order.   Then he said to the
brethren: "I have helped you on your feet, now raise
the money and hire some one else to preach for you,
and let me go and help some other needy church."

Mr. Hastings and I were married in 1870, and had
settled at Farmington.   From that time Mr. Hastings
had taken much of the care of the Farmington church.
The church at Pardee had revived, and had been doing

well under the care of Prof. N. Dunshee; and, later on, by the assistance of Prof. J. M. Reid, and of Mr. Hastings. But, about six years ago, being left without a leader, they begged father to take charge of them, although they were unable to offer him much remuneration. He told them that it would cost them nothing, so far as he was concerned; but that, if he took charge of them, they must promise to support the Sunday-school liberally, and to build a church. He, and his family, therefore, changed their membership from Farmington back to Pardee, where he was elected elder—for he believed that every pastor of a church should be one of its elders—and he preached for them five years. He not only gave largely of his means to build the church, but spent the whole summer in collecting the money, and overseeing the building of the house. He looked after the buying of the materials, and sent his teams to do much of the hauling, and never stopped until the building was furnished, the insurance paid, and his own hands had put the stoves in place.

About a year before his death, however, owing to disagreements about the manner of conducting the Sunday-school, father resigned his eldership, and preached at other points until his death.

But his work for others was not confined to preaching, or church work. He had never tried to make a large town of either Farmington or Pardee. He knew too well the perils of the city. When he helped to lay out Pardee he made it a part of the charter that if liquor should ever be sold on any lot of the town the deed to that lot should be forfeited. His idea was to have a small village, with a good church and school, as the center of a moral and intelligent farming community. He took great interest in schools, Sunday-schools, literary societies, and temperance work ; in everything, in fact, which tended to the moral and intellectual improvement of the young, or to the well-being of society in general.

He spent much time in writing and lecturing on temperance, both before and after the passage of the Prohibitory Amendment. His articles in the papers denouncing the violation of the prohibitory law as rebellion against the Constitution, and all the sympathizers with the law-breakers, as rebels, stirred up such an excitement that when he went to Atchison he could scarcely walk the streets on account of the people, both friends and opponents, who stopped him on every turn, to talk of prohibition. The Germans all wanted to discuss the matter with him ; but one of the leading Germans said to him one day, "You must not expect us old Germans, who have brought our habits from the old country, to change ; but go ahead, Mr. Butler ! Go ahead ! The young men are with you."

Father was sometimes accused of "dabbling in politics." If that means that he was an office-seeker, the charge is false. Though often urged by his friends to run for office, he invariably refused, telling them that he considered the office of a Christian preacher the highest office on earth. But he did think it his duty to attend elections and primary meetings, and work against the whisky ring. He often spent much time, in the fall, speaking and writing to secure the election of temperance men for county officers. The final effort by which he succeeded in arousing a public sentiment strong enough to compel the county officers to close the saloons, was a stirring speech he made at a temperance meeting in Atchison, in the spring of 1885.

Some have thought that father was hard-hearted. Plain-spoken he certainly was, and sometimes harsh in dealing with those whom he thought to be doing wrong. He was so thoroughly in earnest that when he thought a certain way right or wrong, it was hard for him to understand that some other way might be equally right or wrong.

Naturally high-tempered, with a very excitable, nervous organization, it was often a matter of wonder to me to see how much self-control he exercised, under irritating circumstances. He sometimes lost his self-control, and said things that would better have been left unsaid ; but when he saw that he had done so he was ready to beg pardon for the offense. But he was kind-hearted and forgiving, and ready to forget injuries done to him.

No matter how harshly he might speak of an opponent, or wrong-doer, he would often turn right around and do him a kindness.

One of the men who helped to raft him wrote to him three or four years ago, saying that he was writing an account of the Kansas troubles, and asking him for some information on points that he had forgotten. Father readily complied with his request, telling him that he freely forgave him, and all the rest of his old-time enemies.

Father was always ready to help the poor, the oppressed, or unfortunate. It was that spirit of sympathy for the weaker party that led him to side with Horace Greely in 1872, because he thought the Republicans were too hard on the conquered Southerners. But when he heard of the widespread Ku-Klux outrages, he concluded that he had been mistaken, and returned heartily to the Republican party.

I heard a neighbor say a few years ago : "If any one needs help, just go to Bro. Butler. I never heard of him refusing to help anybody that was in trouble, no matter how much time or trouble it cost him."

Another neighbor had his house burned. He was old and feeble, and unable to rebuild. Other neighbors thought they had done their part when they raised a subscription to build him a new house. But cold weather was coming on, necessitating haste. Father, not content with giving money, looked after buying materials, and putting up the building ; sent his teams to do the hauling ; and, because the ground was freezing up, worked until late at night, digging out sand to plaster it. And this was but one of the many instances of his practical kind-heartedness.

He attended the State Meeting at Hutchinson about a year before his death, where he had been invited to deliver a historical address, sketching his own life and work, and the history of our churches in Kansas. He was urgently requested to publish it, and from that circumstance came the publication, in the *Christian Standard*, of his "Recollections."

Bro. F. M. Rains said of that address, "That was the grandest speech ever delivered on Kansas soil."

The Hutchinson *Daily News* spoke of it as follows :

"The address was a happy blending of church history, and personal reminiscence, full of fact, humor and pathos, and, most of all, devotion to freedom, morality, temperance, and godliness. Few people of today are able to appreciate the privations, and sacrifices, and dangers, with

which the pioneer was beset, and these dangers came with special near-
ness to the man whose mission, courage and conscience made him the
open and avowed foe of all sorts of wickedness. The house was packed
with intense listeners, and from beginning to end he held the great audience in close attention, and when he finished, the hope that grand old
Pardee Butler might live a hundred years was the unexpressed wish
of all."

Father was always fluent in prayer, and his peti-
tions earnest and timely ; but in the last year or two of
his life his prayers seemed to grow more fervent and
impressive. Mrs. Hendryx, of Wichita, writing to me
since his death, speaks thus of a prayer offered by him
at the Hutchinson Convention : '' Never, while consciousness shall last, will I forget the ring of your
father's voice in prayer, at Hutchinson. I asked,
' Who is that aged veteran ? he seems almost inspired.'
And they told me it was Pardee Butler."

The earnestness and appropriateness of his prayers
were most noticeable on several funeral occasions, and
numbers spoke of being affected by them, particularly
at Bro. Locker's funeral.

He preached his last sermon at North Cedar, a week
and a half before his accident. The following Saturday, September 15, he attended Bro. Locker's funeral.
The next day he attended Bro. Parker's meeting at
Pleasant Grove, where he presided at the Lord's table.

He had several appointments ahead at the time he
was hurt. One of these was to preach the funeral of
his old friend, Caleb May, who had died in Florida,
August 27. His children in Florida had sent a request
to his son, E. E. May, of Farmington, that father
should preach a memorial sermon at Pardee.

Father had not done any heavy work for two years,
but he still did much light work, and choring, although

his health was gradually failing, milking eight or ten cows a day, and driving a young team from ten to twenty miles to his appointments, almost every Sunday, seldom stopping for bad weather.

It was reported that he was thrown from a colt at the time he was hurt. My brothers wish that report corrected. They think he never was thrown from a horse in his life. They had seen him break many colts, and had never seen him thrown. He had been using the most spirited colt on the place for his riding horse all summer; but that day, September 19, it was in a distant pasture, and finding my brother Charley's colt in the stable, he thought he would ride it to the post-office. It would not stand for him to mount, and he put the halter around a post, holding the end in his hand. As he mounted the saddle the colt jerked both halter and bridle from his hand and trotted off. Unable to reach the bridle he hastily dismounted. As he swung his right foot around to the ground the colt kicked it, crushing the ankle joint. He quietly called mother; and Brother May, who happened to be passing, helped him into the house, and sent for a surgeon.

We feared no worse result at the first than a crippled ankle. He said to Bro. White, who visited him a few days after he was hurt, "Oh, I will get up all right; a Butler never was conquered, you know. My only concern is that I shall not become a permanent cripple."

The first week he was hopeful, though suffering much pain. The second week he was delirious, with high fever. Then he was prostrated with a severe nervous chill—his already over-wrought nervous system was exhausted by pain. From that time he lay in an unconscious stupor the greater part of the time. He passed quietly away at half-past three A. M., October 19, 1888, at the age of seventy-two.

His funeral took place the following day in the church at Pardee. The services were conducted by Elders John Boggs, of Clyde, and J. B. McCleery, of Fort Leavenworth. The house was full, notwithstanding it was a stormy day, raining continuously from morning until night. Word had been sent to all the churches in this and adjacent counties, and hundreds who were preparing to attend the funeral were disappointed by the inclement weather.

CHAPTER XL.

PRO-SLAVERY HINDRANCES.

By Elder John Boggs.

Although our dear departed brother, Elder Pardee
Butler, was never classed with the Garrisonian Abolitionists, he began his ministerial life when the demands
of the South were being felt in all the North, both in
church and State. If slavery could not be advocated by
the Northern conscience it must at least be ignored by
all candidates for popular favor. It had divided some of
the most popular religious denominations; and was the
most exciting subject of discussion known to the religious world at the middle of the present century. Among
the Disciples of Christ the slavery question was peculiarly perplexing, as there was a large per cent. of the
membership who were actual slaveholders, and the
leaders among us, although publicly committed against
"*slavery in the abstract*," were endeavoring to soften the
hard features of slavery in the Southern States by
arguing that the relation of master and slave was not
sinful *per se*, as it was recognized and regulated both
in the Jewish and Christian scriptures.

Bro. Butler was ordained as a minister of the gospel of Christ, among the Disciples, at Sullivan, Ohio,
some time in the year 1844, by A. B. Green and J. H.
Jones, at that time two of the most efficient evangelists in

Northern Ohio. He had a good conscience, which passed judgment upon his actions in accordance with the great law of love inculcated by the Lord himself and his apostles, and he did not allow the application of any "hot iron" so as to sear it. Although he did not come in direct antagonism with the pro-slavery power while he labored in the gospel ministry east of the Missouri River, yet it is evident that the slavery question was a most important factor in making up his decision to leave his field of labor in the Military Tract in Illinois, where he gave up present usefulness and ministerial blessedness for a prospective missionary field and a humble home for his family. He had spent four years there in active ministerial labor; and in the second number of his "Personal Recollections" he calls them "the golden days of my life!"

That the hand of God directed the footsteps of Pardee Butler to Kansas just at the time he went there, and to the place where he took a homestead and improved it, and lived on it with his family for a third of a century, no one who believes in an overruling providence can for a moment doubt. At the risk of his life, and at the cost of great privation in his own person, and that of his wife and children, he unfurled the blood-stained banner of the cross, and never allowed it to trail beneath his feet through the long years of "border ruffianism," and the dark days of detraction and misrepresentation. He was the man for the hour; while on the one hand he was not forgetful of the obligations resting upon him to his family—he laid the foundation for a happy home—on the other hand, he was always ready, both in season and out of season, at home and abroad, to preach the unsearchable riches of

Jesus Christ to a lost and dying world.   To him more than to any other human instrumentality is the brother-hood of Christ's disciples indebted for the early intro-duction of Christianity in the now grand State of Kan-sas; and his name will be honorably and lovingly re-membered by all the good and the true, who shall learn of his unselfish life and his untiring devotion to the cause of the Master.

In the summer of 1858, after he had been in the new Territory over three years, Bro. Butler, in the *Luminary*, writes as follows: " To teach, discipline, and perfect the churches we have already organized; to gather into churches the lost sheep of the house of Israel, scattered over this great wilderness of sin ; to watch over those who are still purposing to tempt its dangers, and to lay broad and deep the foundations of a future operation and co-operation, that shall ultimate in spreading the gospel from pole to pole, and across the great sea to the farthest domicile of man—this is the purpose which we set before us."   This brief quo-tation shows the broadness and completeness of the work, as contemplated by him, and which is now go-ing forward to its accomplishment as never before; and to his almost alone labors at first the work in Kansas can be legitimately traced.

During this year a Territorial Board was formed, and Bro. Butler was appointed as their evangelist; and a correspondence was had between him and the corre-sponding secretary of the General Missionary Society in reference to affording aid to the Kansas Board to help sustain him in his evangelical labors.   It was conducted in the most friendly manner and in a true Christian spirit, until the slavery question came to the front and prevented the accomplishment of what was hoped for on the one hand, and contemplated on the other. The following extract from Bro. Butler's third letter will present the issue in the briefest manner possible:

DEAR SIR:—You say in letter before me, " It must, therefore, be distinctly understood that if we embark in a missionary enterprise in Kansas, this question of slavery and anti-slavery must be ignored." I respond: This reformation is pledged before heaven and earth, and under covenants the most solemn and binding into which men can enter, to guarantee freedom of thought and speech to our brotherhood—not indeed on subjects purely abstract, speculative and inoperative, but on Bible questions—questions which involve the well-being of humanity. This matter of slavery is a Bible question—a question of justice between man and man—of mercy and humanity. It is what Jesus would call one of the weightier matters of the law, and demands, therefore, a large place in our investigations.

.   .   .   .

The brethren here in Kansas have made no such stipulations with me They have left me to my own discretion in preaching the gospel to sinners, and teaching the saints according to the Bible. They have shown themselves too magnanimous to impose on my conscience a restriction which their own manhood would forbid, under similar circumstances, that they should suffer to be imposed on themselves.

For myself, I will be no party, now or hereafter, to such an arrangement as that contemplated in your letter now before me. I would not make this "Reformation of the nineteenth century" a withered and blasted trunk, scattered by the lightnings of heaven, because it took part with the rich and powerful against the poor and oppressed, and because we have been recreant to those maxims of free discussion which we have so ostentatiously heralded to the world as our cherished principles.

In explanation of the first letter received by Bro. Butler from the corresponding secretary, a second one was sent, from which it is necessary to make the following extracts:

I reply, that nothing has been said against teaching a master his duties according to the Bible, nor (what is just as important) against teaching servants their duties to their masters, according to the Bible—

according to the instructions given to evangelists—I. Tim. vi. 1-4. My remarks, as the whole letter will show, had reference to the question of slavery *in Kansas.* The forms it takes on there are very different from the duties masters owe their servants according to the Bible. It is whether a slaveholder is necessarily a sinner, unfit for membership in the Christian Church—a blood-thirsty oppressor, whose money is the "price of blood," and would "pollute" the treasury of the Lord, etc. etc. And, on the other hand, whether American slavery is a divine institution, the perfection of society for the African race, and essential to their happiness—while all Abolitionists are fit only for the mad-house or the penitentiary. These and such like are the *forms* the question of slavery assumes in Kansas, as well as in many of the free States, where there are no "masters and servants" in that sense to be taught their duties, in reference to which it was said the question must be entirely ignored. And we can not consent that on one side or the other such pleas shall be made under the sanction of the American Christian Missionary Society.

I did not then, nor do I now, suppose that if you were employed by the A. C. M. S. to preach the gospel in Kansas, it would fall to your lot to furnish instructions to many masters and servants. If in any churches you may raise up in Kansas—evidently destined to be free—you find masters and slaves, of course it will be your duty to instruct them both "according to the Bible." But to furnish such instruction, and to go through Kansas lecturing on anti-slavery, or mixing up any pro-slavery or any anti-slavery theories and dogmas with the gospel, or to plant churches with the express understanding that no "master" shall be allowed to have membership in it, are very different things. And I had this very matter in view when I wrote to you, for I had somehow heard that the church of which you were a member was about to take just such a stand, and I wanted to have it distinctly understood that so far as action under the direction of the A. C. M. S. was concerned, all such ultraisms must be ignored. . . . . . . You felt anxious to have help to preach the gospel in Kansas. I felt anxious to assist you. I saw danger in the way, growing out of the fact that I represent a society whose membership is in the South as well as in the North, and that some factious ultraists are constantly on the watch to sow the seeds of discord. I knew the state of things in Kansas as bearing on the slavery question. I knew something, too, of your treatment there, and of your feelings. I saw that if you were employed to preach there, an effort would be made to herald it, as in Bro. Beardslee's case, as an anti-slavery triumph. This would be unjust to us. And as the practical question of master and slave does not exist there to any extent, I spoke of ignoring the question altogether. If you still insist on the right to urge that question, and take part in the controversy raging in Kansas, *under the patronage of the A. C. M. S.*, I have only to say it is outside the objects contemplated in our constitution. But if you wish simply to preach the gospel and instruct converts in a knowledge of Christian duties, "according to the Scriptures," there was certainly no occasion for your second letter to be written.

To the foregoing a rejoinder was written by Bro. Butler, which closed the correspondence with the A. C. M. S., and from which the following extracts are taken, that the readers may understand his position correctly:

I reply, 1. In your former letter I find no reference to the *forms* the agitation of this question assumes in Kansas. I presume you had not a copy of that letter before you when you wrote this one. But you do allude to "forms" the agitation of this question had assumed in Cincinnati, and in reference to Bro. Beardslee and the Jamaica mission. I was also instructed that " our missionaries" must not be ensnared into such utterances as the *Luminary* can publish to the world, to add fuel to the flame. The utterances against which I was guarded *seemed* to be in Cincinnati rather than in Kansas. I had already published a piece indicative of my views in the *Northwestern Christian Magazine*, and that appeared to be the obnoxious "utterance." 2. You are misinformed relative to the "forms" the agitation of this question assumes in Kansas. The question, Shall slaveholders be received as church members? has hardly been debated at all. 3. Neither myself nor any person associated with me has at time proposed to organize a church to exclude slaveholders. 4. Slaveholders have been members of our churches from the first day until now. How, then, could I understand you as referring to anything else than to my own published Cincinnati utterances?

. . . .

As respects slavery, the whole power of the master and the obligation of the servant is found in the proper meaning of the words of such precepts as these " Masters, render unto your servants that which is just and equal;" "servants, obey your masters," etc. All within such limits is the doctrine which is according to godliness—all beyond, whether on the part of the master or the slave, and which is attempted to be foisted into the church as a part of the apostolic doctrine, is schismatical, and

essentially fills up the picture drawn by Paul : " If any man teach otherwise, and consent not to wholesome words, even the words of our Lord
Jesus Christ, and to the doctrine which is according to godliness; he is
proud, knowing nothing '—from such withdraw thyself." In these precepts no right is given to the masters to buy and sell, to traffic in slaves;
no right to enslave the children, and the children's children of his servants; no right to hold them in a relentless bondage which knows no
limit but the grave, and in which the heritage transmitted by the slave
to his children, is a heritage of bondage to all generations.

On the 26th of August, 1858, the same season that
the foregoing correspondence took place, Bro. Butler
wrote to the editor of the *Christian Luminary* the following letter, which is given entire, as showing the
exact position which he occupied ministerially at that
time :

OCENA, ATCHISON CO., KAN., Aug. 26, 1858.

DEAR SIR :—Three churches—one meeting at Leavenworth City,
another at Mount Pleasant, Atchison county, and a third at Pardee,
same county—have formed an organization for the purpose of propagat-
ting the gospel in Kansas. For four months I have been in the employ
of these churches. My first business was to travel over the Territory
and ascertain where we have brethren in sufficient numbers to make it
expedient to organize churches. To that end I have traveled over that
portion of the Territory north of the Kansas River, and embraced in
the counties of Leavenworth, Atchison, Doniphan, Jefferson, and Calhoun; also, to some extent south of the Kansas River.

I will not say that this has been the pleasantest labor of my life.
A long and wearisome ride across wide prairies, under a burning sun,
has often been followed by a fruitless effort to excite interest enough to
justify established preaching. I would not convey the idea that this
region is not full of promise to the missionary, notwithstanding I am fully
persuaded that we are not to expect such *immediate* results as have followed my own labors elsewhere. We must first sow, and then, in due
time, we shall reap, if we faint not.

The M. E. Church reports 120 preachers in Kansas and Nebraska;
the U. B. Church, 9, sustained in part by contributions from abroad.
The Missionary Baptists make good their right to the name they have
chosen, by sustaining four missionaries. I confess it is a matter of pro-
found humiliation to me that the demonstration that ours is primitive,

apostolic Christianity, is found in the fact that we can afford but one missionary in Kansas, and that to his support not one dime has been contributed from abroad. The brethren in the Territory, under an unexampled pecuniary pressure, and out of their deep poverty, have done all that has been done. Two new churches have been organized—one at Big Springs, Douglas county, numbering twenty-eight members; the other at Cedar Creek, Jefferson county, of eleven members. We have also the nucleus of a congregation at Atchison, and another at Elk City, Calhoun county. Thus we have in this part of Kansas the foundation laid for eight churches, all of which are steadily increasing in numbers; and the brethren composing them, in all the elements of future growth, and in moral and in religious excellence, are at par value with the brotherhood in any of our States or Territories.

If the older churches, blessed with such abundant means, would aid us in this hour of our need, it is my opinion they would be no poorer on earth and much richer in heaven. But whether they aid us or not, I trust we shall hold our own, and ultimately prove that the weapons of our warfare are not carnal, but mighty through God to the pulling down of strongholds, casting down imaginations and every high thing that exalts itself against the knowledge of God. We have a number of young preachers, who are giving promise of future usefulness.

Very truly, your brother,

PARDEE BUTLER.

P. S.—Five persons in this congregation, and one at Big Springs have been recently added by baptism; also two from other denominations.

On the 1st day of July, 1859, Bro. Butler made a very interesting report of his labors, and especially of his tour in several of the free States—mostly where he had labored in the gospel before his removal to Kansas. As the document is too long for publication entire in this volume, only the more important extracts can be given. The first two paragraphs being only a fuller statement of what is already written, the first extract will show the voluntary indorsement of Bro. Butler by the churches for which he had been laboring, as follows:

WHEREAS, Bro. Butler has faithfully and diligently performed the labor assigned him as our evangelist; therefore,

Resolved, 1. That we do most heartily approve of his labors and general course of conduct during his term of service. 2. That the officers of this Board be directed to procure the services of Bro. Butler, or some other suitable person, to solicit aid in the States for this society.   ·

Bro. Humber, as president of the Board, did not call it together to complete the arrangement contemplated. On my own part, I felt unwilling to importune him. I went on my tour, therefore, simply under the indorsement and approval of my own congregation. I left home December 16, 1858, and returned May 12, 1859. I visited the Military Tract of Illinois, Northeast Iowa, Southwest Michigan, Central and Eastern Indiana, and Northern Ohio. The amount of money realized was $365; expenses, $110, leaving a balance on hand of $255, as the first installment of the fund of our begun mission.

Of all the churches in which I sought a hearing only one, the church at Bedford, Ohio, gave me the cold shoulder. In response to my request for the privilege of delivering a lecture before them, in development of our wants and condition in Kansas, they responded that they considered it "political," and they had resolved that their house should not be used for political lectures! . . . . In all the localities visited by me, I found the masses of the people with such convictions as will constrain them to treat slavery in the United States as a moral evil, and to patronize only such societies as assume toward it a similiar position. It is asked: What have we to do with slavery? I reply: We, as Christians, should have nothing to do with it. But we in Kansas are placed under compulsion to have something to do with it. We have slaveholders in our churches; and if the time should come when there will be no slaves in Kansas, still we have something to do with it, for within one day's ride of us in Platte county, Mo., is the largest body of slaveholders in that State. Discipline is special to each congregation, but that sense of justice which always stands as the basis of discipline, is common to all the churches of one communion. This public opinion is created by a mutual interchange of sentiment—the books we read and the preachers we hear. For years past slaveholders have ceased to hear those suspected of abolitionism or to read their writings. I will bear very long with error where mutual discussion and free interchange of sentiment promise ultimately to bring all to be of the same mind. Am I told that the safety of slave property requires that Abolitionists should not be heard in the slave States? I reply: The more shame to

those who perpetuate an institution that demands for its security the tyranny of such proscription; and that the human soul of the black man should be so cruelly dwarfed and robbed of his manhood. . . .
. . . . Such are the not very flattering impressions made on my mind during a five months' tour in Northern Ohio, after an absence of nine years. There must and will be a reform; it has become a public necessity. Temporizers are proverbially short-sighted. God gives only to the pure-hearted the divine privilege of foreseeing the coming of those beneficent revolutions, which exalt and dignify humanity. Ambitious and selfish men are left to go blindly on and fall into their own pit. At present there will be chaos! The people will not follow those who have been accustomed to lead, notwithstanding those leaders will have power greatly to embarrass the action of those who do not follow them. We have three pressing wants: 1. A *sustained* paper that will not bow the knee to the image of this modern Baal. Such a paper we have, but it should not be concealed, that it must pass through a fiery ordeal, and can only be sustained by the timely efforts of its friends. 2. We need a convention made up of men who regard slavery as a moral evil, and are disposed to make their own consciences the rule of their action. 3. We need a missionary fund, which shall be placed in such hands that it shall not be prostituted to the vile purpose of bribing men into silence on the subject of slavery.

I am not commissioned specially to speak for the *Luminary*, nor to prophesy concerning any convention which may hereafter assemble. I only speak for myself. Let it then be candidly admitted that the fund which I have been able to collect is a rather unpromising beginning, and that it does not augur that this mission will be well sustained. I remark, then, I never was adequately sustained. I have been a frontier and a pioneer preacher, and have shared the fortunes of such men. To keep myself in the field I have labored very hard, I have toiled by day, and have subjected my family to the necessity of such labor, privation, and close economy as, perhaps, calls for rebuke instead of praise. The churches at Davenport, Long Grove, De Witt, Marion, and Highland Grove, in Iowa; and Camp Point, Mt. Sterling, and Rushville, in Illinois, can be addressed as to my former manner of life. I would speak modestly of myself; and have not obtruded these matters before the brethren until rudely assailed as though I never made any sacrifices. I do not complain, and what I have said is offered as evidence, in some sort, that money appropriated to this mission will not be squandered.

In this connection it is thought proper to insert a single quotation from a letter which appeared in the *Review*, a paper which published editorially, the most unscrupulous slanders in reference to Bro. Butler's work in Kansas, which letter was written by Bro. S. A. Marshall, of Leavenworth—both an M. D. and a preacher, and than whom no more honorable gentleman ever lived in that city. His testimony is incidental, and therefore so much the stronger:

The brethren of the four churches named have tried to co-operate together to sustain Bro. Pardee Butler as home missionary for a little while. He is an able evangelist and generally beloved; and being on the ground and well acquainted with the country, and the manners and customs of the people, could be obtained at much less expense, and perhaps be as useful and acceptable to the people as any other available evangelist.

In harmony with the suggestion made by Bro. Butler in his report, for a convention of our brethren who look upon slavery as a moral evil, call was made for such a meeting to convene in the city of Indianapolis on the 1st day of November, 1859. About six hundred signatures were attached to the call, including many of the most intelligent and influential members of our churches in the North. After much misrepresentation and denunciation, the convention was held in the Christian chapel in Indianapolis; a constitution for a missionary society adopted and the necessary officers appointed. Many of the churches gave it a most hearty endorsement. It was deemed expedient that Bro. Butler, before returning to Kansas, should visit as many churches as practicable. Accordingly, he wrote to the *Luminary* under date of December 26, 1859, from Springville, Ind., as follows:

I have thought best, before returning to Kansas, to make a short visit to this part of Indiana, where, according to report, almost all the brethren are opposed to our recent missionary movement. In twenty-three days I have preached thirty-two discourses. For the mission we raised, cash, $55; pledges, $43. Three have been added by baptism, and one from the Presbyterians who had formerly been immersed. Some of our preaching brethren in this part of the State conclude to take the advice of Gamaliel: "And now I say unto you, refrain from these men, and let them alone; for if this counsel or this work be of men, it will come to naught; but if it be of God, ye can not overthrow it; lest happily ye be found even to fight against God." In the cause of a common piety and a common humanity.

Bro. Butler returned to Kansas, and resumed his labors wherever a door of entrance was opened to him. Angry clouds thickened across the political and religious horizon, until, shortly, the storm broke forth in unwonted fury, and swept away from the national statute book every vestige of American slavery. For a quarter of a century longer he continued in the service of the Master, laboring successfully in every department of the ministerial work—evangelical, pastoral, and in the advocacy of all moral reforms, and especially as a leader in the warfare waged against the saloon interest in Kansas. He lived to see his adopted State take an advanced position in the legal prohibition movement, slavery in the United States abolished, and the cause of Bible Christianity flourishing as it had never done before. He commanded the respect of all who knew him, and was regarded as one of the chief founders of the church. His presence at all the Christian conventions in and out of the State was always hailed with tokens of gladness. Still he was aware that there were individual members, and even some churches that never forgave him for the active part he took against the extension of slavery, and his indictments against it as a moral evil—a sin against God and man. Fifty years of his eventful life were consecrated to the service of the Master and the good of humanity. He died with the ministerial harness on. At the time of the sad casualty which proved to be fatal, he had arrangements for continued work in the churches, both at home and abroad. He finished his course with joy, for he knew there was laid up for him in heaven a crown of righteousness. He labored assiduously in life, and now enjoys the sweet rest which remains for the people of God.

CHAPTERL XLI.

TEMPERANCE AND CHURCH WORK.

By Eld. J. B. McCleery.

ANALYSIS OF CHARACTER.

1. An indomitable will.
2. A sublime courage.
3. A never-satisfied hungering and thirst for knowledge.
4. An intense love for truth, and hatred of shams.
5. A tireless worker.
6. An advanced thinker.

In presenting this analysis it is by no means thought to be complete. There are many phases of his well-known character left untouched, because this chapter would become a book, if all were presented in detail. We touch upon these more salient ones, as presenting the well-known outlines of his later life, and trust the picture will find faithful recognition among his host of admirers.

Those who have known him ever since the past Territorial days of Kansas, will concede that, for the accomplishment of a purpose unto which he had once deliberately put his hand, no man ever breathed the fresh air of these broad prairies who followed the trail

with more determination and keen, intelligent acquaintance with all bearings, overcoming difficulties, meeting
objections, accepting temporary defeat (pnilosophic-
ally), but never relinquishing his purpose until victory crowned his effort, or failure was absolutely inevitable, than he.

Suited to this was a courage as heroic as Leonidas'
and sublime as Paul's. The stormy days of the fifties
and sixties gave evidence of the physical side of this
quality, and his entire life, of the moral. He "feared
no foe in shining armor," and rather courted than
avoided a passage at arms dialectic. Eminently a man
of peace, and loving the pursuits that make for it, he
would see no principle of right unjustly assailed without girding himself for the conflict, and standing where
the blows fell thickest.

Coming to this unknown country at an age when
the ordinary mind takes firmest grasp of all intellectual
things, and being thus deprived of that mental food
necessary to satisfy and make strong, there was ever
after a hungering for the things he did not have, that
would not be satisfied. I remember talking with him
once, while sitting on his lumber wagon, resting his
team in the cotton-wood bottoms east of Atchison,
and he bewailed as much as a man of his fiber could,
the fate that compelled him to toil day and night while
his soul was starving for that intellectual food which
lay all around him, but which he did not have time to
gather and devour. This, however, was not abnormal;
for, even to the day of his death, he was a devoted disciple, sitting at the feet of every true Gamaliel.

An intense lover of truth, and a like hater of shams,
he analyzed mercilessly; not for the sake of opposing,

but in search of kernels and the source of things.   If
he found the tree was bearing, or destined to bear
evil fruit, he would do his utmost that there should be
left of it neither root nor branch.   Accepting good in
every presented form, if he suspected evil in the garb
of good, there was no waiting for a more opportune
time than the then present, for such stripping and exposure as his vigorous logic, sarcasm, wit, pathos, and
personal presence could produce.   Humble, and exceedingly retiring in ordinary, when the truth was assailed, or wolves in sheeps' clothing appeared, he became a lion, fierce and towering; and woe betake the
man or system that then became the object of his
righteous wrath.   Such torrents of invective as fell
from his tongue; such flashes as gleamed from his gray
eagle-eyes; such scorn as glowed in his thin, pallid
lips, made every one tremble—an avalanche that swept
all before it.

To toil, of some character or other, he seemed to
be destined.   For no sooner did he find a little rest
from the field or herd, than all his Hurculean energy
was thrown into some cherished and waiting mental
project.   His life is an example of the statement that
" genius is the result of labor."   Neither did he travel
in thought alone upon the surface of things.   There
were subjects, the philosophy of which no contempor-
ary understood better; and upon the social and
organic relations of the religious reformation with
which he always stood identified, he was twenty years
ahead of his confreres.   He was a veritable Elijah in
many things, but he was never known to flee from the
face of his enemies.

His was a mighty nature ; the soul of honor and the embodiment of truth.

There are two features of his Kansas life, which marked the man, that I wish to portray, viz: His *temperance* work, and his *religious* work. These were not in any sense divorced, as though they were not always righteously allied ; but, as all know, the prohibition question holds a prominent place in the history of this proud young queen, with her "*ad astra per aspera*," and from the time she was admitted to a place among the sisterhood of States, up to the date that the comparatively little majority of 8,000 votes placed her squarely in opposition to the saloon, with all its interests and iniquities, he labored, watched, and prayed, for such a consummation. In this, as in his religious conceptions, he was always in the advance, running new lines and opening broad highways, and inviting fields for the less sturdy but oncoming multitude. As he had battled to prevent this, his adopted State, from being dessecrated by the blot of human slavery, so now he voted, preached, lectured, wrote, that it might be delivered from the body and soul destroying curse of the rum power.

I have before me his temperance scrap-book, beginning with the proposed amendment to the State Constitution, March 8, 1879, and coming up to the time of his death, in which I find fifty-five newspaper articles written by him, of from one to three columns in length, presenting, in his own terse, humorous, glowing, vigorous, convincing way, all sides of this chameleon-hued question ; now analyzing the amendment and the laws to enforce it, turning aside here to answer the cavil of some carping critic, then to demolish and bury some blatant political defender of the whisky element; arraigning the Governor, Senate and House of Representatives for their gingerly treatment of the great question, and sending a trumpet-call to the honest, brave, and sincere temperance workers, both men and women, urging them to greater vigilance and closer compact. These, with numerous short and pithy articles, added to all his sermons and lectures on the subject, occupying a much larger space and far more time, will give an idea of the labor of heart and brain bestowed upon this one question, during this one decade. We have room in this chapter for only one short article from his pen, as an example of the many, indicating how he felt, thought, and wrote during those stirring years. The title of the article is, "The Prohibition of the Liquor Traffic. The Constitutional Amendment in Kansas." He says:

This is, perhaps, the first case in which any government in the world has incorporated into its constitution a clause prohibiting forever the sale of intoxicating drinks as a beverage. This is a struggle in which the churches, the preachers, and the Sunday-schools are arrayed in mortal antagonism to the saloons and saloon-keepers. Both parties are instinctively conscious that this is a contest in which the issue is to kill or be killed. No truce or peace is possible. 'I will put enmity between thy seed and her seed.' The people are drawn into one or the other of these parties by a sort of elective affinity. One class goes with the churches and the Sunday-schools; another gravitates to the drinking-house. The one class are swayed and controlled by the law of love— "Thou shalt love thy neighbor as thyself;" the other by the principle that governed Cain—"Am I my brother's keeper?" "Who cares?" "Let every man look out for himself?" "If a man chooses to make a beast of himself, it is none of my business."

One of the peculiar things connected with this movement is the fact that by far the most determined and effective opposition to this law comes from foreign-born and naturalized citizens. They have, so to speak, monopolized the liquor traffic; they are bound together by a kind of free masonry, and with small regard to whom they vote with, Demo-crats or Republicans, they give the whole weight of their political influ ence in favor of free liquor.

With here and there a notable exception, the Roman Catholic Church throws its influence on the same side; hence its church fairs are carnivals of drunkenness.

The two extremes of our American society do also largely join in this clamor for free liquor. "The upper ten thousand," those that arrogate to themselves that they are par excellence, the *élite* of the nation—albeit that their assumed gentility is sometimes but a shoddy or shabby gentility—make the road from the top of society to the bottom, and from thence to hell, as short as possible, by assuming that it is aristocratic to tipple.

When from these so-called upper circles, we go down to the bot-tom of society, what shall we say of that great multitude of men and women, crushed into poverty, helplessness and ignorance, groping as the blind grope in darkness; and who find in the dram-shop a momentary oblivion to their miseries?

To these elements of opposition to prohibition we must add another class of men—the professional politicians. These, like the chameleon, take the color of every object they light on. To them the good Lord and the good devil are equally objects of respect, and possible worship; and, having all mental endowments accurately developed, except the en-dowment of conscience, they hold that all things are legitimate that bring grist to their mill. These will be good prohibitionists when prohibition dances in silver slippers; but now they do duty on the other side.

The above picture contains a very fair analysis of the elements of the vote in opposition to the prohibitory amendment, except that, per-haps, we ought to add the vote in opposition to a well-intended class of men who have no proclivity for liquor, and who, perhaps, could give no better reason for their vote but that they abhor innovations, and are con-tent to do as their fathers and grandfathers did before them.

Notwithstanding, prohibition carried in the State by eight thou-sand majority. It is noteworthy that six counties, lying along the Mis-souri River, and having in or near them the cities of Atchison, Leaven-worth, Wyandotte, White Cloud and Kansas City, and which also contain the largest foreign-born population in the State, gave heavy majorities against the amendment.

It is self-evident that if the execution of this law is left to the municipal authorities of the above-named cities, or to the officers elected in the above-named counties, then the saloon keepers and liquor dealers will, without let or hindrance, trample under foot both the constitution and laws. The proof of this lies in the fact that, in time past, the liquor dealers have ridden rough-shod over all laws enacted in the interest of temperance. For example, the law provided that they should not sell to boys under age; the law provided that they should not sell on the Lord's day. The law forbids bribing at elections; but the bribery of strong drink at elections, in the cities, has been just as common as the elections; and church members, and even preachers, who were candidates for office, have been blackmailed to get the money to buy the liquor.

It will be asked, What, then, do we gain who live in these river counties, and in these cities, by the passage of this prohibitory law? We gain much.

1. Thus far these law-breaking liquor dealers have acted, in carrying on their business, under the shadow and protection of law. This protection is now withdrawn.

2. The government has hitherto been in partnership with liquor dealers in the infamous business of making drunkards. This partnership is now dissolved.

3. The appetite for strong drink is not a natural appetite. It is an appetite artificially created in children, boys and young men. It is not for the public welfare that it should be created at all. The scheme and plan of the popular saloon is to create this appetite, and to strengthen and foster it after it is created.

The whole business of the saloon looks in this direction. To this end are its flashing lights, its glittering decanters, its rainbow tints, its jolly good fellowship and boon companionship, and the *bonhomie* of the portly saloonkeeper. All these, in the purpose and intent for which they exist, mean the death of the body and the soul of the man that enters these gates that lead down to hell. The saloon is a serpent, with the serpent's fascinating beauty and power to charm, but with the serpent's deadly bite. "At the last it biteth like a serpent and stingeth like an adder." Kansas has wisely ordained that it will not maintain by the public authority and at the public expense poisonous serpents to sting the people to death.

4. Men object: "The selling of liquor will go on, but you will drive the business into dark places and into the hands of disreputable men." To this temperance men reply: "That is just what we want. We wish to take away every vestige of respectability from the man that sells liquor. We intend that it shall be sold—if it must be sold at all—in dark cellars and in back alleys, and that the men that sell liquor shall take rank among the law-breaking and dangerous classes of society."

5. The one potent charm and omnipotent argument that has served as a gift to blind the eyes and an opiate to lull to sleep the consciences of the municipal authorities of our cities has been the revenue they have derived from liquor license laws.   For example, the city of Atchison has derived from this source a revenue of $10,000.   This revenue was paid not alone by her own citizens, but by all men who were drawn to the city for purposes of business or pleasure and who could be induced to patronize the saloons.   And this has been a perpetual menace to the safety of families living in the country who did business in the city. This revenue is gone.   It is hopelessly and irrecoverably dried up.   The Missouri river will turn and flow backward towards its source before this revenue, which is the price of blood, like the thirty pieces of silver for which Judas sold his Master, will ever come back again.   After Jesus had cast a legion of demons out of the demoniac that dwelt among the tombs, this man was far more impressible with regard to motives addressed to his better nature than while he was possessed by these demons; so we may charitably hope that now, after ten thousand evil demons have been cast out of the hearts of the mayor and common council of the city of Atchison, these dignitaries will be more impressible with regard to motives of morality, humanity, and of the public welfare.

Meantime, temperance men look on the whole business of liquor license as an unspeakable madness.   Regarded simply as a question of dollars and cents, they look on it as a horrible nightmare—a hallucination fallen on men nearly allied to that form of mental abberration which carries men to mad-houses and insane asylums, a strange and mysterious perversion of the human faculties.   Regarded in its economical aspects, they hold that it would be just as good economy and as much the dictate of common sense, to obtain a revenue by licensing murder, theft, burglary, robbery; and harlotry, as it is to license the sale of intoxicating drinks as a beverage.

It will be seen, then, that prohibition incorporated into the constitution of Kansas, does not, by any means, give us the victory; it only places us in a position to fight a fair and equal battle hereafter.   We are, like Israel, shouting triumphantly, "I will sing unto the Lord, for he hath triumphed gloriously; the horse and his rider hath he drowned in the Red Sea."

But beyond us are parched and desert sands, poisonous serpents, savage wild beasts and mortal enemies.   All these must be conquered before we finally rest in the happy Canaan.

It is now conceded by the best informed actors in this great drama or tragedy, that Pardee Butler, as much or more than any one man, made the prohibition movement in Kansas the marvelous success it is. The generation is yet to come that will rise up to do him rightful honor.

From '54 to '60 Pardee Butler was the Moses to the church in this wilderness, and for years following he was in some sense like Paul, "having the care of all the churches." But from the beginning he was the foremost man by virtue of natural and acquired ability, although a reluctant following was often given because of former habitudes and shibboleths, socially. There were other men in different localities who battled grandly for the truth and sowed the seed of the kingdom with firm and loyal hand: Brethren Yohe and Jackson, of Leavenworth, followed by the Bausermans, Joseph and Henry, Gans of Olathe, Brown of Emporia, White of Manhattan, and others equally worthy,—all pioneers in every good sense, and now all gone to their reward, with the exceptions of Brethren Yohe and the Bausermans. Without being formally chosen Pardee Butler was the recognized leader of these sanctified few, and no home where they entered was too humble, or field where they toiled too barren, for the light of his countenance to cheer, or the strength of his arm to be felt. In the polity and development of the church, as in other fields of moral and social struggle, he was far in advance of the time ; and up to the day of his death, this was one of the great burdens that rested upon his heart.

The membership coming to the Territory, and which, of course, formed the nuclei of churches, was a heterogenous compound. In many respects there was no possible assimilation ; but so far as the simple tenets of the primitive faith were concerned, there was little or no difference. But as to plurality of bishops in the congregation, their tenure and jurisdiction of office, the relations of comity between sister churches, the duties and powers of an evangelist, the laying on of hands in induction into authority, instrumental music in the congregation, the Sunday-school and its organization, the order of social worship, the mid-week meeting for prayer, and numerous other matters of scriptural life, there were as many shades of opinion as there were of dialects ; and the tenacity with which they were maintained, those not familiar with the time and its environments can hardly hope to know. Yet upon all these and kindred questions, Bro. Butler had singularly clear-cut and advanced opinions. He has often said to me, "How very obtuse the churches seem to be on the plain teaching of Scripture. And the preachers are equally ignorant, or else they are willing to go limping and halting, when they could as well and better be easily marching and leading their sanctified hosts to marvelous victory."

He did not feel, or even make manifest, that he recognized his greatness in these directions only as he labored to bring the congregations and their officers up to his ideals.

In the first struggles to bring the scattered congregations into co-operative unity, he was the head and heart of the movement ; and through all the varied successes and failures of those non-cohesive times and men, he never lost courage or intimated aught else than the success which now crowns the work.

I regarded him as the finest ecclesiastical historian among us, and because of his knowledge here, coupled with the philosophy that grew out of it, linked to the genius of Christianity itself, he was, by educational intuition, a missionary zealot.

Carey and the Judsons, and Barclay and Livingstone, with all others of like character, were what he termed "ripe fruit" from the Good Tree. He was to the churches in Kansas what these men and women were to the people among whom they labored. Visiting every outpost, gathering the straggling sheep into folds and striving to secure shepherds for them, stripping the fleecy garments from the wolves, uncovering the sophistries of the various polytheisms, immersing the converts and exhorting the saints, the thirty-five years he spent in Kansas were years of severest mental, moral and physical labor; and from which he asked no respite until God called him.

Truthfully this Scripture may be written as his epitaph: " Blessed are the dead who die in the Lord from henceforth; Yea, saith the Spirit, for they rest from their labors and their works do follow them."

CHAPTER XLII.

The following tributes of friendship were published in the *Atchison Champion*, after father's death :

TWO KANSAS PIONEERS.

BY JOHN A. MARTIN, EX-GOVERNOR OF KANSAS.

Rev. Pardee Butler, who died at his old home, near Farmington, on Saturday last, was, for a full generation past, one of the most prominent figures in Kansas history.   He was a minister of the Christian Church, and located in this county early in 1855.   He came to Kansas to fight slavery. He was a sincere man.   He was a brave man.   He had in him the stuff of which martyrs are made.   He deliberately chose, on coming to the young Territory, the county in which the advocates of slavery seemed to be strongest and most violent.   He made no secret of his opinions on the question of slavery, nor of his purpose to oppose the attempt to make Kansas a slave State.   He was not a fighting man, in the worldly sense of that word ; but in its broader and higher significance, he was an aggressive, fearless, tireless fighter.   He would not kill, but he did not hesitate to brave death.   He would not shoot, but he did not quail or cower before guns, or knives, or ropes.

The *Champion* publishes, this morning, some extracts from its own columns, when it was a newspaper with another name and other principles, narrating some of the incidents of his early life in Kansas.   They are historic.   During a marvelous era they stirred the heart and aroused the conscience of the Nation.   This humble preacher, coming to the Territory for a cause, and bravely enduring the pangs of martyrdom for his opinions, became, at once, the representative of millions of men. The story of his wrongs was told in every newspaper of the land, and was discussed around the firesides of a million homes.   The brutal proslavery mob of Atchison saw in him only an impudent and absurd opponent of an institution that controlled courts, legislatures and congress; the awakening Nation saw that he stood for Free Speech, for Liberty, for Law, and for Humanity; and the indignities heaped upon him touched and stirred the heart of the North in its profoundest depths. Pardee Butler, facing the drunken, ignorant, howling, brutal pro-slavery mobs of Atchison, must have been, to them, a unique figure. They could not understand him. The writer has heard men who were present, but not participants, when the mob had him in charge, say that the mingled hatred and respect with which the ruffians regarded him, was singularly manifest. He bore himself with quiet dignity and composure. He did not attempt to resist, nor, on the other hand, did he manifest the slightest evidence of fear. To their loud and violent threatenings, he made answer with quiet, manly dignity. It would have gratified the ruffians beyond measure if they could have induced him to recant, or to make some pledge that would compromise his frankly expressed opinions—some promise of silence concerning or acquiescence in, or non-interference with, their cherished purpose to establish slavery in Kansas. If he had yielded even so much as this, they would gladly have let him go. But never for a moment did he falter, or waver, or equivocate. He refused to make any promise. He stood upon his rights as an American citizen. He was opposed to slavery in Kansas, and intended to oppose it as long as he lived. He came to Kansas to aid in making it a free State, and no fear of personal injury would change his purpose. He was one man among hundreds, but he intended, then and at all times, in Atchison or elsewhere, to express his convictions, and with voice and vote maintain his opinions. All this he said, quietly and without a trace of boasting, but with a firmness that won from the mob a most unyielding respect.

And this saved him from a worse fate. If he had quailed or equivocated, they would have triumphed; if he had boasted or threatened, they would have hanged him. He did neither. And so they first set him adrift on a raft, and again tarred and feathered him; and on both occasions manly courage and sincere faith were victorious over brute force and mad passion.

Mr. Butler lived his life, during all the years of his residence in this county, illustrating the same lofty purposes and sincere convictions. He was not always correct in his judgments, but he was always earnest. He was interested in every good cause. During his whole life he was an ardent temperance man. He was a practical, as well as an ardent, advocate of temperance, and the organization of the so-called " Third party " prohibitionists, excited, at once, his indignation and contempt. He was one of the first prohibitionists of Kansas to distrust St. John, and to denounce him as a self-seeking, ambitious demagogue. He had no use for any man who was not entirely sincere, or who was not willing to subordinate his own personal interest for the sake of principle.

Among the free State pioneers, of Atchison County, Pardee Butler and Caleb May were first in influence and usefulness. The latter died only a few weeks ago, in Florida. The *Champion* made notice of his death at the time. The two men, in their personal characteristics, had nothing in common. Col. May was a man of very limited education ; Mr. Butler was schooled in books. Col. May had lived all his life on the frontier; Mr. Butler came from one of the oldest communities in Ohio. Col. May believed in the weapons of carnal warfare ; Mr. Butler put his faith in the power of reason. Both were men of approved and unquestionable courage, but if the pro-slavery mob had attempted to capture Col. May, a revolver, held with a steady hand, would have blazed his defiance; Mr. Butler submitted, without resistance to the mob's will. The ruffians did not understand this peaceful but resolute antagonist, but they were compelled to respect his determined purpose. When Col. May wrote to their leader a letter telling the pro-slavery rulers of Atchison that his home was his castle, and if any man attacked it, he would meet with a bloody reception, and that he (May) intended to come to Atchison whenever he pleased, and meant to come armed, they laughed at his rude chirography, and made merry over his " spelling by ear," but they understood his meaning perfectly, and knew, also, that he would do exactly what he said. And they never disturbed him. In his personal appearance Col. May was an ideal " Leatherstockings." He might have sat for a portrait of Cooper's famous frontier hero and Indian trailer. Over six feet in height, angular, muscular, somewhat awkward in repose, with cool, bright gray eyes, deep set under shaggy eyebrows, and having immense reach of arm—his was an imposing figure. Mr. Butler was a born Puritan; Col. May was a born frontiersman.* Mr. Butler opposed slavery on moral grounds, and because he hated injustice or wrong in any form. Col. May hated slavery, and fought it,

---

* Mr. May was not the blustering rough that many people suppose a frontiersman to be. He was a quiet, hard-working farmer, kind and neighborly, but ready to defend his own rights, and those of his friends, or of the poor and downtrodden. His proverbial phrase was, " Whatever I do, I want to do it so well that the world will be none the worse for my having lived in it." His son, E. E. May, says that he used to say that he learned from his Bible to hate slavery. He could lead a prayer-meeting as easily as he could lead a regiment , and he could defend the Scriptures as readily as he could defend his home. I once heard him say that he had never kept a hired man for any length of time, but that he succeeded in persuading him to join the church before he left him.   Mrs. R. B. H.

because he believed the institution was detrimental to his own race. Born in Kentucky and reared in Missouri, he had seen the effects of slavery all about him, harming him and his, and so he hated it.

Kansas owes both of these pioneers a debt of respect and gratitude. The world was better that they lived in it. Freedom found in them devoted loyalty to her cause. They both loved Kansas, and their lives were inseparably associated with the stirring events of the most momentous years of her history. They served her well. Brave and strong and useful, they fought a good fight and kept the faith. Honor to their memory.

A WREATH OF TRIBUTE.

By Rev. D. C. Milner,
Formerly Pastor of the Presbyterian Church at Atchison, Kan.

Editor of the Champion:—Having read, with much interest, your sketch of Pardee Butler, I am moved to lay a wreath of tribute upon the grave of the old hero. He was a man of most invincible courage. Earl Morton, by the open grave of John Knox, said, "Here lies one who never feared the face of man." Mr. Butler was a John Knox sort of man. Those who have visited him at his home of late years will remember how modestly, yet with some pride, he would tell the story of that day in Atchison when the mob started him down the river on the frail raft, and how he would exhibit the banner so carefully preserved. It would be of much interest if we could have the full story, told by himself, of the raft journey; of the after "tar and cotton" affair; and also, of the night, some time after that, when some of the very men who helped to mob him, assisted him across the river with his loaded team when he was in some trouble.

He lived to see the overthrow of the slave power, which he hated with all the intensity of his nature. He also witnessed the revolution in Kansas as to the liquor power. The files of the *Champion*, for the spring of 1885, have an account of a notable meeting in the court-house at Atchison of the friends of law and order. The friends of the saloon, for nearly five years after prohibition was the law of the State, had ignored the law, and challenged its enforcement. This convention was the first general gathering of the citizens of Atchison County to protest

against this lawlessness, and demanded that the officers of the law close
the saloons.   Pardee Butler was one of the leading spirits in the convention.   Many will recall his fiery speech of that day.   He spoke of the
thirty years of his life in Kansas, and of the great events that had happened.   He then denounced the actual rebellion then in existence, and
called for its suppression.   That convention was the beginning of the
end of the downfall of the organized saloon pewer in Atchison.

Pardee Butler was in sympathy with good men in every good cause.
While a born controversialist, and strong in his convictions, he was
glad to work with Christians of any name in building up the kingdom of
God in the world.   He identified himself heartily with the Sunday-
school work, and was anxious that everything should be done for children and youth, not only to make them believers, but good men and
good citizens.   I agree heartily with what Noble Prentis has recently
said of him: "We knew him well in his later years; a brave and earnest man ; full of ideas for making this world better, and confident that
they would succeed. He has gone to the company of those who, on every
field for these hundreds of years, where the battle for the sacred rights of
man was to be fought out, have cried, 'O Lord, make bare thine arm!'
and have bared their own."

Manhattan, Kan., October 26, 1888.